Billy Hopkins, who is better known to his family and friends as Wilfred Hopkins, was born in Collyhurst in 1928 and attended schools in Manchester. Before going into higher education, he worked as a copy boy for the *Manchester Guardian*. He later studied at the Universities of London, Manchester and Leeds and has been involved in school-teaching and teacher-training in Liverpool, Manchester, Salford and Glasgow. He also worked in African universities in Kenya, Zimbabwe and Malawi.

Billy Hopkins is married with six grown-up children and now lives in retirement with his wife in Southport. His two bestselling autobiographical novels, *Our Kid* and *High Hopes*, are also available from Headline.

Acclaim for *Kate's Story*:

'I enjoyed reading your first two books about your life, and have just finished *Kate's Story*. Again, I enjoyed this immensely. I should like to thank you for your authentic and compelling book' Molly Boyes, Hatfield, Herts

'As I sit here writing this note to you, my wife, Anne, has begun reading *Kate's Story* and within a few minutes, there was first of all laughter followed almost immediately by weeping! My turn to read the book next and I can hardly wait' Angus Greenhalgh, Perth, Australia

'I feel I must write to thank you for the pleasure I got reading your books. How true to life, as it were, they all are!' Mrs Margaret Roberts, Keighley, Yorkshire

'My congratulations on the freshness of your memory, the richness and generosity of your values, and the liveliness and sincerity of your creative touches' Dr Con Casey, Retired Head of Education, Hopwood Hall

'There are a hundred things I could congratulate you for on your books. I have read lots of things that appeal . . . but they have not touched my heart as you have' Mrs Helen Carter, Morpeth, Northumberland

'Your books have given me a real insight into what life was really like for our grandparents and great grandparents. Thank you so much from another satisfied customer' Mrs Maria Hobain, Newcastle, Staffordshire

Acclaim for *High Hopes*:

'I would just like to say I thought your books were fantastically written; they made me laugh out loud and they made me cry. I have finished *High Hopes* and couldn't put it down' D. Gilbert, Uxbridge, Middlesex

'Everyone will enjoy *High Hopes* . . . The book reflects the exuberance of youth in those early days of post-war Britain. Thank you for providing such a good read and for bringing so much pleasure to all who enjoy tales of Manchester' Bernard Lawson, M.B.E., Retired Private Secretary to the Lord Mayor of Manchester

'A little masterpiece' Dr Darragh Little, GP and writer

'*High Hopes* is very readable, unpretentious and brimming with humour. It lifts the curtain on life in the '40s – as it was for students and for a young teacher in an inner-city school' Joan Kennedy, Retired Teacher, Manchester

'It was a great pleasure to read this highly entertaining sequel to *Our Kid*. Its mixture of fact and fiction, class divisions, failures and triumphs, set in the aftermath of the war recalls vividly memories of a Manchester I knew' Dan Murphy, Retired Teacher, Manchester

'I have read *High Hopes* and *Our Kid* – my kind of books. I laughed and cried, and thought, 'been there, done that'. They reminded me so much of my childhood in the '40s and '50s. Whatever you write, we will buy. Please keep on writing' Mrs Thelma Morris, High Peak, Derbyshire

'The pawkish humour of Billy remains and bubbles out frequently in unexpected places . . . This latest book is a wonderful sequel to the life and career of Billy the Collyhurst Kid' Dr Jennie McWilliam, GP, Staffordshire

'I read *High Hopes* faster than many books I've read all year. I both laughed and cried throughout . . . Billy is a loveable character with an irrepressible sense of humour' Mrs Kathleen Rawcliffe, Infants Teacher, Fleetwood, Lancs

Acclaim for *Our Kid*:

'*Our Kid* . . . was the funniest book I have ever read – it had me laughing out loud, it was so great. You sure have the gift of writing' Isobel Fox, Doncaster, Yorkshire

'The book is like a best friend – no one likes to see the friendship come to an end – and that's just how I felt when I read [the last] page' *Visiter*

'Reading *Our Kid* was a very moving experience! I was born in Salford and so you can understand my deep emotion at reading your wonderfully written, deeply touching, extremely heart-warming memoirs. Congratulations!' John Sherlock, Hollywood Producer

'To say I couldn't put *Our Kid* down is an understatement . . . I kept laughing at the truly funny incidents and had to read some out to my husband. I really didn't want to finish *Our Kid* but knowing *High Hopes* was waiting in the wings was a bonus' Mrs K. Pearson, Gosport, Hampshire

Also by Billy Hopkins

Our Kid
High Hopes

Kate's Story

Billy Hopkins

First published in 2001
by HEADLINE BOOK PUBLISHING

First published in paperback in 2002
by HEADLINE BOOK PUBLISHING

23

ISBN 0 7472 6852 5

Typeset by Avon Dataset Ltd, Bidford-on-Avon, Warks

Printed and bound in Great Britain by
Clays Ltd, St Ives plc

HEADLINE BOOK PUBLISHING
A division of Hodder Headline Limited
338 Euston Road
London NW1 3BH

www.headline.co.uk
www.hodderheadline.com

For my five sons
Stephen, Peter, Laurence, Paul and Joseph

Acknowledgements

Kate's Story is the first in a trilogy, though oddly enough it was the last to be written. I have many people to thank for their help along the way. I owe a debt of gratitude to all those relatives and friends who gave valuable advice, in particular my brother Alf for carrying out research in Manchester (especially with regard to the Swinton Industrial School), to members of the General Practitioner Writers' Association, especially Dr Darragh Little of Limerick for his expertise, to my daughter Catherine for her insightful comments and feedback, and to her husband Steve for tracking down documents, to the staff of Ainsdale Library for their ever-willing help in answering my many inquiries, and finally to my wife Clare for her endless patience in listening to early drafts and for her unfailing encouragement.

I could not possibly end this section without mentioning the inspiration given by Isobel Dixon of the Blake Friedmann Literary Agency, and Marion Donaldson of Headline Publishing. They have always been there ready to give professional support whenever I needed it.

Foreword

This is the story of my mother Kate. When she was eighty-nine years old, I took a tape recorder into her room and asked her to tell me her life story. How she could talk! Her story filled two ninety-minute tapes! This book is based on what she told me and whilst I have taken a certain poetic licence with names and characterisation, the events themselves – all of which took place before I was born – are true. Life in the early part of the twentieth century was tough but Kate was a survivor and retained an optimistic outlook right to the end of her life. There is no doubt in my mind that it was this outlook that enabled her to live to the ripe old age of ninety-two.

I want to say finally that I found writing this story to be one of the most moving experiences of my life. If you share some of these emotions in reading it, my labour has been worthwhile.

Billy Hopkins,
August 2001

Chapter One

If you were to ask me which was the happiest day of my life, I think, looking back, I'd probably pick my eleventh birthday. It was also the diamond jubilee of Queen Victoria, and at school we'd been given special mugs with her picture on them and, what's more, we'd been given the day off as well. I can see it now. But let me tell you a little about myself first.

My name's Catherine but everyone called me Kate, except teachers and priests who always gave me my full title, Catherine Lally.

We lived in Butler Court, a little cul-de-sac with a gutter running down the middle, off Butler Street in Ancoats, Manchester. There were only three terraced houses on the court, the two-up, two-down, scullery at the back kind – you probably know the sort. Next door to us lived old one-eyed Annie Swann who kept a flea-bitten, mangy dog called Pug which was supposed to guard her, and a fat lot of good it was too. Why, our black cat Snowy only had to arch its back and spit and it ran off down the court howling in terror. Annie wore an old battered hat with tatty artificial flowers round the rim and I think it was welded to her head for she never took it off, not even when she went to the lavatory. Mam said she was the district layer-outer who put pennies on your eyes when you were dead and she was also a pawnbroker's runner – whatever that was. I think the hat was her badge of office. Danny and me were always tormenting her by playing black rabbit, that is tying cotton to her door knocker, pulling the string to make it knock, and hiding when she opened her front door to see who it was.

Old Annie may have been the layer-outer but I was the letter-writer, not only for our court but for a few streets beyond. Many of the people round there couldn't read or write and so they thought I was a scholar because I was the only one with a fountain pen – one of the new Waterman's which Dad had bought me at Christmas along with a book of fairy tales by the Grimm Brothers. So people came to me when they wanted a form filled in or a letter written applying for relief or that sort of thing; they usually gave me a penny but I was only too happy to do it for nothing if they had no money.

The end house was occupied by Mr and Mrs Sam Hicks, a drunken pair if ever there was one. I hardly ever saw them sober and they were always bickering and screaming at each other, usually over money. I don't think Sam Hicks had a job and Mam used to wonder where they got their money from but at six o'clock every night, Sam's missus, Ivy, went out dolled up to the nines. Dad said she was on the game but I never saw her playing any games, not once. Not like Dad who'd play hide-and-seek with us if he wasn't at work and he wasn't too tired.

In the back entry behind the houses, we had one cold tap between the lot of us – the kind that had a button to press – and we all shared the one lavatory, though not at the same time, thank goodness. Each house had its own big key so as to keep the privy private like, as we didn't want strangers in there messing it up. Outside the lavatory door, there was a hook with a big wooden curtain ring on it and when you went, you had to take the ring inside with you to let everyone know there was somebody in. For Annie Swann, though, there was no need for the ring because her poxy dog used to stand outside on sentry duty. She sat in there singing songs like 'Home, Sweet Home' and us kids clung to each other giggling. I never went to the lav at night, though, as I was too scared of the dark and there was no candle. I was terrified as well that Mrs Swann would catch me and lay me out with pennies on my eyes. If any of us needed to go during the night, we used the chamber pot.

We took turns to clean the privy and cut up fresh newspaper squares to hang on the nail. Saturday morning was my turn to wash out and donkey-stone the place, worse luck, 'cos it usually stank like mad from the night before when the Hickses had been on the beer. Late on, the night-soil men used to come round with the cart to empty the privy. We always kept the windows closed when they went past but just the same we couldn't avoid getting a strong whiff of the terrible pong, no matter how late it was.

We lived in a quiet court but Butler Street and Oldham Road were near and they were always busy with people and traffic of every kind – horse trams, coal carts, delivery vans, hansom cabs. At the corner of the two big roads there was a massive hoarding with thousands of bills stuck all over it and I was always fascinated by them, for they told of things I'd never tasted, places I'd never been to or even heard of, stage shows I'd have given anything to see. CAMEO CIGARETTES; THE BEST TEA IN THE WORLD 1/10 PER LB AT SEYMOUR MEAD'S; MEADOW SWEET CHEESE; KOMPO FOR COLDS; MOORE'S LADIES' COSTUMES 10/6D AT JOHN NOBLE'S; ZEBRA GRATE POLISH; IN ITS LAST WEEK AT THE PRINCE'S THEATRE – *BABES IN THE WOOD*; AT THE QUEEN'S

THEATRE – MR LOUIS CALVERT IN A GRAND PRODUCTION OF SHAKESPEARE'S *ANTONY AND CLEOPATRA*; SINGER'S SEWING MACHINES; HE: 'OXO?' SHE: 'RATHER!'; BOVRIL CURES INFLUENZA; COLMAN'S STARCH AS GOOD AS COLMAN'S MUSTARD; VAN HOUTEN'S COCOA – SIMPLY THE BEST AND IT LASTS LONGER; PREPARE TO MEET THY GOD; DEVON & CORNWALL FOR HOLIDAYS BY G.W.R.; SAVED BY VIROL; AT THE CASINO: VESTA TILLEY AND DAN LENO ADMISSION 2D TO 6D.

There were lots of shops on Butler Street but we went to Greenall's at the corner because it stocked everything you could think of from food to firewood, medicine to mousetraps. On the wall they'd pinned up one of those notices which said: 'Please do not ask for credit as refusal often offends' but they were always happy to let you have something on tick as long as you paid them at the end of the week.

Though Butler Court was a small alley, there was always something going on. Apart from the Hickses tearing each other's eyes out, we had other entertainments and visitors, like the street singer, the knife-sharpener, the Gypsy with her snotty-nosed kids selling paper flowers and God help you if you didn't buy something 'cos she put a terrible curse on you, the terrifying old rag and bone man who swapped old clothes or old iron for a donkey stone or scouring soap, the door-to-door salesman with his case of razors, safety pins and shoelaces, the club man to collect the funeral insurance money, and the tallyman to collect the weekly payments. And every morning, we had the milk cart with its massive churn and the milkman ladled out a pint or a gill or whatever you wanted into your own jug. We always gave his horse, Ben, a treat – an apple, a carrot or a jam butty – and he refused to go on until he'd got it. Sometimes we offered him a sugar lump on a flat hand but that took a lot of nerve and I was the only one who would do it.

In the morning of the day I'm talking about, we were playing the usual games in the street. When I say 'we', I mean my younger brother Danny who was eight, my little sister Cissie who was five, and Lizzie Brennan aged nine who lived with her mother, my Auntie Gladys, in our cellar. Lizzie was not only my best friend but my cousin as well 'cos she was the daughter of my Uncle Jack who'd been killed when he fell off a ladder. Oh, yes, and there was our baby Eddie an' all, but he was only two weeks old, too young to play, and besides, he thought of nothing but his next meal at the breast. Mam and Auntie Gladys were sitting on chairs outside our door enjoying the sunshine and Eddie was fast asleep in his bassinet.

As I said, we were playing in the street. Danny spent his time falling off the homemade stilts which Dad had made out of two tin cans and pieces of string while us girls were playing hopscotch in the squares we'd chalked on the flags. Much to our surprise, Luigi Granelli appeared with his barrel organ and his monkey and began churning out 'Little Dolly Daydream'. Funny that, 'cos he didn't usually come down Butler Court – 'There's no enough bambini,' he'd say. I think my dad must've slipped him a tanner because of my birthday. Anyway, we left off our games, and we danced and sang in a ring to the wobbly piano sound of Luigi's barrel organ.

Little Dolly Daydream
Pride of Idaho
So now you know.
And when you go,
You'll see there's something on her mind,
Don't think it's you
'Cos no one's gonna kiss that girl but me.

We laughed our socks off at the antics of Pongo, his pet monkey, which ran round with the hat collecting the pennies. While we were doing that, we had a second surprise 'cos Antonio Rocca and his ice-cream cart suddenly turned into the court. The first time he'd ever done that. I knew for certain then that Dad had fixed it.

'I'm not kidding,' Mam said, 'it's like Little Italy round here.'

'Mam, Mam, can we have a cornet?' I pleaded. 'Please, Mam. It's my birthday today, remember.'

'Oh, very well, Kate,' she said. 'Go and get my purse off the kitchen table and bring two cups for me and Gladys here. And we'll need two teaspoons as well.'

'It's good of you, Celia,' said Auntie Gladys. 'Ice cream's just what the doctor ordered in this scorching weather.'

I ran down the lobby and into the living room. There was the scent of cedarwood as I pulled out the heavy drawers in the big sideboard, rattling the statues in their glass shades. I was soon back with the two cups, the spoons and the purse. Mam took out a tanner.

'Right, Kate. Get ice cream in these two cups for me and Gladys and five cornets. And ask Antonio there to put raspberry on 'em.'

'Ooh tar, Mam. But why five?'

'Don't forget Luigi. It's hot work turning that handle.'

Antonio filled five cornets and gave each one a big helping of raspberry. He handed them one by one to me and I passed the first one to my young sister. 'First one's for you, our Cissie, 'cos you're the youngest. Next one for you, Lizzie.' Lizzie was a beautiful girl with rosy cheeks and shoulder-length golden hair like her mother's. I handed the next two to our Danny. 'And one for you, Danny, and take this one over to Luigi and tell him to change the tune. You know which one I mean,' I said, giving him a wink.

'Leave it to me,' Danny grinned, taking an almighty lick at his cornet.

'God bless you and your bella famiglia, Mrs Lally,' Luigi called across as he began a frontal attack on his ice cream.

Finally I handed one of the cups now charged with ice cream to Lizzie. 'Take this over to your Mam, Lizzie. And I'll take the other cup to mine.'

'Thanks, Mam,' the young 'uns chorused.

'Tar ever so, Auntie Celia,' Lizzie said ever so shyly.

Antonio made a tiny cornet for Pongo 'cos we'd forgotten about him.

Soon, we were busy devouring 'Rocca's delicious ices' as it said in the bright curly lettering on the side of his cart.

Luigi obeyed the whispered request from Danny and laughingly turned the pointer of the organ to change the tune.

'By special request of Caterina and Daniele, the favourite song of Signor and Signora Lally,' he announced and began turning the handle. The strains of the new tune went round Butler Court and, still licking our ices, we lifted our voices to sing the chorus.

The pale moon was rising above the green mountains
The sun was declining beneath the blue sea
When I strayed with my love near the pure crystal fountain
That stands in the beautiful vale of Tralee.

By the time we had finished, both Mam and Aunty Gladys were in tears. The song never failed to have that effect. They said it always reminded them of Ireland and the times that used to be.

'*Adesso, devo andare,*' Antonio laughed as he trundled off with his cart. '*Arrivederci.* Now I musta get a move on to maka sure I get my place on Market Street. I see everybody at the big parade, maybe?'

'Yes, yes, Antonio. We're going later this afternoon,' Mam answered.

Luigi Granelli was next to go, leaving behind something of an anticlimax. The other kids went back to their games but I sat on the step next to my mam. I liked to listen in to adult conversation though I didn't understand much of it.

'I'm so grateful to you, Celia, for all you've done for our Lizzie and me,' Auntie Gladys was saying. 'If you hadn't taken us in and given us your front cellar, I don't know what we'd have done without you, I really don't.'

'Don't mention it, Gladys,' Mam said. 'It's the least we could do for you. We look on you and Lizzie as part of the family. I only wish we could have given you the parlour but as you know, we have to keep that nice in case we have important visitors, like the doctor or the priest.'

'The cellar's fine for us, Celia. It's nice and warm there, especially when you've done the washing on Monday morning. My job at the soda works pays me only one and six a day and so if you hadn't come to the rescue, we'd have been in Queer Street and no mistake.'

Queer Street! What a strange name, I thought, and I wondered where it was and if it was anywhere near Butler Court but I didn't ask in case they told me to run away and play.

'When Jack was killed in that accident,' Gladys said, 'I thought my life had come to an end, I really did. The world doesn't take kindly to an unmarried mother. Not even the church would help us. A fallen woman, they called me.'

I was puzzled by this. What did she mean when she said she was a fallen woman? I'd never seen her fall, not once.

I looked at both her knees to see if she had any scabs but I couldn't see any.

'That's in the past, Gladys,' Mam said. 'I should try to forget it if I were you. After all, it's nine years ago. And there's no shame in any of it 'cos Jack would have married you if he'd lived.'

'Try telling that to the gossipy neighbours,' Auntie Gladys said. 'They used to say some right nasty things about me, like "He died leaving a bun in the oven" and "He's left her in the pudding club".'

I'd never realised that my late Uncle Jack had been a baker as everyone'd told me he was a bricklayer. And what were they doing in a pudding club and why had he left her there?

'Little pitchers have big ears,' Mam said, flicking her eyes and her head in my direction.

My mam always said this when she thought I was listening to adult talk. Thought I didn't know what it meant. She must've thought I was daft.

'I take your point, Celia,' I heard Auntie Gladys saying. 'Anyroad, if you hadn't taken us in, we'd have ended up in the workhouse.'

'Don't even breathe that word in this house.' Mam picked up the baby and clutched him to her breast as if to protect him. 'The mention of it sends cold shivers down my spine. I'd rather give myself and my kids an overdose of laudanum than go into one of them places. You've had some rotten luck, Gladys, and I only wish we could've done more for you but never wish yourself into the workhouse. Pray to God that it'll never come to that. We've been lucky up to now, touch wood. As you know, Mick has a good job at the Poland Street glassworks, being a gaffer now with his own chair.'

I visited my dad at the works a lot and so I knew better

than they did that a gaffer with a chair was a foreman in charge of a team.

'He's gone up in the world, has Mick,' Auntie Gladys said. 'And good luck to him. He deserves it – he works that hard.'

'He does an' all. There's no denying he has a good job but they work such funny shifts at that glassworks – twelve hours on and twelve hours off. One week he's on nights and on days the next. It has something to do with keeping the furnaces going, he says. Today, though, he finishes at dinnertime and he's got the day off because of the jubilee. So we mustn't grumble. He works all the hours God sends but he earns good money. Last week, he came away with thirty-two shillings in wages with overtime.' Mam gave a deep sigh of contentment.

'Our rent's only seven and six a week and we've even started to save a few bob. If we go careful, one day we might be able to afford a bigger house with our own yard, our own lavatory, and even our own water tap. That's pipe-dreaming, I suppose.' She laughed at her own joke. 'Mick has even talked about buying a piano on the never-never. He loves a bit o' music, does Mick. New, they're twenty-five pounds but we've seen a second-hand Broadwood for only three pounds – that's three bob a week from Worsley's on Rochdale Road. And who knows? One of these days we might manage a little holiday back home. I'd love to see Tralee again.'

'That'll be the day, Celia. Holidays in Ireland, your own tap, your own lavatory, and a piano. That's asking a lot.'

'Talkin' of Mick,' Mam said suddenly, 'that reminds me. I promised to send his snap over to him by ten o'clock. He'll go mad if he doesn't get it.' She hurriedly put baby Eddie back in the bassinet. 'Instead of listening in to things, our Kate, you can run a couple of errands for me. Take your father's snap to him; he'll be waiting for it. Tell him I've managed to get him some nice boiled ham and there's a brew of tea and condensed milk in his billycan. And on the way, go to your Auntie Sarah's with this half-a-crown. I promised to help her out till Friday. And here's a bowl of broth for your grannie. Tell her to warm it up in the oven for her dinner.'

'Right, Mam. And I wasn't listening in. Are we really going to get a piano?'

'Never you mind, Miss Big Ears,' she said. 'Now get going.'

I collected the items and set off. My Auntie Sarah was a little, short-tempered woman who lived with my Uncle Barney in a one-up-and-one-down in Portugal Close a few streets away; and there was no question of who was boss in that house. She had only to give him one of her looks without even uttering a word and he was already saying 'Yes, dear, yes, dear' over and over again. And even though Auntie had a part-time job in a bagging factory somewhere on Shudehill, they were always short of money as Barney was only a casual builder's labourer and was in and out of work. Mostly out.

Barney's one escape was his rabbits which he kept in a hutch in the yard. Everybody in the district knew about them. Understandably, 'cos you could smell them a mile away.

'I'm not joking,' Aunt Sarah said, 'he thinks more about them bloody rabbits than he does about me. He's given them names and is out there talking to them all the hours God sends. He could be dead out there and I don't think anyone'd notice for a couple of days until he stopped coming in for his tea. One of these days, I swear I'll serve them up to him in a pie.'

We saw Barney every Friday when he came over to our house to borrow the tin bath.

'Ta, love,' Auntie Sarah said when I handed over the money. 'You're a good girl. And your mam tells me it's your birthday. So here's ha'penny for you. Get yourself a few toffees.'

A ha'penny bought a sherbert, with a twist of liquorice that you dipped into the powder. It tasted nice but it left a sticky mess round your mouth.

'Ta,' I said to my auntie and I went over to my gran's in Bengal Street across the road. She lived in a furnished room that used to be someone's parlour but she'd made it her own by filling it with her old furniture and a great big aspidistra.

I didn't like going to my gran's 'cos she was a bit strange, was my gran. I was told that she and Grandad came over from Kerry because there'd been a famine there. Sometimes I thought Gran hadn't changed her frock since because as long as I'd known her, she'd always dressed in black from head to foot with a cameo brooch at the neck and a silk mob cap stuck on the top of her head. On her sideboard she had a grim-looking photo of my grandad when he'd been a soldier in the Dublin Fusiliers. His name was Henry and he had a face like an ox with one of those big droopy moustaches. I'd never met him 'cos he'd been killed in Africa before I was born. Gran was always going on about Zulu warriors and how they loved sticking spears in people, especially people like my grandad. She had a good army pension of seven shillings a week but since she'd lost my grandad she'd gone a bit funny and the only thing she wanted to do was sit in her chair talking to herself. That wasn't so bad but she was always wanting to give me advice, and when she started I made for the door and quick. One thing I'd say for her, though, she told me things my own mother was too shy to talk about. Anyroad, I gave her the broth. She said, 'The only broth worth having is the kind you can stand your spoon up in.' She had some right funny ideas, if you ask me.

I told her I couldn't stay as I had to take my dad's snap. 'Don't you worry yourself about me,' she said. 'I won't be bothering any of you much longer. Leave the basin on the sideboard. Call in tomorrow after school and do my errands.'

Not so much as a please or a thank you. Didn't smile. Never did. There was gratitude for you. I left her and walked down George Leigh Street to the glassworks.

I loved going over to the works as it gave me the chance to watch the men turning out all kinds of glass objects. It was like magic. The man on the gate knew my face and always let me go straight onto the factory floor as long as I didn't go too near the furnaces. And Dad always made some little thing for me. At home, I had lots of glass stuff he'd blown for me – little toys, or friggers as the glass-workers called them – a bell, a dog, a deer, and even a horse. Maybe today, I thought, he'd make something extra special.

I waited on the edgings for a horse and coal cart to go past and then I went down Silk Street, taking a short cut along Radium Street. Over the road, on the Portugal Street Rec, the Sanger's Carnival Company was setting up their fairground of stalls, sideshows, and roundabouts. I always felt a thrill of excitement when I saw the men unloading the tents, running about, hammering stakes into the ground, shouting instructions to each other, hoisting up poles, cranking handles, and creating a wonderland before my eyes. I loved fairgrounds – the lights, the piped music, the smell of the food and the oil of the machinery. There were the booths with the freak shows: the bearded lady, the three-headed animals, the mermaids. Was there any chance of Dad taking us? Maybe if I reminded him about my birthday, he might.

I crossed over Poland Street and went into the works. The glassworks was a large, funnel-shaped building on a small industrial estate. In the glass-blowing department where Dad worked, there were twelve men in two teams of six, all of them stripped to the waist in the heat. They sweated like mad because of the furnaces which were kept hot by the teasers who stoked them up. I'd watched them before many a time. The team worked together like dancers, turning ever so gracefully from furnace to chair, swinging the long irons with the white-hot tips which they dipped into buckets of water before blowing and working them into lovely long-stemmed wine glasses, ready for the polishers and the engravers to add the finishing touch.

'Time for a break, me boyos,' my dad announced when he saw me coming. 'Ah, there she stands, my beautiful little Kate,' he said. 'A sight for these poor sore eyes, if ever there was one. Is she not like an angel from heaven? Have you ever seen such a lovely creature, lads?' He broke out into song. '*She was such a lovely creature, boys, that nature did intend/To go right through the world my boys without the Grecian bend.*'

I paid no attention to his singing and his praises because I felt so embarrassed in front of those men. I handed over the lunch box and the billycan.

'Sit down there, me little darling,' he said, pointing to a bench some way off from the furnace, 'while we have our break and then you can take the empty can home.'

He turned to the young lad who was sweeping up the bits of rubbish on the floor

'Alfie, run and fetch me a gallon of water like a good boy for haven't I a terrible thirst on me. I could drink the River Irwell on my own.'

Alfie, a young twelve-year-old, grabbed the brown jug and ran off to get the water.

'Alfie's going to make a bloody good glass-blower one day,' Dad remarked. 'He's a smart lad.'

'Never mind about Alfie,' said Shaun, the teaser. 'What about your own son? Young Danny'll soon be ready for work, I'm thinking. You could teach him yourself, Mick, for what you don't know about glass-blowing isn't worth knowing.'

'No, no,' Dad said decisively. 'I'll not have any lad of mine in this business. There's the question of health. Look at the damage we're doing to our eyes looking into that furnace and the molten glass all day. I think I must have more cataracts than Lake Victoria.'

The men laughed. Maybe they were nervous 'cos they all had trouble with their eyes.

'Sure, they should give us them protective goggles to shade our eyes,' said Shaun, 'but our firm's too bloody mean.'

'They'd be no good anyway,' Dad said. 'For they'd soon get misted over and we wouldn't be able to see what we're doing. Apart from the damage to our eyes, there's the bits of glass we pick up into our joints. And since we went over to lead crystal, God knows what poisons we're taking into our lungs. No, I'd like my lad to get a job where he can breathe God's clean air.'

'Then he'd better move away from Manchester, Mick,' said Fergus O'Leary, one of the team. 'Perhaps a job back home in Ireland?'

'Ah, there's no work to be had in Ireland. Do you think any of us would be here if we could get a job there?'

'But you must agree,' said Shaun, 'the money here's good and well-paid jobs are not easy to come by.'

'That's my cue for another song,' Dad laughed and he broke out into the tune of 'Mountains of Mourne'.

Ah, the Glassworks, my boys, is a wonderful place
But the wages they pay are a bloody disgrace,
And for all that I'm saving I might as well be
Where the Mountains o' Mourne sweep down to the sea.

Everyone roared at Dad's singing. I was that proud to see my dad was so popular.

'Ah, the money's not that good, Shaun,' Dad went on, 'especially when we think what the bosses are making. I read in the paper that a mill in Salford is celebrating the jubilee by giving its two thousand workers the day off and a pound each. They must be making big profits if they can afford to give all that away.'

'That's more than Manchester and Salford are doing,' said Fergus 'As far as I can see, the councils are giving themselves a big feed in their town halls and a bit of a tea to the needy and the destitute old people – but just for the day, mind you. The rest of the year, they can bugger off and starve. When it comes to this jubilee, I'll be staying at home. All this talk about the British Empire and the Queen's loyal subjects! Slaves conquered by the British is more like it. Besides, she's not the Queen of Ireland as far as I'm concerned. Today every true Irishman should be wearing not red, white, and blue, not even green but black like the patriots in Limerick.'

'Ah, it's only a bit of fun and excitement and the kids love it,' Dad said. 'The decorations on the town hall in Albert Square are something to behold, so I'm told.'

Alfie was back with the water and Dad tipped the jug to

his lips and drank greedily. His Adam's apple rose and fell as he noisily gulped the water down. The drink triggered a fit of coughing.

'There. What did I tell you?' Dad exclaimed. 'Hasn't the water brought up the stuff I've been breathing. Here I am forty-four and sometimes I feel like seventy-four. No use complaining though. I suppose we've got to thank the Lord and His Holy Mother that we have jobs at all.'

'You're right there, Mick,' said Shaun. 'Pity the poor jobless people on outdoor relief. I read today in the *Evening Chron* that the authorities in their generosity are going to raise their money from six shillings and sixpence to seven and six a week in honour of the jubilee.'

'And that extra shilling is not permanent but is only for one week,' added Fergus who seemed to have 'it's only for one day' on the brain. 'I'm sure Her Gracious Majesty the Empress Victoria will be pleased when she hears her destitute subjects are to be given such a magnificent sum to keep body and soul together. Especially when we hear that she's to spend a few million quid on her own celebrations.'

Dad took another long draught of water which set off his hacking again.

'There I go again,' he spluttered. 'God knows what stuff is in my lungs. If someone were to blow into my gullet, I'm sure they could shape a couple of fine glass ornaments down there.'

I thought it was time to remind him that I was still sitting there.

'Mam said that you were to come straight home at dinnertime, and no going into the Lord Napier with your mates,' I said.

'As if I would even contemplate going into a pub on a day like today.'

'Do you know what day it is today, Dad?' I asked shyly.

'Of course I know what day 'tis. Do you think I'm the village idiot? 'Tis Tuesday, is it not?'

'Not the day, Dad. The date! The date!'

'I don't have a calendar with me, Kate, but if I'm not mistaken 'tis Tuesday, June the twenty-second, eighteen ninety-seven. Am I not right, boys?'

The 'boys' signified their agreement with grunts, mumbles and laughter. They loved these little games Mick played with me each time I came to bring his snack.

'Not just the date, Dad. A special date. One that you mustn't forget.'

'Ah, well now, Kate. Let me think. I suppose you thought you'd catch me out with that one. Have we not been talking about the very thing. 'Tis the diamond jubilee of Her Gracious Majesty, Queen Empress Victoria.'

'No, no, Dad,' I said, exasperated. 'It's even more special than that, and you know it. Stop teasing me.'

'Teasing you, begorrah. There's only one teaser in this place, young lady, and that's Shaun there whose job 'tis to tease the furnaces.'

Shaun laughed good-humouredly.

'It's my birthday, Dad. I'm eleven years old today!'

'Well, would you believe it?' Dad grinned. 'Here's me with a daughter who's nearly middle-aged and I didn't even know it. I suppose you'll be wanting some kind of present.'

'Make me a flip flap, Dad. That's all I want.'

'Your wish is my command,' he said. 'Right, lads, you heard what she said. A flip flap the young lady said but I think we can do better than that.'

I took several steps back and watched as the men went to work.

Fergus, the gatherer, walked swiftly over to the furnace and thrust the long tube into the molten glass. With great skill, he drew off a glowing bulb and handed it across to Dad in his chair. I gazed fascinated as he swung and rolled the long iron to and fro making the fiery gob of metal change shape with its flip-flap noise. When he was sure the shape was right, he dipped the glass into a bucket of water, raised the tube to his lips and blew.

'Pass me the procello, Fergus,' he called between breaths.

Fergus handed him a pair of tongs and, using these, Dad shaped the cooling glass into the body of a cat. He detached the animal and took it to the leer, the long cooling tunnel.

'Now, that should be ready in a couple of days, me darlin' Kate, and I'll bring it home to you then, that is if the polishers and the engravers don't smash it with their clumsiness.'

He saw the look of disappointment on my face and he said, 'But I suppose you'll be wanting something now since it's your birthday today and not in two days' time.' He turned to the young apprentice. 'Alfie, run up to the engraving department and see if they have that special thing ready – the one we made last week.'

He grinned. 'Right-o, Mr Lally.'

Alfie was back in two shakes. He was carrying a box tied with ribbon.

'Here's a special some*thing* for a special some*body*,' Dad said, handing me the box.

Watched by the workmen, I opened it. There in its custom-made cardboard holder, I found the most beautiful glass swan. On the side of the bird, the engravers had inscribed a birthday message: TO KATE LALLY ON HER ELEVENTH BIRTHDAY JUNE 22ND 1897

'Oh, Dad,' I said. 'This is the best present I've ever had. I'll look after it for the rest of my life.' I kissed my dad on the cheek and gave him a tight hug. 'I love you, Dad,' I said. An unusual thing for me to do and say because we were not the kissing kind.

'That kiss and the hug are the only reward I need,' he said, eyes glistening. 'Now run along home with you. We've got work to do.'

'All right, Dad. But don't forget we're going to town this afternoon for the big parade. And, Dad, Sanger's Carnival are setting up their fairground on the Rec. Do you think we could . . .'

'Ah, go along with you, you young madam,' he laughed. 'We'll see about that later today.'

I left the factory floor and hurried home. I had to get ready for the afternoon and our little family outing.

Chapter Two

Going to town was a special occasion in our family and the prospect filled us with such excitement, we could hardly eat the 'tater-ash' which Mam had cooked in the fireside oven. She had to keep threatening us with, 'If you don't eat up your dinner, there'll be no trip into town or anywhere else.' We didn't believe her but we did as we were told and cleaned our plates with rounds of bread. After that, our attention was on the business of getting ready. Washing us lot in cold water was a major operation as Ancoats seemed to rain specks of soot, morning, noon and night.

At two o'clock, the grown-ups gave us the final once-over. Young Danny was dressed in his Whit Friday serge trousers held up by colourful braces, a white shirt with St Michael's School tie, grey stockings and gleaming black boots. Cissie and I both wore dresses in bright pink taffeta with silk sashes in red, white and blue. For Lizzie, they had chosen a gold satin dress with a matching ribbon in her hair. Young Eddie in his bassinet wore his usual blue.

'Well, what do you think?' Mam asked of Dad and Auntie Gladys. 'Do they pass?'

'With flying colours,' replied Auntie Gladys.

'As beautiful as their mothers,' Dad gushed. 'Though a

bit too much of the red, white and blue and not enough of the green.'

'Away with you and your blarney,' Mam said, giving him a playful dig in the ribs.

'You'll pay for that,' he laughed. 'Wait until I get you alone.'

The adults, too, looked smart. Dad wore his best black shoes, blue suit, silk white shirt, a smart green tie and his straw boater tilted at a jaunty angle; he had a watch and chain in his waistcoat pocket, and he carried a silver-headed cane. Like a toff.

The ladies wore their 'special occasion' rig-outs which meant large hats and long woollen coats as a change from their workaday shawls.

It was clouding over when we set off and we wondered whether we should've taken the large umbrella that Dad had bought at Lewis's for the Whit walks. We decided to take a chance. Mam pushed the bassinet and Dad carried Cissie high up on his shoulders. The streets leading to town had been blocked off and so there were no trams or horses to worry about. We walked along Oldham Road to New Cross where there was a Salvation Army band with choir singing 'Rock of Ages'. A woman in the army uniform rattled a tin box at Dad and he put in a few pennies. 'You never know when you might need the Sally Army,' he said. In Tib Street Dad bought us paper Union Jacks from a hawker's barrow. Even baby Eddie had one tied to his pram.

'I don't know what my Irish friends at the glassworks would say if they could see me buying flags of England, the country which has oppressed us for the last seven hundred years.'

Hundreds of people streamed towards Piccadilly and as we got nearer, the throngs got thicker. Market Street was a sight to behold. Bright bunting was festooned from lamppost to lamppost, and banners and flags fluttered from every building; there were flowers and plants everywhere. Office clerks hung from upstairs windows and kids clung to the lampposts. Thousands of people lined the route of the procession and the crowd was six deep on the pavement. They waved their flags and joked with the police.

'Watch out for pickpockets,' one copper said.

'They'll be wasting their time here,' Dad replied. 'For indeed the ladies have no pockets and I have nothing worth stealing except maybe my watch and chain and I'll break the face of the owner of any hand that tries to take 'em.'

Dad elbowed his way though the mob and pushed us kids to the front to give us a better view. A brass band playing 'Soldiers of the Queen' was approaching; we could hear it faintly but not see it. A cheer began and it rippled along the street like a wave until those around us joined in the patriotic chorus. Even the birds in the trees seemed to be whistling it.

. . . when we say we've ALWAYS won,
And when they ask us how it's done,
We'll proudly point to every one
Of England's Soldiers of the Queen!

'That song was written by Leslie Stuart, organist at the Holy Name Church on Oxford Road,' Dad told us. 'Did you know that?' He was always giving us titbits of information like that. Anyroad, nobody did know that. And I don't think we cared either.

Then came the shire horses – beautifully decorated with their manes and tails plaited in red, white and blue braid and even their hooves polished black – stamping and snorting, leading the floats at the front of the procession.

And what floats they were! All had as their theme 'The Queen and her Glorious Empire'. First came the wagons from Sharp Street and Charter Street Ragged Schools with their scholars dressed up as flowers to make up a bouquet for the Queen. Next, the boys from Chetham's Hospital in their cassocks and flat hats marching smartly in line and carrying and playing full-sized musical instruments. Such excitement everywhere that I couldn't understand Fergus at the glasshouse saying he wouldn't join in anything to do with the Queen. He must have been daft, that's all I can say. There was no end to the boys and men in uniform – the Church Lads brigade, the fire brigade, the police, and the soldiers of the Manchester Regiment. Finally came the Lady Mayoress in an open carriage, waving her hand from side to side as if she was the Queen herself, surrounded by prancing horses and plumed helmets.

'Where's the Lord Mayor?' somebody asked.

'He's down in London with the other mayors,' another answered.

'Yeah, feeding his face, smoking cigars and drinking whisky at our expense,' said another.

When the last carriage had passed, Dad moved quickly.

'Come on, everybody, we'll make our way to Albert Square to hear the police band.'

He picked up Cissie and forced a way through the dense mob of people. We followed the end of the procession until we reached John Dalton Street. The roar of the people was even louder there. I looked about me and saw young men clinging dangerously to the balconies and railings around the square. Some of them must have been toffs for they were wearing striped blazers and whirled their flat straw hats over their heads. As the parade finally came to a halt, the band played 'Rule Britannia' and the vast crowd joined in. I felt proud to be English even though Dad had told me a hundred times that I was Irish 'cos I had an Irish father and mother. But the music was so stirring, I didn't feel Irish at all.

At half past three, a bugle call rang out to signal that faces were to turn towards the conductor on a raised platform outside the town hall steps. The band played the opening bars of the National Anthem and at a second bugle call everybody stood to attention and joined in singing 'God Save the Queen'. Then miracle of miracles, as the band struck up, the sun came out from behind the clouds and shone in all its glory. 'Queen's weather!' everyone said. There were three cheers for the Queen, the men took off their hats and the great crowd sang 'All People That on Earth Do Dwell' to the tune of 'The Old Hundredth'. As it was a Protestant hymn, I knew it was a sin to join in but as everyone else seemed to be singing it, I took the risk of going to hell and let rip.

What a day it had been. Tired but happy, we made our way back to Butler Court where Mam gave us butties spread with dripping, pineapple chunks with custard and a big cake with eleven candles. I blew them out in one go. The day might have ended there but there was more to come.

Lizzie and me sided the table and Mam and Gladys washed the pots. Dad had us mesmerised with his card tricks and his magic. He told us to pick a card and hide it from him and then he told us what it was. He wouldn't tell us how he did it.

'You can tell the card from marks on the back,' I said.

'Is that so, my little clever madam?' he answered. He opened a new pack, closed his eyes, and told me to take one card and hide it. He opened his eyes.

'Jack of diamonds,' he said immediately.

'Come on, Dad, tell us how you did it,' said Danny.

'Easy,' he said. 'Take a look at the rest of the cards.'

We did. The whole pack was Jack of diamonds.

'That's cheating, Dad,' I laughed. 'You really are daft.'

He pulled a toffee out of Cissie's ear, a penny from Lizzie's golden hair, a whistle from Danny's jersey, and a sixpence from my shoe. At the end we thought he was going to be sick when he started to make lots of gurgling and clucking noises, only to produce a boiled egg from his mouth. We couldn't stop laughing at his antics.

He's the best dad who ever lived, I thought.

Then he said, 'The night is still young. What would you like to do? There's going to be a big fire on Kersal Moor with lots of fireworks. Let's go there.'

He was always teasing me, was Dad. He knew I wanted to go to the fair.

'Aw, Dad,' I said, 'stop messing about. Kersal's miles away and the fair's just round the corner.'

He laughed. 'Don't be serious, Kate. Life's too short. Since you're eleven today, your wish is our command.'

As we stepped out of the front door, we could see the bright glow and hear the piped music from the fairground.

'That's called a calliope,' Dad said, 'and it's driven by a steam engine.'

We didn't care what it was driven by as long as we got across there. From the streets around, people – some wearing funny hats and red, white and blue rosettes – streamed towards the light like moths to a candle. The fair was a madhouse of stalls, barrows, sideshows, and merry-go-rounds, and people, people everywhere with the naptha flares throwing a funny, eerie light over their faces. Like everyone else, we jostled our way around, dazed by all that was going on around us. Mam used the pram she was pushing like a battering ram, forcing a way through the crowd.

'The first thing we buy,' Dad said, 'is hokey-pokeys for everyone.'

The seven of us must have looked a right sight as we wandered about licking our ice creams and gawping at everything. But I didn't care what we looked like even when I saw sneaky Eve Ogboddy from my class at St Michael's School. I felt proud of our little family.

'Show-off,' she hissed, as she went by, tossing her head.

We had a go at everything – well, nearly everything. Dad handed each of us threepence and that gave us a lot of things to choose from. And I had the extra money that'd been given to me. Danny spent most of his money on a helter-skelter slide called 'Slipping the Slip' and the ghost train, but us girls preferred the horses on the merry-go-round. I had to sit behind Cissie to make sure she didn't fall off.

'You look after your little sister, Kate,' Dad called, looking at me steadily. The adults watched us go round several times, waving and laughing each time we went past. Next we switched to the boat swings, with Lizzie pulling the rope on one side and Cissie and me on the other. The adults spent most of their money trying to win prizes – the Hoop-La, the Roll a Ha'penny – but no one won anything as it seemed impossible to get your ha'penny exactly in the square. Dad had better luck on the darts, winning a kaleidoscope for Danny, a doll for me and a teddy bear for Cissie. When he saw that Lizzie had nothing, he had a shot at the 'Test Your Strength' stall by swinging a great big mallet and ringing the bell – which won a big furry dog for her. The only trouble was the effort started off his coughing again.

At half past nine, it was time to go home and it was a

happy little band that made its way along Oldham Road. We reached Bengal Street and as we were about to pass the Shamrock Club, Dad said, 'How would you two ladies fancy rounding off the day with a glass of stout before we finally turn in?'

Mam and Auntie Gladys did fancy.

'Take the children home, Kate, and put the kettle on for the cocoa. We'll be home in half an hour.'

'Yes, Mam.'

I didn't mind them going to the Shamrock for a drink, not one bit. They were entitled to their bit of pleasure 'cos they worked so hard during the week. Mam, Dad and Auntie Gladys often went to the *ceilidhe* there on a Saturday night if Dad wasn't working, and they always left me in charge. One thing I'd say for them was they didn't go to the pub every night like some of the rough people of Ancoats. One or two girls from my class at school, like Fanny Butterworth or Florrie Moss, were left hanging around outside the pubs every night with their young snotty-nosed brothers and sisters, hoping to cadge a few coppers when the boozers shut.

I took over Eddie's bassinet and we walked back to Butler Court. The adults kept their promise and were back in half an hour, though Dad had brought a few bottles back to keep up the celebrations. I noticed, too, the sweet smell of stout on their breath when they came through the door and they were in a happy, laughing mood as they always were after the Shamrock Club. Mam turned up the oil lamps and made us kids a mug of Van Houten cocoa – the best. We never went to bed without first saying night prayers and everyone knelt down in the living room while Dad led us in a decade of the rosary, counting off the prayers on our beads. I was always glad when we got to the Glory Be 'cos it meant we were coming to the end.

Auntie Gladys took Lizzie down to their furnished room in the cellar, and us three Lally kids went to our own bedroom – Danny to his iron bed in the corner, and Cissie and me to our big double bed with the patchwork quilt. Mam and Dad had their room at the front with Eddie in his cot.

Dad came in to give his goodnight hug and tell us one of his many Irish fairy tales – they were usually about fairies, fairy rings, giants, goblins and hunchbacked men but that night the story was about a little girl on her birthday and how she was visited by leprechauns who gave her all kinds of magic presents and magic spells.

'Time to settle down,' he said when he'd finished. 'We've had a busy day.'

'Ta for the teddy bear, Dad,' said Cissie as she cuddled into it.

'Yeah, and for the kaleidoscope as well, Dad,' Danny called out.

'Ta for everything, Dad,' I said. 'The swan, the parade, the fair, the doll, the story, the charades, for everything.'

'Glad you enjoyed it, Kate,' he said. 'All birthdays are important but those with two ones at the end are the most important.'

'I'll remember that, Dad, when I'm a hundred and eleven. It's been the happiest day of my life. I wish it could be today for ever. I wish time could stand still.'

'That's the one thing you can never wish for, Kate,' he said with his serious face. 'Time and tide wait for no man.'

He blew out the candle. 'Goodnight, childer.'

'Goodnight, Dad.'

Chapter Three

Next day, Wednesday, it was back to the routine and for us kids that meant school, St Michael's Elementary School. We had to be there at nine o'clock and God help us if we were late. Two of the cane on the hands for the girls and two on the bum for the boys. Getting to school on time wasn't always as easy as it sounds. Mam made porridge with milk and sugar, and after getting it down, we were ready to go. But that morning, two things slowed us down. First the lavatory. Only one between three houses. The Hickses were no problem as they were usually in bed till twelve o'clock, Gladys had gone to the soda factory at six o'clock and Dad was on nights. No, it was old Annie. She was sitting in there singing one of her songs. '*Be it ever so humble, there's no place like home.*'

Her mangy dog sat outside howling in harmony.

'Please hurry up, Mrs Swann,' Lizzie shouted, knocking on the door. 'We're going to be late for school.'

'*Mid pleasures and palaces though we may roam,*' she warbled, ignoring us, '*there's no place like home.*'

It was quarter past eight when she came out, which didn't leave us much time.

'We'll get a good hiding if we don't get a move on,' I said.

Then Danny said, 'I've just remembered, it's Wednesday and we have swimming today. Mr McCarron takes us to

Osborne Street Baths on Rochdale Road, for a good fumigating, he says. And I can't find my cozzy anywhere. I've got to have it or I'll get belted.'

Danny was proud of his cozzy because on it he had a badge saying he'd swum ten lengths.

'Rubbish,' Mam said. 'You don't have to have a cozzy. You can swim in your birthday suit.'

'Aw, Mam,' he said. 'I don't like to. Everyone'll be looking at me. Anyroad, you can get locked up for swimming nude.'

'Rubbish,' she said again. 'It's lads only and what you've got is only the same as the others have. So I don't know why you're mythering us about such a little thing.'

But Danny went on moaning about it so much that we started turning the house upside down to find his lousy cozzy.

'As if I don't have enough with a young baby and your father coughing his lungs up half the night,' Mam said.

We looked everywhere. In the wardrobe in the bedroom, under the bed, in the pile of clothes waiting to be ironed, on the drying rack hanging in the living room. As a last resort, I said a quick prayer to St Antony, who's in charge of heaven's lost property office, though you're supposed to put a penny in the poor box if he finds your lost article. No use. No sign of it. It was half past eight and we were into danger time.

'When was the last time you saw it?' Mam asked.

'Last Wednesday when we went to the baths,' he cried. Suddenly he stopped whinging, clapped his hands to his stomach and said, 'Wait a minute! I've still got it on!'

'Thanks, Antony,' I said, raising my eyes to heaven. 'I owe you a penny.'

But Mam didn't share my gratitude for she gave Danny

a clout. 'You daft little bugger, worrying us like that. Now get to school the lot of you.'

We had ten minutes to get to school and we knew it was impossible to make it in time but, just the same, we ran all the way. We got to the big front door of the school at five past nine, where Mr Rooney, the head, was waiting with a cane hanging by a crook over his arm.

'Late!' he said in triumph. As if we didn't know. 'What's your excuse?'

I didn't know why he asked 'cos he never accepted excuses.

As I was the oldest, they looked at me to answer. 'We've only one lavatory, sir, and the next-door neighbour wouldn't come out. She kept singing "Home, Sweet Home".'

'Never mind what she was singing,' he said. 'It won't do. Hands out, the girls.'

We put our hands out and all of us, including little Cissie, got two of the cane. Danny got it on his bottom. The cane caught the tips of Cissie's fingers and she started to cry, sucking her fingers at the same time.

'Come on, Cissie,' I said. 'No crying. You're a Lally, remember. Head up.'

'Can't help it,' she wailed. 'It stings.'

Cissie had a lot to learn about life.

'Let that be a lesson to you,' Mr Rooney announced, as we knew he would. 'If you've only one lavatory, you must get up earlier and get in there before your Home Sweet Home neighbour. Do you think the British Empire would be as great as it is today if we were late reporting for duty? Do you think I would be where I am today if I came late every day? The country, the Empire, the world, the universe must run on time. Now get to your classes.'

'Yes, sir. Thank you, sir,' we chorused.

Rubbing his backside which was still wearing the rotten cozzy, Danny went to Mr McCarron's, a tearful Cissie still sucking the ends of her fingers went to Miss Tunney's infants class, and Lizzie and me still wringing our hands went along the corridor to Miss Gertrude Houlihan's – Shirty Gerty we called her. She weighed about two tons and her mousey hair was curled at the back in a schoolma'am bun.

There were about forty girls in our class and every one of us hated school, every minute of it. We sat three to a desk and Lizzie and me had to sit next to the spiteful Eve Ogboddy. Gerty sat perched on her high desk looking down on us over her nip-nose glasses.

In my exercise books, she'd made me write: 'Catherine Lally is my name, England is my nation, Manchester is my home town, the Church is my salvation.'

Round the walls she'd pinned up all kinds of religious sayings, like THE DEVIL FINDS WORK FOR IDLE HANDS and SUFFER THE LITTLE CHILDREN TO COME UNTO ME. We didn't understand much of what she taught but we weren't there to understand but to memorise. We knew what the last one about suffer the little children meant all right. Or we thought we did.

I was sure that in another life Shirty Gerty had been in charge of a dungeon in a castle. She had five kinds of torture: the treatments, we called them. First, she cuffed you over the head or, if in a bad mood, boxed your ears. Second, slapped you hard on your wrists. Third, belted you on both hands with the leather strap she'd had specially made in the West of Ireland. Fourth, made you kneel all morning on the cold stone floor. Last, and the one we hated most, made you wear the dunce's cap. Some days there were more girls kneeling and standing at the front than sitting at the desks. Which punishment you got depended on the way she was feeling that morning and that depended on the state of her stomach. If she gave a good belch first thing, we knew we were going to be all right; otherwise we had to watch out. We wished her mother would give her a big spoonful of gripe water.

Her lessons were mainly learning by heart and that meant reciting together in a sing song chant, stuff like the thirteen multiplication tables, and yards and yards of poetry. I loved learning long poems, though, like the one about daffodils or the Lady of Shalott, but I hated the thousands of other useless things she knocked into our heads. God help anyone with a bad memory, and that meant nearly everyone in the class. You got one of her treatments if you couldn't spell, didn't remember things like the Kings and Queens of England from Alfred to Victoria, or didn't know about bushels, pecks, rods, perches and poles and other weights and measures, or couldn't recite sentences like, 'The terrestrial core is of an igneous nature'.

I'd had all Gerty's treatments except the dunce's cap, not like my poor friend Lizzie who'd once had to stand on a chair in front of the class all morning wearing the big pointed cap because she couldn't list the bits of Africa that belonged to Queen Victoria, and couldn't name and point to the capital of Bechuanaland. It used to be Gaborone, in case you're interested.

That morning, when we got there, Houlihan was giving her favourite lesson, religion, which meant learning the catechism. We didn't understand any of it. You will one day, she said. She didn't like being asked anything in case she didn't know the answer. A few daring girls like Fanny and Florrie enjoyed tormenting her with awkward questions. She'd written a verse up on the blackboard and the class was busy copying it onto their slates.

I must not play on Sunday, because it is a sin.
Tomorrow will be Monday, and then I can begin.

The girls did their best to make the chalk squeak on the slates 'cos that always got her mad and she could never tell who'd done it. As we walked in, she was marching round the class, cuffing heads where girls were too slow.

'Put your chalk down now,' she barked. 'Right. Now that Catherine Lally and Lizzie Brennan have favoured us with their presence, perhaps we can start our religious instruction.'

As I said, religion was her favourite subject but if she had a favourite topic in religion, it had to be heaven and hell, especially hell because it was something she knew a lot about.

'Now today,' she began, 'we're going to learn about how God punishes sinners. So wiggle the wax out of your ears and we'll see if we can't get something into your thick skulls. And while we're on the subject of sin, remember that Father Muldoon will be coming to hear your Wednesday confessions at the end of the day when we go to Mass.'

How I hated these weekly compulsory confessions, mainly because I couldn't think of any sins to say. I couldn't very well go into the box and say, 'Bless me, Father, for I have not sinned. It is a week since my last confession and since then I've done nowt.' So I made a few up and said, 'I've been cheeky to my dad, refused to go errands, and I pinched a penny out of my mam's purse. Lastly, I've just told lies.' The priest never twigged it. I don't think he was even listening. I was sure if I'd said 'I've committed murder', he'd have said 'How many times, my child?'

Lizzie and me went to our desks and sat down. The desk seats had no backs – to stop us from slouching,

Houlihan said – and we'd learned to sit up straight without any support. Otherwise she was only too ready to give you a dig in the small of your back to remind you.

'First, what will Christ say to the just?' she asked. She looked round the class; her eye landed on Ada Davis, a little nervous girl who was knocked about something shocking at home.

'Please, Miss Houlihan, Christ will say, "Come ye blessed of my father, possess ye the kingdom prepared for you." '

'Good,' Shirty Gerty said, hiding a belch with the back of her hand.

It looked as if we were going to have a trouble-free morning but we hadn't counted on Fanny Butterworth, the class blabbermouth.

'What's heaven like, Miss Houlihan?' Fanny asked, giving the rest of us a sly look.

'Oh, heaven is a lovely, happy place,' she raved. 'That eye hath not seen, nor ear heard, neither hath it entered into the heart of man, what things God hath prepared for them that love him.'

'What about those saints with the funny names like Barnabas, Marcellinus and Anastasia that the priest reads out at Mass. Will they be in heaven?'

'Oh, yes indeed. They'll be there waiting for us.'

'What about animals, miss? Can we take our cats and dogs in?' Fanny was in top form.

'Certainly not! No pets allowed. Animals don't have souls like us.'

'Then I don't want to go, miss. It sounds dead boring with all those men with the beards and the funny names. And if I can't take our Scamp, I'd rather go to hell.'

'And that's where you and your mongrel will end up, Miss Fanny Butterworth,' Shirty rasped. 'Along with the other sinners. Now, there are two kinds of sin,' she continued. 'Original and actual. You're born with original sin on your soul and so there's nothing you can do about that except get yourself baptised by a priest or someone else if there's no priest about. Who knows what original sin is?'

Eve Ogboddy, the teacher's pet 'cos her mam was the school cleaner, how we hated her – Eve, not her mam – put her hand up. 'It's the sin committed by Adam when he pinched an apple off the tree and took a dirty big bite out of it.'

'Is it true you can use tea or Guinness if there's no water, miss?' Fanny Butterworth asked. No doubt about it, Fanny was the cheekiest and the daftest girl in the class 'cos she was always trying to rattle Shirty. She was begging for it with questions like that.

'You could,' Shirty snapped, 'if there's no holy water about but who in your family would waste good Guinness when there's plenty of water in the standpipe outside?'

'What happens to babies that die before they get baptised?' Fanny persisted. She really was asking for it.

'Tell her the answer, Catherine Lally,' Gerty said. Now I was being dragged into the stupid argument.

'Limbo, miss. They go straight to limbo.'

'And limbo is . . . ?' She clucked her tongue and let her gaze wander round the room, looking for a victim. It settled on my friend Lizzie.

'Limbe is . . .' Lizzie began nervously.

'Not Limbe, you stupid girl,' Shirty bawled. 'Limbe is a town in Nyasaland. LimbO is what we're talking about here. Eve Ogboddy, go and point to Limbe on the map.'

Her toady tripped out to the front and put her finger somewhere in the middle of Africa on the scruffy map hanging on the wall. 'That's it, Miss Houlihan,' she simpered.

'Please, miss, limbo,' Lizzie faltered, 'is a place of rest where the souls of the just who died before Christ were detained.'

'Does that mean,' asked Fanny, 'that the old codgers who snuffed it before Christ died on the cross were let out but that the unbaptised black babies who died afterwards had to stay?'

'That is the teaching of the Church and you will accept it, Fanny Butterworth, whether you like it or not.'

'Aw, miss. That's not fair. All them babies haven't done nothing and it's not right that they should have to stay while the others go upstairs to heaven.'

Houlihan blew her top. 'Come up here!' she yelled. 'I'll teach you to argue with the Church, you insolent girl.'

She gave Fanny two stinging strokes of the strap and told her to kneel at the front.

Then she got on to her 'doom and gloom' subject which put the fear of God in us. We shivered in fearful delight 'cos we knew what was coming.

'The world is an evil, sinful place and there will come a time on the day of the Last Judgement when God will have his revenge,' she proclaimed, her finger pointing upwards. 'The sun will be darkened, the moon will turn to blood, and the stars will fall from the sky.'

'She sounds almost glad,' Fanny whispered across the class from her kneeling position.

'What was that, Fanny Butterworth?' Shirty barked.

'I said it sounds awful bad,' Fanny replied.

'It'll be bad all right,' Shirty said, 'but especially for the wicked. Out of the clouds will ride the four horsemen of the Apocalypse. The first will bring war, the second, death, the third, famine; and the last, the worst of all, pestilence.'

'What's that – pestilence, miss?' asked a trembling Lizzie.

'It means a terrible disease like the Black Death, and people will break out in terrible suppurating sores before they die a painful death. And then it'll be hell for the lot of them for eternity.'

We were petrified at the thought of going into the furnace and being shovelled about by devils with big spades and pitchforks.

'As long as your bad deeds are venial sins,' she continued, 'you go to purgatory.'

'How long do you have to stay in purgatory?' I asked.

'There are no clocks or calendars in purgatory,' she grunted.

'Then how does God know when you've done your time?' Florrie asked, looking round the class for support.

'All right, all right,' Houlihan snarled, 'if you must have a figure, let's say about a thousand years.'

'Do you mean to say,' said Florrie, 'that if I pinched a penny from my mam's purse and then got run over by a horse and cart, I'd go to purgatory for a thousand years?'

'That is correct,' Houlihan leered through her yellow teeth, 'and you'd well deserve it.'

'That can't be right,' Florrie protested. 'The magistrate at Minshull Street gave my mam seven days for swiping a pair of boots but I'd get a thousand years for pinching a penny.'

'That's bloody unfair,' Fanny said from the floor.

'Right, you!' roared Houlihan, cuffing her across the head. 'On with the dunce's cap and up on the chair.' But Fanny had rattled Shirty Gerty's cage and she was happy.

'When you're in purgatory, miss,' Florrie said, 'do you ever get time off for good behaviour like they do in Strangeways?' Florrie seemed to know about courts and prisons and matters like that.

'We can help the souls in purgatory and so reduce their sentence,' Shirty sighed, 'by gaining indulgences for them. Who knows what an indulgence is?'

There was little point in trying to answer, for the little Ogboddy sneak was in there quick as a flash.

'An indulgence,' she recited, like a parrot, 'is a remission, granted by the Church, of the temporal punishment which often remains due to sin after its guilt has been forgiven.'

'Good answer, Eve!' Houlihan said. 'We can always depend on you.'

'Does that mean, miss,' I asked, 'that when we go to confession, our sins are not really forgiven and that we don't go straight to heaven if we die?'

'Is it a bit like when me mam does the washing?' asked Florrie. 'The sheets are still a bit grubby even after she's put them through the mangle.'

'You should buy some decent soap,' said Agnes Scully, a red-haired girl with a face full of freckles and a head full of nits, 'like Sunlight instead of that dog soap your mam gets from the rag and bone man.'

'Kneel down at the blackboard, Scully!' bellowed Houlihan. 'Who asked for your opinion? I'll deal with you later.'

'I heard somewhere,' said Fanny on the chair, 'that people used to buy indulgences like tickets to be let off time in purgatory. So much money for so many days, like.'

Shirty ordered Fanny to turn away from the class and keep quiet.

'Stupid men in the past did think they could buy indulgences,' Gerty continued, 'but the best way to earn indulgences is by prayer and suffering.'

'What kind of suffering?' I asked.

'For example, people used to go up the sixty-six and the seventy-seven steps in Collyhurst on their knees to earn days of indulgence for their loved ones who'd passed away.'

We were impressed. Everyone knew about the steps in Collyhurst.

'I'll bet they didn't half have scabby knees,' I laughed.

'Right, that's it,' she barked. 'We'll see about scabby knees, Catherine Lally. Kneel down at the front and earn a few scabs and get yourself an indulgence or two at the same time.'

Not again, I said to myself. I must have spent half my life on my knees, scrubbing, praying, and being punished.

'How much time would you be let off for going up the seventy-seven steps on your knees?' Lizzie asked quietly. She was thinking of her dad in purgatory.

'It's hard to say,' Houlihan said slowly. 'About a month, I should think.'

'That means we'd have to do it thousands of times to be let off for knocking off a penny!' gasped Florrie. 'That's daft.'

'Kneel down with the others,' Gerty growled.

She rounded off her religious instruction with a revision of the main prayers: the Our Father, the Hail Mary, the Glory Be, the Hail Holy Queen, the Memorare.

Finally she asked, 'How should you finish the day?'

'By kneeling down and saying my night prayers,' we chanted.

'After your night prayers what should you do?'

'I should observe due modesty in going to bed and occupy myself with the thoughts of death,' we chorused.

For me, the thoughts of death were one-eyed Annie Swann washing me down and putting pennies on my eyes.

Chapter Four

In the mornings at school I learned about religion, the British Empire, the Kings and Queens of England, and how to calculate by counting with my fingers on my chin. But after school in the afternoons I learned about sex and where babies came from. And my teacher was my gran who'd gone a bit off her rocker even though she was always on her rocker, if you know what I mean. She thought I was about sixteen, though I'd told her a million times I was nowhere near that old. Perhaps she thought she'd better tell me in case she snuffed it 'cos she kept saying how my own mam would never have the guts to do it.

After school let out, I went round to my gran's in Bengal Street to see if she wanted any errands doing. It was a chore my mam made me do every day even though she knew I hated it. The one consolation was that Gran sometimes gave me a piece of cake. As usual, she was sitting in her rocking chair, mumbling to herself. When she said she didn't need anything, I heaved a sigh of relief and got ready to make a quick getaway.

'Wait,' she said suddenly. 'Sit down in that chair. I want to have a serious talk with you.'

I didn't much like the sound of this but did as I was told.

'It was your birthday yesterday, wasn't it?'

'Yes, Gran'ma. I was eleven,' I said, even though I knew

it was a waste of time and would go in one ear and out the other.

'You're a lovely girl with lovely brown hair. Why, it stretches right down your back. It's your crown of glory.'

'Yes, Gran'ma. Thank you, Gran'ma.' Not a patch on Lizzie's golden hair, I thought.

'Make sure you don't get any nits in it, that's all,' she snapped. 'You're quite the young lady now, eh? Getting to be a big girl now and it's time we had a heart-to-heart talk.'

Where was this leading? With my gran you never knew.

She looked at me and suddenly said, 'Have you started your monthlies yet? I remember your mother started early and she hadn't a clue either.'

Uh-oh, I thought. Here we go. My face went bright red as I'd treated this matter as a guilty secret and I didn't want to talk about it. A few weeks back, I'd started bleeding and I'd been worried out of my mind in case it was serious. Fanny Butterworth, of all people, who was a year older than me and had had the same problem, explained what it was and told me what to do. But I wasn't sure that Fanny had had the right answer.

'Sorry, Gran'ma,' I said, pretending not to understand her. 'My monthlies? I don't know what you mean.'

'You know very well what I mean,' she grunted. 'I can tell by your face. It's what we call the woman's curse and you'll have it every month from now on. You must cut up some sheets into strips and use them to wrap yourself up down there.' She pointed to the lower part of my body.

It was a relief to know that Fanny's advice had been correct. Still, I was embarrassed to be talking about it. Why hadn't my own mam warned me? I knew that if I ever had a daughter I would tell her 'cos I had truly thought there'd been something wrong with me.

'Anyway,' Gran went on, 'it means you're becoming a young woman and it's time you knew about the facts of life. It's up to me to tell you 'cos I know that mother of yours is too daft to do the job.'

I looked towards the door and wondered if I should rush out and shout out some excuse, like our chimney's on fire.

'If you're going to be a respectable young lady, there's certain things you must never do. Are you listenin'?'

'Yes, Gran'ma.'

'Never eat in the street. Never put on jewellery that makes a noise and never pluck your eyebrows. You do as I say and you won't go far wrong.'

'Yes, Gran'ma.'

'Now you're starting to become a young woman,' she continued, 'it means you can have babies and you'll start attracting the boys. Do you have a boy?'

I went even more red. 'Me? A boy, Gran'ma? I'm eleven. I'm much too young.'

'Don't try to kid me. You're never too young for that sort of thing. And I see you're beginning to develop a little bust on you. That'll catch the boys' eyes for a start. So the first thing you must do is flatten your bust so it can't be noticed.'

'Flatten my bust, Gran'ma? I haven't got a bust.'

Trust Gran'ma to try and make mountains out of molehills. To tell the truth, though, I *had* noticed that I was developing a bosom. Furthermore, I wasn't the only one who'd noticed. As we lay in bed one morning, Cissie said, 'Eh, our Kate, I've been looking down my nightie and I haven't got two lumps like yours. All's I've got are two little pimples. It's not fair. Why can't I have lumps?'

'You will one day,' I'd said to reassure her. 'When you're eleven like me.'

'Get your mam to bind your bust to flatten it,' Gran'ma

was saying, 'so it won't cause wicked boys to have wicked thoughts. And don't let boys kiss you, that's another thing.'

'I won't, Gran'ma.'

'Do you know where babies come from?' she asked sharply.

'My mam says they come from under the bed but the girls at school say the nurse brings them in her black case.'

'Nonsense,' she snorted. 'Babies are made in your belly. Do you know how they get there?'

I didn't.

'They're put there when you let a boy hug and kiss you and put his thing in you.'

What was she talking about? She was trying to shock me. Was she saying that my Mam and Dad did such things? And what about Queen Victoria? Surely Gran'ma didn't think that the Queen had done these terrible things with Prince Albert? Gran really had gone off her trolley.

'How does the baby get out?' she rapped out.

'I dunno,' I said. 'Through your belly button, I suppose. It must open like a flower.'

'Babies come out from the same place they went in,' she said.

I knew for certain then that Gran had gone off her head.

'So you mustn't let boys hug and kiss you and put their thing in you, do you hear? You let a boy do it and next thing you know, you'll be having one of them there illiterate babies like Lizzie that your Auntie Gladys got from your Uncle Jack.'

The photo of my late grandad glared at me from the sideboard and he seemed to be agreeing with his widow. I was sure I saw him nod.

Her next question knocked me over.

'What kind of knickers are you wearing?'

I turned scarlet. 'Knickers?' I faltered. I wanted to say, 'What's it got to do with you, you old witch?' Instead, I said, 'Ordinary ones that my mam bought on Tib Street market. The kind with a little pocket for your hankie.'

'What colour?'

'Pale blue – they were the only ones they had.'

'I want you to promise me never to wear black underwear.'

'Promise, Gran'ma.' Anything for peace.

'Any lace?'

'No lace. They're plain.'

'That's good. Now you've started your monthlies, you'll have to stop playing them skipping and ball games where you tuck your dress into your knickers. You mustn't show off your legs to the boys. You're a young lady and you must start behaving like one. Now then,' she went on, 'it was your birthday yesterday and you thought I'd forgotten, didn't you? Well, I didn't. Look in that cupboard in the sideboard.'

I went over to the big sideboard, pulled the drawer open, releasing a smell of mothballs. Now I was sure my grandad's picture was smiling. I found a brown paper parcel.

'Open it!' she ordered.

I did so and found a huge piece of navy blue cotton material. She's bought me a tent, I thought.

I was wrong. It was the biggest pair of bloomers I'd ever seen; they had elastic all round, at the waist and at the legs.

'That elastic is there for a purpose,' she said. 'We call these bloomers "hand-trappers". Wear them and you'll have no trouble with boys.'

I was sure she was right. What could I say except, 'Thank you, Gran'ma.'

Chapter Five

It was during the long summer holiday that I sensed that something was wrong. It was a Monday morning – washday. In the cellar, Mam was scrubbing clothes on the washboard and Lizzie and me were helping by putting the washing through the mangle. Lizzie was feeding the clothes between the rollers and I was turning the big iron handle. I noticed that Dad's hankies were stained brown.

'Mam,' I said, 'I think we'll have to put these hankies into the boiler again 'cos I don't think they're clean. Why are they that funny colour?'

'That's because your dad has been doing a lot of coughing into his hankies. I can't get them clean nohow.'

'What's wrong with Dad?' I asked. 'Why is he always coughing like he does?'

'It's his job, Kate. He says it's because of the stuff he breathes in when he's blowing the glass but I think it's bronchitis.'

When I heard that word 'bronchitis', I got worried. I'd heard Mam say to Auntie Gladys that bronchitis could be dangerous if it turned into pneumonia. When I came to think about it, Dad had got thinner and he'd not been his usual bright and cheerful self. Not only that, he'd had a few days off work and that was something he never did 'cos he didn't get paid if he was off. And Mam must've worried about us all getting it 'cos she'd lapped our chests up in brown paper with wintergreen oil and nutmeg. That had solved the problem of the bust flattener all right but I'd felt daft going to school with that round me. Not only did it make a funny crackling sound but it didn't smell nice either. The other girls were always laughing at us. Eve Ogboddy said we smelt like her old grannie just before she'd died.

'Is bronchitis serious, Mam?' I asked.

'It could be if it's not looked after. I've made your dad wear lots of hot mustard poultices and I've dosed him with Veno's Cough Cure. Last week, he followed that tar-making machine along Oldham road and had a good snuff up of the hot pitch, so he should be all right.'

When Dad came home that night he looked tired and older. He was about to speak but a shudder passed through him, followed by a fit of shivering.

Mam poured him a cup of steaming hot tea. He swallowed it in two massive gulps.

Mam asked, 'How're you feeling, Mick? Is your cough any better?'

'Ah, Celia,' he panted, 'don't worry about the cough for it's doing very well. It's getting stronger and stronger whilst I'm getting weaker and weaker. Now I have pains in the chest and a terrible headache. It's that dust and lead I'm taking into my lungs every day in the glassworks. There'll be no improvement till I get a job in the fresh air.'

'There's not much chance of that,' Mam said. 'We've tried the poultices and the cough cure. Now it's time to try something else.'

'If you don't mind,' he said, 'I'll not have any dinner. I'll be off to my bed. What I need is a good sleep. I'm sure it'll do me the world of good.'

'We're not beaten yet,' Mam said. 'There's lots of other things we can try. In Ireland, folk used to swear by kerosene rubbed on the chest. But tonight I'll put a hot fire brick in your bed and I'll bring you up a hot drink of cabbage tea. Tomorrow, we'll try Friar's Balsam. That should do the trick.' She sounded desperate.

Next day, Dad was worse and he coughed nonstop. He was for ever spitting into the chamber pot that Mam had placed by the side of his bed.

A Gypsy called at the front door and for a few bob advised Mam to collect snails, boil them and rub them anti-clockwise on Dad's stomach.

It didn't work. Dad spluttered and retched as if he was bringing the whole of his insides up.

'I'll have to get up and go to work, Celia,' he gasped between bouts of hawking and spitting red mucus. 'The men will be depending on me.'

He heaved aside the bedcovers, struggled out of bed and began hurriedly to dress.

'What do you think you're doing, Mick – you a sick man?'

'I must go to work.'

'You'll do no such thing,' Mam said, feeling his forehead. 'Let the glassworks do without you for a few days. Shaun can do the blowing for you. You have a fever. So now we'll try Fenning's Fever Mixture. That should bring your temperature down.'

It didn't and it was time for stronger measures.

'I'm going to get Dr O'Brien,' Mam said. 'He can start earning the shillings we've been paying into his Sickness Club all these years.'

Mam once called the doctor before when Dad had the flu. She told us to keep out the road and she shooed us into our bedroom. But she'd forgotten that the walls in our house were that thin you could hear all that was going on in the next room, especially if you put your ear to the wall.

As we awaited the arrival of the doctor, Mam went into hysterics about the state of the place.

'The room's a disgrace,' she said to Dad. 'What'll the doctor think when he sees it?'

The bedroom got a going-over. A fresh runner on the dressing table and her best set of silver-backed hairbrushes and hand mirror were placed where the visitor could see them. Dad had to get out of bed whilst she re-made it with immaculate sheets and a silk pillow case. He was made to put on a clean nightshirt and his clothes were picked up from the back of the chair where he always hung them and dumped on our bed until the doctor had been and gone.

Dr Eugene O'Brien was a plump middle-aged man with a full beard and a no-nonsense manner. He was a good friend of Dad's – I think they used to go drinking and playing billiards together in the Shamrock Club. Anyroad, on this day, he examined Dad's chest with the telescope thing he carried round his neck, all the time making funny *aha* noises. Finally he had the rotten job of examining the phlegm in the chamber pot. Who would be a doctor?

'Bronchitis, is it not, Eugene?' Dad wheezed. 'This is what I get for that glass-blowing these last twenty years.'

'Bronchitis it is not, Mick,' said the doctor. 'I think it could be a little more than that.'

'You always were a pessimist, Eugene. Even when we played billiards. So, tell me now, what are my chances?'

There was a long pause before the doctor answered. 'About fifty-fifty,' he said.

I felt as if an icy hand had been placed on my heart when I heard this.

'What the hell do you mean, Eugene? Fifty-fifty? You're supposed to tell me I'll be back at work tomorrow.'

'Look, Mick, you're an old friend. Do you want me to give it to you straight?'

'I do.'

'I've seen a lot of cases like yours lately, Mick, and I can tell you that what we have here is a clear case of primary consumption, sometimes called galloping consumption.'

'Galloping consumption?' Dad echoed. 'What in God's name is that? It sounds like the name of a horse in the Irish Derby.'

'How serious is that, doctor?' Mam asked anxiously.

'It's extremely serious,' Dr O'Brien answered. 'Though Mick there seems to think it's a big joke.'

'Always look on the bright side, that's my motto,' Dad said with a laugh. I knew Dad's laugh and somehow this didn't sound right. 'You said my chances were fifty-fifty, Eugene. What must I do to get the right fifty?'

'The only medicine I can offer for your condition is plenty of fresh air and rest. From now on, you understand, work is out of the question.'

'There is no way I can give up work, Eugene,' Dad said. 'Not if I'm to go on feeding my family. How long have I got? A year? Two years?'

'Who can say how long? A year, maybe more. Depends on how you live from now on. A year's holiday in Switzerland or southern Italy or a Mediterranean sea cruise might slow it down a bit.'

He knew full well that such things were out of the question.

'I'll make sure my passport's in order,' Dad answered, still trying to be funny.

Ignoring Dad's attempt at humour, the doctor said, 'Even Blackpool where you can get some sunshine and fresh air would certainly give you a little more time. Failing that, a good dose of laudanum which you can get at Wise, the chemist's on Butler Street. That at least will give you some relief. Take consolation in the fact that many great people have suffered from the same complaint – John Keats, Frederic Chopin, the Brontë sisters.'

It didn't sound much of a consolation to us kids listening in the next room.

When the doctor had left, we were in a state of shock. Surely Dad couldn't be dying. Not *my* dad! I felt a pain at the pit of my stomach. But then again I couldn't help thinking that maybe he'd lived to a good age. After all, he was forty-four.

Mam and Auntie Gladys wept and wailed nonstop when the news finally sank in. As for us young 'uns, well, we refused to believe it. Dr O'Brien wasn't God. He could be wrong.

Dad joked about it all the time.

He took off his wedding ring and gave it to Mam. 'At least,' he said, 'you won't have the miserable job of trying to get this off after I'm gone. Maybe you can get a few shillings from Solly, the pawnbroker.'

Which set Mam and Auntie off all the louder.

Next Dad took it into his head to start arranging his own funeral as if he was fixing to take that holiday in Blackpool.

'I want a good send-off,' he gasped. 'I was pallbearer at my brother Jack's funeral and he had two priests at the Requiem. I'd like three. My insurance policy should cover it.'

'Glory be to God. Three priests will be fearful expensive,' Mam said through her tears. 'Two priests will be enough but stop talking like that, Mick. You're not dead yet.'

'We've got the honour of the name of Lally to keep up,' Dad said.

'Don't worry, Mick,' Mam said, humouring him. 'If you die, you'll have the best, I promise you.'

There was no stopping Dad once he got an idea in his

head. He even arranged for Mr Stiles, the undertaker, to come round and measure him up for his coffin. 'Be sure it's long enough and wide enough,' he said. 'And I'd like silk cushions. May as well be comfortable on the ride up to the cemetery.'

'Talking of cemeteries, Mr Lally,' Mr Stiles said, 'have you decided where you'd like to be buried? You can choose between Moston and Southern Cemeteries.'

'If I had my dearest wish, I'd be buried back in Ireland but I suppose I'll have to settle for a place here in Manchester. I'll leave it up to you. Why not surprise me?'

Whenever there were people around, Dad had to have his little joke. But once or twice in quieter moments when he didn't know I was watching, I caught him looking sad as if he knew deep down that it might not be long before he'd be saying his final goodbyes to us.

'Don't forget the mourning women,' he said cheerfully one day, putting on his act. 'Try to get Mrs O'Dea and Mrs McNally from St Michael's – they're the best keeners in the district. I'd like the fanciest funeral and the noisiest wake the parish has ever seen. We've got plenty of time to arrange it. The doctor said I've got a year, maybe more.'

As it turned out, he didn't have a year.

It was November and I'd had the usual day at school. As soon as word got round about my dad having TB, the other girls refused to play with any of us Lallys. The same went for Lizzie Brennan as she lived in the same house. We were treated like lepers. Shirty gave Eve Ogboddy permission to move her place from our three-seater desk to one at the back and she even moved her own high desk nearer the window. That was another thing – Gerty kept the windows open all day even though it was freezing cold. I said a silent prayer to the Holy Ghost for Houlihan and Eve Ogboddy to get pneumonia. But I don't think he was listening.

On the day I'm talking about, there was thick fog, a real pea-souper and you couldn't even see your hand in front of you. It was so bad, Gerty kept the windows closed and the school let us out at half past two. The four of us groped our way home through the smog.

Men with oil lamps walked slowly in front of the horse and carts. Once or twice horses stumbled onto the pavements and we had to stand right back to the walls to avoid being trampled. It took us over an hour to find Butler Court and when we reached home, the front door was opened by Auntie Gladys.

'Your dad's gone,' she said.

'Gone? Gone where?'

'To a better place.'

They've moved him to Blackpool, was my first thought.

'He's passed away,' Auntie said. 'Your mam's inside but she's best left alone. Best not to upset her.' When I heard this, I swallowed hard and a lump came to my throat.

Mam was sitting at the table sobbing quietly, her head in her hands. We didn't care what Auntie Gladys had said. We went to her and, weeping, we clung together for dear life.

'There'll be no piano now,' Mam said through her tears. 'No more trips to the fairground. No more nothing.'

We had to bring in Annie Swann from next door to help lay the body out. She arrived wearing her old battered hat as usual but we soon saw that she was an expert. First she bound up his jaw, closed his eyelids, and put pennies on his eyes. She washed down his body, and the three women, Mam, Auntie Gladys and Annie, dressed him in his best suit, along with his watch and chain, to wait for the undertakers to fetch the coffin which had been ready in the shop for weeks.

'I've bought him new underclothes – a vest and long

johns,' Mam said. She had a thing about underclothes. 'Always make sure you have clean undies,' she was fond of saying.

'Why?' I asked her one day.

'In case you're run over and have to go to hospital.'

That was all very well but new underclothes when you were dead! I could imagine my dad at the pearly gates and St Peter saying, 'You've led a blameless life, Michael, and you've done your time in purgatory but we can't let you in 'cos your long johns are a disgrace.'

'I thought of buying him a new suit as well,' Mam said. 'He's lost a lot of weight and that suit is hanging on him but I don't think anyone will notice.'

They put a soft downy pillow under his head. Last, they polished his best black shoes but it was a struggle to get them on him.

'He never liked those shoes,' I told them. 'He preferred the brown ones. He said the black ones were too tight.'

'Doesn't matter now,' Mam said. 'He won't be walking to the cemetery.'

Blinds were fixed to the windows and the curtains of the house were drawn, a wreath was hung at the door, the furniture was shrouded in white sheets and the mirrors were covered so no one could be spending time looking at themselves and primping up their hair.

Dad lay in state in front of the parlour window. Underneath the coffin Mam had placed a pan containing Jeyes Fluid, and on the table a bunch of potpourri. One or two nosy neighbours, some with their kids, called and asked to see the body. Mam invited them in for a look.

On the day of the wake, the coffin was carried into the living room and placed upright with the lid off so that Dad could oversee the gathering. Not that he was in a position to give his approval. The wake lasted two days and two nights. There was food and whisky galore and from all round the district of St Michael's there was a constant stream of visitors with wreaths and black-lined cards of condolence – the McBrides, the Walshes, the Dugans, the O'Learys. Even the Hickses from next door but one came round to join in the feasting. They brought one bottle of Irish whiskey and drank three. From the corner of my eye, I noticed that Mam, too, was drinking more than she usually did. But she'd been so close to my dad, it was understandable. There was a lot of singing of Irish ballads. Auntie Sarah sang a song called 'Barney Take Me Home Again'. It was hard to know whether it was a request or an order but the words were:

Oh Barney dear, I'd give the world
To see my home across the sea,
Where all the days were joy impearl'd

The tears ran down Uncle Barney's cheeks. Why this should have been so was anybody's guess. Edna O'Leary warbled about Killarney where Dad came from, and Seamus Walsh gave a powerful rendering of 'The Snowy-Breasted Pearl'.

But a kiss with welcome bland and a touch of thy fair hand
Are all that I demand would'st thou not spurn
For if not mine, dear girl, oh snowy breasted pearl
May I never from the fair with life return.

This last performance nearly caused a punch-up when Seamus's wife, Sheila, who by this time had put away two or three sherries, accused him of making goo-goo eyes at Ivy Hicks in her daringly low-cut dress each time he sang the word 'breasted'.

'If you look at that woman's bare bosom again, Seamus Walsh,' she said, 'I'll break your jaw, so I will.'

A riot was avoided only when Denis Dugan reminded everybody that we were there to pay our respects to poor Michael who, not yet cold in his coffin, was standing there watching our every move.

It's a terrible thing to say but us kids enjoyed this excitement and the attention everyone was giving us, patting us on the head, and giving us money.

'Ach, the poor wee childer. What will become of them now?'

We did our best to look sorrowful as that usually meant more money.

Even our milkman came round with a wreath. 'Mr Lally was a good man and he never failed to pay his bill on time. It's a mystery to me how he came to die as he did for he always looked so hale and hearty and he drank a lot of our wholesome, health-giving milk. As for this bronchitis thing, there's an awful lot of it about nowadays. Mr Lally is the third one on my round to die of the coughing this week.'

The two hired mourners, Mrs O'Dea and Mrs McNally, cried nonstop and were worth every bit of the smoked hams they received for their trouble.

'The loveliest funeral I've ever cried at,' Mrs McNally said. 'Look at Mick over there sleeping in his coffin like a babe. He makes a handsome corpse, don't you think so, Mrs O'Dea?'

The two keeners were right. Dad did make a lovely corpse. He had an amused smile on his lips as if he was enjoying the wake with the rest of them. He didn't look dead and I expected him to step out at any time and say, 'That tricked you.'

I spoke to him when no one was looking. 'Why did you

have to die, Dad?' I asked. 'Why, why did you have to die now?'

No answer. He simply went on smiling. For me, the penny slowly began to drop. Dad really had gone for good.

The funeral was held at St Michael's in George Leigh Street. It was a miserable rainy day, in keeping with the way we were feeling. The church was filled and I'd never seen so many flowers apart from in a flower shop or Smithfield Market. My dad had been an important man in Ancoats – one of the best glass-blowers at the Poland Street works. The family sat in the front bench. Mam, pale, her eyes heavy with weeping and lack of sleep, sat with the rest of the family, Gran'ma, Auntie Sarah, Uncle Barney, and Auntie Gladys, along with us kids. The women wore deep black crepe and the rest of us were dressed in new clothes with black armbands, all bought on Dad's death policy with the Co-op. When I looked around and saw the sad faces, I realised that Dad's death had upset not only me and our family but a lot of other people as well. His death was going to change so many lives apart from our own. There was Dad's glass-making team and I think they were nervous about what the future might bring. It was going to be worse for our own little family and that included Auntie Gladys and Lizzie. What was to become of us? I pushed these thoughts out of my mind. We'd face the music after the funeral.

At the head of the middle aisle stood the coffin draped in black. The little choir sang the plainchant Requiem and Father Muldoon gave us a lovely sermon saying how Dad had been a good man, a member of the Men's Confraternity and a regular attender at Mass and the Sacraments.

'I am sure that Michael Lally,' he said, 'will end up in heaven after he has served his time in purgatory. So we must offer up our prayers and our troubles for him so that he may be soon released and taken up into paradise. We can earn time off for him by saying special, indulgenced prayers, like "Jesus, Mary and Joseph, I offer Thee my heart and my soul" which is worth twenty days. Better still, when we suffer little hardships, we can offer them to God to earn him remission.'

He came down from the altar to sprinkle holy water on the coffin and say lots of prayers in Latin. Next he frightened off any lurking evil spirits by walking round the bier, clinking the thurible against the chain and sending a lovely aroma of incense around the church.

Dad's team of glassmakers were bearers. They were dressed in their Sunday black, the stiff, uncomfortable suits they wore only for church. Out of the glassworks they somehow looked strange and unnatural, their faces scrubbed clean of the grime which went with their job. They came forward and lifted the coffin onto their powerful shoulders and, with young Alfie leading the way, took Dad on his final grim journey. The coffin was carried slowly past and our family and the mourners followed on behind. The solemn music of the organ filled the church. It was a long, sorrowful procession to Moston Cemetery. The horses had their hooves covered in pads to deaden the noise and as we made our way up Oldham Road, men removed their hats, and other people stopped and bowed their heads, some making the sign of the cross as we passed.

'I've been thinking about what that priest said,' little Cissie whispered. 'Will Dad have to stay in purgatory long, Kate?'

'I don't know,' I answered through my tears, 'but our teacher said maybe a thousand years.'

'That's a long time,' Danny said.

'Is it hot in purgatory, Kate?' Cissie asked.

'I'm not sure,' I said, 'but Miss Houlihan said that when

we die we are the Church suffering and our venial sins have to be burned off us. I think it must be as hot as hell 'cos this month we pray for the dead and sing a special hymn for them. Two of the lines are, *Pray for the holy souls that burn/This hour amidst the cleansing flames.*'

'Poor Dad,' Cissie said. 'I wish we could get him out of that fire and up into heaven. What did the priest mean when he said we can get remission? What's that – remission?'

'It means we can get time off from having to burn in purgatory. We can be let off so many days or months or even years.'

'Maybe there's a way,' said Lizzie, 'to get both our dads out of there. Remember what the priest said about indulgences.'

'The priest mentioned a certain prayer giving us twenty days' remission,' I said. 'We'll have to say it millions of times to earn a thousand years.'

'I don't know what you're going on about,' Mam sobbed. 'All that rubbish about your Dad burning in purgatory. I'm sure he's now in heaven with his cough cured.'

At Moston Cemetery, the small group of mourners followed the coffin to the graveside. In the Catholic section, crowded with tombstones, two grave-diggers had dug a fresh pit in the yellow clay and were respectfully standing back, holding their shovels, ready to fill in the grave when everyone had gone. We gathered round the hole and with heads bent watched as the men in our group gently lowered the coffin into the grave. The women sobbed and moaned. The men hunched their shoulders, bowed their heads and looked lost. The priest said the final prayers,

'Forasmuch as it hath pleased Almighty God of his great mercy to take unto himself the soul of our dear brother here departed, we therefore commit his body to the ground; earth to earth, ashes to ashes, dust to dust; in sure and certain hope of the Resurrection to eternal life, through our Lord Jesus Christ.'

Together we recited the prayer for the dead: 'Eternal rest give unto him, O Lord, and let perpetual light shine upon him. May he rest in peace. Amen.'

Mam tossed a single rose into the grave. The priest sprinkled the coffin again from the brass container carried by the altar boy. After that each of us had a go with the holy water brush and then it was over.

At that moment, I thought of Dad cold in his coffin. I wondered if he was still smiling.

It was getting dark and it looked as if the November fog was coming down again. The funeral cortege took us slowly back to Ancoats.

There was a small ceremony in the upstairs room of the Shamrock Club for the family and those who had been to the cemetery. Everyone said again what a great man Dad had been.

'Sure, he'll be missed something awful in the glassworks for there wasn't another man in the whole of Manchester who could blow glass like Michael Lally,' Shaun said.

This time the occasion and the talk were quiet and sad and everyone spoke in whispers. A couple of hours later, our little family walked back through the gloom to Butler Court and an empty house.

We opened the door, and were met by a strange eerie silence. The fire was dead in the grate and the place was cold and depressing. Mam lit the oil lamp. Only then did I realise deep, deep down that I had truly lost my dad, and I broke down and cried for all I was worth, which set the others off, including baby Eddie.

Now Dad was gone, there was one big question on our minds.

What now?

Chapter Six

For some time after the funeral, everyone in the family was miserable as if a light had gone out of our lives. Nobody did anything. Mam lay in bed staring at the ceiling and weeping quietly to herself. The rest of us moped about the house, getting more and more depressed. Everywhere we looked there were things that reminded us of Dad.

'Here are the cards he did those tricks with,' said Danny sadly. 'And look, I was right. He had marked the cards.'

'You'd better tell him then,' I said, 'that he was a twister.'

'No matter where I turn,' Mam said after a while, 'there he is. All the little things he left behind – his cuff links, even his collar studs.' She pulled out his straw boater and his silver cane. 'He won't be needing these any more,' she sighed.

'Oh, I don't know,' I replied, trying to be cheerful. 'Maybe he's entertaining them in heaven or purgatory or wherever he is, doing his song and dance act.'

For Cissie, it was the same. She clung to that big teddy bear he'd won at the fair. I thought it was worse for me though. I had those glass friggers he'd made for me – the dog, the cat, but specially the swan he'd made for my birthday. They reminded me of the glassworks and the happy times I used to have watching him and his team at work.

Us kids in the family tried playing games in the court but

it was no use, our hearts weren't in it. We wouldn't have dreamt of doing 'black rabbit' on Annie Swann's door – not after all she did for us laying Dad out in his coffin.

One day I said to Mam, 'This could go on for weeks and we're getting more and more miserable. Someone's got to do something.'

My words must've hit home, for Mam made the first move. One Sunday after Mass, about a fortnight after we'd buried Dad, she called us together, including Auntie Gladys and Lizzie.

'Kate's right. We've got to snap out of this grieving. I'm sure Mick wouldn't have wanted us to go round with faces as long as fiddles for the rest of our lives. It'll soon be Christmas and we've got to start looking on the bright side. So I've made some plans for the future. First of all, Auntie Gladys and Lizzie are coming up from the cellar to live with the rest of us. Gladys can sleep with me in the big bed in the front room and Lizzie can go into the girls' bed, top and tail.'

'That's great, Mam,' I said. 'Lizzie's my best friend and it can't be healthy down there in the cellar – it's so damp.'

Auntie Gladys already knew about the new arrangement. She smiled and nodded.

'Thank you very much, Mrs Lally,' Lizzie said in her quiet voice.

'The next thing we've got to realise,' Mam went on, 'is that the ride in the gravy train when your dad was earning good wages is over. We're almost broke. I think I've got about fifteen shillings left in my purse and that's got to see us through the week. The money from the insurance has gone on the fancy funeral and the new clothes. Now we have to get some cash from somewhere.'

'I have tuppence,' said Cissie, 'and you can have that if you want it.'

Mam smiled and patted her on the head. 'That's good of you, Cissie. I know you mean well, love, but we need a lot more than that.'

'We could get Saturday jobs,' I suggested.

'Sell firewood or run errands,' Danny said.

'They don't pay much and anyroad there's no need,' Mam said. 'I've got myself a job working with Gladys at the Magadi Soda Works in Angel Meadow. The wages are twelve shillings a week and if Gladys and me pool our money we should be all right. We'll have twenty-four shillings altogether; our rent is seven and six and that'll leave us over sixteen bob a week. That should be enough.'

'What about Eddie there?' I asked, pointing to the baby. 'What do we do with him?'

'That's where you come in, Kate. Now that your father's dead, you're going to have to grow up fast. I'm leaving you in charge of the house and the family while me and Gladys are at work.'

'But what about school? I'll have the School Board after me.'

'We don't have much choice, Kate. You'll be leaving school when you're twelve next year. So it won't make much difference.'

I didn't like the sound of any of this. Not one bit. I might do my share of moaning about school but deep down I loved going and I was doing so well in the weekly tests, especially in English and arithmetic. Besides, there was the School Board and everyone knew about the School Board – they were worse than Mr Rooney and Shirty Gerty rolled into one. According to Florrie Moss in our class, they'd hit you with a big stick if they caught you playing wag.

On the Monday morning, we started the new routine. At five o'clock, we heard Joe Gatley, the knocker-up, banging his pole on the front bedroom window. 'Come on, get up with thee,' he called. 'You're not born to lie in bed all day.' At half past five, Mam came into the bedroom and dumped Eddie into the bed with us. They had to be at work in time for the six o'clock hooter.

'I'm leaving you in charge,' Mam said. 'Bring Eddie over to the works at twelve o'clock and I'll feed him.' From the breast she meant. Mam didn't believe in bottle-feeding. 'Nearly all the bottle fed babies die,' she said. She finished giving her orders and she was gone. I couldn't go back to sleep after that and anyroad Eddie needed his nappy changing.

No use moaning about it, I had to get up and get on with it. I set the fire using wood and the cinders from yesterday. I soon had a cheerful blaze going. The nappy was next. I removed the dirty one, put Vaseline on his bum, wrapped the fresh one and fixed it with a safety pin, taking great care not to stick it in his bottom or I'd never have heard the end of it. Next, breakfast and that meant only one thing – toast. I cut slices of bread and raked the mixture of coal and coke till I had a nice glow right for toasting. I gave Danny and Lizzie the job of spearing and holding the bread to the bars while I made the tea from the big iron kettle on the hob. I helped Cissie to get washed at the slopstone. She moaned about the cold water. 'Mam always uses warm.' 'Well, I'm not Mam, and anyroad, there's no time.' I made sure that Danny got washed properly, especially his neck as he seemed to forget that he had one. At half past eight, they were ready for school. Lizzie promised to look after Cissie. I told Danny that I'd be out at dinnertime taking Eddie to be fed and I warned him not to lose the front door key. 'What's for dinner?' he asked. 'Bread and dripping', I told him. I couldn't think of anything else. I hoped there was enough dripping. We'll have to get ourselves better organised, I said to myself.

When they were gone, I sided the table, washed the pots, and swept up. The fire was going out and I had to go for a shovelful of coal in the bunker at the back. It was all slack and I had to be careful not to put the fire out. A few lumps of coke put that right. Mam had left me a pile of ironing and so I put the iron on the hob. It took me the rest of morning to get through it. Meanwhile, Eddie was yelling the place down and I took him on my knee and gave him a bottle of sugar and water to keep him quiet. I'd rather have been at school, I thought, even kneeling at the front of Gerty's class.

At half past eleven, it was time to take Eddie across to Mam at the soda works in Angel Meadow. I wrapped the baby in his warm coat and his woolly hat. He wasn't too heavy and as it was quite a way to go, I decided to carry him as it was quicker than pushing the bassinet which had a rickety wheel. I set off, making sure I closed the front door behind me. I only hoped Danny didn't lose the front door key or we'd be in big trouble. To get to Angel Meadow, I had to cross two busy main roads. I walked quickly down Oldham Road and at the Victoria Square Buildings I crossed over to Thompson Street and past the railway goods yards until I reached Rochdale Road. It was an area Danny and me knew well as we often came over this way with the pram to buy coke at the Gould Street depot. I managed to get over the road opposite Ludgate Hill and a short walk brought me to Angel Meadow. A funny name, I thought, and I wondered who decided the names of the streets as there was no sign of a meadow and certainly none of any angels.

At twelve o'clock, the factory hooters went off and soon I saw Mam and Auntie Gladys coming out of the soda works. I handed Eddie over to Mam. She sat on a stone step and gave Eddie the breast. He sucked greedily. Anyone would've thought he hadn't been fed before. Mam brought up his wind by putting him over her shoulder and patting his back. Eddie obliged by giving a belch that could be heard several streets away. She handed him back to me and I could tell from the smell and the farting noises he was making that it would mean a change of nappy when I got him back home. 'Take him home now and put him to bed,' Mam said. 'Close the curtains when you get back and don't open the door to nobody or you'll have the School Board after us. I'll be back after six o'clock.' She went off with Auntie Gladys to get her own dinner of bread, cheese and a bottle of stout in the Angel Inn at the corner.

I wondered how Danny, Lizzie and Cissie were getting on at home. Had they managed to find the bread and dripping I left for them? Still worrying about them, I hurried back. I reached Sherratt Street off Oldham Road. And as I turned into George Leigh Street, there he was! The School Board! A tall man with a droopy moustache and dressed in a uniform with a peaked cap like a postman and carrying a large stick. 'Hoi, you!' he shouted. 'Come here at once!' I was terrified. We'd heard such stories about them and what they did to you if they caught you. Clutching the baby, I ran and ran. In Silk Street there was Mrs Sullivan standing outside her door. I must've changed to a frightened colour.

'What's to do, Kate?' she asked.

'The School Board's round there and he's after me.'

'Quick,' she said, 'come in here.' It was a lobby house. 'Take the baby into the scullery. Whatever you do, don't let him cry.'

'He won't. He's still asleep.'

As I was cowering in the kitchen saying my prayers to St Jude, I could hear the School Board outside. 'Did you see a little girl with a baby in her arms pass here?'

'Not while I've been stood here,' Mrs Sullivan replied. 'Why, what's she been doing?'

'Playing wag from school, missing her lessons, that's what she's been doing. If I catch her, I'll teach her a lesson she won't forget.'

I waited till he'd gone but my heart was thumping madly as I crept along the last few streets to Butler Court. God, I hoped I didn't get this every day or I'd soon be a nervous wreck. I made it home in one piece and put Eddie to bed. I made sure the other three had something to eat and I got them off to school for the afternoon session. How I wished I could have gone with them!

We got through the rest of the week without any further mishaps but I noticed that Mam and Auntie Gladys were getting home later and later. They finished work at six o'clock and it shouldn't have taken more than half an hour to walk home. On the Monday they were back at seven but by Friday night – the day they got paid – it was half past eight. I had already got Eddie and Cissie to bed when Mam and Auntie got back. There was that sweet smell of stout about them like the whiff of a saloon bar when you're walking past the open door. They'd both taken to sniffing snuff and they talked a bit funny and kept repeating themselves. Not only that, they sounded that cheerful – too cheerful.

'You're a proper little mother, our Kate,' Mam gibbered. 'A real saint if ever there was one. No wonder you were always your dad's favourite.'

I didn't like this talk and I wasn't my dad's favourite or anything of the kind. If he'd had a favourite, it was Cissie. I didn't say anything. I'd found it was best to keep quiet when people had had a drop.

It was on the Saturday that things came to a head. It

was seven o'clock and I had Eddie and Cissie in the tin bath in front of the fire, with Lizzie helping. The bath water had gone a bit cold and so I asked Danny to put some more water in the big kettle. He picked up the heavy iron kettle from the fire and, as he was going over to the slop stone, he tripped over the coconut matting and not only spilt hot water on his foot but bashed his head against the bolt on the scullery door. What to do? He was yelling the place down. 'Help! Help! I'm bleeding to death.' The two in the bath joined in in sympathy. I got his stocking off and sprinkled flour on his burning foot. Next I put lint and bandage on the cut on his forehead but I could see he was going to need a couple of stitches in the wound.

'Quick,' I said to Lizzie, 'take Danny over to Auntie Sarah's in Bengal Street and ask her to take him to Ancoats Hospital. I'll have to stay with the young 'uns.'

When Danny heard those words 'Ancoats Hospital' he bawled even louder 'cos like the rest of us he knew about Ancoats. There was a giant of a nurse there with one of those massive headdresses. She was one of those no-nonsense types. And there was something about that hospital that was terrifying – the funny-shaped glass bottles with all kinds of coloured liquids, and a sickening smell of ether or chloroform or something. And what was even more frightening, if you had to have stitches, there was no painkiller or anything like that and the big nurse had to hold you down while the doctor did his fancy needlework on your flesh.

I got the two small ones out of the bath, dried them and got them into bed. At half past eight, Auntie Sarah returned with a sorry-looking Danny. He looked as if he'd been in the wars and the only thing that would console him was a big jam butty. Auntie Sarah sat in front of the fire and waited. She may have been a little woman but she had a fiery temper and I could tell from the way she was scowling that she wasn't happy.

Half an hour later, Mam and Gladys rolled in breathing stout and snuff fumes all over the place. They'd both got silly smiles on their faces but Auntie Sarah's expression soon wiped them off.

'You stupid, stupid pair,' she shouted. 'Fancy leaving a young eleven-year-old girl like Kate in charge of the house while you two go off gallivanting. I've half a mind to set the cruelty man on you.'

'There's no need for that nastiness,' Mam said, turning sober in a matter of seconds. 'Gladys and me have put in a hard week's work in that terrible soda factory and we've a right to take a little time off to enjoy ourselves.'

'It won't do,' Sarah yelled. 'You can't work and rear a family at the same time. You'll have to give up the job and stay at home to look after your kids.'

'And what are we supposed to use for money?' Mam shouted back. 'Since Mick died, we haven't two ha'pennies to rub together. What can we do? Maybe you could do some baby-sitting for us?'

'No use coming to me for your baby-sitting for haven't I a job of my own to hold down. You'll have to apply to the parish for outdoor relief.'

'That's one thing I'll never do,' Mam said. 'I'd sooner die first than go on the parish.'

Next afternoon, matters were taken out of her hands. It was Sunday afternoon and things were quiet. Mam and Auntie Gladys had both gone for a snooze, taking Eddie with them. The others were playing outside in the court. There was a loud knock at the front door. I left off black-leading the grate and looked through the curtain to see who in God's name would be visiting us on a Sunday afternoon. My heart skipped a beat when I saw who it was.

The School Board man still in his uniform and wearing his peaked cap! 'Mam! Mam!' I called up the stairs. 'Come quick, it's the School Board!'

She soon came hurrying down the stairs, pausing at the mirror to primp up her hair before opening the door.

'Mrs Lally?' the Board man said in a stern official voice. 'Mrs Celia Lally?'

'That's right, sir. That's me.' Mam was shaking like a leaf.

'You have a daughter by the name of Catherine Lally?'

'That's correct, sir. Why, what's she been doing?' she said, looking accusingly at me.

'It's what she hasn't been doing,' he sneered. 'Why has she been away from school?'

Mam was flummoxed but only for a minute. 'She's got no shoes.' The old, old story, the School Board must've heard it a thousand times.

'She can come in her bare feet – as long as they're clean. But it has been reported to us by Mrs Ogboddy that you have been keeping her home while you go out to work and I distinctly saw her during the week running away carrying a baby.'

'It must have been someone else,' Mam lied. 'Our Kate hasn't stirred out of the house. Have you, Kate?'

'No, Mam.' That lie was going to cost me at least a couple of thousand years in purgatory, I said to myself.

'Be that as it may,' the Board man said in that funny way he had of talking, 'but I have to inform you that in accordance with the Education Act of eighteen eighty, attendance at school is compulsory for children until the age of twelve. Failure to comply with the law can mean a fine of up to five pounds. If you continue to break the law, it will result in a prison sentence.'

He took out an official-looking notebook and filled in a

lot of details. He tore off the page and handed it to Mam who took it with trembling hand. 'What is it?' she asked.

'This is a formal order that you ensure your daughter attends school. Failure to comply with this order will result in proceedings being taken out against you.'

'What does that mean?' Mam faltered. 'We've done nothing.'

'It means,' he said, 'that I shall expect to see your daughter at St Michael's School first thing on Monday. Otherwise, I shall have no alternative but to issue you with a summons. Good afternoon.'

That word 'summons' was enough for Mam. It was a word much feared in the district. It meant court, solicitors, police, magistrates, fines and maybe even Strangeways.

Next day, Mam gave up her job at the soda factory and I went back to school. I filled in a form of application for outdoor relief to the Board of Poor Law Guardians. It was a form I was familiar with as I'd done it for dozens of neighbours. Two weeks later, we had a visit from a member of the district relief committee. Mam told the young 'uns to go out and play but she let me stay to give her support 'cos she was jittery when she had to talk to any kind of official. Our visitor was a small man with large bulbous eyes which didn't look at you straight. I thought he had some disease like St Vitus dance until I realised that his head and his eyes were darting about the place taking stock of everything in the room.

'My name's Mr Gillespie,' he said, turning his head from side to side like the beam from a lighthouse. 'I'm one of the guardians for your district. I'm here to look at your case and see if you qualify for outdoor relief. It's also my job to see that we don't give away the ratepayers' money to undeserving cases.' He smiled nervously as if expecting someone to punch him. Maybe on some previous visit someone had.

'Can I get you a cup of tea, Mr Gillespie?' Mam asked, partly to make him feel welcome and partly to hide her own jangled nerves.

'That would be welcome, Mrs Lally,' he said, flicking his eyes in every direction.

Mam brought out her best china – something she only did for special people like priests or doctors.

'Bone china?' he asked, scribbling in his notebook.

'A wedding present I've managed to keep in one piece all these years,' Mam said proudly, handing him his tea with trembling hand.

'Let me explain the position,' he said. 'It's the job of the relief committee to give help where there's genuine hardship. Do you think you come into this category, Mrs Lally?'

'I don't know what genuine hardship is,' Mam said, speaking up bravely, 'but I have four young children and since my husband died no income whatsoever. My rent's over seven shillings a week, and we need money for food, coal, paraffin, and the bare necessities to keep body and soul together.'

'That may be so,' the little man said, 'but I think you're far from being destitute. We can only give relief to the poorest of the poor. You said on your form that you have a lodger – a Mrs Gladys Brennan – who is helping you out with the rent and so I'm afraid you don't qualify for aid from the rates.'

'But I have no wages coming in and I have four mouths to feed.'

'That may be so,' he said, 'but we can only give relief when we see a person is completely without any means. That is to say, only cases where an applicant has used up her own resources and has no choice but to come to us for support.'

'You mean when she's reached the end of her tether and is dying of starvation?'

'Exactly,' he said, swivelling his head in a full circle. 'Looking round your lovely home, Mrs Lally, it's obvious you have many valuable possessions and it would be unfair to the deserving cases we have on our books if we were to give you help when you have the means to help yourself.'

'You're saying we have to sell everything we have before you can give us relief?'

'That is correct,' he said, grimacing as if he'd got belly ache. I felt like grabbing the cup out of his hand and giving him a clout.

'From where I'm sitting, I can see a whole range of beautiful objects. Your furniture, sideboard, table and chairs, the statues in their glass shades, the grandmother clock and the pictures on the walls, the ornamental teapot and those lovely blown-glass things on the mantelpiece, your china tea set. And that's only in this room. You have your beds and your bedding. Even your clothes and those of the children are of good quality. I could go on but you can see it's obvious that you're nowhere near being a genuine case of poverty.' He put away his notebook.

'So, only when we have nothing left will you consider us?' Mam said angrily.

'I'm afraid that is so,' he replied, putting down his cup hastily and sensing maybe that this was where things might start to turn nasty. He stood up. 'If ever you do reach the point where you have exhausted your own resources, don't hesitate . . .' He was already moving towards the door. A minute later he'd gone.

It was from the day of that visit that we started to slide downhill.

Chapter Seven

Whenever we needed help we always went to the one place we knew we could get it, like we did when my dad died. The church, you think. But at St Michael's, Father Muldoon would send us on our way with a blessing and a sprinkling of Holy Water. And we couldn't live on Holy Water. What about our relatives living nearby – Gran'ma, Auntie Sarah and Uncle Barney? No use. They'd got nowt to offer but advice. No, for down-to-earth practical help, we turned to the old lady next door, Annie Swann, the pawnbroker's runner. Why did we need her? 'I can't be seen taking our things to the pawnbroker,' Mam said. 'I'd be too ashamed. What would the neighbours say? Imagine the gossip if they saw me pushing the bassinet loaded up with our things! Best to get Annie – she doesn't mind what the neighbours say.' Mam still had her pride. How long could she keep it?

Annie came into our living room with her mongrel dog nervously looking around in case our cat should put in an appearance. Annie cast a professional eye around the room. 'You've got some lovely things, Mrs Lally,' she said. 'They should keep you going for some time.' She picked out our prize possessions – a wall clock which Dad had inherited from his parents before he was married, and on the mantelpiece a boat-shaped teapot, a wedding present from

– as Mam was always telling us – 'my grandmother, Mary Molly McGinty'. We thought we'd miss that clock if it went, for it was part of the family and we were so used to hearing it chime out the hours and register the passing of the years. We wouldn't miss the teapot as much because Mam never brewed tea in it. But what could we do? Annie took the clock and the teapot down and put them in the bassinet, covering them up with a blanket.

An hour after Annie had left, Mam turned to me and said, 'I'm leaving Lizzie and Danny in charge while you and me go to get some money from your uncle.'

'Uncle?' I asked. 'Which uncle? It's no use going to Uncle Barney, he never has nowt.'

'No, you daft ha'porth. Uncle Solly. Annie should have the stuff there by now. We'll sneak into his shop by the back door.'

Solly the pawnbroker had his shop on Butler Street at the corner of Mellor Street. There was a big sign in his window which gave his name in gold lettering: SOLOMON GOLDSTEIN: MONEYLENDER AND PAWNBROKER. PLEDGES TAKEN IN STRICTEST CONFIDENCE. Underneath that it said: I BUY ANYTHING. I used to wonder about that 'Anything' bit when I passed the shop on the way to school. Would he buy the hefty blue bloomers gran'ma had forced on me? Would he buy the jam jar of tiddlers our Danny caught in the River Irk last Saturday? If the answer was no, he should have taken that sign down and changed it to 'Almost Anything'. Hanging from the wall, I saw three golden balls.

'What do they mean, Mam?' I asked.

'People in Ancoats say they mean the chances of ever getting your stuff back are two to one. But if you want to know, you'd better ask inside.'

At the corner of Mellor Street, Mam stopped and looked nervously over her shoulder. Shifty-eyed was the expression that came to my mind. 'See if you can see anyone coming,' she muttered. 'I don't want to be seen going into the shop.' When we were sure the coast was clear, we moved quickly down a side street to the back entrance.

Behind the counter inside the shop was a wall of shelves right up to the high ceiling. To reach the top levels there was a sliding ladder and a long pole with a hook on the end. Everywhere we looked we saw thousands of labelled bundles, each one someone's prized possession, someone's family heirloom, someone's best clothes, someone's dignity. A young assistant showed us into one of the many cubicles to await Uncle Solly.

'This is like going to confession,' I whispered.

'Shush, someone might hear you.'

I expected a grille to open and to hear Solly greet us in Latin, '*In nomine Patris, et Filii, et Spiritus Sancti*. How can I help you, my child?'

'Bless us, Father Solly, for we are broke,' I would say. 'It's over a month since we had a decent meal.'

After five or six minutes, the great man himself joined us. He was little and shrivelled-up with yellow skin and beady, watery eyes.

'So your clock and your teapot I've seen,' he began. 'To borrow on them you're asking what kind of money?' Solly had this funny way of asking questions backwards.

'The clock cost over twenty-five pounds a few years ago, and the teapot was a present,' Mam faltered. 'I thought maybe ten pounds for the two.'

'I should live so long,' Solly chuckled. 'They're not worth that much today. The clock's a cheap japanned model that runs on springs and it's finished in poor quality black lacquer. As for the teapot, who needs one shaped like a boat? The most I can give on them is fifty shillings.'

'That's only two pounds ten,' Mam gasped. 'A tenth of what they're worth.'

Solly shrugged. 'Take it or leave it.'

We took it. He handed over five grubby ten shilling notes and a numbered pawn ticket.

'*You* may redeem your clock any time you wish by repaying the loan with interest. After a year, *I*, if I wish, may sell it to recover the money I've lent you.'

Mam nodded her agreement. As if she had any choice.

On the way out, I asked him the meaning of the three golden balls.

'They're the coat of arms of a famous money-grasping Italian family called the Medici – crooks who used to cheat the poor by lending money at crippling rates. Not like me. I charge only a shilling in the pound per week.'

'That's five per cent per week,' I said. At school Gerty had been ramming percentages down our throats.

'Clever girl,' Solly said, sounding as if what he meant was, 'Too bloody clever by half'.

'That's twenty per cent per month and two hundred and forty per cent per year,' I persisted. I was showing off. Gerty would have been proud of me.

'Yes, yes. Very clever,' Solly snapped. 'Maybe you should be running your own shop.'

He ushered us out by the same door we came in.

'If you need me again,' he said as we departed, 'remember I'm here to help, especially if you have rings or precious stones. I'm Solly, the people's friend.'

The wall clock and the teapot were the beginning of a long line of items that found their way onto Solly's shelves: the fancy crockery, the statues in their glass shades, the brass fire irons, even the glass toys Dad had made at the Poland Street works but not, I'm glad to say, the glass swan he had made for my birthday. Solly wasn't having that, no matter how broke we got. We reached a stage, though, where there was more of our home in Solly's shop than in our house at 6 Butler Court. After the ornaments, our clothes were next to go, sometimes before we even knew about it.

Danny spent one Sunday morning looking for his best trousers. 'I can't find my Whit Friday pants, Mam,' he moaned. 'Do you know where they've got to?'

'You ate 'em yesterday,' she said.

As we got nearer to Christmas, things got tighter and tighter and to feed the great pawnbroking monster that was Solly's, we scraped the bottom of our barrel and turned to the furniture. For this he had to pay a personal visit. He walked around the house, pursing his lips and making little tut-tutting noises, which meant he didn't think much of any of it. He slipped on a pair of half-moon glasses and wrote in his little black notebook.

'There's no call for big heavy sideboards like that,' he said, shaking his head. 'People don't have rooms big enough to take them. Twelve bob's the most I can offer.'

'But Solly,' Mam said, 'it cost five pounds and there's not a scratch on it. Have mercy on us, Solly, it's coming up to Christmas.'

'So for Christmas I should make special concessions. Tell you what,' he said finally. 'I like you and your family, Mrs Lally. You're honest and straightforward. So I'll give you fifteen and that's my last offer.'

'So what can we do?' Mam said, shrugging her shoulders. She was already beginning to pick up Solly's mannerisms.

The fifteen bob kept us going for another week. In the third week of December, we were on our uppers and we wondered what kind of Christmas we could expect.

Cissie still believed in Father Christmas.

'Maybe this year,' Mam said, 'she'll have to grow up. Then again, perhaps we'll not ruin her childish dreams of Santa Claus and his reindeers. Growing up can wait till January.'

'Father Christmas may not be able to come this year,' I told her. 'For a start, our chimney's much too narrow for him to climb down. He's a big fat man and likely to get stuck.'

Cissie listened to this and looked solemn and with a sad expression nodded her head to show she'd understood.

Mam was determined to have as good a Christmas as she could afford. She took two wedding rings to Solly's – her own and Dad's. They were both solid gold and so for a couple of weeks we were flush. She bought a few bargain-priced presents from the pawnbroker to put in our stockings.

'This is the first Christmas without your dad,' she said. 'It's miserable enough without him and so I'm going to splash out with the last money we're likely to get from Solly. I'm sorry to lose the rings but we need food more than we need bits of metal. Maybe one day we'll get them out of hock.'

Some hopes.

About this time, we lost our front door key. Naturally we blamed Danny who was always losing things. 'I haven't seen the rotten key,' he protested. 'Why do I always get the blame for everything?'

The mystery was solved a couple of days later. The postman in his red robin uniform came knocking at our door with a letter addressed to 'Father Christmas, North Pole'. In it was the missing key. Cissie hid under the table as the letter was read out.

'Deer Fathr Christmass, Are Kate sez you cant get down our chimley becos its two small. So here Is the key to are front door. Pleaz come in.'

Christmas Eve, we hung up our stockings hopefully. Even though we knew it was Mam and Auntie Gladys who were Santa Claus, we went along with it for the sake of Cissie who had been told that maybe Santa had lost weight and would squeeze down the chimney after all. Us bigger ones tried to stay awake until stocking-filler time but we didn't make it. Next morning, we were up bright and early to find that each of us had got an apple, a tangerine, half a bar of Fry's chocolate, and a present – a Raggedy Ann doll for Cissie, a torch for Danny, a pencil set for Lizzie, and a book called *Little Women* by Louisa May Alcott for me. Oh, I almost forgot, and a rattle for Eddie.

On Christmas Day, Gran'ma, Auntie Sarah and Uncle Barney came over for dinner. Mam and Auntie Gladys came up trumps with a lovely meal of chicken, roast potatoes, sprouts, and stuffing, and we even managed to have crackers to pull though Gran'ma fell off her chair with the effort.

After the dinner, we sang the carol, 'We wish you a merry Christmas' and when it came to the bit 'We all want some figgy pudding', we let rip. Mam and Gladys took out the pudding from the oven and with a big helping of custard, we soon made short work of it. Lizzie and me sided the table and washed up while the adults dozed off. There followed a treasure hunt for toffees which were hidden around the house.

That night we went to bed happily. My only regret was that Dad hadn't been there. On second thoughts, maybe he *was*.

Chapter Eight

When the Christmas celebrations were over, we came down to earth with a bump – a big bump.

For one thing, it started to snow heavily. Fun for us kids, you think, but we had no coal and we'd used up the slack we had in the cellar. Using our coal shovel, we kept warm by clearing a pathway through the snow for our own house and for Annie Swann and the Hicks. They gave us a few pennies for doing it. Then us three big kids – Danny, Lizzie and me – had this idea of going over to Gould Street Gasworks with a sack to pick up lumps of coke that the carts dropped as they came out of the gate. Cissie cried to come with us but we didn't let her.

'You're too small,' I told her.

'I'm not,' she protested. 'I'll soon be six.'

We left her behind anyway, still crying her eyes out.

We took our old pram with the wobbly wheel that seemed to have a mind of its own, and when we got to Gould Street, we found we were not the only ones with the idea. As a cartload of hot steaming coke came out of the yard, there was a mad scramble. The Collyhurst kids were too quick for us and they snaffled the lot. But when the second load appeared, we were ready and quite a few lumps dropped in our path. We got a little more coke by appealing to the carters' better nature. 'Got any spare coke, mister? Please, mister. We're freezing at home.' Some of the drivers told us to bugger off but one or two threw a few handfuls our way. We followed the carts for a few hundred yards and whenever the carts gave a jerk or a jolt we thanked God 'cos a few more lumps fell off. Then I had a brainwave.

'Why wait for these jolts?' I said. 'Let's make 'em happen. Danny, go and find a good sized rock – not too big and not too small.'

Danny soon found one on a nearby croft. We placed the rock on the cobbled roadway and every time a cart rolled over it. Abracadabra! Pieces of coke fell right into our lap.

Half a day of this and we'd collected half a bag. We went home happy with our haul 'cos it meant we could have a warm fire and make toast. Some of the kids hanging around the gasworks told us that it was better at the railway sidings in Collyhurst Road 'cos you could pick coal and clinkers on the tip there but you had to keep your eyes skinned for the Railway Police who'd grab you for trespassing.

The following weekend we decided to try our luck. Cissie started her skriking again and so we let her come with us this time even though it was a long walk across two main roads. We made her promise not to get in the way. 'I won't, I won't,' she said.

We turned off Collyhurst Road and crossed over the Canal Cut by an iron bridge. Behind Collyhurst Dwellings we came to the big railway fence; it was about seven feet high and made of thick wood. There were little holes in the wood which let you see what was happening on the other side. Danny got up in two easy jumps like a frog when it's had a stick poked into its backside. Straddled across the fence, he hoisted first Cissie, next Lizzie and lastly me. On the other side we couldn't believe our eyes. Treasure! There was a big rubbish tip and we could see straightaway that along with broken LMS crockery, it had rich pickings of coal, coke and clinkers dumped from the trains in the Red Bank sidings. We even found one or two cups and saucers still in one piece. There were lots of other kids there but there were enough goodies for everyone.

With a whoop of delight, we went to work and soon had a bag filled with a wealth of mixed fuel. We were like hens scrabbling and scratching for grubs. Our faces and our clothes were black, our fingers were cut and bleeding but we didn't care. We started work on the second sack. We'd got it about half filled when there was a terrified shout from the other scavengers. 'Railway cops! Run for it!' There was a mad scurrying and scrabbling as everyone tried to run down the tip to make for the fence. 'Grab the bags!' I bawled to the others. Danny picked up Cissie, and Lizzie and me got the bags, then we ran for all we were worth. We threw the bags over, losing half our swag in the process, but Danny pushed us over to safety. It took a bit more effort to get Cissie over as we had to catch her on the other side. What a relief as we helped her down! Danny was not so lucky. He was snatched by the Railway Police and taken away by the scruff of the neck across the railway sidings.

My heart was beating wildly as we dragged our two sacks – still half filled with coal and coke – along the streets and back to Butler Court. Mam and Auntie Gladys were filled with horror when we told them the news. 'Oh, poor, poor Danny!' Mam moaned. 'What'll they do to him? I wish you'd never gone near the bloody place. We'd rather shiver with the cold than have this trouble with the police.'

That night a big burly copper called round and knocked loudly on the front door. He told Mam that she had to go to Willett Street police station to collect her son. Worried out of her mind, Mam put on her shawl and took me with her. I think I'd become her support whenever there was trouble.

At the police station, a desk sergeant took down our particulars and we were told to sit on a hard wooden bench. There were all kinds of roughs around us – drunks, mad-looking men, wild-eyed women who screamed abuse at the sergeant and everyone else. After an hour, the police brought out a sorry-looking Danny. His face was puffed up from crying and he had a red mark on his cheek where they'd belted him. We were called to the desk and the big sergeant read out the charge. 'Daniel Lally, you have been charged with trespass on railway property. We have decided to let you go on this occasion as it's your first offence. But it has been noted in our books and you now have a criminal record against your name. I must warn you that if you are ever brought before the police or the courts again, you will be punished most severely. Do you understand?'

Danny, racked with sobs, could only mumble 'Yes' through his tears.

At home, Mam gave us a severe telling-off. 'I want you to stay away from gasworks and railway sidings. Whichever way we turn, it all goes wrong. I try to work, we have the School Board on our back; I apply for relief and I'm told I must first sell all we've got; we go to the pawnbroker and have to give away our things for a pittance; and now, we try to scavenge a few scraps of coke and we're in trouble with the law. It's getting that I don't know which way to turn. If we didn't have Auntie Gladys lodging with us and bringing in a little help with the rent, I don't know what I'd do.'

It was true that bit about Auntie Gladys helping us a little with the rent. It hadn't been so long ago that she'd been thanking us for taking her and Lizzie in. But now the boot was on the other foot. She was the one with the job – not much, admittedly, but it was *something*. The five shillings a week she gave to Mam was helping us to keep our heads above water – if only just.

Over the weeks after Christmas, our house was gradually emptied and Solly Goldstein's horse and cart became a familiar sight outside the house. Mam no longer cared if the neighbours knew. The chest of drawers and the wardrobes from both bedrooms went the way of the others. Finally our bedsteads were taken away and we were left with straw palliasses on the floor and our coats became our blankets. We managed to survive into February but it was bitterly cold and when the water in the standpipe and the toilet froze over, we found ourselves shivering all the time. It was even a relief to go to school as, despite Gerty's cruel 'treatments', at least there was some heat there. Even the strap was welcome as it warmed our hands.

We were hungry most of the time but Mam wouldn't hear of us going to one of the charity soup kitchens run by the Salvation Army.

'Selling everything to the pawnbroker was bad enough but not the soup kitchen! I'd be too ashamed to be seen going into one of them places. What would the neighbours think?'

'I couldn't care less what the neighbours think,' I answered. 'Let's get some of that hot pea soup inside us.'

She agreed to let us go but only after five o'clock when it had turned dark. We took a small pan in case the soup-makers thought we were greedy. We were soon back and Mam heated the soup up on the kitchen fire. It was thin watery soup but who cared? Thank God for the Sally Army, I said to myself. A thought struck me. Solly and Sally – our two saviours.

Auntie Sarah and Uncle Barney came round to see if

they could help. As usual, Barney was out of work and so they had no money but they brought us a bucket of coal and half a bag of coke so we could at least boil a kettle to make a hot drink. Mam told me to go to the corner shop for a jar of Bovril. 'Tell Mrs Greenall to put it on the slate,' she said. Soon we were drinking the lovely beef stew from the jam jars and the railway cups. Our own crockery had long since gone to Solly. Things didn't seem so bad when we had the Bovril inside us. At least, things couldn't get any worse, we thought. Not much.

Auntie Gladys caught a bad cold because of the icy weather and our empty grate. She tried the usual things – hot bread poultices, Friar's Balsam, Veno's Cough Cure, but it was no good. She went on coughing and wheezing. I hoped she wasn't another one with bronchitis or consumption like my dad's. But Auntie recovered and after a week in bed went back into work. We sighed with relief as we'd come to depend on her little wage. Later that morning, she came home – sacked for having so much time off. The factory explained that they couldn't employ someone who wasn't a hundred per cent fit and they'd had to find a replacement for her. They were nice about it, though, and gave her a week's wage – twelve shillings and sixpence.

'They say that troubles come in threes,' Mam said, 'but I think in this family they're coming in fours and fives. We've run out of money, run out of things to sell, and I've run out of ideas.'

'I'm sure we'll think of something,' I said, but not too hopefully.

That same day, I came home from school to find a hen party in progress. Mrs Hicks from next door but one had come round and the three ladies were jugging it – drinking ale from the jam jars. I wondered where they'd got the money from.

Mam sent me and Lizzie round to Greenall's for a loaf of bread, cheese and a quarter of bacon – on tick as usual. I returned with the bad news.

'Mrs Greenall said she can't let you have any more in the book, Mam, as you owe her over two pounds already.'

Mrs Hicks came to the rescue with a ten shilling note.

'Take that round to the shop, love, and get what you need. We can't see you go hungry.'

'As I was saying,' the Hicks woman continued, 'if you're short, I can let you have a few bob till your luck changes. But the best thing you can do is take up my offer. You two ladies are still young, both good-looking and you've still got your figures. I can soon show you how to make money – pots of it. Night work, of course.' She laughed. 'Think it over.'

Mrs Hicks was right about them being good-looking. Mam had lovely chestnut-coloured hair and Auntie Gladys wasn't called Golden-Haired Gladys by people in the district for nothing.

Auntie looked as if she'd been thinking it over, for she said, 'I'd have to be at the end of my tether to take up your offer and it's not come to that – yet.'

'I don't need to think it over,' Mam replied. 'I'm sure it's not our line.'

'Anyroad, the offer's there,' Mrs Hicks replied. 'It's better than starving.' She looked over at Lizzie and me. 'And another thing,' she said, 'those two young girls could make a fortune if they went on the game. Lovely young faces. There's lots of men like a bit of young, fresh stuff and will pay through the nose for it.'

'I don't think so,' Mam said. 'I'd rather feed my kids arsenic than have them go on the game.'

Mrs Hicks said she had to love us and leave us as she had to go to work. When I asked her where she worked, she gave me a funny look and started to laugh. 'I do community work, love, and have an open-air job in Piccadilly.'

She must have one of those jobs on the open-air stalls, I thought, like the ones I've seen on Tib Street market.

When she'd gone, Mam said, 'We may be desperate but we're not that desperate. We'll have to apply for outdoor relief and call that funny little man from the Guardians back. What was his name again?'

'Gillespie,' I told her.

A few days later, he was back in our sitting room. He sat stiffly on the edge of a straight-backed chair and he didn't look at all comfortable. Mam offered him tea which he accepted though without enthusiasm. Little did he know that the coal we used to heat up the kettle was our last.

'I see you've been on your holidays,' he said, examining his cup.

'Holidays? We can't afford no holidays,' Mam said. 'What makes you say that?'

'The cups,' he replied. 'They have London Midland and Scottish Railways printed on the side.'

'Oh, those! No, they were found by the kids on some-body's tip.'

The adults went on a tour of the house, with Gillespie taking notes in every room.

'Well,' he said when they returned. 'Things are looking a bit different from the last time I was here. You've sold most of your furniture, I see.'

'We've managed to keep our heads above water for six months,' Mam said. 'We've nothing left to sell or pawn as all our belongings are now in Solly Goldstein's shop.'

'Not quite all,' he said. 'The children still have good clothes.'

Mam flared up when she heard that. 'The only clothes they have are the ones they stand up in and they have to serve as blankets as well. Surely you don't want them to go round naked.'

'No,' he said nervously. 'We're not that bad. Tell me how the Guardians can best help you and we'll see what we can do.'

'We need help with the rent,' Mam said, 'with food, and with shoes for the kids – the ones they have let water in and we have no money to repair them or buy new ones.'

'We don't give actual money,' he told her, 'as many of you people are tempted to spend it on drink. We can give you tickets to help with part of your rent, your fuel, and your food. As for footwear, we can give you a chit to get clogs from Briggs's on Swan Street. You'll find they're special clogs with a brass iron fixed round the rim to stop them being sold or pawned. That's been tried before.'

'Can we use the tickets at Greenall's corner shop?' Mam asked. 'It's only a few yards away.'

'No,' he said. 'The tickets can only be used at designated shops on Oldham Road.'

One of our neighbours once told us that the Guardians used only their own favourite shops 'cos they were in a clique together and they gave the poor the scrag ends of meat and left-over bread. We didn't know whether to believe her but it was beginning to sound true.

The allowance he gave us covered half the rent, half the food and half the fuel bills. He didn't say where we were to get the other half. The tickets were just enough to keep us on the edge of starvation.

'What do we do if we can't survive on the paltry sums you've given us?' Mam asked bravely.

'You can apply to go before the Board for supplementary funds but I don't hold out much hope there. I've given you all that's within my powers as parish overseer.'

Auntie Gladys now came forward and asked, 'What

about me and my daughter Lizzie, sir? We are lodgers but since I lost my job, we are destitute.'

'What about your husband?'

'He's dead, sir.'

'Did he not provide for you? Who was he? What was his job?'

'He was my brother-in-law, Jack Lally,' Mam said quickly, answering for her. 'He died in an accident on a building site.'

'Why is Mrs Brennan called Brennan if her husband was Lally?' Gillespie asked, looking from one to the other suspiciously.

Auntie spoke up for herself. 'He died before we could be married, sir, and I've had to bring up my daughter myself.'

Gillespie tut-tutted. 'You and Mr Lally jumped the gun, as it were. Your daughter then is a . . . a . . .' He couldn't bring himself to say the word. 'I'm afraid the Board doesn't look kindly upon mothers with illegitimate offspring. Can you not get a job cleaning or taking in washing?'

'We've tried, sir, but everyone round here is like us – penniless.'

'I'm sorry,' he said, 'there's nothing I can do. My hands are tied.'

Things were little better after Gillespie's visit, despite the tickets. We got our clogs from Briggs's and we had a fine time making sparks fly by stamping along the pavement. The other kids at school laughed at us and poked fun. 'You look like Hansel and Gretel,' Eve Ogboddy sneered at me and Danny. 'Where do you live now – in a windmill?' We took no notice of her. At least we were better off than Florrie Moss who didn't have any shoes at all. On Sundays, though, we didn't wear the clogs – it's not respectable,

Mam said. Instead she put cardboard in our shoes to cover the holes. Fine as long as it wasn't raining.

The neighbours in the surrounding streets started a bit of a subscription for us and several people put their names down for a shilling. It was a big surprise and Mam and Auntie Gladys were touched by the gesture. When Mr Dugan came round with the fifteen shillings in an envelope, Mam and Auntie burst into tears. The rest of us did the same 'cos we thought it was yet more trouble as every calamity in our life seemed somehow connected with men with envelopes appearing at the front door. The collection helped us survive for another two weeks.

As the days went by, though, it became more and more obvious that we couldn't manage on the pitiful allowance Gillespie had left us. It wasn't enough to feed us or keep us warm and only half the rent was paid. We borrowed a few shillings from Auntie Sarah and Gran'ma but they couldn't afford much as they were nearly as skint as we were. I asked Mam why we couldn't borrow from Mrs Hicks but Mam wouldn't hear of it. She tried to pawn the clogs but Solly wasn't born yesterday and he recognised the brass irons on the rims.

'I'd love to help you,' he said, holding out two upturned hands, 'as you've been such good customers but the Guardians would send me to Strangeways if I lent money on their property.'

We raised a little cash, enough for a few days' grub, by selling our chairs and we made do with a couple of orange boxes from Greenall's. But even the boxes had to go in the end as we needed a fire to boil the kettle for tea. Danny didn't seem to suffer as much as the rest of us 'cos he was always out with his pals and I was sure he cadged bread and jam at their houses.

It was Cissie and the baby I worried about most. Eddie

cried constantly and Mam tried to keep him quiet by giving him the breast but somehow that didn't seem to satisfy him.

Cissie cried quietly. 'I'm hungry, Kate. Can't we have some bread and jam?'

'Later, later, Cissie,' I told her. 'As soon as Mam gets back from Solly's. Offer your belly ache up for Dad in purgatory.'

As if being hungry wasn't enough, we fell behind with the rent. That's the most serious thing of all, Mam wailed. The rent collector called one Friday to tell us we were five weeks in arrears and if we didn't pay what we owed by the following Friday, we were to be evicted.

'If it were left to me,' he said, 'I would turn a blind eye but this property belongs to the Earl of Derby and if he doesn't get his rents, many people will find themselves out of work, me included.'

'We've reached the end of the line,' Mam said tearfully when he'd gone. She looked crushed, like a beaten dog. 'There's only one thing left to us now. I want you to write one of your letters to the Board of Guardians and apply for supplementary relief.'

Apart from my glass swan, there were two things I'd managed to keep from Solly's shop – my fountain pen and a bottle of Waterman's ink. I always knew they'd be needed one day.

'Of course I'll write the letter, Mam,' I answered. 'But what happens if the Board turns us down?'

'God only knows,' she sobbed. 'It's too awful even to think about it.'

Chapter Nine

A few days after my letter, we were told to report to the town hall to 'go before the Board'. This meant not only our own little family but also Auntie Gladys and Lizzie because they were lodging with us. We were told to turn up at nine o'clock but we were so worried about being late, we set off at quarter to eight for the long walk to Albert Square. We didn't take the bassinet in case it slowed us down and Mam and Auntie took turns carrying the baby. It was trying to snow and the pavements were a bit slippery but we managed to arrive at the town hall at half past eight in plenty of time. Or so we thought. We found we were not the only ones with the idea of turning up early, for there was a long line of people stretching from inside the building to the end of Mount Street. I think the whole of Manchester must have been applying for relief because people were jammed into the staircase five or six deep. They were a real mixed bunch of worn-out people: the respectable and the rough; the old and the young; the infirm, the sick, the blind and the lame; tramps with stubble chins, sluts who screeched and cackled at each other; lunatics and imbeciles who cursed and swore or burst into fits of wild, hysterical laughter. Some of the kids wore thin, scanty clothing and the piercing cold March wind had many of them shivering. The queue moved oh so slowly.

We were lucky in one respect though – the people near us seemed all right. In front of us was an old grannie with a walking stick. She was dressed in a tattered coat and a fur boa which looked as if it had the mange. She introduced herself as Norah Clynes. She looked and sounded like a frog.

'They won't give you nowt, you know,' the old lady croaked to those around her.

'What makes you say that?' Mam asked.

'I know this lot,' she said, pointing her stick up the stairs. 'A mean set of bastards. Chairman of the Board is Sir Josiah Grimshaw, the meanest of them all.' Peering at Mam for the first time, she said, 'Is this your first time applying for relief, love?'

'No,' Mam answered in a friendly tone. 'We've been on outdoor relief for six months but we couldn't manage no longer and so we're applying for supplementary.'

'You'll be lucky,' Mrs Clynes said. 'I read in the *Evening News* the other night that they're cutting down on outdoor 'cos it's too dear, especially where there's kids.'

'I hope not,' said a man behind us in the line. 'I've got a wife and two young lads and we don't fancy the idea of going into the House. We've heard some right tales about it, I can tell you.'

'All true,' said Mrs Clynes, the self-appointed adviser. 'And it's the Board that'll make the decision, not you. These Guardians have got only one idea on their mind and that's to save the ratepayers' money.'

'I'm a carpenter by trade,' the man said. 'Had my own little business. Foley and Sons – not that my sons are old enough to do any carpentry, mind, but I was looking to the future. Then we had a fire which wiped us out. Now, no home, no business, no money. The workhouse is our only hope.'

'If I were you,' said Mrs Clynes, 'I wouldn't use the word hope and workhouse in the same breath. A few years ago, I was an inmate in the Union Workhouse and I know what it's like. I'd do anything not to go back there but I've no choice.'

The little section around the old lady was all ears and she obviously enjoyed being a source of information and advice. Her account of life in the workhouse filled us with fear.

'You sound like a real Job's comforter,' Mam said.

'And with good cause, missus,' the Clynes lady said. 'You wait till you get into the Bastille, you'll find out.'

'I'm hoping and praying it won't come to that,' Mam said.

It was noon and we'd been queuing for over three hours but at least we'd reached the main hall. There we saw dozens of hard, wooden benches with no backs, but every seat was taken. Most of the people waiting looked like hospital cases. Here was an old man with an eye patch; there, an old crone cackling to herself; and babies, babies everywhere. One of them started to howl and the others began to wail in sympathy until the mothers, including my own, responded to some invisible command and put them to the breast.

All that feeding reminded us that we hadn't eaten since early morning.

'I'm hungry, Mam,' Cissie said.

'Don't worry,' Mam said, and she produced from her shopping bag rounds of bread and dripping and a large bottle of water. Good old Mam, she thought of everything.

We were now a little nearer the office where the Guardians were settling everyone's future. We could hear them summing up their morning's work.

'Paddy Cox, married, four children. Iron Street . . . Workhouse. Freda Parkins, imbecile . . . Workhouse. Alfred Noakes, baker, Red Bank, wife and seven children. Applied for relief. Workhouse. Edna Bates, widow, Dalton Street, five children. Applied for outdoor relief. Rejected.'

We heard one Guardian protest at the last case. 'Edna Bates was a most deserving case. She has worked hard all her life and we should give her help.' His plea was overruled.

What chance did we stand?

Around twelve thirty, a Guardian came out of the inner office. He was a well-dressed man with a waxed handlebar moustache like in the advert for cut-throat razors and leather strops.

'There will now be a break until two o'clock to allow members of the Board to have their lunch as they have been hard at work all morning.'

What about us? we thought. We've been waiting in this terrible place all morning.

No use moaning about it. We had to sit it out.

At quarter past two, the cut-throat razor man re-appeared and the interviews began again. After a little while, a man came out. He looked unhappy.

'Rejected,' he said, shaking his head. 'They've sent me and my family back to Durham. They said my case has nothing to do with them.'

'There, what did I tell you?' Mrs Clynes said. 'They'll do anything to save ratepayers' money. Anyroad, let's see what they've got to say about my application. At least they can't send me off to another parish. I've lived in Manchester all my life.'

We were now sitting outside the office door and we could hear every word that was said.

'What's that you said, Mrs Clynes?' laughed a male

voice. 'Rheumatism and arthritis, eh? The House is the finest cure in the world for those conditions. Old Jock'll soon fix you up. They say a change is as good as a rest. A holiday in the poorhouse will soon heal your aches and pains. Workhouse! Next!' We heard the rubber stamp punched on the paper.

Mrs Clynes came out crestfallen. 'Best of luck,' she said to us as she hobbled off.

It was our turn. Hearts fluttering, we waited for the moustachioed man to appear. It was all new and unfamiliar and very frightening. He came out at last and called our names.

'Lally family and Mrs Brennan and daughter Lizzie.'

We crowded into a little office and found ourselves in front of the Board of six Guardians – four men and two women in large picture hats. One of the men was our Mr Gillespie. There were chairs but nobody asked us to sit down and we stood around feeling uncomfortable. And even though we'd been waiting outside for over five hours, nobody asked if we'd had anything to eat. Why should they? They'd just come back from a splendid pub lunch in The Boot and the Slipper. The chairman was a dried-up looking old man in a tweed suit and a flat cap. He gazed over his wire glasses, sniffed, and inspected us as if we were a species of nasty insects. He mumbled as if it was costing him a great effort to speak to people like us and we could hardly hear what he was saying but from the adoring looks on the faces of the rest of the committee, it seemed as if he was taking dictation from God Himself. He checked our names to make sure he'd got the right people and began his cross-examination. We felt like criminals in the dock.

'We, er, are known, er, as the Guardians,' he said, 'and, er, people think that, er, we are guardians of the poor.' He looked round at the others for approval.

The rest of the board laughed as if it was the best joke they'd heard that day. I had the feeling they'd heard it before.

'But we're nothing, er, of the sort,' he continued. 'No, er, we are the guardians of, er, the *rates* and we're not here to give out money to ne'er-do-wells and worthless idlers. Our job is to make sure that public funds go only to deserving cases. We've got to distinguish between the incorrigibly idle and the deserving unemployed. Which one are you, madam?' he asked, pointing to Mam.

'I'm sure I don't know, sir,' Mam said nervously, 'but my husband was a respectable man who always paid his way and his rates and taxes. He died in November and I have four young children to care for, sir. We're five weeks behind with the rent and we don't have any wages coming in. We've sold our possessions, everything we have, and now we're destitute.'

'Quite, quite. Mr Gillespie has filled us in with the details of your case. You state on your form that you have a lodger, a widow, Mrs Gladys Brennan. Does she not pay you rent?'

'Not any more, sir. Not since she lost her job in the soda works. Now she's also penniless.'

'Yes, yes. We shall come to Mrs Brennan shortly.'

Gladys shuffled uncomfortably from one foot to the other.

'Your husband, Michael Lally,' the chairman continued, 'had a well-paid job. Was he not insured? And did he not provide for you?'

'His insurance was just enough to cover his funeral expenses, sir. After we buried him, there was nothing left.'

'Disgraceful,' the chairman said, looking round at his fellow members for support. 'Mr Gillespie tells us it was a lavish funeral with no expense spared. Pity your husband didn't think a little more of his surviving family.'

Mam flushed with anger when she heard this but bit her tongue and said nothing.

'You said you have four children.' He looked at his notes.

'Yes, that's right – four,' Mam said defiantly.

'Do, er, you know the Reverend Thomas Malthus?' he asked.

'No, sir,' Mam answered. 'The only reverend I know is our parish priest, Father Michael Muldoon.'

'Thomas Malthus,' he continued, ignoring her, 'was a great thinker who told us that people like you breed too many children and if we all go on like that, soon there won't be enough food for any of us.'

'I'm sorry, sir,' Mam said, as if she was responsible for causing world famine.

'It's too easy to have children,' he said, looking at his fellow Guardians. 'In fact, it's an enjoyable activity having children, eh what?' His partners on the bench were nodding and smiling like those wind-up Japanese dolls I'd seen advertised. Encouraged by his cronies, he warmed to his subject. 'It's all very well for you people to marry and breed children like rabbits but you do not seem to appreciate the need to make provision for emergencies like sickness and death. No, you'd rather leave it to hard-working ratepayers to foot the bill. It's damned irresponsible. Damned irresponsible. You should be grateful that our government in its generosity has more forethought than you and your late husband appear to have had. I hope you are truly grateful.'

'Oh, yes, sir. Indeed I am.' I'm sure the words stuck in Mam's throat.

'Anyway,' Sir Josiah Grimshaw continued, 'the good news is, we have considered most carefully Mr Gillespie's report on your family and we have no hesitation in offering you the House.' The rest of the Board smiled and nodded agreement.

On hearing the decision, Mam broke down in tears and began sobbing uncontrollably, I didn't understand why. If it was good news, like the man said, she should have been smiling.

'As I am sure you are aware,' the chairman droned on, 'whether you go into the House or not is entirely up to you. It's your decision. But of course payments of outdoor relief will now cease.'

'Very well, sir,' Mam said through her tears. 'We have no choice but to accept the Board's kind offer and go into the workhouse.' Mam looked so upset my blood ran cold when I heard her say this.

'Good,' said Sir Josiah. 'Then it's settled. The Union coach will call at your home on Friday afternoon to collect you and your family and the one trunk we allow you. Now we come to the case of your lodger, Mrs Brennan. Or more correctly, *Miss* Brennan. This is a different kettle of fish, I'm afraid.' Addressing Auntie Gladys directly, he said, 'We can take you and your daughter but the conditions are different.'

'How are they different, sir?' Auntie asked, anxiously biting her lip.

'First, mothers of illegitimate children are housed in a separate institution so as to avoid contact with the young. There we try to return such wicked women to the path of virtue.'

'You mean I would have to live with a crowd of prostitutes and be cast out like a leper? I think this is harsh treatment, sir.'

'Women like you bring such treatment on yourself. Our aim is to make young girls think twice before they bring a bastard into the world. You fell away from virtue by anticipating marriage as you did. Now you must take the consequences of your sinful behaviour. As Guardians, it is our job to protect the young from depraved and degraded women and to train them for a dutiful and industrious life. You may rest assured that we shall look after your daughter and raise her virtuously.'

'What happens, sir,' Auntie asked, 'if I accept your conditions? Do I never see my daughter again?'

'Your daughter is over eight years of age and so you may leave her with us whilst you try to earn your living outside, if that is your desire. When you are in a position to look after her yourself, you are at liberty to take her back whenever you wish. If you decide, however, to come into the House yourself, you must reside in the section of the House reserved for unmarried mothers. Our training there consists of wholesome discipline, productive industry and reformation. In addition, you would wear the special clothing provided for women of your status.'

Auntie Gladys had now turned deathly pale. She looked sorrowfully across to a bewildered Lizzie.

'It's all for the best, Lizzie,' she murmured. 'Very well, sir,' she replied, turning back to the chairman. 'I'd made up my mind about this matter before I came today. I can no longer cope with my present situation. May I leave my daughter in your capable hands?'

'You have made the wisest decision,' he said. The rest of the Board nodded. That's not a bad job they have, I said to myself. Nod and smile whenever the chairman gave the signal. Why, even I could do that.

Chapter Ten

Sunday night was our last in Butler Court. The house was bare of furniture, there were no ornaments on the mantelpiece, no pictures on the wall. The place was desolate. When we spoke, our voices echoed through the empty house. I sat before an empty grate with Snowy, the cat, on my knee. It was purring away happily in its ignorance of the terrible blow fate had dealt us. I couldn't help wishing I'd been born a cat, for it doesn't have any problems like us. Mrs Hicks had agreed to take it and so there'd still be no peace for Pug, Annie Swann's dog. We were depressed; the house had so many memories for us. Joyous when Dad was with us and also sad and miserable when we ran out of money and were slowly but surely sucked down the drain.

Mam came into the room and looked around. There was nothing left but rubbish. On the bare floorboards lay a broken compact mirror, an empty cocoa tin, and a few scraps of straw, paper and string. She reached behind one of the orange boxes which had been serving as a chair and brought out an old battered chocolate tin – a memento of happier times. Inside were letters, old bills, a couple of faded photographs, and bits of old jewellery that were of no value, not even to Solly, rosary beads, and a small phial that once contained holy water. For a long time, she sat holding the tin, looking over it, her fingers still on her few bits and pieces. They were all she had left. She bit her lower lip and sighed, thinking and remembering the days that were. At last she made up her mind. She picked out the trinkets and the photos and put them into the pocket of her pinny. She took the tin with the papers and put them into the overflowing dustbin.

Nobody slept properly that night as we thought about what the next day might bring. Early next morning our fitful slumber was disturbed by the sound of hammering. The bailiff's men had come to board up the windows. We finished packing our small trunk with our two blankets, a few hand towels, a change of underclothing, a small crucifix, a statue of the Sacred Heart and my most precious possession, the glass swan. We washed in cold water at the slop-stone and we were ready to go. There wasn't much to eat, half a loaf of bread from yesterday and a little margarine. Nobody was hungry anyway. We took our trunk and waited outside on the pavement for the arrival of the workhouse coach. Annie Swann took us in out of the cold and offered us each a bowl of Irish stew which she had been warming in the oven. Auntie Gladys and Lizzie waited at the Hickses because Auntie had decided to take a job helping Mrs Hicks with her community work in Piccadilly. I wondered why Mam couldn't take a similar job and keep us out of the workhouse. It was no use asking, though, 'cos they'd tell me to run away and play as I wouldn't understand.

A bit later in the morning, Gran'ma and Auntie Sarah came round to say goodbye. There was a lot of hugging and sobbing. Then the workhouse coach with a decrepit old horse in the shafts trundled into the court. It had a big sign painted on the side with the words: UNION WORKHOUSE: HOME FOR THE DESTITUTE. The neighbours from the streets around appeared, tut-tutting. 'Terrible,

terrible,' they kept saying over and over again. Our shame was complete when they formed a gauntlet like they do when an ambulance came to cart somebody off to hospital. When the moment to climb aboard came, Lizzie and her mother clung together so tightly, we wondered if we'd ever get away. Auntie Gladys wept nonstop and promised to send for Lizzie as soon as she'd saved enough money. The coachman cracked his whip and we turned round to take our last look at our old home. In Mam's eyes, there was a look of despair.

'One day,' I said to her, 'I'll get our family back together – the way it used to be. I don't know how but I will.'

As we drove along Oldham Road, Cissie, who had been strangely quiet all morning, spoke for the first time.

'This is like going to Dad's funeral.'

She'd never said a truer word. But not *Dad's* funeral – more like our own.

The coach made its way along Oldham Road taking much the same route that Dad's funeral cortege had taken a year ago. We came to a large building surrounded by high walls which someone had decorated with chalked warning messages: 'ABANDON ALL HOPE ALL YE WHO ENTER HERE' and 'POOR TAKEN IN AND DONE FOR'. We stopped before a huge gate which had a great sign in wrought iron saying: UNION WORKHOUSE FOR THE HOMELESS AND THE DESTITUTE. WORK AND PRAY. Our coach driver applied the brake and got down from his perch. He rang a bell by pulling on a long chain and we waited, trembling in fear, wondering what was going to happen to us. A door in the grating slid back and an ugly-looking man with a twisted face rasped out his words of greeting. 'Welcome to the Bastille.' We heard the sound of bolts sliding back, the great gates squeaked open and our coach rolled into the workhouse yard.

One look and my heart sank into my clogs.

'I want to go home,' Cissie sobbed. 'I don't like this place.'

'Who does?' Danny said nervously.

'Chin up, our Cissie,' I said. 'Remember what I told you about purgatory and the thing called remission, how we can earn time off for poor old Dad who's burning away down there for a thousand years. Every time you're brave and stop yourself from crying, he gets a month off. Maybe more if you're really brave. We were lucky to get places here 'cos God was giving us the chance to get Dad out of the fire.'

'And my dad as well,' added Lizzie.

'Only after we've got our dad out,' Cissie replied tearfully.

The ugly man had a big bunch of keys round his belt. He closed the gate, applied the bolts, and locked it securely behind us. He didn't smile, didn't even look at us. For him we didn't exist. We weren't people – we were paupers.

He led us along a dark, narrow passage and my first impressions were of whitewashed walls, jangling keys, and high, small-paned windows. There was the stench of stale sweat and rancid food, mixed with the stink of leaking privies. Butler Court was a garden of roses next to this.

He unlocked a door and pushed us into a large hall. There were about forty or fifty people queuing before a table where a man in uniform was taking down details. We joined the end of the line.

'Single file, single file!' a man in the workhouse uniform barked, prodding us with a stick to enforce his order. I knew he was a pauper because he had a large letter 'P' printed in red on his back. When I looked around I saw several more of these attendants who were obviously there to enforce discipline and to see that people did as they were told. I noticed one or two women in the grey uniform but they were different 'cos down their backs they had yellow stripes making them look like human humbugs.

We searched for a friendly face but there wasn't one. The people looked metallic and the eyes stared out but didn't see – the eyes of people who had given up hope. After an hour in the queue, we reached the table for registration.

'Name!' the clerk snapped without looking up.

'Lally and Brennan!' Mam replied in a similar sharp tone.

The clerk slowly raised his eyes to examine the specimen who dared answer back like that.

'Why two names? Isn't one enough?' he barked.

'We are two families,' Mam answered.

The clerk snorted and turned to his box of index cards.

'Yes, here you are. You've been before the Board and I've got your details.'

Slowly, as if it was costing him great effort, he copied out our family particulars into a large ledger – names, dates of birth, school attended, last address. He gave each of us a number in his book and he recorded this on a cardboard workhouse badge which he handed to each of us with a safety pin. There was even one for the baby.

Mam's badge read. DORMITORY 11, FTWF.

I looked at my own badge. It said: MANCHESTER WORKHOUSE FOR THE DESTITUTE; CATHERINE LALLY, PTWF. NUMBER 1633. AGED 11+. DORMITORY 16.

'What does that PTWF stand for?' I asked.

'Part-Time Worker Female,' the clerk replied. 'Now pin this badge on your uniform when you get it. Don't lose it or forget it or you'll be in serious trouble.'

Cissie looked worried when she heard this and clutched the badge tightly in case a wind might suddenly blow it away.

'A uniform!' Danny exclaimed. 'We're going to get a uniform. It's like joining the army.'

'Where's Mrs Brennan?' the clerk asked suddenly. 'Why isn't she here with her daughter?'

'She has decided not to accept your kind offer,' Mam said, 'but the Board agreed to her daughter coming in with us.'

'Oh, very well,' the clerk sighed. 'Most irregular.'

I looked over his shoulder at the big tatty ledger he was writing in. I could see three columns: one was headed 'Folln Wimmin', the second 'Popers', and the third 'Hilly Jittimites'.

The Lally family was written under Popers. I didn't know if this was a misspelling of Paupers or if it was another way of saying Roman Catholics. Lizzie was down as a Hilly Jittimite which sounded like some funny religion from up in the mountains.

As we came away from the table, we recognised a couple of familiar faces – Mrs Clynes and Mr Foley who was now with his wife and three boys. I noticed on Mrs Clynes's badge that she was down as IF DORMITORY 16. 'IF', she told us, stood for infirm female.

'Ah, so you accepted the Board's offer of the House,' Norah Clynes said to Mr Foley and Mam. 'I hope you've both made the right choice. If you're going to stick this place, you'll have to be brave souls.'

'They don't seem very friendly,' I remarked.

'You haven't seen nothing yet,' Norah Clynes replied. 'But watch out what you say in front of these people,' she added, indicating the inmate helpers with her stick. 'They're "trusties" and they'll report anything you say to McTavish if they think it'll get them an extra crust of bread.'

One of the trusties rang a bell and all eyes turned towards the platform where a small burly man with a pock-marked face and iron-grey hair had appeared, along with several other people who looked like they might be members of staff.

He blew a whistle and barked, 'Look this way, all of you!' He was swaying a little as if drunk. He had a gruff, raspy voice and spoke with a strong Scottish accent which made him difficult to understand. Like a foreign language. But the tone of his voice was clear enough – it said, 'You argue with me and you're for it.'

At a signal from him, the staff sat down. Us inmates remained standing, mainly because there were no chairs.

The little man looked down at us and started to speak.

'Ma name's Angus McTavish and I'm the workhouse master. I'm told folk call me Old Jock but God help you if I hear any of you sayin' it. Welcome to the Pauper Palace, the Manchester Union Workhouse. You people are here because you're inadequates who couldna cope with life outside. You're now what the state calls "paupers" ' – it sounded like poppas – 'and you're under my care. It's my job to feed you, clothe you and put a roof over your head. As far as I'm concerned, you're a bunch of idle wretches and good-for-nothings. But let me mak' one thing clear from the start. You're no' here to enjoy yoursel'. You're no' here on holiday. This is no' Blackpool or Morecambe. Oh no. It's a workhouse and it's no' called a workhouse for nothin'. You're here to work and by God it's ma job to see that you do or ma name's not McTavish. I'll have no scrimshankers in my House. D'ye hear tha'?'

'I don't understand anything the man's saying,' Cissie whispered to me.

'Don't worry,' I said. 'I'll explain it to you if I can.'

McTavish went on. 'First you should know the names of some of the staff who'll be dealin' with you. First there's ma son, Andrew who's taskmaster here. He will allocate the jobs that need doin' in the House and see that you do them. He acts with my full authority. Woe betide anyone who's reported to me for laziness or swingin' the lead. Next to ma son is ma wife, Mrs Flora McTavish, and she's matron here. Make sure you treat her with respect at all times. If she gives you an order, you'd better hop to it or I'll know the reason why.'

'The old dragon,' Norah Clynes muttered.

Mrs McTavish stood up and glowered at us. If her husband was a dwarf, she was a giant; she towered over him. If ever they lost their job in this workhouse, I said to myself, they could get a job in a freak sideshow at Sanger's Carnival.

Next, was the House doctor, Dr Eugene O'Brien.

I couldn't believe my eyes. It was the doctor who had tended my dad when he was ill. Mam and I exchanged surprised glances. She was smiling broadly when she whispered, 'It's so nice to see a familiar face.'

The only trouble was, I didn't think he would recognise any of us as he'd been too busy trying to cure Dad's illness.

'I sometimes think,' McTavish continued in a sneering tone, 'that the doctor there is too soft wi' all of you. But you'd better not try your malingerin' with me, I can tell you. Salts and senna pods are all you people need.'

I noticed that the doctor was staring straight ahead. His lips were tight and he looked angry.

Our attention was directed to a one-armed man whose head looked as if he could be a model for the skull on a pirates' flag. We were told his name was Harold Catchpole and he was the workhouse teacher. My blood ran cold when I saw him. I was sure my dad in his coffin had looked healthier than he did. Dad had definitely looked happier. Even our old teacher Gertie seemed as merry as a circus clown next to him.

Finally, Old Jock turned with a smile to introduce a plump lady with a rosy complexion. She gave us a nod and a big smile. I liked the look of her. She was Mrs Burns, the workhouse cook. As McTavish introduced her, I couldn't help noticing that Flora McTavish was scowling at her husband. If looks could have killed . . . I made a mental note to ask Norah Clynes what was going on there. She was bound to know.

Our workhouse master dismissed the staff with a jerk of his thumb meaning 'Skedaddle' but what he said was, 'I'm sure you've got better things to do with your time than sit there listening to me.' The staff filed out, with the exception of the old dragon who opted to stay.

McTavish watched them go until the platform was clear. Then he turned his gaze on us and held up a big battered leather-bound book.

'Take a good look at this tome,' he said. 'This is the House punishment book. What I call "The Purgatory Book". Roman Catholics have a prayer which asks, "Lord, send me here my purgatory". Get your name in this book and your prayer comes true. You'll be for it. D'ye hear tha'?'

'I don't understand it,' Cissie whispered. 'He talks funny.' She sounded worried.

'He's explaining how you can get Dad out of purgatory,' I lied.

McTavish cleared his throat, took a big pinch of snuff and chuckled madly to himself. 'You've heard of Strangeways prison,' he smirked. 'Well, we have our very own right here in the cellars of the house. We call it New Strangeways. Break the rules of the house once, you're disorderly and you don't eat. It's chokey and Diet Number Two – bread and water for two days.

'Break the rules twice, you're refractory and you don't eat. It's Diet Number Three – a week of bread and water.

'If you're stupid enough to do it a third time, it's solitary in the dungeon for a coupla weeks.'

'What's he saying?' Cissie asked. 'What does it mean?'

'Sh . . .' I said. 'He's reading out the remission times.'

'And now,' McTavish continued, 'I dare say you'd like to know the rules. Pay attention and memorise them. A full list is posted on the wall of each dormitory. Study them carefully.

'One: you're not to leave the building or go into the yard without permission,' he barked. 'D'ye hear tha'?'

I translated for Cissie. 'Staying in the building and not going into the yard. One year's remission for that.'

'Two: you must wear your House badge at all times. Failure to do so, two days in the cellar. D'ye hear tha'?'

'Wearing your workhouse badge earns one year and two days,' I told Cissie.

'When Mrs McTavish or I go past,' Jock said, 'you must stand to attention and bow your head. Forget and you'll pay the price – two days.'

'Maybe we should make the sign of the cross,' Norah Clynes muttered.

McTavish continued his long list of rules.

'Refusing to work or not finishing jobs you've been set means four days; telling lies, being insolent, using bad language, refusing to eat food, talking at meals – three days; smoking or taking snuff – two days.'

At least, I thought, we don't have to worry about the last rule.

The worst regulation of all, however, was next.

'Finally,' McTavish announced, 'before you go into the cellars for cleansing and your new uniforms, Mrs McTavish and I will select you for your work groups. Each group will live in separate dormitories and during the week there will be no mixing. I canna have the working week disturbed by petty family problems. However, I'm glad to say that the Union has generously set aside a time at weekends when visitors are allowed on the premises. Visiting times are on Sunday afternoons from two to half past three when you're permitted visitors, and families can meet as long as it's in this main assembly hall. I was against this concession mysel' when it was agreed to but I have to abide by the rules just as you have to.'

When this announcement sank in, there was a gasp of horror in the waiting crowd. I felt as if I'd been punched in the stomach.

'Lord, take me now,' Mrs Clynes exclaimed. 'Ready when you are, God.'

'Women and girls to the left,' McTavish bawled over the noises of alarm. 'Men and boys to the right.'

Mothers whimpered and clutched their sons. Mrs Foley clasped her two boys and they had to be prised from her embrace by the trusties who were there for that purpose.

The people moved slowly and reluctantly and the trusties went into action, poking them with their sticks. Poor old Danny was pulled away from Mam and forced in with the other males. He looked utterly bewildered.

That wasn't the end of it, though. A further division was made. The dragon rasped out her own set of orders.

'Full-time women workers to the front. Rest to the back. Mothers with babies may keep them for the time being.'

It was then that I realised the meaning of the letters on our badges. Mam and Eddie were to be taken away from us.

Cissie clung to Mam's legs like a limpet. 'Please don't go, Mam,' she sobbed. 'Please don't leave us.'

'It's all right, Cissie,' Mam said gently. 'I'm only in the next building. We'll see each other on Sunday. You've got Kate and Lizzie with you – they'll look after you. Think of poor Danny over there, he's got no family with him.'

We looked over towards Danny and saw that he had recovered somewhat and was busy talking to the Foley boys. He'd get by, I thought.

Our group of PTWFs and IFs were escorted into the cellars by two female trusties who kept us in line with their sticks. I felt like a lamb being led to the abattoir. As we walked along the dismal corridors in the basement, we passed several dungeons with the faces of the rule-breakers watching our every move. We wondered which rules they'd broken. We came to a sluice room where three women were waiting to receive us.

Young and old alike, we were told to take our clothes off and to put on a thin slip to cover up our embarrassment and our bare backsides.

We sat on wooden stools and the sheep shearing began.

We were ordered to bend down and throw our hair forward while the trusties went to work with their shears. For the next ten minutes there was no sound except snip, snip, snip as our locks fell to the floor. It was bad enough for Cissie and me to lose our hair but how my heart wept for Lizzie as I saw her beautiful golden tresses dropping around her feet.

The three of us looked like plucked Christmas turkeys ready for the oven.

'Why do we have to have this cruel treatment?' I asked my particular trusty.

'Old Jock orders everyone to be cropped to kill any vermin you might bring into the House,' she answered.

'Old Jock's a stickler for bugs and lice. Won't have 'em in the place.'

'Lucky bugs and lice,' I said to her.

Next we were each given a rough piece of carbolic soap and we stood together in the bath-house while a hosepipe was turned on us. The water was freezing and judging by the way the three trusties cackled, it was the funniest thing that'd happened that day. We were given a rough piece of calico to dry ourselves.

I could see that Cissie was near to tears again.

'Come on, our Cissie,' I said. 'Remember you're a Lally. This must be worth at least ten years to Dad.'

'And for mine,' whimpered Lizzie.

'Only five for you,' Cissie snuffled. 'Remember there's two of us.'

The final touch to our appearance came when we were given our drab uniforms – under-drawers, a shift, long stockings and, to cover the lot, shapeless frocks that reached to our ankles. Everything was several sizes too big. 'To allow for growth', our trusty informed us. All items were in the same coarse grey calico. We pinned on our badges and the picture was complete. From now on, everyone would recognise us for what we were – workhouse inmates. We were grateful for one thing – we were not made to wear the little poke bonnets that the old women had to put on their heads, though I suppose we could have done with something to cover up our hideous hairstyles.

'After supper,' the big trusty said, 'come back here and we'll give each of you a towel and a blanket. You take these to your dormitory, and don't lose 'em or you'll be in big trouble.'

When all was finished, we didn't know whether to laugh or cry.

Chapter Eleven

As we came out of the cellar, we heard the sound of a handbell. 'Supper time! Supper time!' a man called as he walked down the corridors.

'Must be six o'clock already,' Mrs Clynes said in her gravelly voice. 'Follow me and I'll show you where the dining room is. Make sure you don't talk or you'll be in trouble. And watch out for Big Bertha at the head of the table. She'll snitch on you first chance she gets.'

We climbed the stone steps to the first floor and joined a long queue in an unlit corridor. I noticed a grubby poster on the wall and even though it was quite dark I could make out that it was a list of food rations we were to be given during our stay. 'Official Diet Number One,' I read. 'Each inmate will receive 137 to 182 ounces of solid food a week. Women and children over nine will get the lower amount and able-bodied men the higher.' Monday's supper was to be a pint of soup and one piece of bread. Other meals were gruel with bread, and the highlight during the week was to be Wednesday when we were due for three ounces of cooked meat and two potatoes. Saturday, too, looked as if it was going to be a big day 'cos we were to get two ounces of mincemeat with the potatoes, but Sunday was the red letter day for we were promised two ounces of cheese at dinner and one rasher of bacon at supper. In big capital letters, the sign told us that water was to be the only drink allowed and that beer was strictly forbidden. That was no hardship for us as we didn't drink the stuff though I didn't know how Mam would take the news. Men and women over sixty were allowed tea and sugar if a visitor gave them any.

'What's it say, Kate?' Cissie asked.

'It's a list of indulgences that you can earn for people in purgatory,' I lied again. Keeping up this pretence was proving to be a hard task but I had to try to give Cissie courage and hope. I wished there was someone to keep up *my* spirits.

I'd just about finished reading this stuff on the wall when I noticed Mam ahead of us in the queue. She gave us a big smile and put her finger to her lips to tell us to stay quiet. I managed to read her lips though. 'See you on Sunday,' she mouthed silently.

The main doors opened and we filed into the huge barn-like dining room. On the rafters there were lots of banners with religious sayings like: 'The Kingdom of Heaven is not eating and drinking', 'Envy and Wrath shorten life'.

At the front of the hall were four large cauldrons of bubbling hot soup. It smelt appetising and we could hardly wait. There were about twenty long tables, each with wooden benches, facing a raised platform. The table layout was like the one you see in pictures of the Last Supper, with the diners facing one direction. Mrs Clynes showed us where our dormitory – Number 16 – sat. At the head of the table stood a huge woman who must have weighed a ton and a half; at the other end was a tall, gangly woman, so tall she had a permanent stoop. When everyone had entered, I could see the arrangement: at the front were the old ladies and the young girls like us; immediately behind, the old men and the boys, and I smiled and nodded when I saw Danny standing there with his new friends; the next row of tables was occupied by the able-bodied ladies, and right at the back the able-bodied men. Everyone remained standing until Mr and Mrs McTavish marched onto the platform. They were accompanied by two big male trusties. Old Jock rang a large bell suspended on the wall by hitting it with a metal hammer to get everyone's attention. Not that it was needed 'cos everyone was staring in his direction anyway.

'Before we begin eating,' he said, 'we have a small matter of discipline to attend to. Freda Williams and Paddy Cox, come to the front.'

The two inmates left their tables and went to the front and mounted the stage. They looked nervous, especially the Williams woman who was trembling.

'These two wretches,' McTavish announced, 'have committed serious breaches of discipline. Last night at supper, this Cox fellow broke Rule Number Eight and Rule Number Ten by daring to leave his own table in order to speak to some woman at Table Twelve. A woman he claimed to be his wife though I think it doubtful they're married. Be that as it may, I won't have the workhouse rules flouted in this way. There must be no fraternisation and no talking in the dining hall. D'ye hear that?'

Cissie turned to me and nodded, holding up one finger.

'This floutin' o' the rules will not be tolerated,' Jock bellowed. 'I sentence Paddy Cox to ten days in New Strangeways. Take him down.'

Poor old Paddy was escorted out of the dining hall while McTavish made a note in his Purgatory Book.

Now he turned his attention to Freda who stood quivering with fear.

'As for this good-for-nothing,' he sneered, 'she broke a

number of rules yesterday. Number Fourteen by stealin' a lump o' bread from the dining room and eatin' it in her dormitory. The eating o' food in the dormitory is expressly forbidden as we dinna want to encourage the breedin' o' mice and rats. Taking food out o' the dining room is stealing. When she was confronted with her crime, she denied it and so not only is she a thief but she's a liar too. For that, she'll have no supper tonight and she'll stand here wearing the card and watching you enjoy your hot, nourishing soup.'

Round the neck of the luckless Fanny he hung a card which said: THIEF AND INFAMOUS LYAR.

After his little ceremony he intoned grace: 'For what we are about to receive, may the Lord make us truly thankful.'

Everyone said 'Amen' and sat down.

Even though McTavish said, 'For what *we* are about to receive,' I noticed that neither of the pair showed any sign of joining us in the meal.

'Forward the table leaders!' Mr McTavish commanded. Twenty inmates went to the front and collected their zinc buckets which were filled with the broth from the taps on the cauldrons.

I hoped the buckets hadn't been used for other purposes.

Next, the soup was ladled onto plates by the leaders and passed down the tables. Our utensils were made of tin – plates, spoons, cups. They didn't break so easily, I supposed.

On the platform, Mrs McTavish began weighing hunks of bread.

'The Poor Law Commissioners insist that we show you that you're getting the right amount of bread. Waste of time, if you ask me, but you can see that each lump of bread weighs the legal five ounces. Deputy leaders, collect the bread!'

The deputies climbed onto the platform. In our case, it was the long, thin woman.

I took one look at the greasy water that was our soup and my stomach turned over. It looked like the water in which rancid meat had been boiled. Or maybe it was water used for boiling clothes. Whatever it was, it was an insult to the name of soup. As for the bread, it was a dirty grey colour and had a musty smell. I saw that Cissie and Lizzie sitting on my left had both turned sickly green.

I tapped Cissie on the shoulder and pulled a face pretending to vomit into my plate. It brought a smile to their lips. I held up one finger and made the sign for year by pointing to her and pulling on my ear. Cissie's face lit up when she got the message and she began drinking her soup.

To my surprise, the elderly lady on my right touched me on the arm and offered her lump of bread. I nodded my thanks and broke up the extra piece of dough into three parts to share. Terrible though the stuff was, we had to eat something.

Throughout the workhouse feast, Mr McTavish read from a tattered Bible.

'Consider the lilies of the field, how they grow; they toil not, neither do they spin: And yet I say unto you, that Solomon in all his glory was not arrayed like one of these.'

I looked around at the workhouse inmates slurping their soup and I thought that maybe the lowest slave in Solomon's palace was not dressed as one of these.

After the meal, we trooped out in silence. There was no mixing and no chance to talk to anyone from our family.

The three of us went back to the cellar to collect our blanket, towel, and carbolic soap and then found our way to our dormitory which was a long narrow room with one window, one door and twenty single beds in rows on each side. At the wall nearest the door, there was a communal chamber pot for use during the night. At the wall furthest away from the door was a fireplace, round which were huddled ten or twelve old ladies with shawls wrapped tightly round them in an attempt to keep warm on that cold March night. In one of the beds a woman was strapped down and in another was an old lady who looked as if she was at death's door.

The big woman who had dished out the soup at supper sat in the large rocking chair near to the fireside.

'I'm Bertha,' she told us, 'and I'm in charge of this dormitory now that old Sal there is about to snuff it. She's taking her time over it, though, for she's had Extreme Unction nineteen times. Do as you're told and you'll have no trouble. As you three are the youngest and the newest, your beds will be at the end nearest the door and the chamber pot, and it'll be your job to empty it each morning.'

'Two years each time we do it,' I whispered to Cissie who looked as if she was about to break down. I felt like breaking down myself when I thought about the horrible job that'd been dumped on us. I wondered how long God was going to keep us in this terrible place.

'Under your bed,' Bertha continued, 'you'll find a box to keep your bits and pieces in, if you have any. The shelf above your bed is yours for any ornaments you might have.'

The statue of the Sacred Heart and my glass swan, I thought to myself. The Sacred Heart to remind me to pray for Dad in purgatory, and the swan to remind me of past happiness.

I saw the old lady who had been so kind as to give us her hunk of bread.

'Thank you for the bread,' I said. 'It was welcome as we were so hungry.'

'Don't thank me for that,' she said with a wild, fierce look. 'The bread in this place is poisoned to reduce the population.'

'I did notice that it had a funny colour and a funny taste,' I said to make her happy.

'This place is a death trap,' she went on. 'Even the pigs get better food than we do 'cos they want to fatten them up for sale. I've heard that the Poor Law Guardians are planning to kill children over three and women are to be spayed. They do it with the bread.'

'Take no notice of what Jessie there tells you,' Bertha said. 'She thinks we're surrounded by devils who are out to get us.'

'It's true,' insisted Jessie. 'I've heard that the Guardians took a lot of children and their mothers on a boat trip down the Irwell and drownded the lot of them.'

What sort of place is this? I wondered. It resembled a madhouse.

The long gangly woman who had dished out the bread now came up to us. More bad news, I thought. This time I was wrong.

'My name's Victoria,' she said in a friendly voice. 'But everyone calls me Queenie on account of me being born on the day of the Queen's coronation. June the twenty-second, eighteen thirty-seven. I don't belong in this workhouse as I've mixed with the highest in the land. Edward, Prince of Wales, was a personal friend of mine – I used to be his courtesan – and I know he would be upset if he knew I was in here.'

Bertha raised her eyes to heaven.

'Why don't you write and tell him to get you out?' Lizzie asked innocently.

'I'd be too ashamed to let him know that I've landed up in a place like this. What would my friend, the Duchess of

Marlborough, think? And I shudder to contemplate what the Duke would say as I used to be his mistress as well.'

Over her shoulder I could see several of the other old ladies pointing to their foreheads, giving the cuckoo sign.

A young, nice-looking lady with a trim figure now approached us.

'I'm Hannah,' she said, holding out her hand. 'Welcome to our dormitory. It's so nice to see fresh faces like yours. I hope you're going to be happy here. I have the bed next to yours.'

I was happy to meet such a normal person for a change. Yet there was something not right about Hannah. Perhaps it was the slight nervous tic or the staring eyes. She seemed to read my mind for she said, 'I should be in with the able-bodied women but I suffer sometimes from epilepsy and I can't work like the rest. But I'm not as bad as Elsie Peters over there who has to be strapped down in the bed as her convulsions are so bad.'

At half past eight, it was time for lights out. Bertha raked down the fire and everyone got into bed. As this was our first night, we three decided to share one bed – top and tail – for the comfort of each other's company and also to share our blankets. Cissie clung to me and her Raggedy Ann doll. Soon everyone was asleep except us.

I looked at the bodies sleeping around us. They were like a lot of corpses. Some were stretched out full length, others lay with nose and knees together; some with arms or legs sticking out of the blankets. Half an hour later, the night was filled with the noises of snoring and coughing. And what strange noises they were! There was every kind of coughing you can think of – the hollow cough, the short cough, the hysterical cough, the bark that came with the regularity of a grandfather clock, even a weird rattling one like the sound of somebody gargling. Coughing from deep within the chest, tickly coughing from the throat – now in singles, now in doubles, now three or four together. A silence and then it began all over again. And in the intervals between the coughs there was the snoring, the hoink-hoinks and the hink-hinks. We traced the culprit to Mrs Clynes in the bed next door.

'Nora the snorer,' I whispered to Lizzie and Cissie in a vain attempt to make them laugh.

'I don't like this place, Kate,' Cissie whimpered. 'All these funny noises – I can't sleep.'

'But listen to it, Cissie,' I said. 'It's like music. You can even fit a song to it.' Softly, I sang to the rhythm of the coughs and the snores:

After the ball is over (COUGH COUGH)
After the dance is through (COUGH COUGH).

I soon had Cissie and Lizzie laughing quietly.

'I love you, Kate,' Cissie whispered, 'more than anything in the world. More than . . .' she searched for the words. 'More than chocolate biscuits.'

The rest of the song fitted beautifully to the coughing attacks and before I'd finished, Lizzie and Cissie were sound asleep. I was left with only one problem – how to get to sleep myself.

I was lying there for about an hour when I heard a voice in the bed next to me. A man's voice. Next I recognised Hannah's voice pleading.

'Please don't, Mr McTavish,' she cried. 'Please leave me alone.'

There was the noise of frantic movements and the squeak of bed springs.

Suddenly the snoring and coughing stopped. Everyone in the dormitory was on the alert. The silence was finally broken when we heard the powerful voice of Bertha from the end bed.

'Listen to me, Mr Andrew McTavish! This is the third time you've been here to disturb our sleep and that poor unfortunate girl. If you're not out of that bed in ten seconds, I shall ring the fire bell and your father will be here to give you merry hell. Now leave!'

There was the sound of scuffling and we saw the shadow of a man leaving the dormitory. Then all was quiet.

The night passed slowly. I heard a church clock strike two and, far off, the sound of a train which for some reason made me feel sad and lonely though the patter of the rain on the roof somehow gave me comfort. I must have dozed off in the end, for I was startled out of sleep by the clanging of a loud bell. Everybody was getting up and dressing though the day had not yet begun to dawn and our light was from a couple of oil lamps. Queenie was setting the fire and I suddenly remembered that we'd got to empty that foul-smelling chamber pot. No use complaining about it. Lizzie and I picked it up and turning our faces away so as not to have sight of it, we carried it outside to the privy where we poured out the contents.

It was a bitterly cold morning but despite our shivering we got dressed and took our turn washing at one of the four dormitory basins. The water was freezing but we were already getting hardened to the workhouse conditions.

'Come back here after breakfast,' Bertha ordered, 'and I'll give you three girls your jobs for the morning.'

With the rest of the inmates, we went down to breakfast. It was the same routine as before except that table heads took a roll call and reported the results to McTavish who recorded them in a big book. Bertha went to the front to report that Table 16 was present and correct. We three kids were feeling hungry and we wondered what breakfast would bring. It brought a lump of bread and a jug of porridge – not ordinary, common or garden porridge, you understand, but workhouse skilly which was in a class by itself. I can honestly say that I don't think I've ever seen a more nauseating mixture. Oats and water, no matter how small the oats, simply boiled, would have been tastier. But this concoction served up was the nastiest dish I had ever set eyes on. I didn't have to look far for the reason. It had been cooked in the same cauldrons that had held last night's soup. I doubt if anyone had washed them out between meals. Skilly was the stuff everyone linked with the workhouse and the Bastille, and after tasting it that first morning, I could understand why. But what could we do? Either we ate it or we starved. But, oh, what I would have given for a pinch of salt or a spoonful of sugar!

With our hunger only partly satisfied, we climbed the stairs back to the dormitories to await Bertha's instructions. There we found everyone in a state of distress for during the night Old Sal had died in her sleep. That explained the rattling noise I'd heard around two o'clock.

At the end of the dormitory, McTavish and Dr O'Brien were in earnest conversation and they seemed to be having a fierce row.

'The old lady must be given a decent funeral,' I heard the doctor say. 'None of your penny-pinching or skimping on a coffin or the tolling of the bell. One chime for each of her seventy years.'

'That's all very well,' McTavish snapped, 'but the Poor Law Commissioners make no allowances for fancy funerals.'

'I know you and your pauper funerals,' Dr O'Brien retorted. 'You're given enough to afford to have the body washed and dressed in a clean shroud as well as a decent coffin. Or does the money go into your own pocket?'

McTavish turned purple with rage and it looked as if they might come to blows until they noticed us kids watching them goggle-eyed.

'Anyway, see that old Sal is buried with respect,' the doctor said finally, 'or I may have to report you to the authorities.'

As Dr O'Brien was coming away, I plucked up courage to speak to him.

'Do you remember us, Dr O'Brien?'

He looked closely at us and said in a kindly voice, 'I seem to recognise your faces but I can't place them. Where've I seen you before?'

I explained that he had attended my father, Michael Lally, before he died.

'Of course I remember you now. Mike Lally was a friend and a fine man, a brave man with a great sense of humour. But what in God's name are you doing in a place like this?'

I felt like asking him the same question but instead I told him our story and how we'd come down in the world, how we'd been forced to sell everything to survive. He listened closely, clucking in sympathy from time to time.

'Look,' he said at last, 'I have to go but I work now in the workhouse infirmary, such as it is. I want you to know this – if ever any of you need my help, don't hesitate to come to me, no matter what time of day or night. It grieves me to see you in such a place as this. Your father would turn in his grave if he knew. I shall try to see your mother and tell her I've spoken to you. Meanwhile, keep your chin up. Remember, it's always darkest before the dawn.'

These words of encouragement cheered us up no end. But that was before Bertha gave us our morning's work.

It was seven o'clock when we began. We were to clean and scrub the whole dining hall – floor, tables, benches. It looked as if the diners had poured their soup and their skilly across the surfaces instead of eating it. In some ways I wouldn't have blamed them. My part was to do the rear portion of the hall and a long, long passage leading to the kitchens. We were given cloths, brushes, buckets and soda but no aprons. We had one kneeling pad between us and this we gave to Cissie. I was used to scrubbing and donkey-stoning Butler Court but I have never in all my days worked as hard as this. We cleaned the hall, the passageway, a whole flight of stairs and the McTavish private sitting room which had to be done with the greatest care if we were to avoid Old Jock's fist. Whilst we were on our hands and knees in that area we heard Florrie McTavish giving Jock hell. It was all about him drinking too much whisky and having it off with Mrs Burns, the cook. It did our hearts good to listen to him getting it in the neck and we hoped his missus would give him one with the poker. It was the only light relief that morning.

We went through four buckets of water for the dining hall and another five for the long passage and the sitting room. We had brasses to clean and paintwork to dust. At dinnertime, one o'clock, we stopped for a break but we were exhausted as we'd been at it for six solid hours. I couldn't touch the food but Lizzie and Cissie managed a small lump of bread with margarine, washed down with cold water. Tired? That word wasn't strong enough. We were jiggered. We'd each of us done a charlady's day's work in one morning. We'd all got sore knees, including Cissie despite her kneeling pad. Lizzie and Cissie could hardly speak and we just about had the strength to crawl up the stairs to our dormitory beds where we collapsed in a heap. We were more dead than alive and every limb ached. We wondered how Mam and Danny had got on and how we were going to survive afternoon school.

'I don't like it here,' Cissie announced, rubbing her sore knees. 'I'm going to run away.'

'Where to?' I asked.

'I don't know – to China or Timbuktu.' The last named was the most faraway place she could think of. 'How do I get there, Kate?'

'Go straight out of the workhouse gate and walk down Oldham Road as far as Great Ancoats Street. Then ask again at the post office.'

'Is it past Albert Square?'

'About another three miles. But if you go, what happens to Dad? You can't leave him burning for hundreds of years in purgatory.'

She considered this for a while. 'How many years off purgatory up to now, Kate?' she asked.

'I reckon that each of us earned about fifty years for that little bit of scrubbing today. If we keep this up, soon we'll be in credit and God will owe *us* time off.'

'Oh, all right,' she said. 'I suppose I'll have to stay.'

Before two o'clock, we dragged ourselves off our beds and prepared to go to afternoon school. We asked Bertha for directions, which she gave along with lots of warnings.

'Watch out for that man Harold Catchpole. He's a bad-tempered old bugger. He used to be a miner – lost an arm and an eye in a colliery accident. Now he has to make do with two substitutes, a glass eye and metal arm. He tries to take out his bad luck on the rest of the world. Him a teacher! I'd be surprised if he can read and write himself.'

Trembling with anxiety, the three of us found our way to the schoolroom where we saw about thirty other kids, boys and girls, standing with Catchpole in their midst. He held a thick hair rope in his right hand. The room was dismal and dark because the only window had been whitewashed to stop people looking in. Or out. Not seeing the usual classroom paraphernalia, like writing slates, wall maps, or a blackboard, we thought at first that we'd come to the wrong place until we saw tattered copies of the Bible and *Dr Mavor's Spelling Primer*.

'Yes, yes, come along,' he bellowed, waving the rope around his head. 'You're new here?'

'Yes, sir,' I said quietly, numb with fear in front of this terrifying man.

'You'll have to speak up,' one of the big boys said from the side of his mouth. 'Lord Nelson there is as deaf as a post.'

'Yes, sir, we're new,' I shouted.

'Stand at the back with the other new ones,' he instructed.

Then we saw Danny and the Foley boys. What a change had come over them. They were wearing the grey workhouse uniform but what made them look so different was their new hairstyle. Like us they'd been cropped but their barber had left them with a tuft at the front, giving them the appearance of a billy goat. We made no comments, however, as all eyes were on Catchpole who was delivering a speech.

'Most of you brats have been dumped here on the parish because your own parents can't look after you. I'm supposed to learn you but most labourers' kids outside don't get much of an education and so I don't see why *you* should. You'll learn two things here – the Bible and spelling. And God help any of you I find slacking.' He brought the rope down heavily on a desk to show what would happen to anyone doing such a thing. 'If you can't read, you must get one of the other scholars to learn you. But there'll be no writing, not in my class. Writing leads to mischief and I'll not have it. We'll begin today with a Bible reading.' He pointed to the big boy who'd told us about his deafness.

'You, McBride, make a start and show them how it's done.'

McBride was standing in front of us. He opened his Bible and began to read in a loud, clear voice.

'In the beginning God created the heaven and the earth. And the earth was without form, and void; and darkness was upon the face of the deep. And the Spirit of God moved upon the face of the waters. And God said, Let there be light: and there was light.'

That's pretty good, I thought. Obviously a good reader. Then I noticed that McBride had the book upside down. He must have memorised the passage.

The rest of the reading lesson went without incident and when it came to my turn, I thanked God for the teaching I'd received at St Michael's Elementary School. I looked back wistfully to those days in Gerty Houlihan's class. Whatever I thought about her at the time, she'd certainly knocked her stuff into our thick heads.

After the Bible, we switched to spelling. Catchpole told us to learn a list of thirty words – some of them easy, some hard. He gave us ten minutes for the task. Holding the book in his good hand, he tested us.

Lizzie was first.

'Spell "receive".' He watched her lips to check her answer.

'R – E – C – E – I – V – E,' she answered.

He consulted the book. 'Correct.' He sounded disappointed.

I got worried when, pointing to Cissie, he ordered her to spell 'cocoa'.

This was where my ventriloquist skills came into play. 'C – O – C – O – A,' I whispered.

'C – O – C – O – A,' Cissie repeated after me.

If I stay in this place much longer, I said to myself, I'll

develop my skills to the point where I don't move my lips at all. Maybe I could go on the stage.

It was my turn next but I wasn't nervous 'cos my spelling wasn't bad. I got the word 'skeleton'. Easy, I thought, as I gave him the answer.

'I'll bet he wouldn't know the answers if he didn't have that book in his hand,' Cissie whispered.

'Don't be silly, Cissie,' I said. 'He's got to have the book. He's not learning – he's teaching.'

Danny was next. No problem as he used to be top of the class at St Michael's. He got the word 'stationary'.

'S – T – A – T – I – O – N – E – R – Y,' he spelt out confidently.

'Wrong! Wrong!' Old Nelson yelled triumphantly. 'That's not what it says in the book. It should be A – R – Y at the end. Get out here, you lazy good-for-nothing. You were told to learn those lists and you've spent your time day-dreaming.'

'But, sir,' Danny protested. 'It can be spelt two ways. The way I've spelt it means writing materials, like paper and envelopes. The one with A – R – Y means standing still – not moving.'

'I can see you're one of them clever dicks. Don't argue with me, lad. Out here!'

Poor old Danny. He was always in the wars. He received two stinging blows of the rope across his shoulders. I used to think Miss Houlihan was a tyrant but compared to this bully, she'd been a kindly old soul.

The rest of the lesson dragged its weary way with more errors, more shouting, and more vicious punishments.

At the end of the lessons, we got a chance to exchange notes with Danny. We told him about our dormitory and the strange characters, the murderous task of scrubbing out the dining hall. He told us how he and the Foley boys had been put on oakum picking.

'What *is* this oakum picking?' we asked.

'Oakum is rope covered in tar. It's used in ships to fill the cracks to make them watertight. Our job is to unravel and remove the tar. We were given three pounds of rope each but after three hours I managed only half a pound. They said I was lazy and I got belted.' He showed us his torn and bleeding fingers.

'You're not the only one, Danny,' Cissie said sadly. She showed him her sore knees. 'That's from kneeling all morning on stone floors. Kate said we'll get Dad fifty years off purgatory if we don't cry.'

'Do you see me crying?' he said. 'But the men tell us that there's something worse than oakum picking and that's bone-crushing. If they put us on that, I don't think we can stand it and the Foleys and me are planning to run away and live rough, like the tramps you see in the brickyards.'

My heart skipped a beat when I heard him say this. No telling what would happen if he tried that.

'Don't even think about it,' I warned him. 'McTavish will put you in solitary confinement in New Strangeways. Or, even worse, they can make you spend the night in the mortuary.'

We parted company but Danny's words had made me anxious.

We went into supper. We were that hungry, we felt that we could eat anything – and we did. Broth! Workhouse broth!

After supper, we returned to the dormitory and wondered how we were going to spend the time. There were no books, no magazines, no games, no toys. I appealed to Bertha for help. She found us an old register and three pencils. 'Black leads' she called them. They were our lifeline and saved us from going mad with boredom. We thought of lots of games to play, like Hang Man, OXO, Consequences, and Your Future Job. You played the last game by making a list of jobs and careers and rolling up the paper. When your partner said 'Stop', you looked at the job they'd landed on and that was what she was going to be when she grew up. We always included a few daft jobs like lavatory attendant or painter of stripes on humbugs. It gave us a laugh or two and God knows we needed them in that Union Workhouse.

At other times, we lay on our beds and listened to the old ladies as they huddled around the fire. Sometimes, that was the best entertainment of all. After half past eight, it was not permitted to put more coal or coke on the fire and as it began to die down, some of the younger women gathered round the fireplace to take advantage of the last bit of heat.

'Well, Old Sal's gone at last,' Bertha sighed. 'She's in a better place now. I'll be taking her bed as it's nearer the door and it's my job to lock it.'

'Fat lot of good that did last night,' Jessie, the worrier, said. 'Didn't stop Randy Andy last night, did it?'

'That's because he has his own master key,' replied Bertha. 'From what I've heard he's been visiting a few ladies' dormitories at night.'

'A chip off the old block,' Norah Clynes said. 'Old Jock likes his oats too and not only with his missus. He's been getting a bit of rump steak with Fanny Burns the cook – if you take my meaning.'

'Apart from that,' Bertha said, 'Old Jock's only other interest is cutting costs. Always trying to save a ha'penny here and a ha'penny there. Did you hear Dr O'Brien going on at him about pauper funerals?'

'Dr O'Brien's a good man,' said Mrs Clynes. 'I don't

know why he stands for McTavish and his penny-pinching ways. Why doesn't he do something?'

'His hands are tied,' Bertha said, 'and he has to watch his step or Old Jock'll have him out on his ear. Then where would we be?'

'What are these pauper funerals they were arguing about?' Queenie asked. 'How are they different from the ordinary kind?'

'I can tell you that,' Jessie butted in quickly. 'It means planks for a coffin, no shroud, a strip of calico, no tolling of the bell, a quick service, inmates in workhouse uniform as pall bearers, and lastly a communal grave. I hope I don't die in this terrible place.' She swivelled her eyes in our direction when she said this and I shivered with fear. But Jessie was half mad and no one believed her. Did they?

Hannah now made her first contribution. 'What I want to know,' she asked, 'is why they separate families. My husband is in with the able-bodied men and I get to see him only for an hour on Sunday afternoons.'

'You are kept apart, my dear,' Queenie answered haughtily, 'firstly as a way of making this place as nasty as possible; and secondly, so that you won't breed. At least not whilst you're in here.'

'We old 'uns over sixty are allowed to see our husbands every day if we like,' Bertha said. 'More's the pity. My old man's such a moaner that five minutes once a month would be quite enough for me.'

The fire had now gone out and the room had turned cold. Time to turn in.

Soon it was back to the snoring, the wheezing and the coughing.

Chapter Twelve

Sunday at last! Oh, what bliss! During our first week in the workhouse, I had been counting the hours and the minutes to this day. And for three reasons. First, according to the menu on the wall, we were due for better food at dinner and at supper; second, we were to go to church today – twice. But the third was the best reason of all. We were to meet again as a family and even though it was only for an hour, it meant everything in the world to us. There was joy for Lizzie as well for she was expecting a visit from her mother.

The day began with the usual skilly but the way we were feeling, we weren't bothered by its funny taste. Besides, we were getting used to it. There was only one chapel in the House and each religion had to wait its turn. The Protestants went first and as we sat in the dormitory we could hear them singing their hymns. I didn't like to admit it but they really could sing and they let rip with hymns like, 'Praise, my soul, the King of Heaven' and 'Holy, Holy, Holy! Lord God Almighty'. Don't think I'm being catty when I say it sounded a bit like the vault of the Lord Napier on a Saturday night. I mean that as a compliment. Whoever said 'The devil has all the best tunes' was wrong 'cos I think it was the Proddy-dogs who'd snaffled the lot and left us Roman Candles with the rubbish. Anyroad, we didn't usually have a sing-song at Mass but left that to when we had Benediction.

At last the singing stopped and a little later, when we heard the bell, we knew it was our turn. Us three girls set off with Mrs Clynes who couldn't walk very fast because of her arthritis. She was carrying her missal with her but I didn't need one as I could recite the Mass backwards, thanks to having it drummed into me at St Michael's. We saw Mam and Danny outside the chapel door but we were not allowed to talk, otherwise we'd have been sent back to the dormitory. We nodded to each other and mouthed the words 'See you later'. There were about a hundred in the congregation and everyone looked happy, as if they were going for a day out at Blackpool. It made such a change to be surrounded by so many smiling faces.

The chapel was set out like St Michael's Church back home and it did my heart good to see the familiar things – the tabernacle, the altar, the candles, the pulpit, the flowers. They gave me a feeling of warmth and security as I knew that the same Mass was being said all over the world. At times during the week, I'd felt miserable and lost but I hadn't been able to show it because of the other two, especially Cissie. Now the sight of these things had me in tears as they brought back memories of those happy times we used to have before we went down on our luck.

The altar bell tinkled and the priest came out with an old miserable-looking inmate as his server. They genuflected and began.

'*In nomine Patris, et Filii, et Spiritus Sancti*. Amen.'

I blessed myself and joined in the prayers happily.

'*Introibo ad altare Dei*,' the priest chanted.

We answered, '*Ad Deum qui laetificat juventutem meam*.' To God who giveth joy to my youth.

The Acts of Faith, Hope and Charity followed. It was the one about hope that I said with all my heart. 'My God, I hope in you, for grace and for glory, because of your promises, your mercy and your power.' I asked God to get us out of this awful place and to help us get back together again. 'I don't care how you do it, God, but that's my greatest wish. I don't want money or things or owt like that. Make it so that we can be a family again.'

Soon it was time for the sermon and we sat back to listen. The priest – Father Hannon by name – was a tubby man with rosy cheeks and there was something comforting about him. A man who knew what life was all about. His sermon was about not wanting things we didn't have but being content with what we had. He told us that man did not live by bread alone but by every word that proceeded out of the mouth of God. He quoted the Sermon on the Mount a lot. Blessed are the poor in spirit: for theirs is the kingdom of heaven, and blessed are the meek: for they shall inherit the earth. He told us how lucky we were to be poor because it was easier for a camel to go through the eye of a needle than for a rich man to enter into the Kingdom of God. I thought: too bad for Solly, the pawnbroker, 'cos he had our furniture; and Jock McTavish the workhouse master, who, according to the ladies of our dormitory, was robbing the Board of Guardians blind.

At home, I used to be bored by the long sermons but here I wanted the sermon to go on so as to put off having to go back into the workhouse proper. But we'd got the afternoon to look forward to.

We finished Mass with a hymn of our own. I was normally too shy to sing out but there in that place, I lifted my voice and let rip.

Soul of my Saviour,
sanctify my breast!
Body of Christ,
be thou my saving guest.
Blood of my Saviour,
bathe me in thy tide,
Wash me with water
flowing from thy side.

I hoped the Protestants were listening up there in the dormitories.

It was time for Sunday dinner and we were due for something special. A piece of cheese with our bread! First, we had to put up with a talk from an Anglican clergyman. I noticed that, like the McTavishes, he did not join in the meal. He reminded us of the great mercies that had been showered down upon us; how lucky we were to have good food, comfortable clothes, and a roof over our heads, all provided by the generosity of the ratepayers and the Board of Guardians. He was saying this while we were eyeing the lump of bread, the small slice of cheese which sat on our plates, and the jugs of water. All that singing had given us an appetite and, although the dinner may not have seemed much to an outsider, for us it was a banquet and we were anxious to get at it. We could have done without the parson droning on. We'd had our ration of sermons for that day, now it was time for grub. He brought his talk to an end and said Grace. For once, we meant it when we said, 'May the Lord make us truly thankful.'

Sunday afternoon brought an hour of wonderful happiness, sixty minutes of heaven. At two o'clock, out of our minds with excitement, the three of us hurried along to the dining hall. Before we even entered, we could hear the babble of dozens and dozens of people talking frantically at the same time. It was like a madhouse as everyone tried to get the most out of this one hour. There was hugging and kissing and crying and shouting. For the inmates, especially those with children, Sunday afternoon shone through the whole week like bright sunshine on a winter's day.

We soon found Mam with little Eddie, and Gladys looking more beautiful and glamorous than I'd ever seen her. Lizzie and her mother went off a little way and were soon deep in conversation. Gladys was looking that rich, I wouldn't have been surprised if she wasn't planning to take Lizzie home with her soon. Lucky Lizzie if she was!

Our own little family sat together at one end of the table but today facing each other which was not normally allowed. I can't find words strong enough to describe our joy. For the first five minutes we simply hung tightly onto each other. Cissie clung to Mam quietly as if she'd never let her go. She showed Mam her sore knees and told her about the floor scrubbing.

'Our Kate says that already we've earned over three hundred years off for Dad in purgatory. Only another seven hundred and they'll let him into heaven.'

Danny showed his raw fingers and described the oakum picking the men had to do. All this time, I held Mam's hands in mine and listened to her account of her week. She'd been put to work in the laundry and wash-house and had to put in a ten-hour day whilst young Eddie was looked after by inmates in the nursery. It sounded as if Mam had been having as bad a time as us.

'Why do we stay here, Mam?' I asked. 'Surely we'd be better off outside.'

'Without money or a home, where would we stay and how would we live? No, we must put up with it and hope that God will see our plight and help us.'

'That's all very well,' I replied, 'but everyone else in this place is hoping for the same thing and God can't help everyone. Why should he give us special help?'

'Have faith,' she answered.

Came the terrible moment when the porter entered the room ringing his bell to let us know that time was up. I think the noise of that bell must be the most hateful, cruellest sound in the world. There were sudden tears and cries of dismay but it was no use arguing with it. If we didn't leave immediately, there would be no supper that night. Before we parted, Gladys gave each of us a bar of Fry's chocolate. We took it gratefully but it didn't take away the sorrow in our hearts as we said goodbye for another week.

There was one consolation. As Holy Roman Candles, we were allowed to go to Benediction later that afternoon. It was back to the regime of no talking but we were in each other's company again for the rest of the afternoon.

The severe-looking server was lighting the candles when we came in and soon the chapel was aglow with their reassuring illumination. I don't know what it is but to me there seems to be something special about candlelight on human faces; somehow they look holy, even saintly. Led by his server, Father Hannon appeared in his magnificent robes and the service began. We sang the Benediction hymns though it wasn't easy to stay in tune with Norah Clynes croaking out her frog-like version beside us. Just the same we sang out lustily.

O Salutaris Hostia,
Quae coeli pandis hostium;
Bella premunt hostilia
Da robur, fer auxilium

Misery-face swung the thurible in a wide arc, releasing a cloud of incense that filled the whole church with its sweet aroma. A gleaming silk cloak was placed on the priest's shoulder and as he turned to bless us with the monstrance, our server made a clinking sound with the thurible against its chain. Next came the Divine Praises.

Blessed be God.
Blessed be His Holy Name,
Blessed be Jesus Christ, true God and true Man,
Blessed be the name of Jesus . . . Blessed be God in his Angels and in his saints.

We filed back to our dormitories feeling refreshed and uplifted.

In our soul-destroying routine, Sundays were like oases in a desert, but one Sunday things were different.

Us three girls hurried down to the dining room as usual, eager to see our parents after a hard week of scrubbing floors. When we got there, we found Mam, Eddie, and Danny there all right but no Auntie Gladys. Instead there was Auntie Sarah looking very serious. When she saw that her mam was missing, Lizzie turned white as if she'd seen a ghost.

'What's happened?' she asked urgently. 'Where's my mam? Why isn't she here? Is she sick or something?'

'Now, now, Lizzie,' Aunt Sarah said. 'Don't go jumping to conclusions. Your mam's not sick or anything like that. She's well but she won't be able to come for a week or two.'

'What's happened? Where is she?'

'I'm not going to try to hide the truth from you,' Aunt Sarah said in a kindly voice. 'Your mam, along with

Mrs Hicks, have had a spot of bother with the law and they've both been given a month by the Minshull Street magistrates.'

When I heard this, I felt sick in the pit of my stomach. We'd heard that kind of talk at St Michael's School from girls like Fanny Butterworth and Florrie Moss when they'd told us how their mam or dad had been given time for nicking something from a shop or from a stall on Tib Street market. We'd never thought for a minute that we'd hear that one of our own 'had been given a month'. But why Auntie Gladys and Mrs Hicks? Somehow I couldn't see them nicking stuff.

We tried to console Lizzie by telling her that a month was not for ever. Her mam would be seeing her after a few weeks and everything would be back to normal. At the best of times, Lizzie was quiet but when this terrible news had sunk in, she went right inside herself as if she'd been struck dumb. She stared into space.

When we told our fellow inmates in the dormitory what had happened and how we couldn't understand why people should be given a month for doing community work on Piccadilly, some of them looked sympathetic but others roared with laughter.

'You girls are dumb,' cackled Bertha. 'They were given a month for being tarts, ladies of the night – prosties. They sell their bodies for money, love. I don't blame 'em 'cos in this world, it's sink or swim, sin or starve.'

'I don't think so,' I protested. 'I can't see Auntie Gladys doing anything like that.'

It was only later when I thought about it that it began to add up. So that was why Mrs Hicks and Auntie Gladys had so much money. That was why our own mam hadn't wanted the work. I didn't report my thoughts to Lizzie, she had enough worries on her plate for the time being.

But looking back, I think that was the night I started to grow up.

Our weekly family meetings after that were never the same. Somehow the joy had gone out of them and we spent much of the time sighing and saying how much we looked forward to the day when golden-haired Auntie Gladys would come again with her gifts and her bars of Fry's chocolate. But she never did. One fateful Sunday, Aunt Sarah turned up again. We knew by her face that she was the bearer of sad tidings. She didn't seem to want to look at Lizzie and addressed Mam instead.

'I've bad news,' she announced. 'On Friday last, Gladys passed away in the infirmary of Strangeways Prison.'

'Oh dear, dear God,' Mam exclaimed. 'What in Heaven's name happened? We were expecting to see her today.'

'It was all over in a week,' Aunt Sarah said. 'Gladys developed bronchial pneumonia whilst she was inside. It was so quick that she didn't have time to suffer or even know what happened.'

All eyes turned to Lizzie. Her face was ashen. No tears. She shook her head slowly, unable to take in the disaster which had befallen her.

I put my arm round her. 'Lizzie, Lizzie. I'm so sorry. But you still have us. We're your family now.'

Mam and Lizzie were allowed by the Guardians to attend the funeral Mass which was held in St Michael's Church. The rest of us stayed behind and said our own private prayers.

'Now we've got another soul to get out of purgatory,' Cissie said plaintively. 'That's three we've got to suffer for now.'

'No, Cissie,' I said. 'I think Lizzie's suffering has been enough to get Uncle Jack out, and as for our own dad, I'm sure he must be up in heaven by now after all we've gone through.'

After that tragic Sunday, we resigned ourselves to being in the workhouse for ever. We were becoming like some of the other inmates who had been there for years and years. In class, old Catchpole once asked the McBride lad what he wanted to be when he grew up.

'I want to be the head of our dormitory,' he replied.

That made me determined never to accept the workhouse as my destiny. Every time I gazed on that glass swan of mine on the shelf above my bed, I was reminded of where I'd come from and I swore that some day we'd escape from this awful place. I looked next at the statue of the Sacred Heart. 'Come on, God. You can do it. Get us out of here. We've scrubbed enough floors to get Dad out of purgatory. Now it's our turn for a leg-up.'

It was all very well begging God for a miracle but I couldn't see how even He could help, apart from sending down a thunderbolt to strike Jock McTavish and his hideous family. Where were those Bible miracles when you needed them? We simply ticked over; the days became weeks, and the weeks months. But God works, so they say, in mysterious ways.

I was constantly concerned about Lizzie. She seemed to have withdrawn into herself completely. Never smiled, never laughed any more, but went round with a sad, grief-stricken expression. A few weeks later, though, my worries switched to my brother Danny.

One Sunday a few weeks after Auntie Gladys's death, we met in the dining hall for our family get-together. We exchanged the usual news of happenings during the week but when it came to Danny's turn, he broke down in tears – a rare thing for him to do.

'They've taken us off oakum picking,' he wept, 'and put us on bone-crushing. I don't think I can take much more of it.'

'Bone-crushing?' I asked. 'What does that involve?'

'They bring in tons of horses' bones which we have to crush into powder and they sell that to the farmers as fertiliser. They make us use a huge rammer which even the strongest men can hardly pick up.'

'So how do you manage it?'

'They put two boys to each rammer. I've been working with one of the Foley boys for the whole of Saturday. It's not only back-breaking but our hands are blistered and the smell is so bad that one or two men have fainted. Andrew McTavish comes round and whips us on the legs with his cane if he thinks we've been slacking.'

We listened to Danny with horror. We knew bone-crushing was sometimes used as a punishment. We'd once heard Old Jock cry out, 'Keep that man well to the bone tub!' instead of sending him to New Strangeways.

'If it doesn't stop soon,' said Danny, 'me and the Foley boys are going to do a bunk.'

Something within me turned to ice when I heard this. Mam looked distraught.

'Whatever you do Danny,' she implored, 'don't try that. They're sure to catch you and you'll be brought back in chains. You'll get solitary and Diet Number Three – bread and water for a whole week.'

Danny didn't answer. I had the feeling he'd already made up his mind.

When we parted after Benediction, I was troubled in my heart and for the rest of that day I was worried sick. I hoped and prayed Danny and the Foleys wouldn't be so stupid as to make a run for it. On Monday morning I was so relieved to see them at breakfast. They've used their brains and common sense has won the day, I thought. But my relief was short-lived for on Tuesday they'd gone. Andrew McTavish was on roll call duty when the absences were reported.

'Table Twenty-five,' reported the table head, 'three missing – the two Foley boys and Danny Lally.'

There was a gasp of horror throughout the hall.

Andrew McTavish was aghast. 'Are you sure?' he asked.

'Absolutely,' the table head replied.

The McTavish son lost no time and ran out of the hall to report the matter to his father. No doubt Old Jock would have a heart attack when he got the news. Young boys absconding from his workhouse! It was unknown!

Oh, the stupid, stupid boys, I said to myself. They're bound to get caught and Old Jock'll make their lives hell.

The rest of the week was pure misery. A cloud hung over me and I was filled with deep disquiet. In the mornings I awoke to a feeling of panic. Something bad was going to happen, I knew it. The days went by but there was no sign of Danny or the boys. Rumour had it that in the early hours of the morning the three lads had climbed the workhouse wall and bolted. Searchers with dogs were out everywhere looking for them.

It was Friday at breakfast when things came to a head. We'd got our skilly and the prospect before us was the usual stint with the buckets and the scrubbing brushes when McTavish with his wife and son in tow strode into the hall and onto the stage. As Jock and his missus stalked past our table, they left a powerful whiff of beer, whisky and snuff behind them. Whatever they intended doing required Dutch courage.

The whole dining hall froze.

'Before you begin stuffing yourselves,' Old Jock thundered, swaying a little as he spoke, 'we have a matter of discipline to attend to. Bring on the absconders.'

Two big male trusties frog-marched our three boys onto the stage. What a sorry sight they were! Bedraggled, dishevelled, and shivering with fear.

'These boys thought they could deceive me by running away. Ungrateful wretches! They thought they could give this workhouse a bad name by telling lies about the treatment they've received here. I've been too soft. I've been kindness itself and this is the way they have repaid me. Well, today my kindness and generosity come to an end. I intend making an example of these three absconders for all of ye to see in case any of ye out there are entertaining similar ideas.'

The audience of diners watched spellbound. For them it was pure theatre.

'For these two boys,' McTavish shouted, pointing to the Foley brothers, 'it was their first offence and so I'm going to be lenient. They will each receive six of the birch. Bring them here.'

One of the trusties dragged the two boys forward by the scruff of the neck.

'Touch your toes!' McTavish growled.

As each vicious stroke hit the mark, the boys cried out in pain. When McTavish had finished, he thrust the boys to one side. 'Now, stand over there while I deal with the real villain, the ringleader of this little episode.'

My blood ran cold. Standing alone, Danny had turned grey and was trembling like a leaf. What was coming? I looked back to see how Mam was taking this. She had covered her face with her hands and put her head on the table. She couldn't bear to look. Danny glanced round the hall and his eye caught mine for an instant in a look of pleading as if he expected me to save him from the terrible punishment that was to come.

'As for this boy,' McTavish snarled, 'this is a different kettle of fish. Not only is he the ringleader, he already has a criminal record with the Railway Police. We are dealing with a wild animal here. I think his rebellious and disobedient nature needs to be tamed and I intend to do it right here and now.' He pointed to Danny with his birch. 'Take off your shirt, you ungrateful wretch. I'll teach you to defy me.'

He turned to the trusties and said, 'Bring on the whipping horse.'

The two men left the stage to carry out his instruction.

'As for you, Master Danny Lally,' McTavish bellowed, 'I sentence you to six of the cat.'

Everyone in the workhouse knew about the cat, or cat-o'-nine-tails. It was like flaying someone alive, they said. We'd heard that it used to be the official punishment in the Royal Navy for serious crimes like rape or robbery with violence but it had been abolished some time ago. Surely McTavish was not reviving it in the workhouse and against a young boy of eleven. For me, this was sure proof that McTavish had gone off his head and was stark staring mad. He was not going to use that whip on my brother, Danny! No, sir! Someone had to do something to stop him. I made up my mind. All eyes watched me as I stood up and dashed out of the room. I had to get help and there was only one person in the workhouse I could think of. Dr O'Brien. I ran along the corridor and up two flights of stairs to the infirmary. I burst into the ward where I found the doctor and a nurse attending a bed-ridden patient.

'Doctor, doctor, please come at once to the dining room,' I gasped. 'Mr McTavish is about to give our Danny a public flogging with the cat and I'm afraid it'll kill him. Please hurry!'

Dr O'Brien took one look at me and saw the urgency. He asked no questions but said quietly to the nurse, 'Take over, sister. I shall be back soon.' Turning to me, he said, 'Let's go! This time, McTavish has gone too far. It's the last straw.'

We hurried back as fast as our legs would carry us. As we got near we heard the sound of a whip on flesh and a scream of pain. In the dining room a deathly hush had fallen and every eye was focused on the stage where Danny had been strapped to a wooden horse. There was a bar of livid flesh across his back. McTavish raised his whip and was about to bring it down a second time on Danny's back.

I winced in anticipation.

'Stop!' Dr O'Brien's voice rang out clearly and with great authority across the hall. 'Enough is enough!'

McTavish froze in the act. 'What the . . .' he blustered.

'You will put that whip down – *now*!' the doctor commanded. 'Or I shall see to it that you are prosecuted for malicious cruelty.'

'Be about your own affairs, sir,' a flustered McTavish shouted back. 'Your remit is to look after the sick.' But his whip hand did not move.

'You will release that poor unfortunate boy immediately,' the doctor cried, 'or I shall be forced to take the law into my own hands.'

'You have no right to interfere in matters that do not concern you,' Old Jock ranted but he sounded less sure of himself.

'Untie the boy!' Dr O'Brien ordered the big trusty who was standing by, bewildered and confused as to who he was supposed to obey. 'Do it – *now*!'

The inmate did as he'd been commanded. Whimpering, Danny got up and rushed from the stage into the waiting arms of Mam in the body of the hall.

'I'll see you in my office, doctor,' McTavish raged. Together they stormed out of the hall.

When they'd gone, a strange thing happened. For the first time, the silence of the dining hall was broken by the excited hum of conversation as the inmates discussed the drama they'd witnessed.

From that day on, our fortunes changed. I don't know the details of what happened between Dr O'Brien and Jock McTavish in the inner office. Perhaps the doctor had been waiting for Old Jock to overstep the mark. I only know that a few days later we had a number of visits from important people on the Board of Guardians and we were asked lots of questions about food, punishments, work programmes, and how we'd been treated. A nice posh lady called Mrs Pankhurst talked to us in Dormitory 16.

'They have no right to keep women and young girls in such dreadful conditions,' she said, and wherever she looked she kept repeating the same words over and over again, 'I'm appalled! I'm appalled!'

She was on our side and it soon brought action.

A full investigation was carried out and a new workhouse master appointed. Mr and Mrs McTavish and their son Andy landed up in clink not only for their cruelty but also for half starving the inmates and putting the food money in their own pockets. Served them right, I thought.

As for us Lallys – and I include Lizzie now in our family – our lives took a complete turn about. Mam got a part-time job in a bagging factory through Aunt Sarah and went with baby Eddie to live in her front parlour. Dr O'Brien came to the rescue of the rest of us kids by getting us places in a school called Swinton Industrial School. He showed us pictures of it and it looked like Buckingham Palace. He even arranged for us to be moved by the workhouse coach, driven by Old Misery himself. Oh, how we looked forward to getting out of the Bastille! The memory of the McTavishes and the nauseating smell of beer and whisky were forever imprinted on my brain.

The Foley family were in luck as well. Mr and Mrs Foley went to live in a furnished room in Jersey Street 'cos Mr Foley had found a job with a furniture firm on Great Ancoats Street, and the two boys went with us to Swinton.

It was sad to say goodbye to our friends in the dormitory – to Mrs Clynes, Jessie, Bertha, Queenie, and Hannah – but at least they were to get a new workhouse master who promised to be kinder and more generous. We were not at all sorry to say goodbye to the other things.

'Goodbye to workhouse skilly and the watery soup,' said Lizzie.

'Goodbye to scrubbing floors,' added Cissie.

'Goodbye to Catchpole and his spelling book,' from Danny.

'And goodbye to our friends, the fleas, bugs, and cockroaches,' I said to round off our farewells.

On the day we left, I said to Cissie, 'It's been worth it. We've got both dads out of purgatory and I'm sure Auntie Gladys won't be long in there. From now on, things can only get better.'

Chapter Thirteen

'*The stranger gazing upon the splendid brick edifice, with its surrounding territory, was surprised when he was told that it was not the seat of an ancient dukedom; but that it was a modern palace for pauper children.*'
Charles Dickens, *Household Words*, on visiting Swinton Industrial School in July 1850.

The ride in the workhouse coach was sheer agony. I think the springs had packed up a long time ago and every bump in the road sent a jolt up the spine. Not only that, we were crammed together like sardines, all six of us kids – Cissie, Lizzie, Danny, the two Foley boys and me. To add to our discomfort we were feeling as nervous as kittens 'cos we didn't know what was going to happen next. Mam and Eddie had already gone to Aunt Sarah's and now we were on our own, riding into the unknown.

'I'm scared, Kate,' Cissie said.

She wasn't the only one but we didn't say it out loud.

'Not to worry, Cissie,' I said. 'We'll get by. We always do.'

As the coach rolled through Shudehill towards Salford, we heard the news boys shouting out the latest headlines: 'Britain declares war on the Boers! All over by Christmas, says Prime Minister.'

'Who are the Boers, Kate?' Danny asked. 'And why have we declared war on them?'

'No idea, Danny. Unless by the Boers they mean boring people. In that case, they've spelt it wrong on their billboards.'

We trundled along Blackfriars Street past Chetham's Hospital and soon we were moving along Chapel Street past Peel Park. Half an hour later we turned off Partington Lane through big iron gates and into a gravelled driveway that wound past green lawns and bougainvillaea bushes. Our first sight of the place did nothing to calm our fears. The building was immense with two twin towers like in those pictures of big haunted castles you see in ghost stories. And the signboard with the words MANCHESTER UNION, MORAL AND INDUSTRIAL SCHOOL FOR CHILDREN OF THE POOR didn't help either.

'I don't like the look of this place,' Danny said.

The coach stopped outside the solid oak entrance and Old Misery, the driver, got down.

'All out,' he shouted. He climbed onto the roof of the coach and handed down the linen bags which contained our bits and pieces. We stood there quaking in our clogs, waiting for someone or something. We must've looked a pitiful sight in our workhouse garb and with our cropped hairstyles. Oh, for a friendly familiar face!

God granted my wish for out of the main door came Dr O'Brien, a big smile on his face and both hands outstretched in welcome.

'Good morning, children!' he called. 'I'm so glad you finally made it.'

Behind him followed a middle-aged couple – also smiling happily. The man was about fifty years old, his hair greying at the temples. Beside him stood a lady around the same age, perhaps a little younger.

'Welcome to Swinton,' he said warmly.

'Let me introduce everybody,' said the doctor. 'Children, meet Mr and Mrs Birkby, the master and matron of the Swinton Industrial School.' We shook hands. This was a new experience for us. Shaking hands with higher-ups! And it was that more than anything else that told me this place was a different world from the workhouse. Deep, deep down, I knew we were going to like it there.

The three adults led us into an inner office where we were invited to sit down. Another thing we weren't used to. Mr Birkby told us about the school.

'Our new medical officer, Dr O'Brien here, has told us about you and we do hope you'll be happy here at Swinton – everyone calls it SIS for short.' He laughed. 'I'm only sorry we couldn't find places for you earlier but it's only now that vacancies have occurred.'

We didn't understand why he was telling us this as we weren't used to having things explained to us. I think he realised this because he changed the subject.

'Thank God you're out of that terrible place, the workhouse. The doctor has told us about it. Now, don't let the grand buildings here frighten you. Why, even Charles Dickens was deeply impressed when he visited Swinton many years ago – he called it a modern palace. We're proud of it. You will be here until you're fourteen and then we shall try to find employment for you. And even when you've left, we'll take an interest in your progress and your general well-being until you're eighteen. Here at SIS, you'll be able to think about the kind of future job you'd like to have and we'll give you training for it – what we call vocational training. For the boys, there's a range of classes available – in the building trades, shoe repairing, farming – also a chance for musical training and to become bandsmen in the army cadets. For the girls, there are opportunities in nursing, cotton mill work and domestic service. You'll be able to talk it over with your tutors and choose which way you'd like to go. The school also has its own farm and you'll be given a small plot of land to look after. But I'm sure you must be feeling overwhelmed and a little bewildered. So I won't tell you too much, not on your first day. You'll pick things up as you go along. Now it's time to meet your personal tutors.'

Mrs Birkby went into the hall and rang a small handbell. In a few minutes, two teachers appeared. One was a sturdily built man, in his forties; the other a tall, dark-haired lady, around thirty at a guess. But for me the most striking thing about them was the friendly smiling way they were looking at us – such a change from our scowling Mr Catchpole.

'This is Mr Maguire, tutor to the boys,' Mr Birkby told us, 'and this is Miss Morrell, Miss *Lucy* Morrell, tutor to the girls. They'll explain how our system works.' There was more hand-shaking and I was beginning to feel like Queen Victoria or the Lady Mayoress.

The boys went off with their tutor to the boys' department and we three went with Miss Morrell to the girls' section.

'This is your bedroom which you will share with nine other girls,' she informed us.

'A sort of dormitory?' I asked.

'No, not a dormitory. A bedroom. We think it's more homely and we try to keep the numbers down so you don't feel lost in a great crowd. My own bedroom is close by in case I'm ever needed.'

'Are we your only group, miss?' I asked, thinking that twelve was a small number for one teacher.

'Oh, no,' she laughed. 'I'm in charge of four bedrooms – that's forty-eight girls in all. Everyone at Swinton calls them Lucy's ladies.'

We went into the bedroom and found twelve single beds, six on each side. Next to each bed was a chair, a locker and a clothes rail with a curtain which served as a wardrobe. Over each bed was a shelf for books or flowers or other ornaments. Mentally, I reserved a place for the Sacred Heart statue and the glass swan.

'Where are the other girls?' Cissie asked. She was worried about what they were like and what sort of reception we'd get when we met. The workhouse had made us nervous and suspicious.

'The other girls are at their lessons but I think you'll find they're friendly and will make you welcome. You'll meet them at dinnertime because you're on the same table.'

The three of us pulled faces, sucked in our breath and gave each other the 'hope so' look.

'The first thing we must do for you girls,' Miss Morrell continued in a kindly voice, 'if you're going to become one of my ladies, is to get you out of those revolting workhouse uniforms, give you a hot bath and into some decent dresses. You'll have three of everything, which I think is right and proper – one on, one for the wash and one in the drawer. We can't do much with your hair until it's grown a little. But when you wash it, make sure you dry it properly; if you go to bed with wet hair, you'll catch your death of cold.' That last comment reminded me of my mother and her endless sayings.

She was as good as her word and soon we were soaking in glorious hot water with a piece of Sunlight soap each – our first good wash since we'd left Butler Court eighteen months ago. The Swinton School uniform dresses were made of a soft cotton material with a blue gingham pattern. We felt like new people and our spirits soared. Already the workhouse seemed like a nightmare from which we'd woken up.

The girls' dining hall, too, was a different affair. For one thing it was nowhere near as crowded, the tables were smaller and the girls sat facing each other. And wonder of wonders, they were talking to each other – quietly perhaps, but the surprise was that they were allowed to talk at all. We new girls sat with our mouths agape. Grace was said by Miss Morrell on the stage. 'Bless us, O Lord, and these Thy gifts . . .'

The girl at the head of our table presented herself as Joan Irving. 'I'm the prefect of our bedroom. I'm responsible for our little group. I'm supposed to see that we behave ourselves and keep the place clean. I have to report back every day to Miss Morrell.'

'I hope these workhouse girls have been fumigated,' sneered a fat girl at the other end of the table. 'I don't want any of their fleas or bugs.'

'You can cut that talk out, Vera Paxton,' Joan Irving snapped. 'Miss Morrell told us always to make newcomers welcome. You were new here once yourself. How would *you* have liked it if people had made remarks about you? Do unto others as you would have them do unto you.'

'I know, I know,' the Paxton girl replied. 'Old Morrell's always spouting old-fashioned sayings but she doesn't have to live in the same bedroom.'

It was time for me to say my piece.

'*You've* no need to worry about our bugs,' I said quietly. 'They like only good solid meat and hate fat.'

My comment caused a titter round the table and Vera went red with anger. If she wants trouble, I thought, she's picked on the wrong one.

'I'd like to apologise for our friend Vera,' a pretty, dark-haired girl said, looking at the three of us. 'Vera's got a chip on her shoulder because of her shape though we're always telling her she's not fat, it's just that she's not tall enough for her weight. My name's Peggy Turner and I think I speak for the rest of us when I say you're most welcome to our set.'

'Thank you, Peggy,' I replied. 'You don't know how glad we are to be here.'

Joan Irving stood up and told us it was our table's turn to go to the central counter to collect dinner. And what dinner! Rabbit Pie! As far as we were concerned it was Gordon Blue or whatever they called it. I never forgot that first meal at SIS, the most delicious dinner we'd eaten since heaven knew when. We picked the bones out and scraped the meat off with our teeth. And since it was Saturday, there was even rice pudding as a dessert. This is living the high life, I said to myself.

The meal concluded with Grace After Meals. 'We give Thee thanks, Almighty God, for all Thy benefits . . .'

We joined in the prayer happily.

After dinner, Joan Irving took us on a tour of the school farm. First we looked at the garden which was divided into dozens of little beds which were assigned as plots for the pupils to cultivate. Many of the girls from other bedrooms were hard at work raking and hoeing their allotments. Joan showed us our own plots which were all next to each other.

'These beds were cultivated by the three girls who left in the summer to take up jobs and they're yours now,' Joan said. 'I should warn you that the school expects you to devote at least two-thirds of your patch to growing vegetables for the kitchen. You can treat your sections separately if you want to but there's no reason why you shouldn't work them as one large plot.'

'Oh, yes, let's do that,' said Cissie. 'We can grow different things and work together.'

'We could have one bed for flowers, the other two for vegetables,' Lizzie said warmly.

It was good to see Lizzie joining in. Since the death of her mother and what with the workhouse regime, she'd been so withdrawn.

'Agreed,' I said. 'Flowers – daffodils, anemones, pansies. Vegetables – cauliflowers, cabbages, carrots. I can see it now.'

To tell the truth, it wasn't easy to see it at that time of the year. It was October and there wasn't a great deal growing but the soil looked a rich brown colour and I was sure we would succeed.

'Most girls cultivate their gardens on Saturdays when they're free from school and if their parents are not visiting them,' Joan informed us.

'You mean parents are allowed to come to visit?' I asked.

'Every Saturday afternoon, if they can make it,' Joan replied. 'Unfortunately, for many it's too far.'

Next we looked at the livestock – pigs, cows, sheep, poultry. It was new to us and we weren't sure we'd fancy the job of looking after them. Besides, that job seemed to be the boys' department.

Joan read our thoughts, for she said, 'Generally we leave the livestock to the boys but there's nothing to stop you from helping to feed them if you feel that way inclined.' She added quickly, 'I mean feed the livestock, not the boys.'

We joined in the laughter.

After the tour of the farm, Joan took us indoors to wash and to our surprise we found it was five o'clock and time for the next meal – suet pudding. We'd never eaten so good.

'Are all meals like this?' I asked Joan.

'Not quite. Saturday's a special day but generally

speaking, the food here is good. Most of the milk and the food comes from the farm and our own bakehouse.'

At nine o'clock, it was time for bed. We put out the oil lamps and by the light of the candles we said our night prayers. Not Catholic prayers but the kind we could all join in. Then it was out with the candles and we lay there in the darkness with our own thoughts thanking God that he had brought us to this wonderful place. It had been a long day and so much had happened that I was ready to drop off to sleep as soon as I closed my eyes. It was not to be. Not right away.

In the darkness came a voice which I recognised as that of Peggy Turner's, the one who'd told us that we were welcome as members of the set.

'Does anyone know any stories?'

The question was left hanging for a while.

'Why not let Workhouse Kate tell us one?' Vera Paxton taunted. 'That is, if these waifs and strays know what a story is.'

'You will stop that sneering, Vera Paxton, at once,' said Joan Irving, 'or tomorrow I shall give you a few extra chores to keep you busy. Well, Kate,' she continued encouragingly, 'do you know any?'

'I know many Irish tales that my father used to tell me when we were younger.'

'What kind of tales?' Peggy asked.

'Fairy tales, and folk tales. They're usually about goblins, leprechauns, giants, demons, fairy rings, and humpbacked men.'

'Tell us one about the humpbacked men,' said Joan.

I cleared my throat, took in a deep breath, and began.

'Many years ago, there lived in County Wicklow two humpbacked brothers named Kevin and Desmond . . .' The tale told how Kevin had his hump removed by the fairies when he helped them remember the days of the week. But when poor old Desmond tried to help, he got it wrong and instead the fairies punished him by giving him an extra hump.

When I'd finished my story, there was silence and I wondered if I'd put everybody to sleep. I heard Joan's voice again.

'That's the best story I've ever heard,' she said. 'Also the saddest. Do you know any more like that?'

'Hundreds,' I said.

'You must tell us them all,' Joan said. 'From this night I appoint you as our official story-teller. You can tell us the next one tomorrow night.'

Hearing that made me happy. We were accepted.

Next day was Sunday and we went to Mass in the morning in the Catholic chapel of the school.

There we met the school chaplain, Father O'Dwyer, a small round priest with a strong Irish accent.

'Dr O'Brien has told me about you and the terrible time you had in the Bastille,' he said. 'Let's hope that you find things a little better here. Remember, children, if ever you need me, I'm here at your service.'

Everywhere we went, we met nothing but friendliness and the offer of help. Looking back, I felt as if we'd had a taste of hell and now it was time for a spot of heaven.

On Sunday evening, we went to Benediction.

'You know,' I said to the other two as we left the chapel. 'I think we've died and come to paradise.'

The second night when the lights were out, I told my second Irish tale.

'Many years ago, there lived the most famous hero in all Ireland. His name was Cuchulain and he was the nephew of King Conor of Ulster . . .'

My story was met with the same attention and I could tell that once again the story had gone down well. The only trouble was that I was beginning to feel like the Sultana Scheherazade in the *Arabian Nights*. I only hoped I could keep going with a story every night, but if I ran out of the tales my dad had told me, there was always the Grimm Brothers and Hans Christian Andersen.

Chapter Fourteen

On Monday morning, we were introduced to the school routine. At six o'clock we were awakened by the ringing of a big handbell and a voice calling, 'Up you get, you sleepy heads. Time to start work.'

'That's Miss Crabtree,' Joan told us. 'Crabby for short. Watch out for her, she's a slave-driver. Come on, I'll show you what to do.'

Some of the girls had already gone to their jobs in the kitchens, the laundries, and the bakehouse, but because we were new, Joan Irving gave us jobs around the bedroom. First we cleaned the toilet and made the beds. Miss Crabtree strode into the room to inspect our work. She was a tall, thin woman with a vinegary face, pale blue eyes hidden behind large spectacles.

'Those beds will never do,' she said at once. 'Did they teach you lot nothing in the workhouse? Straighten out and tuck in the sheets. Snap to it.'

Next we were told to scrub the floor. This was a job we knew something about, or so we thought. She stood over us as we got down on our knees. From old Crabby there issued a stream of grumbles.

'Scrub a bit harder.'

'Yes, Miss Crabtree.'

'You!' she said, pointing to me under a bed. 'Go and

get some clean water – now!'

'Yes, miss.'

When we'd finished the job to her satisfaction, she splashed a sloppy orange-coloured polish on the floor.

'Spread that over all the floor and make sure you rub it in properly. Then polish it with these yellow dusters. I'll be back shortly and I expect to see the floor gleaming.' She stalked off.

We went to work until our arms ached. There was a mat at the door of the room.

'What about this, Kate?' Cissie asked. 'Do we polish under the mat?'

'Crabby said *all* the floor. Better do as she said.'

Ten minutes later, Crabby was back to check on us. As she came through the door, she stepped on the mat and went flying through the air, landing on her backside.

It took superhuman effort not to laugh. We froze the expressions on our faces.

I can't remember what she said but it wasn't nice. Not a good start.

At eight o'clock, it was time to wash and go down for breakfast. It was porridge but nothing like the workhouse stuff. This was rich, beautifully cooked, and what was more we had milk and sugar. To finish, the 'dining-room girls' brought round jugs of cocoa and half filled the twelve mugs at the end of the table.

At nine o'clock, it was time for school. Cissie went off to her junior class. She was worried about this but I wasn't 'cos I was sure she would make friends in this wonderful place.

After we'd helped clear away the breakfast things, Joan Irving took us down to our classroom. Like Cissie, we were nervous about this since our experiences of school had not been good. 'I've got good news and bad news,' Joan said.

'Give us the good first,' I said.

'You are both with me in Miss Morrell's class. She takes us for English, arithmetic, and domestic training.'

'So, we are to be Lucy's Ladies,' I said happily.

'That's wonderful,' Lizzie said, 'but what's the bad?'

'You're both over twelve and so you have to attend classes in the evening after supper.'

'What kinds of subjects?' I asked.

'I think you'll enjoy them and so it's not all bad news. We do things like hairdressing and dressmaking. Lucy thinks that if ever we become ladies' maids, we'll need to know about dressing and primping up the mistresses we work for.'

Both Lizzie and I thought that lessons in the evening were good news but Cissie's nose was put out of joint.

'Why can't I go with you?' she pouted.

'Cos you're only eight, we told her. Besides she wasn't a Lucy Lady.

At nine, we were seated in our places and waiting for the arrival of Miss Morrell. She came in and we got quickly to our feet.

'Good morning, girls,' she gushed.

'Good morning, Miss Morrell,' we chorused in the same tone of voice. Everyone was glad to see her – she had the effect of bringing an atmosphere of joy into the room. She told everyone to sit down.

'We have two new girls today and I know you are going to make them feel at home. Remember how you felt yourselves when you first came here.'

'Yes, Miss Morrell,' the class said in unison and smiling broadly in our direction.

'As I've told you many times before, my job here is not only to teach the basic subjects but to make young ladies of you. When you leave this school, the world will recognise you as Lucy's Ladies and you will be able to take a job as parlour maid or even a lady's maid with the highest in the land. I wish to raise the status of domestic service with a new type of "Lady Servant" who will be better educated and worthy to serve the higher social classes. A Lady Servant must combine the patience of Job, the wisdom of Solomon, the wit of Sheridan, with the dignified bearing of a princess.'

She turned her attention to Vera Paxton.

'Yesterday at dinner I saw you sniff and wipe your nose on your sleeve. Now, Vera, that was not the way a young lady should behave. What should you do if your nose is a little runny?'

'Please, miss, use my 'andkerchief. But miss, I didn't 'ave no 'anky.'

'Vera, a lady is never without a clean handkerchief. Remember that. Dignity and gracefulness in all things. And do try to sound your aitches and avoid those double negatives. Say, "I didn't have a handkerchief" if indeed that was the case, but I hope you are never without.'

'Yes, Miss Morrell.'

After this little exchange, there followed the strangest set of speech lessons I'd ever had. Everything was connected to being a servant girl.

'Now', said Miss Morrell, 'what are the six things you must never do if you are to behave as ladies?'

The class began reciting.

'Never eat in the street. Never dye your hair. Never wear shoes that need heeling. Never pluck your eyebrows. Never shave your legs. Never point to people.'

'Excellent, girls. If you are to take jobs as domestic servants, one day you may mix with the aristocracy and you must know how to comport yourselves. The way you speak, the way you carry yourself, the way you dress –

everything about you – will make you instantly recognisable as Lucy Morrell Ladies. Let us begin today by tackling some of the hideous speech patterns that many of you have developed. For example, many of you said "Eh?" or "Wha'?" when you really mean . . . ?' She indicated a tall girl at the back of the class. 'Tell us, Elsie.'

'Please, miss,' she answered, 'pardon or I beg your pardon.'

'Good. And instead of "Shift you!"?'

'Please move,' the same girl answered.

'And "Scram!" ' she said, nodding to Peggy Turner.

'Please leave,' Peggy replied.

'And now we come to the glottal stop,' Miss Morrell said. 'Who can tell me what it is?'

'Please, Miss Morrell,' said Joan Irving, 'it's when we miss off Ts and slide letters together. Like "lorra" for "lot of" or "darll" for "that'll".'

'Good answer, Joan. Yesterday, I heard some boys on the farm say, "I seen a dir-ee big lurry". What did he mean to say? Anybody?'

To my surprise, Lizzie answered. 'He meant to say "I saw a very big lorry".'

'Good answer, Lizzie!' Miss Morrell rhapsodised. 'Let us say together ten times, "Yellow lorry. Yellow lorry".'

We did as we were instructed and we sounded like Geisha girls learning English. There followed a half-hour reciting tongue-twisters like 'Round and round the rugged rock the ragged rascal ran' and 'Peter Piper picked a peck of pickled pepper'.

We finished with the tongue-twisters and switched to 'spelling'. Ah, I thought, here's a subject I know something about. How wrong I was!

'One day some of you will work with lords and ladies and it's most important that you know how to pronounce some of the historic names you may encounter in your work. Learn them, as there will be a test on them tomorrow.'

She wrote a list of strange names on the board which we had to copy into our notebooks with the correct pronunciation in brackets.

Cholmondeley (Chumley); Marjoribanks (Marshbanks); Mainwairing (Mannering); Meux (Mews); Cockburn (Coburn); Blyth (Bly); Waldegrave (Walgrave); Strachan (Strawn); Gower (Gor); Tollemache (Tollmash); Bethune (Beeton); Glamis (Glams); Home (Hume); and Bicester (Bister).

I couldn't imagine ever working with such high-up people but I learned the list just the same.

After the morning break, we had arithmetic, and domestic training entered even into these lessons. Instead of tables, we learned about cutting up things and what weight they would be. Miss Morrell started off by testing us on fractions.

'I cut up a pound of meat into two parts,' she began. 'What fraction do I have and what weight in each part?'

'Two halves and each weighs eight ounces,' answered Joan.

'I cut again. Now what do I have?'

'Quarters and each weighs four ounces,' replied Elsie.

'And again I cut – what then?'

'Eighths and each weighs two ounces,' said Lizzie.

'And again – what do I have now?'

'Mincemeat, miss,' I answered which made everyone laugh, including Miss Morrell.

The lessons that morning ended when each one of us had to go out to the front and, holding the edges of our dress, curtsy and say, 'Good morning, madam' or 'Thank you, madam' while Miss Morrell corrected our posture with comments like, 'Hold your head up, girl' and 'Keep your back straight, Peggy'.

The afternoons were devoted to practical aspects of domestic service and home maintenance. We learned how to paint and decorate as preparation for the time when we might have our own homes, though that day seemed a long way off. We got to know about other useful parts of the domestic servant's job like cooking, baking, laundry work, cleaning, ironing, black-leading, fire-making, needlework, crochet, and darning. In this last subject, I came top of the class and won a prize of a Bible which was presented to me by the Lady Mayoress of Manchester when she visited us the week before Christmas. As the term went on, I learned a lot from Lucy Morrell and I longed to be one of her ladies and to have grace, dignity and charm.

But we learned more than domestic servant things. Miss Morrell showed me a whole world of literature with books like Susan Coolidge's *What Katy Did*, Anne Sewell's *Black Beauty* and Lewis Carroll's *Alice in Wonderland* and his quaint creatures like the 'Dong with the luminous nose' who 'lost his jumbly girl'. But my favourite work was a poem called 'I Remember, I Remember' by Thomas Hood:

I remember, I remember,
The house where I was born,
The little window where the sun
Came peeping in at morn;
(He never came a wink too soon,
Nor brought too long a day,
But now, I often wish the night
Had borne my breath away!')

On Saturdays, we had a break from the classroom. In the mornings, we three Lally girls attended to our garden. We planted all kinds of bulbs and seeds for flowers and vegetables. We could hardly wait to see the results but for that we had to wait until spring.

In the afternoon, we were allowed to walk to the nearby Moorfield Park. There was a large area of flagstones where we played all kinds of games. For skipping, we tied a long rope to a tree and one of the girls turned it so that anyone who wanted to could skip in. Sometimes there were five or six skipping together and singing to rhymes, 'I like coffee, I like tea, I like sitting on a black man's knee' or 'Jack be nimble, Jack be quick, Jack jump over the candlestick'.

Sometimes we played our old game, hopscotch chalked on the flags, using an old tin as the marker. We three were good at this 'cos we'd had such a lot of practice in those far-off days in Butler Court.

We played hide and seek 'cos in the park there were hundreds of bushes and trees to hide behind. The girls from our bedroom got up a game of rounders and there was tremendous fun and excitement as we hit our home-made ball with our homemade bat. I felt as if I was recapturing the childhood I'd lost in Ancoats about the time my dad had died.

The only cloud on the horizon, the only thing that spoiled our afternoon, was a bunch of snooty nannies who sat on the park benches supervising their snooty kids. I hit the ball near to them and Vera Paxton had to go and get it. One of the posh kids picked it up and was about to throw it to Vera.

'Come away from those charity children, Matilda,' a nanny called. 'You don't know what you might pick up from them.'

I wish you could have seen Vera's face. Serves her right, I thought. She's getting a taste of her own medicine.

I overheard one of the nurses say to the other, 'Those wretched pauper children, you know, have all kinds of diseases and nits in their hair.' But the parks were public and they couldn't stop us going there.

For the first few Saturdays, Mam came to visit with Eddie and it was wonderful to see them. It was always a tearful reunion. Mam had settled into her job at the bagging factory with Aunt Sarah, and Eddie was now a toddler. And beginning to look like a regular human being instead of a puking baby. After a few months, we no longer clung to each other as desperately as we had in the workhouse. Even Cissie had grown up since those days. Same with Danny. They'd both found new friends in Swinton, and they'd both become that little bit independent. It was all right for us having visits from Mam but we felt for our friend Lizzie for she had no one.

After those first few visits when Mam knew we were all right, she stopped coming regularly. 'It's a long way to come, Kate, all the way from Ancoats,' she said. 'And I'm not sure we can afford it every week. The fares cost as much as our rent 'cos we have to catch three trams followed by a three-mile walk from Irlams o'Th'Height.'

'I understand, Mam,' I said. 'Don't worry about it. We're settled here at Swinton.'

Despite saying this, at the back of my mind I still had that vision of getting the family together again. We were separated for the time being, but Swinton had given me new hope and prospects. I could see that my dream was not entirely beyond possibility. Many girls left the school for good jobs in domestic service and were able to save money. One day it would be my turn.

At Christmas, the school organised the most wonderful party. After a great Christmas dinner of turkey, roast potatoes, and plum duff, Mr Maguire disguised as Santa Claus and carrying a large sack ho-hoed his way into the hall. On the Christmas tree, there was a present for every child. Lizzie got a nurse's uniform outfit, Cissie a big doll which said Mama when turned over, and I got a copy of *Silas Marner* by George Eliot. If the day of my eleventh birthday had been my happiest day, this was my second.

A week later, the master of Swinton, Mr Birkby, called the senior girls and boys into the hall. It was New Year's Day 1900.

'My dear children, this is a special day indeed,' he told us. 'Today marks the start of a new century and we should be proud to be British and citizens of the greatest empire the world has ever known. It is an empire on which the sun never sets, an empire which stretches round the globe, has one heart, one head, one policy. And how blessed we are to have the greatest Queen the world has ever seen. At present we are at war and in December we had many setbacks but no one is in any doubt that the fight with those stubborn Dutch peasants who are revolting against Her Majesty Queen Victoria will soon end in victory. General Roberts has gone over there with his army and the relief of Ladysmith is only days away.

'But let us forget the war for a moment. The air is full of promise and we are on the brink of a new, exciting age, with new medical discoveries by Lord Lister and Ronald Ross; we have the telephone, the wireless of Signor Marconi, the motor car and, who knows, one day the motor bus may replace the horse and carriage; we have airships which may fly across seas and oceans; we have the camera and even the possibility of moving pictures. And if we are to believe the writer H.G. Wells, at some time in the future we may have the first men on the moon, though I find that hard to believe. But take it from me, boys and girls, strange things are coming.'

And so Mr Birkby continued. We listened to him fascinated but no one believed a word he said. Airships flying across the oceans indeed! From what we'd heard, the German Zeppelins hadn't even got off the ground for more than a few seconds. And as for them carrying people over the seas – ridiculous. I wouldn't have fancied a ride in one of them. What if the balloon popped!

After Mr Birkby we were given a magic lantern talk on the relief of Mafeking by a councillor from Salford. There was a terrible smell of paraffin from the oil lamp projector. He gave us a blow by blow description of the war. We understood why it had been called the Boer War. The lads in the audience seemed to enjoy it though. The councillor told us how the country had gone mad about it. There were Boer War jigsaw puzzles, Boer War chocolate boxes, and some babies had even been named after the victories. How many kids had been named Mafeking? we wondered. But talk about relief! We were the ones who were relieved when he'd finished going on about it. Luckily, when he had no more to say about the war, he showed us colour slides illustrating the story of Cinderella. How I wished I had a magic lantern to tell my stories in the bedroom.

It's said that when you're happy, time flies by like an arrow, but when you're miserable, time drags like a millstone. That explains why our time in the workhouse seemed like for ever while our stay at Swinton simply shot by. Before we knew where we were, it was September and my time there had come to an end. Danny was twelve and doing well as a junior bandsman in the army cadets, Cissie was nine and happily settled at Swinton with lots of friends,

Lizzie had gone thirteen and a half, and I was over fourteen and of school-leaving age.

Most of the girls in our set were looking for jobs. Peggy Turner, who'd also turned fourteen, was the first to start the ball rolling by attending a hiring fair in Preston, her home town. That night in the dormitory, she gave an account of how she'd got a six-month contract as maid-servant with a rich farmer. We lay there spellbound and also horror-struck.

'The men and boys went to one side of the square and the women and girls to the other. The bosses – you can tell who they are by their glossy leggings – walked around you, looking you up and down. "Are you for hire?" they barked. If you said yes, they fired a lot of questions at you.'

'What sort of questions?' I asked.

'Can you cook? Can you bake? Can you wash? Can you sew? If you said you could, they demanded, "What are you asking?" I asked for six pounds. "Six pounds!" the boss shouted. "We don't even pay a lad that for six months. Will you take four?" I said no and in the end we settled on five. When it was agreed, he lifted up his hand, spat on it, slapped *my* hand and gave me a shilling.'

'What's that for?' a fascinated Joan Irving asked.

'That sealed the bargain and I was tied. It's a legal contract and I couldn't change my mind even if someone offered me more money.'

'I don't think I'd fancy it,' Lizzie said. 'It sounds like slavery.'

'I didn't have any choice,' Peggy replied. 'My mother can't afford to keep me at home and at least this job gives me a little wage and free board and lodging.'

Peggy's story had us worried and we lay there wondering about our own fate.

* * *

At the end of September, Mr Birkby called Lizzie and me to his office. He told us to sit down while he consulted his files. At last, he looked up, smiled and said, 'Miss Morrell has nothing but praise for you two – she describes you as her star pupils. You're under our overall care until you're eighteen but now you've both reached the age when you must leave us and go out into the world to seek employment. I am in no doubt that you will soon find positions with respectable families but we here at Swinton will be sad to see you go. As you're both Catholics, I'm arranging for you to visit the Sisters of Charity who will be able to help you find suitable jobs.'

A fortnight later, Lizzie and I took the tram from Irlams o'Th'Height to Salford Cathedral. We stood in front of the big door of the nunnery and wondered how to get attention since there was no knocker. We noticed a long chain with a handle like the one on a new water closet back at school. We wondered if we pulled whether it would flush a lavatory somewhere inside the bowels of the building. We took a chance and were relieved to hear the sound of a bell somewhere within. The great door was opened by an old withered nun and when we announced our names, she ushered us into the front parlour where there were thousands of leatherbound books, all religious, which went right up to the ceiling: *The Life of the Little Flower*, *Lives of the Saints* by Butler, *Summa Theologica* by Thomas Aquinas.

'Reverend Mother Victorine is expecting you. She'll be with you shortly,' the nun croaked and ambled off.

The Reverend Mother turned out to be a tall, stately woman with a massive headdress which looked as if a yacht in full sail had somehow landed on her head.

'Mr Birkby speaks highly of you,' she said, 'and I am going to try and place you with good Catholic families. To give you some idea of how the land lies, as it were, I have brought copies of the *Servants' Magazine* for you to study. Look at the Wanted ads at the back and you will see the kinds of jobs that are available, the conditions of service, and how much they usually pay. We shall proceed from there once we know the kind of job that interests you. I should tell you that trained girls, especially from Swinton, are much in demand.' Promising to return within half an hour, Mother Superior left us with the journals.

Eagerly we scanned the magazine – our first glimpse of the world which awaited us.

'Oh, Lizzie,' I said, 'there are lots and lots of jobs. Look at these.' We read the first vacancies we came to.

SITUATIONS VACANT
A GENERAL MAID FOR A BUSINESS LADY, LIVE WITH FAMILY, 9 SHILLINGS A WEEK. GIRL (15), WOULD BE TRAINED, 4 SHILLINGS. PROTESTANTS ONLY. WITHINGTON AREA.

KITCHEN MAID (14), LOCAL NOT SALFORD. 2 SHILLINGS A WEEK. METHODISTS ONLY. WILMSLOW ROAD, DIDSBURY.

GENERAL MAID, IMMEDIATELY TO SLEEP IN, PROTESTANT, FOND OF CHILDREN. 9 SHILLINGS. 3 IN FAMILY.

SCULLERY MAID. STRONG GIRL. WAGES 7S. 6D PER WEEK. CHORLTON ON MEDLOCK.

WANTED IN A QUIET, SMALL FAMILY A RESPECTABLE YOUNG WOMAN AS HOUSEMAID WHO WILL BE WILLING TO ASSIST THE MISTRESS OCCASIONALLY IN THE MANAGEMENT OF CHILDREN. WAGES £12 PER YEAR. **NO IRISH NEED APPLY**.'

'I can't see many chances here,' Lizzie said. 'And what about when it says "No Irish Need Apply"? Do we count as Irish?'

'We're not Irish,' I said, 'but with names like Brennan and Lally, they'll take it that we are.'

We continued to read. The only possibility was for a 'young girl to help a lady in Didsbury with her dogs. Catholic' – the lady presumably, not the dogs.

'It's no use,' Lizzie said when she'd read through all the vacancies. 'I can't see any place where I'd like to work.' Then she saw an article about jobs abroad.

' "Australia," ' she read, ' "offers the young woman of the working class high wages, a splendid climate, and greater liberty than she could enjoy at home, either in service or in a workshop, and these high wages can be earned without further qualification other than strong health, strong arms, a willing mind and good character." Look,' Lizzie said, 'here's a letter from a servant girl writing home to her brother from Port Adelaide, South Australia: "I have accepted a situation at £36 per year so you can tell the servants in your neighbourhood not to stay in England for such wages as £8 a year, but come here." I think I like the idea of a job abroad,' Lizzie said enthusiastically.

I was amazed to hear this as Lizzie was so quiet and shy. I couldn't imagine her wanting to go to Australia.

'Why, Lizzie?' I asked.

'Now I've lost both parents, I fancy making a fresh start with a new life in a new country.'

'But think of the journey to Australia,' I said. 'It takes three or four months and there are storms and terrible hardships to put up with. Even when you get there, you may find yourself living in a rough wooden shack.'

'Maybe you're right.'

The Reverend Mother returned to ask if we'd seen anything to our liking.

'Not really, Mother,' I answered, 'but Lizzie was wondering about jobs abroad, in Australia for example.'

The nun looked at us for a long time then slowly said, 'From time to time we do get requests from abroad but I wouldn't recommend Australia, we've had a few bad reports about conditions being rough and ready there. If you're serious, though, we may be able to place you both with a wealthy American family. The O'Hagans are good Catholics and they're over here seeking two young English nannies. If you like, I can arrange an interview for you early next week.'

'Oh yes, please, Mother,' Lizzie answered. 'It sounds like the answer to our prayers.'

For her maybe but I wasn't too sure about leaving England and my family.

The following week, we returned to the convent to meet the O'Hagans. Mother Victorine made the introductions.

Mr and Mrs Elmer O'Hagan were a good-looking, middle-aged couple and, judging from their dress, wealthy.

'Mother Victorine has told us your story,' Mrs O'Hagan began. 'You have the highest references and it seems to Elmer and me that you are the ideal pair for our nursery back at Long Island.'

'Thank you, madam,' Lizzie and I answered.

'What cute English accents,' Elmer exclaimed. 'That's another thing that recommends you – your English speech. We'd love our two kids Zoe and Dorothy to pick up that accent. It's kinda refined.'

Refined! Us? I laughed to myself. We'd soon get their kids to stop saying 'gee whiz'. Instead we'd have them saying 'eeh-bah-gum' and 'get sat down and shurrup'.

The O'Hagans went on to describe the job, their home in Locust Valley, the working conditions, the pay of 96 dollars which at four dollars to the pound amounted to £24 a year – £2 a month. A salary beyond our wildest dreams! The O'Hagans sounded like a gentle, kind couple who would care for us. The perfect job! They gave us a few days to think it over and if we decided to take it, they would arrange for us to travel with them by ocean liner.

When we returned to Swinton, everyone around us told us we must, must take it. It was being presented to us on a silver platter and we'd be idiots to turn it down. Lucy Morrell joined the chorus of approval and at night in the dormitory there was nothing but talk of the marvellous chance fate had put in our laps. Joan Irving, who had landed a job with a well-to-do stockbroker family in Macclesfield, urged us to say yes. She'd be only too willing to take our place if we decided not to go.

Lizzie had no difficulty in deciding. She was going.

But I went through the dark night of the soul. Going to America would mean leaving my family. What about Mam, Cissie, Danny, Eddie? Deep down a voice reminded me. What about your dream of making a home for them like it was in Butler Court before Dad died? After several sleepless nights, I made up my mind. I wasn't going. I couldn't. My family in England needed me.

It all happened so quickly. A week later, my dear friend and cousin Lizzie packed up her belongings and joined the O'Hagans aboard the Cunard liner. We promised to write every week but somehow it didn't seem the same. Joan Irving took my job. After they'd gone, life seemed sad and empty. The only thing for it was to apply for that job with the Catholic dogs in Didsbury.

Mr and Mrs Pratt lived with their animals in a house called 'The Laurels' which was at the bottom end of

Lapwing Lane. To reach it I had to take three trams followed by a long walk. It was a big house and I was scared out of my wits as I rang the bell. The door was opened by the housekeeper, a large woman in a blue uniform. I was put off immediately by the cold reception.

'You must be the new maid,' she said, looking down her nose to inspect me. 'The first thing you must learn is never to come by the front door. That's for important people. *You* must use the tradesman's entrance round the side.'

She took me down into the kitchen where the rest of the staff was waiting and she announced in a loud voice, 'Here's the charity kid.'

They looked at me as if I was a cockroach.

That's enough, I thought. I can't work here. I didn't say anything, however, and 'Cheerful Charlotte' took me upstairs to meet the mistress and her husband. She was an obese woman and she was lounging on a sofa with a fat, overfed poodle on her ample belly and two more at her feet. Mr Pratt sat opposite. I thought she must have smeared fish paste or something on her feet because the two dogs were licking her toes.

'Do you like reading?' she asked

'Oh, yes, madam.'

'In that case I'm not sure you'll suit. I find that maids who read are easily distracted from the job. Our last maid forgot to feed and groom my little darlings.'

I could hardly wait to get out of that dreadful house. As I left, one of the scullery maids had a quiet word with me.

'You may as well take a job with Old Nick as come here. They've had four girls in five weeks. You'd be best to steer clear. I'm going to hand in my notice at the end of the week.'

With a great sense of relief, I caught the tram back to Swinton. I was feeling lost. No job, no friends. Then I had a stroke of luck. About time, I thought. The job in Macclesfield – the one that Joan Irving had decided not to take – was still vacant. The family wasn't Catholic but who cared? Mr Birkby arranged an interview for me.

My life was about to take another turn.

Chapter Fifteen

When the day came for me to leave Swinton, I had mixed feelings. Happy that I had found a job. Sad that I was to leave so many familiar places and faces – the Birkbys, Lucy Morrell, and my school friends, but most of all my brother Danny, and my kid sister Cissie. I wasn't too worried about them, they seemed to have settled in well and they had so many friends; no, I was more worried about my job. What sort of place was I going to and could I cope as a junior maid, or tweeny as it was known in the trade?

Mr Birkby assured me that I was lucky to get the job intended for Joan Irving. 'You'll be going to a good home,' he said. It sounded like the kind of thing you'd say to a dog going to new owners. 'The Lamport-Smythes are a respectable, well-to-do family in Cheshire and you'll be treated most kindly. Mr Derek Lamport-Smythe, your new master, is well-known on the Manchester Royal Exchange and Mrs Lamport-Smythe is celebrated for her charity work.'

Swinton always gave its leavers a lovely present to start them off in their new life and I was no exception. When it was time for me to set off, I was presented with a beautiful mahogany box containing a complete outfit of clothes. I could hardly believe my eyes when I looked through the things they had given me: two chemises, two pairs of drawers, two flannel petticoats, one top petticoat, one pair of stays, two nightdresses, two print dresses, four coarse aprons, four white aprons, two pairs of stockings, one pair of boots, one hat, and a pair of slippers. I'd never been so rich in my life and I couldn't begin to thank them enough. I was also rigged out in a new coat and a new dress so as to be respectfully turned out for my new employers.

As well as these gifts, Mr Birkby arranged for me and my luggage to be taken by dog cart to Salford railway station where I boarded the train to Macclesfield. Two hours later, I arrived at my destination.

I managed to grab a sandwich and a cup of tea at the station bar before beginning the ten-minute walk to my new address at the Beeches, Fence Avenue. It was a tall, imposing house in an elegant Regency style and the sight of it was enough to start me trembling.

I reached the front door but didn't go up to it. Oh no, I wasn't that stupid. I'd learned something from my visit to that terrible house in Didsbury. Instead I looked for the tradesman's entrance and found it down some steps leading to the basement.

There was an old man in a battered hat watering the flower boxes on the ledges.

'G'mornin', missie,' he said, doffing his hat. ''Tis a nice mornin', is it not?'

Unsure of myself, I mumbled agreement with him about the weather.

I rang the bell and it was opened by a big, fat, bald-headed man dressed in a black frock coat, like a funeral director. The usual watch-chain dangled from his fob pocket. I was also struck by his nose which seemed aglow from some inner source of light.

'Yes?' he said, looking down his nose at me. 'How may I help you?'

'I'm the new maid. I think you may be expecting me.'

'Ah, yes. The tweeny from Swinton. Come this way. I'll take you to the servants' hall.'

He led me along a stone-flagged passage into a large room. It was sparsely furnished with one large table, several hard wooden chairs, one rocker, pin-rails for hats and cloaks, a towel roller, and a few lockers. Some hall, I thought. It was really gloomy down there 'cos the single barred window was below the level of the pavement.

He didn't deal with me right away because he had some duties to attend to first. He left me standing in the servants' hall. A middle-aged lady at the large table was shouting orders at a young maid.

'Come along, Susie, for goodness' sake. Those sandwiches you've cut for Madam's lunch are much too thick. Cut the cucumber and the bread thinly.'

'I cut them as thin as I could, Mrs Armstrong,' the young maid answered.

'Well, they won't do. Cut them again and don't forget to remove the crusts. And peel the potatoes and prepare the vegetables for tonight's dinner.'

'Yes, Mrs Armstrong.'

The butler reappeared and took his turn at haranguing the young maid.

'Haven't you got the luncheon tray ready yet, Susie? They'll be back at one o'clock. Get a move on.'

'I've only got one pair of hands.'

I stood there, quietly taking it all in. I looked through the window but the only view I could see was the feet of people passing by above.

Boots – boots – boots – boots – movin' up and down again! I sang to myself. Black boots, brown boots, creaky boots, squeaky boots. Why, you could even see the ladies' ankles under their crinolines. I'd bet the men weren't slow noticing that.

The butler turned to me. 'My name is George Willoughby,' he said. 'I'm the house steward, responsible for the smooth running of the house and for staff discipline. Our staff comprises the cook, Mrs Ruth Armstrong, the parlour maid, Miss Victoria Garrett, and our odd-job and handy man, Ned Dooley – we call him Old Ned.'

'I think I saw Mr Dooley as I came in,' I said nervously by way of making conversation and to show him that I wasn't entirely simple-minded and that I had a tongue in my head.

'Quite,' he answered. Obviously a man of few words.

I asked him about my luggage which was still at the station and he arranged for Old Ned to collect it in his cart.

He took me into the kitchen and introduced the cook. She was busy dicing carrots but she looked up from her work to give me a cheery smile. Although I'd heard her shouting orders at the maid, I took a liking to her right away for not only did she give me a big smile, she put down her knife to shake my hand.

'Thank God you're here,' she said. 'You'll be helping me in the kitchen and lately I've been run off my feet. I'm sure Susie, the parlour maid, will be grateful as well.'

I was puzzled. 'Sorry, Cook,' I said. 'I thought the parlour maid was called Victoria.'

'Please don't call me Cook,' she said. 'You must always call me Mrs Armstrong. As for Victoria, upstairs they thought the name of a queen was too posh for a parlour maid so they renamed her Susie as more in keeping with her position. Same with Mr Willoughby here. George is considered too royal and snooty for a butler and so they rechristened him James, the name given to just about every butler in the land.'

'But wasn't James the name of a king as well?' I said.

'That was the King of Scotland and so it doesn't count,' she replied. 'I hope *you* don't have a posh name, dear.'

'My full name is Catherine.'

'Catherine?' Mrs Armstrong pursed her lips. 'I'm not sure they'll wear that upstairs. Better not tell them that. Best to stick to Kate.'

Mr Willoughby – or should I say James – interrupted our little exchange.

'This morning, the family is out and I'm fairly busy. So I'm going to ask Susie to show you around and give you some idea of your job.'

At that moment, Susie entered the kitchen carrying a pile of plates. James made the introduction. She was a pretty young lady with big brown eyes and dark hair, in her early twenties. She was wearing a silk black dress with a lace-trimmed apron and cap with a long streamer at the back. She had an attractive Geordie accent like one of the girls I knew back at Swinton.

'We're pleased to see you here,' she said, smiling warmly. 'Since Molly, the last kitchen maid, left, we've been carrying a heavy load.'

Susie took me on a conducted tour of the house. We began downstairs and she showed me the scullery which was going to be my main place of work. Then the store rooms, the linen cupboards, and the china closet. We examined the butler's pantry – which was not a pantry at all since there was no food kept there. I could see nothing but plates and glassware. The cook's pantry, however, did have food and lots of it – homemade preserves, cakes, biscuits and pickles, plus more china and glass.

Next, we looked at the wine cellar with its stock of port, sherry, Madeira and table wines.

'This is James's province,' she advised. 'No one, but no one, is allowed to touch any of the bottles in here. Sometimes I think he considers himself the real owner of this booze. He reckons that all wines must be tested and tasted before they're taken up to the master's table. In case they've gone off, he says. Some story! That perhaps explains his nose,' she added with a mischievous grin. 'Downstairs, we reckon he drinks one bottle in every five he takes upstairs. He's not the only one who likes a drop. Mrs Armstrong is fond of a hooch or two when she's making sherry trifle or a dish that requires a spot of brandy.'

She showed me the back stairs which led to the top floor where the servants had their quarters.

'Why do we need back stairs?' I asked.

'We use them to hide things our employers don't want to see. For example, it's your job to empty the chamber pots in the morning.' She laughed. 'We have to cover the pots with a cloth so that the people who filled 'em don't have to see their produce.'

'I seem to have spent half my life emptying chamber pots,' I said, joining in the mirth. 'Perhaps I should be called the chambermaid. But what else do we use the stairs for?'

Susie chuckled at my joking. I liked her for that. 'You'll also carry down the hip baths if they've been used,' she answered. 'They're a bit heavy and awkward but Old Ned usually helps.'

'What about James? Doesn't he help?'

'Not on your Nellie. The heaviest thing he carries is the master's *Manchester Guardian*.'

By this time, we'd reached the top floor and Susie took me to the bedroom that we'd be sharing. It was small with a sloping ceiling and a tiny skylight. Hardly big enough for the double bed, the wardrobe, and the small dressing table. Still, I didn't complain. I'd known worse.

We descended by the main staircase and entered a different world. The one inhabited by the Upstairs people. Everywhere I looked, there was opulence, from the thick carpets and the antique furniture to the display of oil paintings on the walls. We entered the master's study-cum-library with its leatherbound books in shelves right up to the ceiling. On the massive mahogany desk was a strange 'Sherlock Holmes' pipe resting on a little metal cradle.

'I see he likes his tobacco,' I remarked, pointing to the pipe.

Susie looked puzzled. 'Oh, that.' She laughed. 'That's not a pipe. It's a telephone.'

'I see,' I replied, embarrassed by my country girl innocence. 'Isn't it marvellous what they can do nowadays? I suppose he uses it to give orders to us downstairs.'

She laughed again. 'No, they have a special speaking tube for that in the dining room. The master uses this one to keep in touch with the outside world, especially his office at the Royal Exchange in Manchester. We have strict orders never to touch it except maybe with a feather duster. And we must never try to use it.'

I looked at the phone more closely and at the metal label on the base which read: 'Ericsson Skeleton Magneto'.

'I wouldn't dream of touching it. I'll bet you can pick up all kinds of brain diseases with that magnetism going through your head.'

She chuckled. 'You *are* out of touch with the wonders of modern science.'

We went into the main hall. And what a hall! It was as big as a whole house and along the wide staircase were wooden panels with heraldic shields. One had the family motto 'Hope and Pray', which summed up the way I was feeling at that moment. The house was a cross between a wine merchant's warehouse, a museum and an art gallery. Why did one family of two parents and two adult children need so much and so many servants? I thought of my mam living in Aunt Sarah's parlour back in Ancoats.

The thing uppermost in my mind, though, was how I fitted into all this. I asked Susie what my duties would be.

'This is a small household, only five servants,' she said, 'and so we all have to muck in. The Lamports in the Macclesfield district are mainly silk merchants with pots of money. Our family is comfortable but not so well off as the other branches of the clan. I think that's why Madam is sometimes bitchy. Thinks she and her husband are looked down on by their hoity-toity relatives because he's only a stockbroker and not a rich factory owner.'

'But the family's called Lamport-Smythe,' I said. 'It's a funny name, isn't it?'

'I suppose it is. But Madam is a Lamport and the master is a Smythe. When they married, she felt that Smythe was a bit of a come-down and so she added her own snooty name to his.'

'There's nowt so queer as folk,' I said.

Susie chuckled at the Lancashire proverb. 'Anyway, because the family's not quite in the top drawer, we have to share the jobs between us. I'm supposed to be a parlour maid but I have to do chores that only a kitchen maid would do in a bigger household. You're the under-parlour maid – which is the maid of all work, the general dogsbody.'

She produced a list from her pocket and handed it to me without saying a word but watched for my reaction with an amused smile.

It was a long list and my heart skipped a couple of beats when I saw it. 'So that's the list of duties for the staff,' I said. 'Which of these are mine?'

'All of them,' she replied, her grin widening. At first I thought she was joking but then I realised that she meant it. No point complaining about it. Beggars couldn't be choosers.

'Don't worry,' she said eventually. 'I felt the same when I first came but you'll get used to it and you'll develop a routine which'll help you cope. At least we don't have to wash their clothes. They send them out to a laundry. Madam said she couldn't do with all that steam coming up from the basement. But more important, let me tell you something about the people upstairs.'

I was all ears 'cos I knew that the personalities I was going to work for could make the difference between heaven and hell.

'First,' Susie began, 'there's the master, Mr Derek Lamport-Smythe. He's away at work in Manchester most of the time and so you won't see much of him. He's a gentle soul, always kind and considerate. Under his wife's thumb though. If she says, "Today I think we'll tell the gardener to cut the lawn", that means "Today, *you* will instruct the gardener to cut the lawn". Madam regards it as beneath her to speak directly to such a lowly person as a gardener. The master is all for keeping the peace and simply does as he's told.'

'Madam sounds like a proper tartar,' I said.

'That's putting it mildly. At times, she can be a real bitch. Ned and I have nicknamed her 'Her Majesty' but James and Mrs Armstrong disapprove of the term strongly. They believe you should have respect for your betters. Anyroad, it's best to be on your guard when dealing with the Madam. Whatever you do, never answer her back.'

'If I answer at all,' I laughed, 'it'll be to her front.'

Susie joined in the laughter. 'As long as you keep your sense of humour, Kate, you'll do. Her Majesty has delusions of grandeur and tries to behave like royalty. She dislikes face to face meetings with servants as she regards us as inferior beings, like slaves. If you happen to meet her on the stairs, it's best to turn away and busy yourself doing something, to avoid eye contact. You'll see what I mean when you get your first pay. If you do have to speak to her, always curtsy and call her Madam. If she orders you to clean something that you've just cleaned, don't argue, hop to it or she'll sack you on the spot. That's what happened to Mollie, your predecessor. Her Majesty has cleanliness on the brain – she runs her hand down the banisters and along the picture rails to test for dust.'

There's always someone like that in my life, I thought. Why couldn't the world be peopled by nice folk?

'What about the other two adults?' I asked, fearing the worst.

'Emma's fine,' she said. 'A do-gooder trying to put the world to rights. She's one of them suffragists fighting for women's rights. You'll find she's on your side in any dispute.'

'And Harold? What about him?'

'Now him,' she exclaimed, 'you have to watch out for. He's one for the girls and no mistake. Downstairs, we call him Horny Harold. Mrs Armstrong tells me that when Madam was pregnant with him, she used to read Dickens and Shakespeare aloud to her womb, thinking it would make him clever. I think someone on the quiet must have been reading bits out of the *Kama Sutra* instead.'

'What's that? The *Kama Sutra*?' I asked.

'It's one of them sex manual books. Harold studies it every morning. He keeps it in a big brown envelope under the bed but I've looked at it when he's out. It's a real mucky book and by the look of the pictures, you'd have to be made of rubber to do as it said.

'When you take his morning tea,' she continued, 'be on the alert. The sight of a long-legged, good-looking girl like you bending over him in the morning will awaken his early-morning passion and he'll have you in his bed as soon as look at you. I know. He's tried it on with me a few times. It's hard to resist 'cos he's the boss's son and he could get you the sack. To him we're not people; we're only servants and anyone's for the taking.'

'Surely he wouldn't try it on with me. I'm only fourteen and a half.'

'Wouldn't he? Your age won't bother him, believe me.'

'So what do we do?'

'Put his tea down on his bedside cabinet and get out of there double quick.'

After this briefing on the personalities of my employers, it was time to return to the servants' hall.

'Her Majesty and the master are back from Lyme Park,' Old Ned declared as he came in from the garden.

There was a flurry of activity at the announcement.

'Susie, be quick, there's a good girl,' Mrs Armstrong ordered. 'Prepare their tray. You know what *she's* like if she doesn't get her tea straightaway.'

No sooner had she spoken than the drawing-room bell started to ring.

'I think I'll die with the sound of them bells in my ears,' Mrs Armstrong exclaimed.

Susie quickly put the finishing touches to the tray of sandwiches and departed hurriedly from the room. She was soon back and it was time for the servants' midday meal, after which I was to meet Mrs Lamport-Smythe – an interview I was dreading.

At the table, James presided and the rest of us sat round

the sides in order of rank. As the newcomer, I was the lowest. Mrs Armstrong poured the tea and gave us a large slice of her walnut cake, the first I'd ever tasted – so delicious it melted in the mouth.

'You'll like it here,' Mrs Armstrong said to me, 'once you've got used to our little ways. You've got to take the rough with the smooth. Madam's sometimes a pain but her husband makes up for her nastiness. As for Harry up there, he's no problem as long as you keep him at arm's length, if you take my meaning. Miss Emma more than compensates for him.'

Old Ned Dooley thought it was time he put in a word or two at the table.

'The postman tells me,' he said, 'that the horny one has been getting more of that there erratic magazine stuff.'

'How do you know it's erotic magazines?' James asked. 'The envelopes are sealed.'

'As God is my witness, I heard it with my own ears from Sidney, the postman. He recognises it 'cos he delivers a lot of that stuff round here, especially to the gentry. The envelope was marked "TEMA Private and Confidential". TEMA stands for "The Erratic Magazine Association", or so Sidney said. The magazine is full of filthy dirty pictures. May God strike him blind.'

'I think Harold must have sex on the brain,' said Susie. 'And come to think of it, not only on his brain.'

'That's what comes from attending them public schools,' James said. 'Once they let them out of school, it's like a cork out of a bottle.'

'And that's something you should know something about,' Mrs Armstrong said slyly.

'And why not?' James answered her. 'We all have our perks in this house. I have a little drink or two to test the quality. You get your boodle in the form of discounts from the tradesmen. That's not counting the dripping you get from the roast meat.'

'And the rest of us get the cast-off clothes when our betters decide to change their wardrobes,' Old Ned added. 'And don't forget our four meals a day and the leftovers from the meals upstairs.'

'Left-over food! Some perk!' Susie exclaimed. 'Sometimes I find I'm having custard and jelly plus steak and onions for breakfast.'

The conversation continued along these lines for some time and I only wished it could have gone on longer. Anything to put off the evil moment when I should have to face the Madam.

'I've brought your box from the station,' Ned Dooley told me. 'You'll need to get it up to your room.'

'We'll take the box up the back stairs to your room,' said James, 'and then it's time to face the music. I'll take you in to meet your mistress.'

For a minute, I thought James was going to help me carry it. Some hopes!

I took a firm grip on the handles of my box and struggled up the back stairs behind James who was carrying the *Manchester Guardian* on a tray for the master.

I deposited my box in my room and James and I descended the main staircase to the drawing room. He knocked gently on the door and entered.

'Miss Catherine Lally, the new maid, Madam,' he announced.

'Yes, thank you, James,' Mrs Lamport-Smythe replied. 'You may leave us.'

James withdrew and I was left alone with Madam and the master.

I stood there awkwardly. Madam's gaze was directed at an ancestral portrait on the wall above the mantelpiece.

The master was sitting by the window reading his paper and he looked up and smiled reassuringly.

She was a tall, thin, bony woman with a scraggy neck. A real sourpuss if ever I saw one. It was a good three minutes before she spoke. She had a high-pitched, squeaky voice – the kind that sounded as if it needed a drop of oil.

'Your name is Catherine Lally?' she inquired, addressing the picture.

'Yes, if you please, Madam,' I said giving her one of Lucy Morrell's best curtsies. I hoped I was not laying it on too thick.

'Catherine isn't a suitable name for a servant. It's the name of a former Queen of Russia. In this house you'll be known as Kate.'

'Yes, Madam. Thank you, Madam.' The words stuck in my throat.

'You come with good references from Mr Birkby at Swinton. I shall take you on trial for a month, starting work tomorrow. I hope you can live up to Birkby's high opinion of you.'

'I hope so, Madam,' I answered. Should I curtsy again? Maybe that *would* be overdoing it.

'Good. Have you brought your belongings from Swinton?' she asked wrinkling her nose. She made 'belongings' sound like sewage from a privy.

'Yes, Madam. Ned, the gardener, brought it from the station.'

'I hope the box was clean and insect-free. God forbid that we introduce bugs into the house. I read recently that these things can multiply at an alarming rate. It said that a pair of bugs can produce twenty-two million in one year.'

'The box has recently been made in the Swinton carpenter's shop, Madam, and my clothes are new.'

'Very well. Now in this initial meeting I want to lay

down the basic ground rules. First, personal hygiene. I trust you keep yourself clean. Mollie, the last girl, did not. She wore the same thick stockings for a week at a time and I think she washed her feet once a month. She was definitely beginning to emit an offensive odour. As long as you are here, you must practise daily ablutions, applied to the feet as well as the armpits. Remember, cleanliness is next to godliness. For this purpose, you will be allocated a bar of soap a month. See that you use it.'

I'd like to see *you* keep yourself clean on one bar a month, I thought.

'Next, you will not get familiar with the various trades people who call at the house. You must not entertain friends in the kitchen and I do not want to hear laughing or singing above stairs. There must be no romping or horse-play. No sneaking off for unauthorised breaks. If you want a break, you must ask my permission. Finally, I will not tolerate followers or boyfriends of any kind.'

She needn't worry on that score, I said to myself. I've never had a boyfriend and I can't see any prospects of one as long as I'm in this job.

'As to your duties, these will be set by James, the house steward, and you will obey him at all times. You will of course undertake a full share of the monthly spring cleaning of the whole house. When it comes to time off, we are more than generous. You will be allowed one evening per week after dinner, a half-day on Sunday, and one full day every three months. Your pay will be twelve pounds per year, which I believe is more than most maids in your position receive. You will be paid at the end of each month.'

'Thank you, Madam.'

This would be the first pay I'd ever received and to me it sounded like a fortune. Why, I might be able to send a bit home to Mam and maybe even save a bob or two.

Mr Lamport-Smythe looked up from his paper again and gave me one of his smiles. 'I hope, Kate, that you'll be happy here,' he said.

Madam froze him with a cold stare. 'Please leave the servants to me, Derek,' she rasped. 'Very well,' she said, turning back to the wall painting, 'we'll see how you get on. Meanwhile, I'd like you to study this little tract published by the Society for Promoting Christian Knowledge.'

I curtsied and holding the tract as if it was the Magna Carta, I left the room.

In the servants' hall, they were waiting to hear my report.

'They've opted for Kate,' I said.

'Told you so,' said Mrs Armstrong. 'Catherine's much too grand for a tweeny. What else?'

'I'm to have one evening off per week, a half-day every Sunday and a full day every three months.'

'Don't make me laugh,' Susie said. 'The evening off is after you've helped make the dinner and washed the dishes. You'll be so jiggered, the only thing you'll want to do is flop on your bed. As for Sunday afternoon off, that's after you've prepared the vegetables for Mrs Armstrong, washed up after lunch and scrubbed the scullery floor. It'll be two o'clock before you're away and you'll have to be back by half-past six to help with dinner. So much for your afternoon off.'

'Now don't discourage the young colleen,' Old Ned said. 'What other rules has the ould bitch laid down?'

'I'm to keep myself clean and have no followers.'

'They're always going on about that have-no-followers rule,' Susie said. 'They're afraid the lower classes might start breeding and overpopulate the country. There's a joke about that follower business. A Madam ran short of change one day and called down the kitchen stairs: Mary, have you any coppers down there? The reply was: Yes, Madam, but they're both my cousins.'

The company round the table laughed heartily.

After dinner that night, I retired to the little box room to unpack my things, hoping that I was not importing parasites into the home. First thing I did was place my glass swan and the statue of the Sacred Heart on the mantelpiece. The swan was my last link to the old life and I vowed never to forget my roots or my heartfelt wish to get my family together again some day, though Butler Court and my hopes for the future seemed a long way off.

Later I was joined by Susie after she'd finished her duties for the day. Together, we read the tract from the Christian Knowledge Society.

> First, don't think too much about wages; serving in a safe, happy home is of greater consequence.
>
> Second, don't deny faults in a saucy, indignant way. If something has been lost, offer to have your own possessions searched.
>
> Third, don't gossip with trades people or servants.
>
> Fourth, don't get into a temper if the hall or the steps you have just cleaned are immediately spattered with mud by thoughtless people.
>
> Fifth, don't read silly sensational stories in poisonous publications which are brought to the back doors of gentlemen's homes.
>
> Sixth, don't let candles flare away for hours without being of use.
>
> Last, remember to pray carefully and regularly.

We put our candles out by squeezing the flames with our fingers and laughed ourselves to sleep.

Chapter Sixteen

No sooner had I closed my eyes – or so I thought – than my peaceful slumber was shattered by the alarm clock and Susie digging me in the ribs.

'Come on, Kate. Five o'clock. Time to get up.'

I rubbed the sleep from my eyes and got up. It was a bitterly cold morning and I hurried to get dressed. Work would soon warm me up, I said to myself. One good thing about the workhouse was that it toughened you up. It was the *only* good thing.

'Have you got your list of jobs?' Susie asked.

'Right here in my pocket.'

'Good, let's get started.'

I was happy to be working with Susie. Together, we could make the hard graft bearable. And if I hadn't had her to show me the ropes, I'd have been at sixes and sevens.

'Can't we have a cup of tea to get us in the mood?' I asked.

'Not yet. There's far too much to do before we can even think about that.'

We crept downstairs so as not to waken anybody and we went into the cold, empty kitchen where we began the job of cleaning out the grate. We placed a piece of old carpet down and raked out the cinders and laid the fire. Before lighting it, we had to black-lead the range using the special brushes provided because, according to Susie, Mrs Armstrong was most particular about it. After much elbow grease, the range was gleaming so you could see your face in it.

'Let's hope the wood and coal that Old Ned brought down last night are not damp,' Susie said as she applied a match. We were in luck and soon there was a good fire going underneath the old iron kettle.

We went upstairs to the main hall and Susie's next action puzzled me. She began scattering tea leaves right, left and centre over the lovely carpets in the hall and the reception rooms. She's gone mad, I thought.

'To lay the dust,' she informed me.

We gave the carpets a vigorous sweeping. We cleaned, dusted, tidied the main rooms and she showed me how to lay the table for breakfast. We lit another fire as the family expected to see a cheerful blaze in the grate when they came down.

It was now six thirty and we made a quick cup of tea for ourselves.

'You can begin your first day, Kate,' she said, 'by taking Mrs Armstrong her early morning cuppa.'

'But Mrs Armstrong is only the cook – a servant like us,' I said.

'Don't you believe it. She's the most important person on the staff. The early morning tea is her only comfort. The rest of the day she's run off her feet.'

'What about James? Do we take him tea as well?'

'James can get his own bloody tea. He's a lazy bugger.'

I took Mrs Armstrong her tea using the best china.

'God bless you, love,' she said. 'I can see that you and I are going to get along fine.'

I was already feeling tired after this frantic activity but there was no chance of getting off my feet.

'Come along, Kate my girl. No sitting down. We have to take morning tea to the lords and ladies upstairs. I'll take it in to the master and the mistress. Her Majesty always likes a slice of thin bread and butter with her tea to set her up for the day, and I have to light a fire in their bedroom. You can take tea in to Harold and Emma.'

'Harold?' I asked falteringly.

'You'll have to do it sometime. Why not today? You can put him in his place from the beginning. But don't forget, he likes two sugars and Emma none.'

I was worried about this taking tea into bedrooms but I supposed I had to get used to it. I prepared the tea and in my nervousness I put two sugars in both teas. And I couldn't remember who wanted it with sugar and who without.

Trembling, I took the tea into Harold's bedroom. He was sitting up awake reading a big book when I went into the room. A young man of about eighteen, with deep brown eyes, his dark hair falling over his forehead, and blue morning stubble on his chin. Quite nice-looking, I thought. But I'd heard such stories about him.

'Your morning tea, sir,' I said, putting on a brave face. 'Where would you like it?'

He grinned cheekily. 'Where would I like it?' he repeated. 'Now, that's quite a question, young missie. Why here in the bed, of course. Bring it to me.'

I was on my guard. I placed it on his bedside cabinet and was ready to beat a quick retreat.

'You're new here,' he said. 'What's your name, pretty maid?'

'Kate,' I answered, moving towards the door.

'Kate! That's a lovely name, that is.' He held his book out to me, showing me the page he'd been reading. 'Have you ever seen anything like that?'

It was a lewd picture of a naked woman and a man in a state of arousal. My cheeks burned.

'No, sir. I don't look at rude pictures like that.'

He laughed. 'Ah, one of those convent girls, I see. We shall have to see if we can liberate you.'

'Will that be all, sir?' I said, making a beeline for the exit.

'For the time being, my dear Kate,' he leered.

'By the way, sir,' I said with my hand on the door, 'if you take sugar, please stir your tea.'

I got out of there quick. I could see they hadn't been exaggerating in the kitchen.

Miss Emma, too, was sitting up in bed when I entered.

'Ah, you're the new girl, Kate,' she exclaimed, holding out her hand. I put the tea down on her cabinet and shook her hand.

'I hope you'll be happy here,' she said. 'But you seem too young to be a maid. How old are you?'

'I'll be fifteen next birthday, miss.'

'But you are only a child. I don't know what we're coming to in this world when we employ young children as slaves. Sweated labour – and in my own family. One day all that will change, Kate. You wait and see.'

'Yes. Thank you, miss,' I said, and I headed towards the door. 'If you take sugar in your tea, miss, stir it. If you don't, don't.'

As I closed the door behind me, I could hear Miss Emma giggling. At least, I thought, she has a sense of humour.

I returned to the kitchen where Mrs Armstrong was already preparing breakfast for the upstairs. And what a breakfast! Enough to feed an Ancoats family for a month. I couldn't see how four people could eat such enormous amounts of food.

Before breakfast, Susie and I had to take up the master's hot water for his shaving and his hip bath which he liked to take in front of the bedroom fire. We removed the two big pans which had been boiling on the range and lurched our way up the back stairs.

It was all right for some people, I said to myself. If there is such a thing as reincarnation, I want to come back as a man – a rich man.

When I got back downstairs, I found James waiting for me impatiently.

'Come along, girl. Get a move on. You must clean and polish the shoes and put them outside the bedroom doors. And don't forget to clean the instep underneath and iron the laces.'

Iron the laces! This was getting more and more like a loony bin with every hour that passed. But James was ironing the newspaper. What a mad, mad, mad world!

I finished the job and I couldn't for the life of me remember which shoes belonged to who. As I climbed the stairs for the umpteenth time that day, I sang the popular song of the day:

I am only a bird in a gilded cage,
A beautiful sight to see.
Though I seem happy and free from care,
I'm not what I seem to be.

I placed the shoes outside the bedroom doors, hoping they could sort them out for themselves.

As I descended to the kitchen, Susie began beating the gong for breakfast and the whole of the household – upstairs and downstairs – assembled in the dining room for the morning Bible-reading by the master.

I saw the beautiful table that Susie had laid with a

spotless cloth, each place with knives and forks and a table napkin folded into the shape of a mitre.

'A reading from St Matthew,' Mr Lamport-Smythe announced. ' "Lay not up for yourselves treasures upon earth, where moth and rust doth corrupt, and where thieves break through and steal. Where your treasure is, there will your heart be also. Is not the life more than meat, and the body than raiment?" '

I looked towards the sideboard with its bread rolls, toast, butter dishes, jars of jam, the jug of cream, and the china cups and saucers. I thought of the magnificent food that James and Susie would bring up from the kitchen: the bacon and eggs, kidneys, mushrooms, cutlets, broiled chicken, the kedgeree. What hypocrisy! *Is not the life more than meat?* St Matthew asked. For the Lamport-Smythes, the answer was there on their sideboard.

As the family sat down to their sumptuous breakfast served by James and Susie, Ned and I took the opportunity to remove the chamber pots and empty the master's hip bath. I looked at the time. It was half past eight – three hours since I'd got up and I felt as if I'd done a day's work already.

There was a short break while all of us downstairs sat down to our own breakfast. It was only porridge but it was the best I'd ever tasted, rich and creamy, and I ate it with lots of syrup. I tried some of the kedgeree which happened to be extra, thanks to Mrs Armstrong's overestimate of the family's needs. It was the first time I'd ever eaten such luxury food.

Whilst we were at the table, I asked about the family. Where did they go during the day?

James supplied the answers.

'Let's see now. Today is Tuesday. Master goes as usual to the Royal Exchange in Manchester, and at nine o'clock

Ned will take Madam in the dog cart for her coffee morning engagement with Fanny Tunnicliffe and her set. Miss Emma goes to meet her friends the Pankhurst sisters – Christabel and Sylvia – and two other young ladies who go by the names of Annie Kenney and Teresa Billington. They're members of some crackpot society called the Women's Social and Political Union – WSPU for short. It'll get them into trouble one of these fine days, you mark my words. As for Harold, he goes to Chester where he's supposed to be doing research for a book on the history of Cheshire.'

'Harold's a real mammy's boy,' said Ned. 'Madam thinks he can do no wrong and that the sun shines out of his arse. And don't go believing that malarkey about him doing research. We know the class of research he'll be after doing and it won't be the history of Cheshire. As God is my witness, I saw him once chatting up the strumpets in Manchester's Piccadilly.'

'And what, may I ask, were you doing in Piccadilly, Mr Ned Dooley?' asked Mrs Armstrong.

'Wasn't I visiting me old Auntie Eileen in Moston and I happened to be passing that way.'

Mrs Armstrong gave him a 'you can tell that to the birds' look.

'As for that nonsense Miss Emma is wrapped up in,' James went on, 'it should be banned by law. When she was younger, she behaved as a young girl in her station should.'

'And what was that, James?' I asked.

'Dressing up and going to parties and dances and lunch engagements. That kind of thing. Now she's got in with a political lot in Manchester. Women getting the vote! Rubbish! Women are too scatter-brained and more concerned with primping up their hair or trying on the latest fashions than meddling in things they don't understand.

Women should concentrate on making themselves beautiful. They should leave politics to the men. A woman's place is in the home, looking after her husband and her children. Everyone should know their place in society. Why, I've even heard that women have formed a football club! It's not ladylike.'

'I agree with you there, James,' said Mrs Armstrong. 'I'm sure I have enough to do without getting mixed up with them politicians. As for them MPs, they're a bunch of liars and cheats. Promise you anything to get the votes and do as they like when they get in. That Churchill fellar is the worst of the lot.'

'As I see it,' Ned said addressing James, 'it's as plain as the nose on your face.' If there was one thing that was not plain, it was the nose on James's face. 'There's one law for them upstairs and one law for us,' Ned continued. 'Always was and always will be as long as *they're* making the laws. Stands to reason. But mark my words, there will come a day when the common man will make the law. Meantime, I believe in keeping my head down and staying out of trouble.'

Such a long speech from Old Ned left him panting. He looked surprised himself that he'd been able to utter so many words in one breath.

'I don't know about votes for women and that,' Susie said. 'I only know that I'm not going to spend the rest of my life at the beck and call of upstairs people. I'd like to get out of domestic service and set up my own home. Someday, I'll make my fortune and you won't see my heels for dust. Or at least if there is any dust, it won't be me sweeping it up.'

'And how are you going to make your fortune?' I asked. I was interested in case there was a chance I could make mine too.

'I dunno at this moment. Maybe doing them competitions in *Tit-Bits*. You can win twenty pounds if you get it right. Or maybe some day my prince will come.'

'And is there a prince waiting in the wings?' Mrs Armstrong asked.

'Maybe there is and maybe there isn't,' Susie answered. 'At home, there's a certain young man I've known since we were kids but either he doesn't have enough money or he's waiting to pluck up courage to pop the question.'

'And what about you, young Kate?' James asked. 'Do you have a young man?'

I blushed to the roots. 'Oh no, not me. I'm much too young for that. Besides, my great dream is to save enough money to get my family together again. My young sister and brother are still in Swinton Industrial School and some day I'd like to see them back home.' I said nothing about the workhouse or the death of my father. There were some things I preferred to keep to myself.

'In other words,' said Mrs Armstrong, 'you yearn for a stable home.'

'That's it, Mrs Armstrong,' I replied with a serious face, 'but I don't fancy living with a bunch of smelly horses.'

Everyone laughed at my attempt at a joke – even though it was corny.

'Talking of dreams,' James said, 'what I'd like to do is get a job as house steward in the house of some lord or duke. Good pay, good grub, good wine and the life of Reilly – that's for me.'

'I don't know about the life of Reilly,' Old Ned chuckled. 'I'd like to return to Erin and live it up but as myself, Ned Dooley, not this Reilly fellar. A pretty young colleen by my side and a nice little cottage in Kerry. Sittin' beside the turf fire with a pint of porter and a pipe of good tobacco – that's my idea of heaven.'

'I've learned not to make future plans,' Mrs Armstrong said quietly. 'We don't know what's coming tomorrow and I never expect too much. That way I'm never disappointed.'

On that solemn note, we broke up, for the bell was summoning Susie to help Madam dress for her coffee morning. And that was no easy job considering Madam would be wearing three or four layers of clothing, with tightly laced stays, many petticoats and a steel-hooped crinoline.

As for me, I had to wash the breakfast things, after which I had to help Susie tidy up the bedrooms. It was while we were making the bed in the master bedroom that I found half a crown under the master's pillow.

'Here's a bit of luck,' I said to Susie. 'We'll split it. One and three each.'

'We'll do nothing of the kind,' Susie retorted. 'That piece of silver has been put there by Madam deliberately to test you. She tried it on me a couple of years back when I first came here. No, you give it back as soon as she returns from her coffee morning.'

It was a good job Susie had been there with me or I'd have fallen into the trap. In the workhouse, I'd learned that it was every man for himself.

I spent the rest of that first morning cleaning and dusting everything in sight and a few things that weren't. I dusted and washed picture rails, skirting boards, the mirrors, and the insides of the windows. In case I ran out of things to do, Susie told me to scrub the front steps and polish the brass on the door, and there was a lot of it – the numbers 3 and 5, the fancy knocker, the knobs, the door plates.

'Make sure it's gleaming,' Susie advised. 'Madam's most particular about the doorway.'

'But it looks like rain,' I objected.

'Doesn't matter, you'll have to do it as she'll notice when she comes back at lunchtime.'

I worked like mad on it till it shone like the sun; the guards at Buckingham Palace would have been proud of it.

At twelve thirty, it was time for dinner; that is, dinner for downstairs and luncheon for upstairs. It had been a long morning and I was as hungry as a horse, and ready for the lentil soup and rolls Mrs Armstrong had organised. Susie prepared a tray and took it up to Madam. We were about to begin eating when Susie returned and with a jerk of the thumb indicated that Her Majesty wanted to see me after luncheon. I was a little worried as to what it could be about but I didn't let it put me off my food. No fear! Anyway, it might be good news; perhaps she wanted to congratulate me on the radiance of the front doorway.

Before I left the servants' hall, James asked me to take a letter up to her. He had a stupid grin on his face and he was doing a lot of winking to the others. I wondered what he was up to but there couldn't be any harm in taking up a letter to her, surely.

At two o'clock, I went up to see Madam and found her waiting for me in the drawing room.

I gave her my best curtsy and held out the letter.

'James asked me to give this letter to you, Madam.'

'Never, never do that again!' she snapped, frowning at the letter as if it were a dead mouse.

What had I done wrong?

'Never hand me a letter like that. Heaven knows how many germs it might have picked up from the people who've handled it. The sorters, the postman, the servants, and now you. Another thing: it's not your job to deliver letters to me but if ever you do, you should wear gloves and always give things to me on a silver salver.'

'Yes, Madam.' Wait till I see that lot downstairs!

'Another thing,' Madam continued staring at some distant point over my left shoulder, 'I'm not satisfied with the brasses on the door. They look positively green and mouldy. What would one of the Brocklehurst family say if they came to visit us?'

Not knowing who the Brocklehursts were, I couldn't answer this but I did know that I'd shone those brasses to the best of my ability. It must have been the rain that had taken the shine off my handiwork but it was no use telling her that. Best not to argue with Her Majesty.

'Sorry, Madam. I'll try to do better.'

'And there's another matter,' she said. 'I distinctly heard you singing this morning, something about a bird in a gilded cage. Must I remind you, there should be no laughing or singing above stairs. It's unacceptable. Kindly refrain.'

'Sorry, Madam,' I answered automatically. I changed my mind about wanting to come back as a rich man. No, now I wanted to return as a torturer in a dungeon and I wanted this woman on the rack with me turning the screw until she begged for mercy.

I dismissed such evil thoughts. Instead, I held out the half-crown I'd discovered under the pillow. 'I found this coin under the master's pillow when we were making the beds this morning, Madam.' Uh-oh, I thought. I've put my foot in it again. Should have offered the coin on a tray.

She studied the half-crown. 'At least you're honest. Put the coin with the others that I've given to Susie. She'll tell you what to do.'

When I got back to the kitchen, they were still sitting round the table and as soon as I appeared they broke out laughing.

'The tray, the tray! You forgot the tray! Also the white gloves!' James guffawed. 'You'll learn in time.'

Some joke! On this occasion, I didn't share their humour.

Susie handed me a box containing about three pounds in silver to which I added the decoy half-crown. The rest of the afternoon I spent cleaning anything that had not been done in the morning. I didn't think there was anything left but there were the staircases and the ledges. Surely now that was the end of it. Then Susie gave me a job which confirmed my view that I was working in a madhouse.

'Madam has asked that you clean and polish the silver coins in her handbag to make sure all germs are exterminated.'

All afternoon, Mrs Armstrong had sweated over her range preparing the evening meal. Towards four o'clock, I helped her cut cucumber sandwiches for Madam and the friend she was entertaining.

'Always cut the cucumber in the middle first,' she instructed. 'Next take a fine knife and peel the skin ever so carefully without losing too much of the cucumber.'

Susie took up the tray and for the next two hours I worked with Mrs Armstrong putting the finishing touches to the five-course dinner she'd been working on the whole afternoon. As the evening approached, it was all hands to the pump and soon there was chaos as everyone ran around attending to their own particular chores. Mrs Armstrong, who was normally so calm and collected, now became the short-tempered and irritable woman I'd seen on my first day. She snapped at everyone, including the house steward.

When James found that his own hob was not hot enough, he placed a kettle on the cook's range.

'You will get that bloody kettle off my range and quick or I'll hit you with this pan, so I will!' she screamed at him.

'One of these days,' James muttered when safely out of her hearing, 'I'll plonk that bloody woman down on her own hot stove.'

Around six o'clock, when things seemed to be under control, the domestic staff sat down to supper in the servants' hall. We ate early so as to be free to minister to the family. Needless to say, we had small tastes of the courses that would be served later that evening. I got to sample foods I'd never heard of and some that I couldn't even pronounce: consommé, Dover sole, entrecôte steak with asparagus tips, sherry trifle, and a board with a wide selection of foreign sounding cheeses like Brie, Camembert, Parmesan.

'I love these rich foods,' I remarked to Susie.

'I hope you do,' Susie laughed softly, 'because you'll be eating some of 'em for breakfast tomorrow.'

'But the waste,' I said. 'All this rich food for a small family whilst people in the workhouse are starving on food you wouldn't feed to the pigs.'

'The waste in this house,' said James, 'is nothing next to what I saw in my last employment. Our master was Sir Charles Lancaster and there were fifteen servants, each with his own particular role, and it was God help anyone who tried to trespass on another's job. The food we threw into the dustbin each morning was enough to feed an Indian village for a week. But fifteen's a small staff next to the big houses like that of the Duke of Westminster who employs about three hundred. You can well imagine the extravagance in a place like that. As for Buckingham Palace, I shudder to think what goes on there. The Queen has a separate staff of Indian cooks to prepare a curry lunch each day whether anyone wants to eat it or not.'

After our meal, the kitchen once more became a scene of frenzied activity. Mrs Armstrong showed me quickly how to set the cook's table with its vast array of knives, forks and an endless list of other implements like fish slices, tongs, spatulas, whisks. The table was set out like a hospital's operating theatre – I was the nurse and cook was the surgeon.

'Knife! Fork! Fish slice! Pepper mill!'

I slapped them into her hand as she called.

'Holy spoon! Ladle! Paring knife! Scissors!'

Using the dumbwaiter, we sent the various courses up to Susie and James in the dining room. The lift was soon back with the dirty dishes. Ned and I filled a large sink with piping hot water and for the next two hours we were hard at it washing and drying. Many of the cook's instruments had to be washed quickly as they were required several times over.

'Come along, Kate! Quick! Quick!' Mrs Armstrong yelled. 'You'll have to learn to speed up!'

'I'm going as fast as I can!' I shouted back. 'I'm not a machine!'

At nine thirty, the pace slowed down as James took up coffee and the cream.

Phew! What a day! And that was a normal day serving four people. God help us if they ever held a dinner party.

As we sat at the table having our cocoa before retiring, I asked, 'Why don't the Lamport-Smythes invest in some of the labour-saving devices I've read about in the *Servant's Magazine*?'

To my surprise, everyone found this funny, especially when Mrs Armstrong declared, 'I'll not have any of them new-fangled inventions in *my* kitchen!'

James said, 'If you mean things like gas cookers, the new electric water heaters or the carpet sweepers, the answer's simple – rich folk would rather rely on our strong arms than pay out good money on mechanical contraptions. The only one they might put their cash into is one that was displayed at the Great Exhibition of eighteen fifty-one.'

'Must have been good,' said Mrs Armstrong, 'if you think they might put their hands in their pocket. What in heaven's name was it?'

'A bedstead specially designed for servants.' James laughed. 'At a set hour, an automatic clockwork device removes the support from the foot of the bed, throwing the occupant out onto the floor. Good for sleepy-heads like Susie and Kate at five o'clock in the morning.'

'Better still for butlers and house stewards,' Susie retorted.

At last we retired to our rooms. Susie and I undressed quickly and collapsed into bed.

My legs were like wobbly jelly. I was so exhausted by my first day at work, I could hardly keep my eyes open.

'Jiggered?' Susie asked.

'No, not jiggered. Buggered!'

I turned over and within seconds I was asleep.

Chapter Seventeen

That first day at the Lamport-Smythes' was typical of the days that followed. The only relief was a few hours after breakfast on Sunday mornings when Susie and I went to Mass at St Alban's and listened to Father Carton's sermons on the fourth commandment, 'Honour thy father and thy mother', which meant we had to obey everyone above us, including our lawful superiors, and how we were never to give old buck. We never managed to get to confession 'cos it was held on Saturday mornings when we were doing the obeying. Besides, we were so busy, there was no time for any sinning.

My early exhaustion passed and it wasn't long before the work became routine. I developed an attitude of 'one day at a time' and learned to take things in my stride. Mrs Armstrong, who described herself as a plain cook, as opposed to a fancy one, turned out to be a good teacher and I learned how to deal with meat, fish, and poultry, and to understand the difference between such things as roasting, braising, grilling and stewing. Most important, she taught me about baking – cakes, scones, biscuits and bread.

Despite Madam's occasional flash of temper, life at the Lamport-Smythes was pleasant enough though I found the routine on my first pay day strange. It was the end of

September, and one by one we were called to meet Madam in the dining room. She sat at a big table facing the large gilt mirror and I was told to stand behind her chair. She didn't look directly at me but addressed my reflection in the looking glass. I was aware that Madam didn't like addressing servants face to face but this seemed totally barmy. Naturally she was wearing gloves since handling money might have contaminated her. It's all straight out of *Alice in Wonderland*, I thought.

'You have been with us now for one month and generally speaking we are satisfied with your work though we can do without your singing and a little more elbow grease on the door brasses would not go amiss. Here is your pay of one pound.'

'Thank you so much, Madam,' I said. I curtsied behind her chair and collected the twenty shillings she had placed in a little pile. I was bubbling with joy for I'd never had so much money. I almost skipped out of the room but resisted the urge.

Downstairs, I couldn't take my eyes off the fortune I'd earned. I spread it out on the table and let it trickle through my hands like Silas Marner. Twenty shillings, eight half-crowns, ten florins, forty sixpences, two hundred and forty pennies, four hundred and eighty halfpennies, nine hundred and sixty farthings! I was rich!

That afternoon, in my short break, I went to Macclesfield post office and opened a savings account with ten shillings. I sent a postal order of five shillings to Mam and I kept five for myself for personal expenses. The great advantage of domestic service was that you got free board and lodgings and so the wage was free of other demands. No wonder I felt like a millionaire.

I wished I could have got home more often to see Mam and little Eddie who was now a toddler of three. It wasn't easy; I only got Sundays off and by the time I'd finished the morning chores, there were hardly any hours of freedom left. To add to the problem, the Sunday train service to Manchester was terrible. Getting there was not so bad but returning to Macclesfield in the evening was a nightmare. The only train back was at five o'clock and this meant I could spend only an hour or two at home. It was hardly worth the effort. When I'd been working about three months, I'd managed to pay a flying visit to Ancoats. Both Mam and Eddie seemed to be doing well. Two things concerned me though. Mam seemed to be off drinking each night with her cronies in The Land o' Cakes and, secondly, there was a new man in her life. Frank McGuinness was a widower whose wife had died of angina, leaving him with two grown-up sons. He was a friend of Uncle Barney's who'd brought him home one night and introduced him to Mam. They told me he was well-off 'cos he had a pension of ten shillings a week from the army. He was a thick-set man, formerly a sergeant in the Lancashire Fusiliers till he'd been wounded in South Africa. He'd have had quite a handsome face had it not been for his mournful expression. When I met him, he was unshaven and looked a bit rough and the deep dark bags under his eyes gave him a haunted look. A visit to a tailor or a jumble sale wouldn't have gone amiss either. Apart from his stubbly chin and untidy appearance, I was not happy with this latest development as I still missed my dad and I didn't like this stranger hanging about the place. I hadn't given up on that vision of getting the family back to the way it was before poverty had driven us into the workhouse. And my vision did not include this ragpicker my Uncle Barney had brought home.

Cissie and Danny were still at Swinton School and, according to their letters, were making good progress.

Cissie, going on nine, had many friends and was hoping to follow in my footsteps and go into service. Danny was now a lance corporal in the school's army cadets and doing well on the clarinet. Not bad for a young boy of twelve. Who knows, perhaps one day he would start his own band.

And so life ticked over. Along the way, there were memorable occasions, some happy, some sad.

The saddest day was the death of Queen Victoria in January 1901. She'd been ill for some time and so the news was not unexpected. All the same, it came as a shock when we saw it in the paper. That morning, because of the gravity of the event, the Lamport-Smythes took delivery not only of their usual newspaper, the *Manchester Guardian*, but *The Times* as well. *The Times* was twenty pages thick and all the columns were edged in funereal black which meant James was kept busy ironing to stop ink getting on the master's hands. Listening to James curse at having to do this extra chore gave us a laugh but it was the only laugh we heard in the house for a fortnight.

James read out snippets to the rest of us as we went about our work.

'It was with the most profound sorrow that we record the death of our much loved Queen.'

Edward's message set us off blubbering by the simplicity of its statement:

> Osborne House, Tuesday, January 22nd, 1901, 6.45 p.m.
> The Prince of Wales to Lord Mayor
> My beloved mother, the Queen, has just passed away, surrounded by her children and grandchildren.
> ALBERT EDWARD

The medical bulletin which followed confirmed it:

Osborne House, Tuesday, January 22nd, 1901, 6.45 p.m.

Her Majesty the Queen breathed her last at 6.30 p.m. surrounded by her children and grandchildren.

James Reid, M.D.
B. Douglas Powell, M.D.
Thomas Barlow, M.D.

The paper contained nothing else. There was even a poem with a French title, '*La Reine Est Morte*', which we didn't understand until James, who had learned a little French at school, told us it meant 'The Queen Is Dead'. Why can't they say it in English? we asked. The poem we liked best was written by some unnamed Hindu poet.

Dust to dust, ashes to ashes,
Into the tomb the Great Queen dashes.

The end of the old Queen left us with a queer feeling. She'd been our ruler as long as anyone could remember – sixty-three years, the paper said. They claimed she had blood links to nearly every throne in Europe. Another poem by Alfred Austin, the Poet Laureate, printed in *The Times* the next day, summed up the effect her passing had on us: 'Dead! And the world feels widowed.' The whole country went into deep mourning. Flags flew at half-mast, horses had their hooves padded and wore black plumes like they did at funerals. In Macclesfield the churches tolled a slow solemn knell all day long. In the Lamport-Smythe household, it was as if someone in their own family had kicked the bucket. We were told to draw the curtains, cover the mirrors, and to hang a wreath at the door. We were ordered to put on mourning clothes – the men black ties and armbands, the women black silk dresses with no hint of white or colour. Everyone spoke in hushed tones and wore a melancholy expression. No joking, no laughing, no singing – neither upstairs nor downstairs. By order, everyone had to put on a long face. This lasted for ten days till after Queen Victoria's funeral on 2 February. I loved and respected the old Queen as much as anybody but in my opinion the country and the Lamport-Smythes were overdoing it.

On Monday, 4 February, I thought it was time not only to start a new week but to snap out of the misery.

At breakfast, I picked up one of Mrs Armstrong's cakes and began dancing across the kitchen floor, munching and singing at the same time. Old Ned got the idea and joined me, striding in line by my side to the strains of 'Lily of Laguna'.

'What are you two dafties doing?' Mrs Armstrong laughed. 'And why are you munching on that cake?'

'It's called the cakewalk,' I said, 'the latest dance from America.'

Susie entered into the spirit of the thing and soon three of us were performing an act which had James and our cook in stitches. It was good to hear the sound of laughter once again.

We looked forward to having the Prince of Wales, Bertie as he was known, as our new King. At the same time we wondered what sort of monarch he would make as he had the reputation of being a bit of a lad – a playboy, a card cheat, and a womaniser. Everyone knew about his goings-on with Mrs Keppel and Lillie Langtry. But who could blame him for sowing his wild oats? He'd had to wait fifty-nine years to get his bum on the throne.

Life wasn't all doom and gloom, there were happy days as well. One that we would always remember almost didn't happen. It was 1902 and the date 31 May, the end of the Boer War, and the whole country went mad. All day long fireworks were let off at every street corner, the whole of the town centre was bedecked with bunting and Union Jacks, and special services were held in every church. Special editions of newspapers with the headline 'Peace Is Proclaimed' sold like hot cakes at sixpence and a shilling a time. Susie and I were given afternoon leave to go and join in the celebrations in Victoria Park where there was Maypole and Morris dancing and where the Macclesfield Cycling Club put on a wonderful parade with bikes decorated in every colour of the rainbow. From there, we made our way to Macclesfield Town Hall to mingle with a great crowd in festive mood. There was singing everywhere we went, the strains of the hymn 'Now thank we all our God' from the churches merging with the beery voices from the pubs bawling out patriotic songs. Along Chester Road, there were so many drunks trying to slobber over us, we thought we might be safer celebrating quietly in the basement at home with the rest of the staff.

But that was not the end of the jubilation. There was more to look forward to – the crowning of our new King! The first coronation since Victoria's in 1838 and for the great majority of people, the only one they had ever known. How we looked forward to it! The troopships were coming home in triumph and the British flag flew – as they kept telling us – on an empire on which the sun never set. How proud we were to be British! The date was set for 24 June and from our *Daily Mail* we learned that rehearsals had begun in Westminster Abbey. Edward Elgar, the composer, had written a coronation ode to be called 'Land of Hope and Glory'. It was my favourite song and I learned the tune from the street barrel organ, and when I was cleaning and dusting upstairs, even though I knew Madam didn't like it, I couldn't help breaking out with:

Land of Hope and Glory
Mother of the free,
How shall we extol thee,
Who are born of thee?

And here was a funny thing: I didn't get a single complaint from anyone.

In the *Daily Mail*, we read that dignitaries were coming to London from all over the world, a gathering of emperors, kings, queens, princes, with their crowns, tiaras, bracelets, and diamond rings. The whole country was to have a five-day holiday and even in little Macclesfield, Mr Lamport-Smythe had hinted that he had a special surprise for us.

Then it all went wrong.

Three days before the great event, it was announced that the King had appendicitis and had to have a serious and dangerous operation. I was at St Alban's Church when I got the news. On the way home as I walked down the 108 steps from the church, I passed a man and his wife decorating their balcony with bunting.

'I wouldn't bother putting any more of that up,' I called up to them.

'Why not?' the woman asked.

'The coronation's off,' I said. 'The King's been taken ill with appendicitis.'

That same day, the newspapers announced that the operation had been performed. The churches were full again, this time with services asking God to intercede. Bertie had only an outside chance of pulling through. For the second time in eighteen months, faces were as long as fiddles. Everyone prayed that we were not to lose a second member of our royal family. The flags and the bunting came down and the foreign dignitaries went home. Mr

Lamport-Smythe cancelled our surprise. What a disappointment!

But praise God, our prayers were answered and we had to wait only six weeks for our postponed festivities. Our King had a quick recovery, the foreign royalties came back, up went the flags and it was all on again though Edward was warned not to overdo it. The funny thing was that it was not the King who collapsed with the strain of the ceremony. No, it was an exhausted Archbishop of Canterbury who had to be helped off the altar. That gave us a laugh downstairs.

The day of the coronation, Mr Lamport-Smythe invited the staff to the drawing room. The whole family was there smiling broadly – even 'Her Majesty'. First, Madam handed each of us a week's wage as a gift – in envelopes, of course. Secondly, we received a porcelain mug with a picture of Edward and Alexandra, another keepsake to put beside my glass swan. We were each given a glass of champagne to drink the health of our new sovereign. Mrs Armstrong had a fit of coughing as the bubbly went down her nose – which set the whole company into gales of giggling.

Finally, Mr Lamport-Smythe unveiled the biggest surprise of all. An Edison phonograph! He had two cylinders and he proceeded to demonstrate this technical miracle by playing them. He turned a handle to wind up the clockwork motor and applied a needle. The cylinder on the contraption went round and from the inside of the tin trumpet came a voice which sounded as if its owner was being strangled. Mr Lamport-Smythe informed us that the singer was a famous Italian called Enrico Caruso. The name reminded me of the ice-cream seller who used to come down Butler Court when I was a kid. This Enrico was singing in his own language and so we didn't understand what it was about but our master told us it meant 'Thy tiny hand is frozen' and I thought it was right for Susie and me at half past five on a frosty morning. It was from an opera written by another Italian named Puccini and this was one of the first recordings ever made. It sounded like it. Mr Lamport-Smythe also told us that the record company had paid Caruso one hundred pounds for half an hour's work. They'd been robbed.

The second cylinder was more to our liking. The first song was by Albert Chevalier and it was one we all knew:

We've been together now for forty years
And it don't seem a day too much
There ain't a lady living in the land
That I'd swap for my dear old Dutch.

The second one was even more popular. Hamilton Hill singing the Boer war ditty, 'Goodbye, Dolly Gray':

Goodbye, Dolly, I must leave you,
Though it breaks my heart to go.
Something tells me I am needed
At the front to fight the foe.

We had a lovely time and we were grateful to the upstairs people for their kindness. But there was a price to pay for little parties like this. The Lamport-Smythes had arranged a celebratory dinner party for their flash friends, Mr and Mrs Chadwick, and two friends of Emma's – Teresa Billington and Bernard Sheridan, a handsome young man of about twenty-one, with dark hair and laughing blue eyes. It was such a big shindig, we had to bring in extra staff to help with the washing-up. We returned to the kitchen and for the next three hours the usual chaos reigned, with Mrs Armstrong shouting and snarling at everyone. No wonder, for she had to prepare a six-course dinner. Madam had written the menu cards herself not only in fancy writing but partly in French as well. This might give you some idea.

1. Prawns wrapped in Smoked Salmon.
2. Watercress and Pear Soup finished with a Chervil Cream.
3. Tournedo of Beef Rossini topped with foie gras served with a sauce Perigourdine. (Pomme Dauphine; Broccoli with Hollandaise Sauce; Sautéed Courgettes; Carrot Timbale.)
4. Raspberry Crème Brûlée with a Brandy Snap Basket of Apricot Sorbet.
5. A selection of English Farmhouse and French Cheeses.
6. Cognac and Liqueurs. Coffee and Petit Fours.

With each course a different wine was served.

What would my friends in Dormitory 16 have made of this? How would cognac have gone down with their gruel? But the Lamport-Smythes and the workhouse inmates lived in two completely different worlds.

I helped James and Susie to serve and they promised to return the favour by helping to clear up afterwards. As the upstairs people stuffed themselves with the rich food, us three servants stood quietly in the background like waxwork dummies in our starched uniforms, ready to minister to their every need. They talked loudly as if we weren't there. As far as they were concerned we were like the furniture – non-people without ears, eyes or brains, in other words, lackeys or menials. There were two topics of conversation – the new King and the 'servant question'. Our master said that our bicycling King should have been called the Prince of Wheels. This caused big laughs round the table. Of course we three puppets didn't join in, didn't even smile; it wasn't our place and we were not part of the company. It was generally agreed by our betters that Bertie would be a great improvement on his mother who'd been mourning her Albert for forty years and had made the whole country miserable by hiding away in Osborne House on the Isle of Wight.

It was a bit much, though, when they got on to the 'servant problem'. They'd completely forgotten that we were standing there taking it all in.

'Securing the services of a good maid is becoming more and more difficult,' complained Mrs Chadwick. 'And they're so demanding. I don't know what the world is coming to, I really don't. Why, one saucy applicant for a place in my household stated that she must have scented soap to wash with, and could only eat delicate puddings. Well, I ask you.'

'I blame Queen Alexandra,' our Madam said. 'She's started having servants' teas in the capital. I believe the first to be held provided for over twelve thousand from all over London. Why, mistresses even served their maids!'

'No good will come of it,' grunted Mr Chadwick. 'Servants will get ideas above their station.'

'Oh, I don't know,' protested Bernard Sheridan. 'Role reversal won't do the mistresses any harm. It should do them a power of good to feel what it's like to be a servant for a change.' Bernard, I noted, was not only well-spoken but had a gentle, kind voice.

'I agree, Bernard,' Emma said, holding out her wine glass to James for a refill. 'There's too much of this social class thing as if working-class people are a different species.'

'One day,' Teresa Billington said, joining in the debate, 'the working class will rise up and demand social justice.

In my own house, I've seen Ma-Ma call our servant all the way up from the basement to perform some trifling task, like drawing a curtain or replacing a book on the shelf. A task she could have easily done for herself.'

Bernard chuckled. What a lovely laugh, I thought. 'Like the old duke,' he said, 'who called up his butler to tell him to move his leg away from the fire as it was burning.'

The young people shared the merriment. Not so the oldies, who looked most displeased.

As for me, my face didn't flicker even when my eye caught Susie's and it took all my self-control not to burst out laughing or to start clapping my hands because our own Madam had often called us up from the kitchen to do some piffling little job.

The rest of the evening passed quickly and at eleven o'clock, the last guest left. In the basement, it was all hands to the pump to clear things away and wash up. It was midnight before we got to bed and of course Susie and I had to be up at half past five as usual to make the kitchen fire and to take cook's morning tea.

As I closed my eyes that night, in my mind's eye I could see that young man Bernard Sheridan and I could still hear him defending the servant class. I'd taken a fancy to him but I dismissed such thoughts right away. I must have been going off my head.

Chapter Eighteen

After the excitement of the coronation, things went quiet. I became so engrossed in my job that time slipped by unnoticed. I was learning something new every day and more and more responsibility was being placed on my shoulders. On my seventeenth birthday, I was given a rise in pay and my new salary was fifteen pounds a year, or one pound five shillings a month. I was in clover. I worked hard and the months flew by. Before we had time to look around, pouf! It was 1904.

At Easter that year, the master and the mistress took their usual annual holiday in Cornwall, taking Susie with them. I was left in the temporary position of acting parlour maid – not a big job as there was only Harold and Emma to look after. When it came to Harold, things hadn't changed much. I still took his tea in the morning but I'd become clever at dodging out quickly before he could start his hanky-panky. One morning, however, when he was particularly insistent that I join him in the bed, I accidentally upset tea on the crotch of his pyjamas. The hot treatment cooled his ardour.

Emma continued to go to her meetings with the WSPU in Manchester but when her parents were away, she invited her friends to meet at home and I was given the job of waiting on them with tea and biscuits. It was a task I enjoyed for the group wasn't a bit snooty and they talked to me as an equal. Apart from Miss Emma, there were three other women – Christabel Pankhurst, Annie Kenney, Teresa Billington. And one man – Bernard Sheridan!

The talk at the meeting was about opening a charity shop which Miss Emma had agreed to run in Macclesfield town centre.

'Instead of giving our cast-offs to the servants,' Christabel said, 'we could sell the clothes to raise money for the poor and the cause of women's suffrage.' When I took their tea into them, they asked my opinion.

'Do you think such a shop will work, Kate?' Christabel asked.

I curtsied before I answered. 'I don't know, Miss Christabel.'

'No need for that bowing and scraping, Kate,' she smiled, 'and you can call me Isabel.'

'Yes, Miss . . . er . . . Isabel. Depends on what was being sold,' I answered, 'and the prices being asked.'

'Good answer,' said Bernard warmly. 'It's what I've been saying. We must only buy goods that are saleable. It's no use buying things like ladies' hats which are personal objects. We need to concentrate on objects like ornaments, books, good furniture.'

'I think you'll find there's a ready market for, as you put it, things like ladies' hats.' Miss Emma laughed.

'I'm sure I can persuade many of our richer supporters,' said Christabel, 'to part with some of their unwanted items to further our objectives.'

'The matter is becoming more and more urgent,' Teresa added. 'This parliament won't budge on the matter of women's franchise. An MP recently said that it wouldn't be safe to give us the vote as we have different mental powers and we're too fickle. I ask you! How did people like that get into parliament? I often wonder what working-class women think about insults like this. I'd like to ask Kate here what she thinks about women getting the vote.'

'I'm sure I don't know, miss,' I replied nervously. 'I'm kept too busy earning a living to be able to think about such things.' What a smarmy answer, I said to myself. What I really thought was that it's all right for rich young things like you lot drinking tea and playing politics. For you, it's a way of filling in your time and amusing yourselves – an escape from boredom. You put charitable work on a par with going to dances and parties.

'How many hours a day do you work, Kate?' Bernard asked.

'Depends, sir. A normal day is about fourteen or fifteen hours but if there's a dinner party on, it can be as much as sixteen or even seventeen.'

'Exploitation!' my handsome hero exclaimed. 'Let me see your hands, Kate.'

He took my hands in his. His were soft and warm. He examined the palms of mine.

'Look at those,' he said to the other ladies. 'A beautiful young lady like Kate with red raw hands. It's not right – it's social injustice.'

Christabel agreed. 'Women in all walks of life will be exploited until we can win power at the ballot box.'

Their debate continued as I sided the table. No one offered to tackle social injustice by helping me. But they were discussing, not doing.

For the rest of the day, I could feel Bernard's gentle, sensitive touch on both my hands. And hadn't he called me beautiful? I was sure he fancied me.

Emma opened her charity shop and she was kept busy every day. It was soon doing well, for the items for sale were of good quality and going cheap. From time to time,

Bernard called at the house to help Emma with the book-keeping. How I looked forward to him coming, for he never forgot to greet me and shake my hand.

Around this time, I started to look more closely at myself in the looking glass. I was a frump. What horrible-looking clothes I had. I'd never bothered too much about my personal appearance as it had never seemed important. Who would have looked twice at a servant girl from Ancoats? One morning when everyone was out, I stretched out on Miss Emma's bed to feel what it must be like to be her. I picked up a copy of the *Illustrated London News* and studied an advertisement telling the reader how to be beautiful and healthy.

ALL IN SEARCH OF HEALTH SHOULD READ THIS

> The lady who wants to be beautiful keeps her system well regulated, is careful of her diet, sleeps nine hours a day, takes a cold plunge every morning upon rising, and then exercises a little time with her two-pound dumb-bells. She wears a Harness' Electric Corset which makes the most awkward figure graceful and elegant. Her stockings are held by suspenders from the shoulders, thus allowing for free circulation of the blood. She avoids strong beverages, and spicy dishes. After each meal she takes Vogeler's Curative Compound, the greatest blood purifier and strength restorer known to pharmacy and medicine.

Fine, I chuckled to myself, but where was I going to get an electric corset and a pair of two-pound dumb-bells?

I examined her clothes, especially her silk and satin underwear, and for the first time I felt envious when I realised how dowdy my own stuff was. Mine was coarse calico that tickled every time I wore it. Serviceable but lacking in elegance and refinement. Then I had a stroke of luck. If you could call it that.

I was cleaning the grate in Harold's room when I found a pound note all screwed up. I thought, this represents four weeks' wages to me and I wondered if Madam had put it there to test me out. Surely not. I'd been working there for three years and I had an unblemished record; she wouldn't still be putting out decoy money. I agonised about it for the whole of that morning. I smoothed the note out and studied it 'cos I'd never possessed a pound note as such. Whenever Madam paid us, it was always in silver coins. Back in my room, I caught a reflection of myself in the wardrobe mirror and saw once again my shabby outfit. I made up my mind.

'Bugger it,' I said aloud. 'I'm keeping this.'

That week, I drew out three pounds from my savings and, putting it with the pound, went into Macclesfield and bought myself a new rig-out, including a silk nightdress. And that wasn't all. I bought a bike for two guineas, a straw hat and a set of knickerbockers, known as Rationals, to go with it. The new look Kate. I was in with the latest fashions. Time, I thought, to loosen my stays, get on my bike and make my presence felt. Back in my room, I tried on the new outfit and studied myself in the looking glass. Not bad, I thought, not bad at all. New clothes gave me an uplift and I felt as if I was as good as the upstairs people.

When the staff saw me in my new apparel and riding my mechanical steed, they couldn't resist making cracks and singing in chorus:

Daisy, Daisy give me your answer do
I'm half crazy all for the love of you.
It won't be a stylish marriage.

I can't afford a carriage.
But you'll look sweet
Upon the seat
Of a bicycle made for two.

'Hello, hello,' said James when they'd finished their warbling. 'Something's going on and it's not even spring.'

'What's got into you, young lady?' Mrs Armstrong laughed. 'Have you met a young man? Or have you won the *Tit-Bits* competition?'

'Didn't you read what it said in the *Daily Mail*?' I said. 'Straight-laced corsets and stuffy bustles are to be chucked into the dustbin.'

'I think I have an idea of who she's dressing up in her Rationals for,' Susie commented slyly. 'I'll bet it's that young Bernard Sheridan who's on Miss Emma's committee. You want to be careful there, Kate. Don't go getting ideas above your station.'

'Nothing of the sort,' I answered, blushing deeply. Susie's words had struck home.

'She's right there,' added Mrs Armstrong. 'Them upstairs don't like the idea of you getting dressed up better than them. They believe you should dress according to your position.'

'Well, I approve strongly of Kate's new get-up,' Old Ned declared. 'Don't you be surprised if you have the young men swarming after you like wasps round a pot of jam.'

Ned was right for I found that whenever I went into Macclesfield to do a message at the Shambles Market, I had a chorus of cat-calls and wolf-whistles from the errand boys and the butchers' lads.

I had to admit, though – I liked it.

And Mrs Armstrong was right about them upstairs not

liking my new look. It wasn't long before Her Majesty called me upstairs.

'I am not pleased, Kate,' she said, 'about this cycling of yours. Ladies who do that kind of thing should be ashamed of themselves, going about on those immodest machines. Why, I saw Mrs Whiston on one in town yesterday and her with little children at home. I don't know what the world is coming to. I read the other day that ladies' hemlines are to be raised above the ankle. I hope you'll be careful not to give scandal.'

'Yes, Madam.' I curtsied as usual but I took no notice of her. Paying lip service is what I believe it's called.

In June, Madam and the master went for their usual holiday to Cornwall. This time they allowed Susie to take her annual leave in her home town of Hartlepool. Once again, I was left as acting parlour maid with the responsibility that that involved. It didn't worry me as I was used to the job and knew the routine inside out. The only interesting things in life were the visits of the various tradesmen to the back door. The butcher's boy with his wooden trough and his large joints of meat, the chimney sweep in his top hat, the muffin man with his handbell. They brought not only their wares but the latest gossip from around the district. For a while, life was quiet, with nothing exciting or dramatic happening.

Until my nineteenth birthday.

I awoke at five thirty as usual and went through the daily routine. At breakfast we sat down together and Ned brought in three letters for me. One was a card from Cissie wishing me all the best and telling me that things were going well, that she was now first in class and had been promoted to Lucy Morrell's group. Soon she would be a Lucy Lady. Danny had been promoted again, this time to full corporal, and he was the leader of the woodwind section in the army band. All good news and it made me happy.

The second letter had an American stamp and I was puzzled for a moment until I saw Lizzie's name and address on the front. My dear old friend Lizzie! In my first year at the Lamport-Smythes, I'd had a short note from her telling me that she'd arrived safely and that she had found things strange. She'd seemed more interested in the strange foods they'd had aboard ship and her experiences going through American Customs than anything else, though she had mentioned briefly that their next door neighbours had a yacht and a motor boat. Now, judging by the thickness of the letter, I was to have a fuller account. About time too, I thought.

I went into a quiet corner of the kitchen to read the letter slowly and to savour every word.

Dear Kate,

At last I have found the time to write to you. Joan and I have now become used to life out here. And how different it is to the one we knew in Ancoats and in Swinton. Everything, everything is so different, especially the food. We seem to have blueberries with everything – in the mornings, blueberry pancake for breakfast, at lunch, blueberry pie for dessert, and in the afternoon we take the kids berry picking. Yes, you guessed it, blueberries and so we made blueberry jam. We are slowly putting on weight due to all the fantastic ice cream, the flapjacks, and the jelly sandwiches. It's amazing how much stodge the Americans eat – it's all soft and I'm sure their teeth don't get enough exercise.

The O'Hagans are rich and own a big department store on Fifth Avenue, New York. Their house is enormous and in twenty acres of ground. They also have a house in California which we visit every summer. This year, they're even talking about taking a sea cruise to South America and we're to go with them to look after their young kids. We earn sixteen dollars a month, that's about four pounds or, if you like, one pound a week. Joan and I are saving like mad as the family won't let us pay for anything. As for the kids' nursery, you wouldn't believe it! No expense spared – toys, equipment, bedding, clothing. We've only to ask and we get. Our boss, Mr O'Hagan, is talking about buying the latest automobile and if he does, it means we'll be riding around in style. The family does a lot of visiting and wherever we go, folk keep embarrassing us by asking us to say something so that they can hear our cute Limey accent. If only my poor mother had lived to see it all! We could have had her over for a holiday, or vacation, as it's called here. We miss you too, Kate, and we wish you'd decided to come with us. It's not too late as English nannies here are in great demand because of the way they speak, I think. Let me know if you're interested and I'll ask around. Coming here was the best move we ever made. Joan considers herself so lucky that you turned the job down. It's funny the way things turned out – she got your job and you got hers.

When I think back about the old days and our time in that dreadful workhouse, it makes me shudder. It all seems like a terrible nightmare.

Love to your Mam, Cissie, Danny, Eddie and the rest of your family.

Your loving friend and cousin,

Lizzie

There were tears in my eyes when I'd finished reading. Dear old Lizzie. How I missed her too! Her letter set me wondering. Should I have gone to America with them? It sounded as if they were having a wonderful time compared to my humdrum life in Macclesfield. Then I remembered the glass swan on my bedroom mantelpiece and it reminded me of my dream. I recalled why I had decided not to go.

I turned to the third letter, post-marked Manchester. Unusual to get a letter from home. The only one I'd ever received from Mam was one informing me of Gran'ma's sudden death and telling me about the funeral which had already taken place. I tore open the envelope. The letter was from Aunt Sarah. If there was any lingering doubt in my mind as to whether I'd made the right decision in not going to America, this letter sealed it. I was needed this side of the Atlantic.

Dear Kate,

As you know, your Mam is not a good letter writer and she has asked me to write to you instead. Don't be too shocked at what I am going to tell you but your Mam's had a baby – a little boy and they're going to call him John. The father is Frank McGuinness.

I hope you are happy to hear this news. It means you now have a little stepbrother. But I think it might be best if you didn't come home for a while.

I hope you are well.

Love,

Aunt Sarah

I couldn't believe it. Mam had had a baby! And not married! Oh, the shame of it! I could feel my cheeks burning and it must have been obvious to the staff in the kitchen.

'What's wrong, Kate?' Mrs Armstrong asked anxiously. 'Not bad news, I hope.'

'Not really, Mrs Armstrong. It's my mother back in Manchester. She's given birth to a baby boy.'

'Oh, that *is* good news,' she exclaimed. 'I'm so happy for you and your family.'

The staff didn't know my mam was a widow and unmarried.

'Yes, thank you, Mrs Armstrong, it is good news,' I lied.

I was in turmoil. What was I to do? I couldn't give up my job – we were going to need money more than ever 'cos Mam was broke and Frank McGuinness didn't look as if he had much apart from his pension. The news made me more determined than ever to save and save in order to get the family together again. It meant getting Cissie and Danny out of Swinton and back home where they belonged. But not straightaway. I had to bide my time.

When Susie returned from leave, she seemed different. There was a spring in her step and she looked happier and livelier.

'As you know, Kate,' she said that night when we were getting into bed, 'I hate being a parlour maid and the idea of spending the rest of my life working for Her Majesty and her odious son fills me with horror. I detest both of them and I don't think I can take much more of it here. I'd love to get one over on them.'

'What sort of thing do you have in mind, Susie?'

'I dunno at this moment but I'd do anything to escape.'

'Anything, Susie?'

'Well, almost anything. Look, Kate, can you keep a secret?'

'Hope so.'

Unable to contain herself any longer, she gushed out

her news. 'I've made up my mind. I'm going back home this year to be married, no matter what.'

I felt as if I'd been thumped when I heard this and I didn't know whether to laugh or cry. Too many changes in my life and they were coming too fast. Of course I was glad to see Susie so full of the joys of spring but I was also hurting inside because it meant she would be leaving. Susie had become my bosom friend over the last few years.

'My childhood sweetheart, Bob,' she whispered, 'has finally proposed. He's a policeman in the Durham Constabulary and he's summoned up the courage to pop the question. I wish you could meet him, Kate. He's so handsome. Bright blue eyes and wavy golden hair with a sort of quiff at the front.'

'I'm so happy for you, Susie,' I said and I meant it though I knew I was going to miss her badly. 'And that's a good job Bob has, being a policeman – good pay and a good pension at the end. You're made for life.'

'Ah, but Bob and I are hoping for better things. We'd like to buy a little business that we can run together. We've got our eye on a post office in a pretty village called Ferrygate. That's our big dream.'

'That'd cost a fortune, surely?'

'A small one anyway. We need about two hundred pounds to cover the cost of the property, the good will, and the stock.'

'You seem to have it worked out.'

'All except for the money. Bob has about thirty pounds and I have around twenty. But that's taken us six years of hard saving.'

'That leaves you only a hundred and fifty. Where do you hope to get a sum like that?'

'It's not as bad as that, Kate. We can get a mortgage of a hundred and so that leaves us only fifty short.'

'Still, fifty's fifty, Susie.'

'That's the part of the plan we haven't worked out yet. Bob wants me to leave as soon as possible, especially when I told him about Madam and her bossy manner. Also about our Harold. He hit the roof when I told him about his groping hands and his obscene suggestions. He reckons we should report him to the police and have him prosecuted for molestation or attempted rape.'

'That would be going a bit far, Susie. Madam would have a heart attack at the thought of the disgrace. What's more, we'd lose our jobs.'

'I suppose you're right, Kate.'

'It's those dirty magazines he's always looking at. I think they get him excited,' I said.

'I feel guilty about leaving you with the job of taking him his morning cuppa, Kate,' Susie said, placing a hand on my shoulder. 'Look,' she continued, 'you've been taking tea to him and Miss Emma for a few years now. How about a swap? You take the tea to the master and the madam and I'll take over your chore. A change is as good as a rest, they say. I'll fight him off for a few months.'

'I wouldn't dream of letting you take Harold on,' I replied. 'Harold's as randy as ever and it's a while since you handled him – or didn't handle him, as the case may be.'

'It wasn't fair that I loaded that on your back, Kate. I'd take it as a great favour if you'd let me take over the job again. It's been on my conscience for a long time.'

'Are you sure you know what you're saying, Susie?' I said. 'I mean, I've learned to cope with our young master. He knows he has to watch his step with me or I'm likely to have an accident with his tea.'

'Look, no arguments, Kate. I insist. I'll start taking in his tea tomorrow. There'll be no problem. Remember, I used to deal with him long before you came on the scene.'

'True, but he's a few years older now and he's learned a trick or two.'

'Maybe, but so have I.'

I was only too happy to make the switch. But I was a little puzzled by Susie's insistence. She must be going off her head, I thought. I put it down to her being in love.

I was sure she regretted her kind offer when I saw her looking a bit red and flustered a few times when she came out of his room in the mornings.

About six weeks later, we were settling down to sleep as usual when Susie whispered to me, 'Can I tell you something else in confidence, Kate?'

'Another secret, Susie? I'm beginning to feel like a priest in the confessional box. But you know you can.'

'I'm late.'

'Late? Late for what?'

'No, not late like that. Late with my monthlies, you know. Kate, I think I'm in trouble.'

In our world, that could mean only one thing.

'Impossible!' I said. Not another one in the family way, I thought. This is becoming contagious. 'How do you know?' I asked.

'I know,' she said confidently. 'Don't ask me how. Maybe it's changes in the body chemistry, I dunno. I can tell somehow by instinct.'

'Who . . . ?' The question hovered on my lips.

'Is the father?' she said, finishing it for me.

'Is it your boyfriend, Bob?'

'I doubt it. Bob and I can get pretty passionate at times but no, I don't think it's him.'

'Then who?' I was afraid to hear the answer.

'I'm ashamed to say, Kate, but I've got to tell someone. It's Harold.'

'You're joking.'

'I swear it.'

'What in heaven's name happened?'

'When we did that swap with the morning tea routine, I had no choice. Just before I went on leave, I was packing my case in my room when Harold walked in on me. You know what he's like. Didn't knock. Didn't think he had to being the son of the master.'

'Typical Harold,' I said. 'But what's that got to do with the morning tea business.'

'He saw what I was packing into my case. I had a few items to take home as presents – a bottle of wine, a tin of salmon, some cans of pineapple and pears – you know the sort of thing. They don't have much money at home.'

Susie had been unlucky getting caught like that. All of us on the staff helped ourselves to a few goodies from time to time. James with the booze, Mrs Armstrong with her deals with the tradesmen, and even Old Ned had a secret vegetable patch in the garden. Me too. I had to hold up my hands and plead guilty. On my last visit home, I'd taken a few things for the family. The Lamport-Smythes had so much and our own people so little.

'Harold threatened to spill the beans to his mother,' Susie said, 'and that would have been instant dismissal, as you know.'

'So Harold had a hold over you. Either you gave in to his demands or it was all up with you.'

'Exactly. You can see now, Kate, why I had to do the swap. Harold wanted crumpet with his tea and since he wasn't getting anywhere with you, I was fair game.'

I didn't usually swear but I couldn't help myself on this occasion. 'The bastard! The conniving bastard!' I said. 'It's a form of blackmail and rape.'

'But I'd no idea, Kate,' Susie wept, 'that he'd become so

persistent over the last two or three years. The first morning, I put down his tea on the bedside cabinet and quick as a flash he pulled me into the bed. Before I could say Jack Robinson, he'd done it. Talk about Flash Harry!'

'So tell me something new!' I exclaimed. 'I know the problem only too well. Haven't I spent the last couple of years fighting him off. But why didn't you call for help?'

'How could I call for help at seven o'clock in the morning? The whole house would have been in uproar, upstairs and downstairs alike. Anyway, it wasn't one occasion; he had me in his power, blackmailing me. He was demanding it on a regular basis.'

'Oh, I'm so sorry, Susie, that you've had to suffer this. If I had my way, I'd castrate him. But about this idea of being pregnant, you can't be absolutely sure, can you? You've missed only one period. Maybe it's worry and tension that's caused you to miss.'

'Maybe you're right, Kate. I hope to God you are.'

A whole month went by before we mentioned the subject again.

We'd had an exceptionally hard day doing one of Madam's monthly spring cleans when a tearful Susie reported the bad news.

'No doubt about it, Kate. I'm in the Stork Club all right. Oh, what a rotten kettle of fish! What am I going to do? I'm utterly lost and I feel like jumping into the nearest canal.'

'No need for that sort of talk, Susie.'

'Tell me what to do, Kate. Shall I get rid of it? I've heard that if you take a hot bath and drink a lot of gin, it can remove the problem.'

'Don't even think it, Susie. Besides, not only is it murder but you'd be taking a big risk with your own life. In the old days, there were one or two cases in Ancoats, as I remember.'

'Then I suppose there's nothing for it but to dump the problem in Harold's lap like you did with the hot tea.'

'That sounds like the best solution, Susie. But what can Harold do? He's such a spineless character.'

'Doesn't matter. He'll have to tell the family upstairs and they'll have to take some sort of action.'

'And if he refuses? What then?'

'I've no choice but to report the matter myself. It's time the Lamport-Smythes learned what's been going on. Their little Harold is due for his comeuppance.'

'His mother'll strangle him, Susie. She thinks Harold is the centre of the universe and everything revolves round him. She'll never believe *he* could do anything wrong. She'll blame it on you and say you led him on.'

'I'm going to wait a couple of weeks to be absolutely sure. Then I'm going to confront the family. But Kate, I'm so scared. I don't think I could face that lot by myself. Will you come with me? Madam frightens the life out of me.'

'Of course I will, Susie. And I'll back up anything you say. Her Majesty should learn what kind of little monster she gave birth to – not a boy but a cross between a wolf and a ram.'

A fortnight later, there was no change. Together, we took Harold's morning tea and gave him the news. His skin was pale to begin with but when he heard that he was to be a father, he turned the colour of parchment. One thing I'll say for him, though, he didn't deny it. Instead he kept repeating the same phrase over and over again. 'What will Mother say? What will Mother say?'

Susie and I were more interested in what mother would *do* than what she would *say*. The question was: would Harold have the guts to tell his parents?

It was James our butler who gave us the answer, though

he himself didn't fully understand it. He came down from having served breakfast looking worried.

'I don't like it,' he said to cook. 'Something's amiss up there. Something funny going on.'

'How do you mean "funny"?' she asked.

'Uneasy, tense. You can cut the air with a knife. As if they were angry with each other. I think Harold's in some sort of trouble.'

'They've probably heard that he's been messing about in Manchester,' replied Mrs Armstrong, 'instead of doing his research work in Chester. I always knew he'd be found out one day.'

Around ten o'clock that morning, James came into the scullery where Susie and I were washing up.

'You're wanted upstairs, Susie,' he said. 'Something's going on. Neither the master nor young Harold has gone to work. And they're wearing them funeral faces which I haven't seen since the death of the old Queen.'

'I'll go with her,' I said quickly.

James was right, the atmosphere in the drawing room was like a funeral parlour. Susie and I went through the curtsying routine but our employers hardly noticed. The master looked sick but Madam looked worse as if she'd eaten something that didn't agree with her, like half a pound of lemons.

And unusually it was Mr Lamport-Smythe who did the talking.

'Harold has told us about what's been happening. Is it true?' He chose his words carefully.

'About me expecting, sir? Yes, it's true,' Susie told him bravely. A spade was a spade where she came from.

'And Harold is the father?'

'Yes, sir,' Susie answered. 'I'm so embarrassed and so

sorry about it. But I thought you would want to know about it because the baby will be your grandchild.'

Susie couldn't have picked a better way to hurt Madam. She gave an involuntary gasp. She winced and her face became fixed in a pained expression as if a gobstopper had gone down the wrong way.

Harold hung his head.

'Well, are you, Harold?' Madam exploded at last. 'Are you the father?'

'I'm not sure, Mother,' he stammered.

'Did you or did you not have . . . ?' She was unable to finish the question.

Mentally I completed it for her. *Have her? Have it?*

'Yes, yes, it was me. I got carried away one morning,' he whinged.

'Oh, Harold, Harold! How could you do this to us?' Madam wept.

'I'm so sorry, Mother. It was just on this one occasion. I forgot myself.'

Madam could hold herself back no longer. She turned on Susie. 'I feel sure that our innocent young boy was tempted by this Jezebel,' she rasped, pointing the finger. 'She led our boy astray.' She took Harold in her arms to comfort him. 'My poor little lamb.'

It was time for me to speak up, though I knew it might cost me my job.

'I'm sorry, Madam,' I heard myself saying, 'but I must say something. Susie's not the only one who's been the subject of your son's attentions. Nearly every morning for the last three years I've had to fight him off, and I'm no Jezebel.'

'That's true,' Susie added. 'He's taken advantage of Kate and me and I'm willing to swear as much in a court of law.'

The reference to the court of law was the master stroke. The whole family turned green.

'There's the scandal,' Mr Lamport-Smythe murmured to himself. 'It would ruin us and our family name here in Macclesfield. Why, we'd have to move to another district. And there's my reputation at the Royal Exchange to think of.'

At the mention of scandal and reputation, Madam began to sob.

'Too late for tears, Miriam,' the master said. 'No use crying over spilt milk. What we must do,' our boss continued, unusually decisive, 'is first check that Susie really is . . .' He had the same problem about using grown-up words, like 'pregnant'. '. . . is . . . expecting. We shall arrange an appointment with our general practitioner and, if it's confirmed, ask our solicitor to advise us.' He turned to Susie. 'If it's confirmed, we as a family accept full responsibility and will see to your welfare.'

Later that night Susie and I talked it over.

'What if the family decide to prosecute you, Susie, and me, come to think of it, for stealing items of food? What then?'

'Not a chance,' she said. 'The whole story would have to come out and so would the scandal. If the *Macclesfield Courier* got hold of it, they'd be ruined. No, take it from me. The family will do anything to hush the matter up. They'll have to compensate me.'

'But what can you say to Bob, your fiancé? Surely, he'll want to know about the baby and where the money came from?'

'I'll tell him the truth. How I took his advice and threatened to report the Lamport-Smythes and their son to the police. I can explain any payment they make to me as "hush" money.'

'What about the baby, Susie? What will you tell him about that? Won't he ask a lot of awkward questions?'

'Somehow,' she said mysteriously, 'I don't think Bob will be a problem.'

Her answer puzzled me but I let it pass.

'Let's hope and pray that Bob is understanding and stands by you,' I said. 'Do you think it's going to work out?'

'I'm going to give it a damn good try, Kate.'

The family made the appointment with the family doctor in Prestbury and Susie's condition was confirmed.

A week later Susie and I, both of us nervous, were sitting at the table in the servants' hall. We were wearing our Sunday best which caused a great deal of comment from the other three on the staff.

'Will someone please tell me what's going on!' Mrs Armstrong snapped. 'If there's some sort of trouble, I want to know about it. If it concerns them upstairs, it concerns all of us down here.'

The front doorbell rang and James went to answer it. He was soon back and he looked worried.

'I've admitted Richard Lambert, the family solicitor. He wouldn't be here unless there's something serious in the wind.'

'P'raps that son of theirs has broken the law,' offered Old Ned. 'I wouldn't be surprised if that were the case.'

'That's as may be,' Mrs Armstrong said, 'but why are these two young ladies dressed up to the nines and on a Monday morning? And why has Susie brought her suitcase down? It's not long since she came back from leave.'

I said nothing and hoped that my face gave nothing away.

'You'll all find out soon enough,' Susie told them. 'Until then, you'll have to be patient.'

The drawing-room bell rang and James went to answer it. He was soon back and with a jerk of his thumb indicated that we were both required upstairs.

'Theirs not to reason why,' I said to Susie, quoting Tennyson's immortal lines. 'Theirs but to do and die.' I was supposed to be giving her moral support but I wasn't feeling too confident myself.

We went upstairs into the drawing room where the master, the mistress, Harold, and the solicitor were waiting. Richard Lambert was a frightening figure with a stern, disapproving face.

We both curtsied to show that we knew our place and that we didn't want to cause any trouble. We were left standing there as no one asked us to sit down. We waited for someone to speak. It was the solicitor who broke the silence.

'Now, Susie – I presume I may call you Susie – I've been fully apprised of the situation. The family doctor at Prestbury has confirmed that you are two to three months pregnant.'

'Yes, sir,' Susie replied quietly. She was shaking like a leaf.

'Now I want to be absolutely certain about what happened,' the lawyer continued. 'Did sexual intercourse take place between you and Harold Lamport-Smythe?' Obviously the solicitor had no difficulty in saying the words. He was a cold fish and no mistake.

I kept quiet but my eyes moved from speaker to speaker.

'Yes, sir,' Susie replied.

I looked around and every face in the room had turned red except of course the lawyer's. I had the impression that the man was enjoying embarrassing everyone and savouring the forbidden words.

'Harold has admitted his responsibility in this matter. It only remains for us to come to some amicable arrangement.'

Susie's eyes were fixed firmly on the carpet as she nodded her head.

'The family,' the solicitor said, 'is anxious to do all in their power to help you, and in this regard they have asked me to give them advice.'

'Thank you, sir,' Susie said. 'I'm truly sorry for the trouble that this situation has caused.'

'You do understand,' Richard Lambert continued, 'that there is absolutely no question of Harold marrying you. You have been in domestic service long enough to understand that it's not the done thing for a young man from a well-to-do family like the Lamport-Smythes to marry a servant girl.'

'Oh, no, sir,' Susie said, 'I wasn't considering anything like that.'

The family looked distinctly relieved when they heard Susie say this. It just went to show how out of touch they were. Susie would rather have married Old Ned or Old Nick himself than their obnoxious son.

'Good, good,' the solicitor mumbled. 'Now, we have drawn up a form of contract which we are going to ask you to sign with your friend here as witness. The family has your future welfare at heart and they have authorised me to compensate you for the necessary expenses you will incur. Let me say at once that I think the family has been extremely generous – I would even say over-generous.' Mr Lambert turned his attention to the form.

'What is your full name?' he asked, his pen at the ready.

'Victoria Garrett, sir.'

'There's the matter of registering the birth of the child. Children born out of wedlock usually assume the name of the mother, you understand.'

'Yes, sir.' Susie's eyes were still glued on the carpet.

'The family has agreed that you will be paid the sum of

seventy-five pounds,' the lawyer said, 'subject to the following conditions.'

Ah, here we go, I thought. Here come the whys and the wherefores and the funny legal mumbo-jumbo.

'First, you will undertake to leave Macclesfield and not return, and second, you will give a solemn undertaking never to contact or communicate with the Lamport-Smythe family again. I take it that you have prepared your things as the family requested.'

Susie nodded.

'If you accept these conditions, I have a banker's draft for the agreed amount.'

Susie and I signed the contract where the solicitor indicated. Susie collected the draft, we curtsied and we were out of there.

There was a big hoo-ha in the servants' hall when we told them the story.

'If I had my way,' James muttered, 'I'd serve up his testicles on tomorrow's breakfast tray.'

'And I'd be happy to cook 'em,' added Mrs Armstrong.

An hour later, my dear friend Susie left in a cab for the railway station, and when she'd gone, there was an ache and an empty space in my heart.

Some time after that, Harold accepted a commission in the Cheshire Regiment. Perhaps the army could instil some discipline into his life.

As for Susie, I heard no more for several months until I received a brief letter.

> Ferrygate in County Durham
> Dear Kate,
> You will be glad to know that everything worked out for the best after I left Macclesfield. I married my childhood sweetheart, Bob, and we are both very

happy. It's so nice to feel that my household chores are now for my own home and not someone else's.

Bob left the police force and we bought our dream post office. It keeps us busy but we love it as we meet so many interesting people and everyone seems to bring their problems to us. Sometimes, I think we're more an advice centre than a post office.

I told Bob that the money I got from the Lamport-Smythes was paid to me when I threatened to take Harold to court for molestation. I said nothing to him about 'the other thing'. I couldn't see the point as Bob is happy about the way things have turned out. His only comment was that I should have asked for more money.

One other small piece of news! Last week, I gave birth to a beautiful baby boy (seven pounds). Everyone said he's the image of Bob, his dad, with his golden hair and lovely blue eyes.

Ever your friend,

Victoria (who used to be Susie)

I had to sit down when I'd read this letter. I thought back on all that Susie had done and said before she'd left. The pieces fitted together like a jigsaw puzzle. The scheming little devil! Susie had pulled the wool over everyone's eyes, including mine. I spent the rest of the day chuckling to myself and repeating over and over again a certain Lancashire expression I'd learned as a child. Who'd a thought it?

Chapter Nineteen

With Susie gone, things went flat. The only event worth mentioning was my promotion. One morning about a week after Susie's departure, Madam called me into the drawing room.

'Kate, you've been working here five years and on the whole I have found your work quite good.'

I took note of the 'quite'. Madam never used expressions like excellent or *very* good in case we got ideas above our station. No, it was *fairly* good or *reasonably* good. The highest praise one could get out of her was 'not bad'. If she said my work was quite good, I must have been doing well.

'I've decided that you will take the place of Susie as full parlour maid and your wage will be raised to eighteen pounds a year.'

Eighteen pounds a year! Rich at last! Why, that was thirty shillings a month. I could send a bit more home and save half of it each month. My dream of getting the family together was that much nearer.

'I have also engaged a junior girl to help you,' Madam continued. 'I hope you will train her in our ways.'

That afternoon, the new girl came to the back door. She was about fourteen and she reminded me of myself when I'd first come to Macclesfield. She was poorly dressed and obviously nervous as it was her first job. I did my best to make her feel at home by introducing her to the other staff and sitting her down at the kitchen table with a cup of tea.

She was originally from Greengate in Salford and had come on the recommendation of Mr Birkby at Swinton Industrial School. When she told us her name was Charlotte, Mrs Armstrong and I exchanged knowing glances. Charlotte? Another Queen! As expected, when she returned from her pep talk with Madam, not only had she had the sermon about cleanliness and not encouraging followers, she had also been given a new handle – Lottie.

In the first few weeks, Lottie had difficulty in adapting to the routine and made a few blunders. On her second day, she was ironing bed sheets and when she was told to answer the back door, forgot to remove the iron. The smell of burned cloth filled the scullery for the rest of the day. The breaking of two plates – not the best porcelain, I hasten to add – and her habit of leaving taps running we could forgive but her slip-up over the storage jars was harder to take.

At dinnertime, we sat down to enjoy Mrs Armstrong's delicious chicken soup. She ladled out our portions and was about to join us herself when Old Ned piped up.

'You'll forgive me, Mrs Armstrong, if I say that this soup of yours has a distinctly funny flavour.'

'Funny! How do you mean "funny"?' Mrs Armstrong snapped. She was touchy about her cooking, was Mrs Armstrong.

She sampled a little on a spoon. 'What in God's name is that bloody awful sickening taste?' she spluttered.

'Tastes like sugar,' I remarked.

Mrs Armstrong ran to the storage jars on the shelf and in particular to the one marked 'Salt'. One look was enough.

'Lottie, you silly girl, you've put sugar in the salt jar!'

'Sorry, Mrs Armstrong,' Lottie wept. 'There's so much work to do, I can't think straight.'

That was Lottie's baptism of fire in the Lamport-Smythe household. As the weeks went by, she fell into the routine as I'd done all those years ago. At least she didn't have to take morning tea to Harold. I wondered if he had a batman in Aldershot and if he gave him a quick flash every morning. They'd soon be court-martialling him if he did.

The one break I had in the parlour maid's round of household duties was provided by Miss Emma when she persuaded Madam to release me every Tuesday afternoon to help in the charity shop in the town centre. How I loved this work, for it not only got me out of the house but gave me the chance to meet other people. The things we had to sell were truly amazing; many of Emma's rich friends were generous in their donations and there was a mountain of clothes of every description. Dresses and costumes which must have cost a fortune were up for sale at a quarter of their value. As for hats! All were of the highest quality with original costs of several guineas and they were being offered for ridiculous prices like half-a-crown or five shillings.

On my first morning at the shop, Emma saw me admiring the merchandise.

'It's the best quality, Kate,' she said.

'It certainly is, Miss Emma. We should have no difficulty selling it.'

I was like a child in a toy shop at Christmas. I couldn't resist the temptation. Surely a few items from all that stuff would never be missed. I felt they owed me a few things because I was expected to make up the loss of my afternoon's work in the big house. And for no extra pay. The shop involved sorting out the clothes, selling them and entering them up in the ledger. As I was going through the various garments, one or two items took my fancy. I picked out a coat with a beautiful fur collar, a black velvet skirt and a superb silk blouse to go with it. Then I thought, may as well be hung for a sheep as a lamb. To complete the outfit, I helped myself to a pair of cream kid gloves with imitation pearl fasteners, a pair of drop earrings, and an evening bag.

As usual, Emma went off early, leaving me to tidy everything and to lock up. As I closed the shop for the day, I put the things in a canvas bag and took them home to the big house where I sneaked them up to my room and hid them under the bed.

I didn't know when I'd ever wear such finery but who knows? Perhaps one day . . .

The charity shop was never short of customers and they came from all walks of life. I thought I'd found my niche working in this shop and not only in the selling line either. When I checked Miss Emma's book-keeping, I found it had as many mistakes as a Christmas cake had currants. She may have gone to a college and a finishing school but she hadn't had the grounding in arithmetic that I'd had in St Michael's Elementary School under the strict teaching of Gerty Houlihan. I spent much of my time correcting Miss Emma's errors.

I often wondered why I went to the shop only on Tuesdays because Miss Emma never failed to go on four weekdays. It was some time in September before I found out.

'Kate,' Emma said, 'I'm expecting some important visitors this afternoon and I want you to take over the serving whilst I'm in the back entertaining my guests.'

The visitors turned out to be none other than Christabel Pankhurst, Annie Kenney, Teresa Billington, and Bernard

Sheridan. My heart skipped a beat when I saw him again. I must be mad, I said to myself; he belongs to a different world. They assembled round the big table in the back room and I was not left in doubt very long as to why they were there. A meeting of the WSPU. Madam would have had a fit if she'd known what was going on. She was very much against movements like this. I'd once heard her describe members as crazy wild female agitators with nothing to do with their time but cause trouble.

Emma called for tea and biscuits and as I went into the kitchen to prepare them, I was joined by Bernard.

'Here, let me help you with those things, Kate', he said. 'We're always going on about social equality and that kind of thing, it's about time we put our principles into action.'

'Thank you, sir. Much appreciated,' I said, turning red. Why was it that I behaved like a stupid schoolgirl in his presence?

'And you can cut that "sir" stuff out,' he added, taking the tray from me.

I returned to the front of the shop to deal with any customers but I could hear distinctly what was being said in the meeting at the back.

'The first item on the agenda is a discussion of progress and the actions we must take next,' Christabel was saying. 'I've read a report this week about the upholstery trade where women are being paid fifty per cent of what men are getting for the same work.'

'It's a disgrace,' said Teresa Billington, 'and the trade unions which are run by men encourage this sex discrimination.'

'It was the same in the Oldham mill where I used to work,' said Annie Kenney. 'There'll be no justice till women get the vote and can have a say in the making of the laws.'

'The first thing we have to do,' Bernard said, 'is to break

down this barmy notion that women are in some way inferior beings and cannot be trusted to make intelligent decisions.'

'The root of that notion,' said Christabel, 'can be found in the Bible with its mistranslation of the way woman was created. The word "rib" should have been rendered "side" or "half". The expression "Adam's rib" is sheer nonsense! Woman was created as the other half of mankind, with distinct functions, and she is absolutely equal to the male.'

'And from that mistranslation,' Teresa added, 'has come the notion that in some way woman has a different mind – politicians talk of the "female mind". What's that about? The brain is not an organ of sex. We might as well talk of the female liver or the female kidneys.'

From the sound of things, I gathered that they had finished their tea and I went in to collect the tray and the crockery. Whilst they were having their high-falutin' discussion, someone had to wash and dry the cups and saucers. And that someone was me.

As I collected the tea things, Christabel turned to me. 'What about you, Kate? Won't you join our cause?'

Not a chance, I said to myself. This rebelling lark was fine if you had an independent income but if you had to work for a living, you couldn't afford the luxury of revolting. They didn't seem to realise that us working-class women were too busy trying to keep body and soul together to bother with such things.

'I'm much in favour of the cause,' I said, being tactful, 'but I can't take the risk of losing my job and my livelihood. I'd be happy to sign any petition that you organise. Most domestic servants would do the same.'

'Well said, Kate!' Bernard said. 'You're right about the suffrage movement being run by middle-class women who can afford to take risks.'

Christabel now moved the debate forward. 'I propose we attend the rally of the Liberal Party to be held next week at the Free Trade Hall. Sir Edward Grey will be there. Friday, October the thirteenth. We must make sure it's a date the world will never forget.'

Everyone agreed and Emma, who was acting as secretary, recorded the resolution.

I went to pick up the tray but Bernard had beaten me to it.

'Allow me, Kate,' he said and carried it into the little scullery.

'You made some good contributions to our discussion, Kate, and we're grateful. It's so refreshing to get the view of a working girl.'

He turned me round, took my face in his hands, and looked into my eyes. I melted. His hands were soft and warm and I could smell soap – Pears, I'd say at a guess.

'You know, Kate, you are a pretty young girl. How old are you?'

'I'm nineteen, er, Bernard.'

'A beautiful girl like you shouldn't be doing menial work. You should be enjoying life. I can see you in a punt, lounging back with your parasol whilst some young handsome man rows you along the Thames at Kingston.'

His attention was brought back to the meeting by Christabel calling to him.

'Bernard, we're about to discuss the second item on the agenda – the charity work in Manchester. Emma tells us that Kate is from Ancoats and might have some suggestions.'

They told me that they were proposing to set up a charitable visit to one of the poorer districts at Christmas. The visit would include gifts for the children, parcels of food and a soup kitchen. When I suggested St Michael's

Parish, they were all for it. I was sure Father Muldoon there would be only too happy to make the church hall available. Miss Emma promised to ask Madam to release me for the day.

The following week, James read out an account of the WSPU activities from the *Manchester Guardian*. The paper reported that at the meeting of the Liberal Party, Christabel and Annie had been ejected when they heckled Sir Edward Grey and demanded votes for women.

Outside, the two suffragists addressed the crowd which had gathered. The police grabbed them and they kicked and lashed out but the burly coppers were too strong for them. The two ladies, determined to go to prison, spat at them, though not too skilfully – some of our Ancoats women could have given them lessons. Anyroad, that spittle was enough. Christabel and Annie were bundled into a Black Maria and driven off.

Next day, our two militants refused to pay fines and Christabel was sentenced to seven days and Annie to three for assaulting the police. They'd got the martyrdom they'd desired and their publicity. The newspaper banner headline read: FIRST SUFFRAGETTES GO TO PRISON.

As for me, I had great sympathy for the movement and I would have loved to support them. But if I'd gone to prison as they had, that would have been the end of my job and I'd never have got another.

There was a good old Manchester drizzle in the air when we made our charity visit to St Michael's in Ancoats before Christmas. When word got out that there was to be soup and free handouts at the church hall, a queue of women and children soon formed. They were carrying jugs of every size, colour and style. The people looked damp and bedraggled but they were a good-natured crowd and there was a lot of laughing and joking as we ladled hot chicken broth into their receptacles. It didn't seem that long ago that I'd been queuing up in the same way. Each child also received a present of a toy and each woman a gift of food. Whichever apostle said it was more blessed to give than to receive was surely right, for it certainly made us feel good.

Then I saw them! My own mam with her new baby and young Eddie in tow. Eddie was now a young lad of eight – a nice-looking kid though I couldn't help noticing the holes in his jersey and his stockings. Close behind them were Aunt Sarah and Uncle Barney. Oh, I was so glad to see them after all this time. I ran forward to greet them, we hugged each other tightly and soon we were in earnest conversation, catching up on each other's news.

'How's everything going?' I asked cheerfully.

'Time's have been hard, Kate,' Mam said. 'We've been on short time at the factory. If it hadn't been for that few bob you sent us each month, I don't know what we'd have done. We came to rely on it. You've got on so well and we're right proud of you. Why, you've even learned to talk posh.'

'If I have, Mam, it was purely unintentional.' I turned to Aunt Sarah. 'And what about you, Auntie? How's life been treating you and Uncle Barney?'

'About as bad as it could be, Kate. Barney hasn't worked for the last two years on account of his bad chest. Bronchitis, the doctor said it is, but I think he might have what your poor dad died of.' She lowered her voice and looked around furtively before she said, 'You know, consumption. It's been a struggle to keep our heads above water, I can tell you.'

Barney confirmed Sarah's diagnosis with a long bout of coughing.

'Oh, I'm so sorry to hear that,' I said. I was feeling

guilty because of the comparatively easy life I'd been leading in Macclesfield. Good food, a comfortable bed, a roof over my head and a decent wage. Hard work, but that never killed anyone. My thoughts prompted me to take out my purse and offer Aunt Sarah a few bob to tide her over. Her reaction was not what I expected.

'Wait a minute, Kate. I hope you don't think I'm pleading poverty and asking you for charity. What do you think I am? A bloody Gypsy woman begging for a crust?'

'I'm sorry, Auntie. I didn't mean to insult you. I was only trying to help.'

'You come here to Ancoats with your flash friends handing out food parcels. Like Lady Bountiful throwing a few crumbs to the deserving poor. We've managed without you lot up to now and so you can bloody well get back to your leafy lanes and your stuck-up Cheshire set.'

Mam tried to defend me but there was no pacifying Aunt Sarah once her dander was up. Again, I said I was sorry if I'd offended her and I left it at that.

While Miss Emma and her ladies were busy handing out Aunt Sarah's 'crumbs' to the grateful poor, I grabbed the chance to go back with Mam to have a cup of tea in her furnished room. Perhaps it was the drizzle, but the district depressed me. As we walked down George Leigh Street, I noticed anew how soot-blackened the factories and the houses were. I'd forgotten how many chimneys there were, belching their smoke into the damp air; I'd forgotten, too, about the gutters running with dirty rain-water down the middle of each poky little court.

We reached Portugal Close where Aunt Sarah lived and it was there I got the shock of my life. Mam had the front parlour and was living in the vilest conditions imaginable. Perhaps it was because of my experiences of seeing how the richer half lived but I couldn't think how anyone, least of all my own mother, could live with her young sons in such a filthy place. Maybe my standards had changed and maybe Aunt Sarah was right. Without realising it, I'd become la-di-da but I didn't think so because I couldn't remember our early home in Butler Court ever being as bad as this. In the old days, Mam used to be so house-proud. As we approached the house, I saw that the steps had not been cleaned or donkey-stoned for a long time, and as we walked down the lobby, there was a smell of sweat and unwashed bodies. The parlour itself was such a mess, it looked as if a gale had blown through it. In one corner was an unmade bed, in the other a horsehair sofa with the stuffing sticking through, and the empty grate, which hadn't been black-leaded since heaven knows when, was surrounded by a fire guard that was draped with damp clothes. The table was covered with a stained newspaper and the slop-stone contained the pots from the morning's breakfast. I noticed, too, the collection of empty Guinness bottles under the sink. I felt like rolling up my sleeves and getting down to it.

I couldn't spend more than half an hour with Mam as I had to get back to the church hall to catch my ride back to Macclesfield. I took a peek at the new baby – he was a Lally all right, with Mam's nose – but my feelings were confused because of the circumstances. I slipped Eddie a bob and Mam a ten shilling note, hoping it would be spent on something for the baby and wouldn't go to the Guinness family fortune.

I was so upset at what I'd seen, I was more determined than ever to build a decent life for my family. I had saved twenty-two pounds during my time in service. Was it enough to rent a house and buy furniture? Should I try to bring Cissie and Danny out of Swinton and back into the family or was it best to leave them where they were? My mind was in turmoil and I spent the following week in a daze. Unwittingly Miss Emma helped me come to a decision.

I took her morning tea into her and as usual left it on her bedside cabinet.

'Good morning, Miss Emma,' I said cheerily

I was about to depart when she called me back.

'Kate, something wonderful has happened and I've got to tell someone. You're going to be the first. Can you guess what it is?'

'No, Miss Emma. I haven't a clue,' I said happily. I felt flattered that she had chosen me to hear her good news. Perhaps it was something to do with the suffragette movement.

'Bernard Sheridan has asked me to marry him. And I've decided to accept.'

The news was like a slap in the face. My mouth went dry and I felt the bile rise in my throat.

'I'm so glad, Miss Emma,' I mumbled. I hoped she couldn't detect the bitter disappointment in my voice. My heart was beating wildly. 'I'm sure you and Bernard will be very happy.'

I left the bedroom but I couldn't go back downstairs. The others were bound to notice the utter misery on my face. Instead I went to my room and sobbed my heart out. What a fool I'd been to think that someone like Bernard Sheridan would even take a second look at a servant girl like me. I had completely misunderstood his kindness and his courteous manners. He'd held my face in his hands and told me I was beautiful. And me like an idiot had picked up the wrong message! But enough of this weeping. I got off the bed and went to wash my face. I squared my shoulders and held my head high. Mustn't let the others see I'd been crying. Come on, Kate Lally, I told myself.

Pull yourself together. At least the news has helped you to make up your mind.

The next day, I went in to see Madam and to hand in my notice. She was shocked that I could even think of leaving. I explained that I wanted to go home to help my own family but she was more concerned about the effect my going would have on her domestic arrangements. Why was I unhappy? Was it something that one of the family had done? Did I want higher pay or more time off? How could she possibly get a replacement, and as for Lottie, she had a lot to learn. Madam begged me to stay but my mind was made up. Eventually she accepted the situation and agreed to give me a good character, telling me that if ever I wanted to go back, there would be a place for me in Macclesfield.

At the end of January 1906 I packed my box and after a sorrowful goodbye to Old Ned, James, Lottie and, most of all, to my good friend and teacher, Mrs Armstrong, I hired a cab to the station and took the train to Manchester. Now all I needed to do was find some decent digs – and also a job.

Chapter Twenty

The sun was shining when I came out of Manchester's London Road Station that January afternoon. A good omen, I thought, for the start of my new life. For the second time that day I took a hansom – which made me feel guilty at the extravagance. I was not exactly used to travelling around in cabs.

At the Young Women's Christian Association, I booked myself in for a week as I needed a place to stay and to store my luggage until I found my feet. I looked for furnished digs in the *Manchester Evening News* and I was spoilt for choice as there seemed to be hundreds of them if I wanted to live in one of the posh districts like Didsbury, Chorlton, or Whalley Range. Half of that part of Manchester seemed to be renting its rooms to the other half but it wasn't so easy locating something suitable in Ancoats. Eventually I found a furnished room in Sherratt Court off Oldham Road, not far from my mam's and Aunt Sarah's. The 'digs' were nothing to write home about since they consisted of a small front parlour and the use of the lavatory in the back yard. Still, for three and six a week they would do until I could fix up more permanent arrangements.

The landlady, a Mrs Hudson, was a sourpuss and a fusspot. She was a small, thin woman of about fifty. She implied she was doing me a big favour letting a room to me.

'I don't let rooms as a rule but my husband's an officer in the merchant navy and is away a lot. So I like a bit of company in the house.'

Anyone would have thought she was running the Ritz Hotel the way she inquired into my background, my family history and asked to see references. She was taken aback when I showed her one on printed notepaper from a Macclesfield family. Just the same, she couldn't resist reciting the rules of the house.

'You must not entertain men in your room.' She sniffed. 'You must not bring drink into the house. There must be no eating of food in the bedroom. Finally, you must keep your room clean and you must be in at night before ten because I lock the front door at that time.'

'What if I'm visiting my mother and I'm a bit late?' I asked. 'If you'll trust me to have a key, I would creep in quietly.'

'No, it wouldn't work,' she replied, giving me a tight smile as if she was in pain. 'I'm a light sleeper and I'd hear you. I'm sorry but I don't issue keys to all and sundry.'

It didn't sound promising but I had no choice. There was nothing else so near to Mam's.

I promised to pay her two weeks in advance and to take up residence the following week.

The job market in Manchester was easy, though most of the jobs offered to women were the boring and repetitive kind – putting squiggles on chocolates, laundry work and that kind of thing. I rejected any idea of taking up domestic service again even though there were lots of posts for parlour maids and cooks available in places like Victoria Park and Fallowfield but five years of slavery had been enough for me. No, I wanted to be free to help my own family, and servants' jobs were too tying. Apart from that, the pay in Manchester looked poor because many of the households were small and employed only one or two servants.

As I sat in my little room in the YWCA, I looked at the Situations Vacant advertised in the *Evening News* and considered the possibilities. It seemed strange to be making career choices at the ripe old age of twenty-one. The opportunities seemed endless.

There were pages and pages of jobs for seamstresses in the Cheetham Hill district, making rainwear for firms like Weinberg's, Greenberg's, Frankenberg's and all the other bergs. Hours: 8 a.m. to 6 p.m. and the pay was piecework which meant sweated labour to make a living wage. I'd been top of the class in needlework at Swinton Industrial School but I had seen the effects of years of close stitching on some of the Ancoats women – many of them almost blind by the time they reached thirty. Definitely not for me.

What about a job with my mam in a bagging factory? Long hours in a stuffy atmosphere breathing in fuzz, hairs, and God knows what else. No thank you.

A barmaid in one of the many thousands of Manchester pubs? Once again, long hours but this time dealing with drunks, ruffians, and other forms of lowlife. And if by some mischance I landed up in a pub serving Chesters beer – the so-called fighting beer – it would be a matter of sorting out screeching women and brawling men at closing time every night. I'd no vocation for work like that and anyhow I associated bawdy drunken behaviour with McTavish in the workhouse.

The rest of the list seemed as gruesome. Corset and surgical appliance maker? Upholstery stuffer? Carding machine operator in a cotton mill? All equally loathsome. Then I saw a vacancy as an assistant in a large emporium. That was more like it, I said to myself – until I saw the hours and pay. Eight shillings and sixpence a week for a ten-hour day. A genteel way of starving oneself to death. I'd about given up when my eye caught sight of a job at Westmacott's, the mineral water firm in Ancoats. Hours: 8 to 6 with an hour off for dinner. Wage offered: fifteen shillings a week. Ideal, I thought, especially since it was only a stone's throw from my own room and Mam's place. Besides, Westmacott's were famous in that part of Manchester. Everyone had heard of their tonic water and ginger ale.

Next day, I presented myself at reception and introduced myself to the boss, Declan Dowd, who welcomed me with open arms. Well, almost. He was a big, lanky, red-headed man with a ready smile, a loud laugh, and a walrus moustache. As we discussed the job, I was conscious of the noise of machines and the rattling of bottles from the works behind the office. One encouraging sound was the cheerful singing of the women as they did whatever it was that mineral water operatives did. The strains of 'Lily of Laguna' rang out, drowning the noise of the steam engine.

He looked at me closely. I suppose I was a bit too well-dressed for the job and I think I'd picked up a bit of a refined accent in Macclesfield.

'Are you sure this is your sort of work?' he asked. 'It's quite rough.'

I assured him I wanted the job as the wage was good and, most important for me, it wasn't far from my mam's.

'Very well,' he said at last. 'We'll take you on trial to see how you get on. We've been short-handed for weeks and so you'll be most welcome. When can you start?'

'Before I agree to take the job on,' I replied, 'can you tell me what it involves? I've not had training for work like this.'

'No problem. We'll give you training on the job. We also supply suitable clothing.'

'Suitable clothing?'

'For a start, you'll need a waterproof overall and clogs as you'll be working a lot in water. You'll soon pick it up.'

I agreed to start on the Monday of the following week. I couldn't help wondering what my old friends back in Macclesfield would have thought of my change in circumstances. Old Ned would have approved – 'Good on you, Kate, me darlin' '; Mrs Armstrong would be disappointed that her culinary training had been wasted on a skivvy now labouring in a mineral water factory; James would look down his nose at such menial work; and Mrs Lamport-Smythe would be aghast that one of her ex-employees had sunk so low in the world. But who cared about them? It was a matter of survival in the rotten old world.

'One thing I'll say,' laughed Declan Dowd. 'We're a happy ship and have a happy crew.'

'No need to tell me that,' I said. 'I can hear it for myself.'

Before starting the new job, I had a week free to get myself and my mam organised. The sight of Mam's furnished room was enough to fill anyone with dismay but I drew a few pounds out of my savings and we got down to beautifying the place.

Under the sink, under the table, and under the bed I found enough Guinness bottles to fill several crates and our first job was to collect them together. I lugged them round to the snug at the Land o' Cakes and collected five shillings on the empties.

'I'm not kidding, Mam,' I said, as I loaded the crates on baby John's pram, 'you've enough bottles here to open up a brewery of your own.'

'I didn't drink that lot by myself,' she protested. 'I had help.'

Help, I thought. She meant Frank McGuinness and her stout-drinking cronies. I hoped we'd seen the back of them.

Mam was busy looking after her new baby, and so, I roped Uncle Barney in to help, despite his coughing and spluttering. The weather was dry and so we carried the big items of furniture – the table, sofa, bed, chairs – onto the pavement outside while we stripped the walls of the dark, depressing wallpaper.

'People round here will think we're doing a moonlight flit,' Mam joked. I couldn't remember when I'd last heard her trying to be funny and it did my heart good to see her laughing again.

Eddie joined in the fun of tearing off the five layers of paper we found stuck to the walls.

'You know, our Kate,' he said, 'this wallpaper's probably been holding up the house for the last fifty years. It belongs in a museum.'

'A museum! Noah's Ark more like. We'd better be quick and get the new stuff up,' I said, 'before the house falls around our ears.'

We dislodged a few bugs lurking in long-term residence behind the paper but we soon made short work of them with Jeyes Fluid. We visited a decorator's shop on Butler Street and bought the things we needed – brushes, scrapers, paint, paste, and Mam chose a lovely paper with bluebells and buttercups.

We got back to the room, and standing on a table, I slapped the Walpamur on ceiling and upper walls. Next came the painting of the cornice, the picture rail, and the skirting board.

When all was dry, it was on with the bright flowery paper. Silently, I said a prayer of thanks to my teachers back at Swinton for their practical training. The room was taking on a clean, fresh aspect and Mam was beaming with happiness. So was young Eddie.

Next, we bought new lace curtains, a linen tablecloth, and for the floor a colourful congoleum square and a patterned peg rug. We added the finishing touches with a new mirror and a picture of a stag entitled 'The Monarch of the Glen' by Sir Edwin Landseer which we unearthed at a second-hand stall on Tib Street market. Finally, I returned the jam jars they'd been using as cups and bought a willow crockery set from Shufflebotham's on Rochdale Road and, while I was at it, a basic canteen of cutlery and a burgundy chenille table cover.

When all was finished I looked over our handiwork. Somehow, it didn't look right. I'd missed something. What was it? Suddenly I saw what was wrong. Their clothes! They were shabby and out at the elbows. Didn't go with the new décor. There was nothing for it but to take Mam and Eddie out to May's, the outfitters on Butler Street, and buy them a completely new rig-out. And not wishing to leave out baby John, a layette and a pram set. Now the picture was complete.

This was a happy time for me. How I loved helping my family get things back together again, to see the light in Mam's eyes as her place was transformed from a slum to an attractive living room. It set me back a few pounds and made a big hole in my hard-won savings, but what did it matter! For years I'd dreamt about this day of putting things right again. Then I thought, in for a penny, in for a pound. I took Mam back to Solly's pawnshop on a special errand, though, to be honest, I didn't expect to have much luck in our quest. But miracle of miracles, the two items we were seeking were still there hidden away at the back of the shop, covered in dust but, amazingly, intact and unsold! Mam's wall clock and her most precious possession, her boat-shaped teapot! Although it cost me five pounds to redeem them – still the same old Solly, as tight-fisted as ever – it was worth every penny to see the delight on Mam's face.

In the midst of this joy, though, there was a fly in the ointment. Frank McGuinness. Every day he put in an appearance. Heaving a big sigh as if the task of breathing in and out was too much for him, he flopped down in one of the chairs. With a large mug of tea in one hand and a Woodbine in the other, he kept up a flow of criticism and suggestion.

'I'm pouring in sweat here watching you. I hate to say it but you've missed a bit there, Kate. I don't think much of the colour you've chosen. You can see the joins in the wallpaper, Kate.'

I was ready to throw the paint tin at him.

'Instead of pontificating,' I said, 'why don't you get a brush, climb on a chair, and give some help.'

'I'd love to help,' he wheezed, puffing on his fag, 'but I can't do a thing because of my war wound.'

'Where were you wounded?' I asked impatiently.

'Mafeking,' he replied.

'No, I mean which part of your body?'

'Left buttock. Nearly had my arse shot away. It takes me all my time to stand up, never mind climb onto a chair with a bucket of whitewash.'

I noticed that he managed to drag himself round to the boozer each dinnertime, to spend some of his war pension. I wished somehow I could wave a magic wand to make him disappear from the scene but Mam seemed to put up with him well enough. Understandable, I supposed. After all, he was the father of her child. Maybe I was being unfair and misjudging him but when we'd been going through hell in the workhouse, and in my lonelier moments in service, I'd had lots of time to imagine this blissful moment when I would begin restoring the family home. Somehow, Frank McGuinness had never been part of that picture. I hoped Mam didn't decide to marry him as I didn't want him as stepfather ruling over us. The situation was complicated by the fact that he had two sons of his own living with his sister on Red Bank. In fairy tales, step-parents never seemed to work out. Was it the same in real life?

Chapter Twenty-One

On Sunday afternoon, I moved into Mrs Hudson's furnished room in Sherratt Court. She was a little more friendly on this occasion. Perhaps it was because, in the hope of making a good start, I decided to lash out and pay her a whole month in advance.

'I'm sorry, love,' she whined as she pocketed the cash, 'if I sounded a bit suspicious when you first came. But I have to be careful who I take in, being so near to Piccadilly where the ladies of the night hang out. They'd turn this place into a brothel as soon as look at you.'

The following day, I was up with the lark and the adventurous part of me was looking forward to starting the new job at Westmacott's but the nervous Nellie in me wondered how I'd get on with my fellow workers. If their rendering of 'Lily of Laguna' was anything to go by, they were a happy-go-lucky crowd. I dressed in the waterproof overall and big clogs I had been issued with after my interview, ate a breakfast of porridge and toast, and then clickety-clacked my way up Oldham Road, along with the other women workers who were going to jobs in mills, factories, and warehouses. I felt strange in this uniform and I half expected the other workers to point a finger at me and say, 'Look at that girl pretending to be one of us.' But there was no problem; many of them greeted me with a 'Good morning, love. Nice day,' which told me that I was accepted and part of the scene.

At Westmacott's I had to wait outside the office till Declan was free to explain my duties to me. At half past eight, he bustled in with a cheery 'Top o' the mornin' to you, young Kate. We'll waste no time in getting you started.'

He introduced me to Mr Foden, the office clerk, who wrote down my details in a big register, after which Declan took me into the works to show me the job.

'Let me tell you what happens here,' he began. 'We produce various mineral waters in this factory, as you probably know. The most popular are Sarsaparilla and Dandelion and Burdock. The men on the floor above prepare what we call the syrup, made up of sugar, flavour, herbs, and colouring, and we dilute that with water. We have the latest machinery from America and most of the processes are done automatically. We have to keep up with the competition. The Americans have brought in a new drink called Coca-Cola but I don't think it'll ever catch on. It sounds too much like cocoa and who wants a bedtime drink when they're gasping with thirst?'

'This talk about automatic machinery, Mr Dowd, sounds complicated. Where do I fit into this?'

'Nothing to worry about. You'll be working in the bottle-washing department.

Ah, bottle-washing. That was more my line.

'Come along,' he said. 'I'll introduce you to your fellow workers. The bottle-washers work in teams of three.'

He took me into a large open room that reminded me of a laundry wash-house because all round the sides were lots of big sinks, at each of which a group of women were sloshing water about. The floor was already several inches deep and now I understood why I had to wear clogs. The noise of the machinery and the clatter of thousands of bottles was deafening.

'You'll be working here,' Mr Dowd yelled, pointing to two ladies busy rinsing out bottles at one of the sinks. 'Next to Angela, one of our best workers, who'll show you the ropes, and Hilda who's new like yourself.'

'Flattery will get you everywhere, Declan,' Angela laughed, giving him the glad eye.

'That's enough of that come-hither look from you, Angela, and me a respectable married man,' Declan joked.

'Married, maybe,' called another woman. 'I don't know about the respectable bit.'

'You get on with your bottle-washing, Brigid Riley,' Declan roared, 'and stop casting aspersions.'

When Declan had gone, Angela showed me the basics of the job. I was to do the first rinse, Hilda the next using a bottle brush, and the final check and shake was done by Angela.

'Doesn't the noise in here get you down, Angela?' I called.

'Noise? What noise?' she yelled back.

'I thought it was deafening when I first came,' Hilda shouted as she brushed vigorously at a brown-stained bottle, 'but after only two weeks I'm getting used to it.'

'Hey, you lot!' Angela bawled, addressing the rest of the bottle-washers. 'This is Kate and she'll be working with Hilda and me.'

'How do, Kate!' the cries came back. 'You're welcome, love. But don't take too much notice of Angela there. She'll lead you astray.'

'Hey, Kate,' a middle-aged woman yelled across. 'What do virgins eat for breakfast?'

'I don't know,' I replied, falling for it.

'I thought so,' the woman replied, which caused a ripple of guffaws around the room.

'Take no notice of Tessie, Kate,' Angela said. 'They're all man-haters here, always making dirty cracks about them and saying that men think of nothing but sex.'

'It's true,' screeched Tessie. 'Men think of nowt but sex.'

'There's only one way to stop a man from wanting sex all the time,' Brigid shrieked.

'Well, clever clogs, and what's that?' Tessie roared.

'Marry him!' Brigid shouted.

'You're talking rubbish,' said Angela. 'My boyfriend Jimmy treats me with great respect and puts me on a pedestal.'

'You know why he puts you on a pedestal,' Brigid leered. 'It's so he can look up your clothes.'

The women held their sides, cackling like a lot of hens.

'If my old man ever puts *me* on a pedestal,' bawled Tessie, 'it's so I can bloody well paint the ceiling.'

The rest of the morning continued along these lines – loud-mouthed banter and a great deal of leg-pulling. They were the happiest, and the bawdiest crowd I'd ever met. When they ran out of wisecracks, they broke out into melody, their repertoire including every popular song of the day: 'After the Ball', 'Down at the Old Bull and Bush', 'She's a Lassie From Lancashire', and 'Stop Your Ticklin', Jock'. Good innocent fun although this last song contained a number of verses which had me blushing to the roots because it wasn't 'ticklin'' that Jock was asked to stop. What would the upstairs people back in Macclesfield have said if they'd heard the singing in this place? I have to say that I preferred the honest atmosphere of the Westmacotts' mineral waterworks to the stuffiness of the Lamport-Smythes.

That first day at work, Angela, my bottle-washing companion, told me her life story: how she lived with her retired parents in Angel Meadow, had worked at Westmacott's for three years, and had a boyfriend named Jimmy Dixon who she was hoping to marry in the near future. Jimmy was a mechanic and had a good job at Henry Wallwork's on Red Bank. By the time Angela had finished, I felt I knew as much about her and her background as I did about my own family. Hilda was more reserved – the kind who did more listening than talking – and didn't say too much about herself. As for me, I kept my own counsel – there would be plenty of time for talking in the days ahead.

'I think maybe we're going to make a good team,' Angela said as the hooter sounded, signalling the end of my first day.

'I'm positive we're going to be a good team,' I answered.

'What makes you so sure?' Hilda asked.

'Because,' I said smilingly, 'you, Angela, are tall and dark – why, you could be half Italian – whilst you, Hilda, are petite, blue-eyed, fair-haired and could be Swedish or German. As for me, I'd say I'm somewhere in between the two of you – in age, height and even in my colouring 'cos my hair is auburn and my eyes green. That's my Irish origins, I suppose.'

'You're right about me being half Italian', said Angela. 'My full name is Angela Rocca and my father used to be an ice cream merchant before he retired.'

'And you're not far wrong about me, either,' added Hilda. 'My grandparents came from Germany many years ago and my full name is Hilda Muller though we're hoping to change the Muller to Miller by deed poll. So now we have an international team of workers – Italian, German and Irish.'

My route home took me down Oldham Road, past my Aunt Sarah's, and I developed the habit of calling on them after work. Mam was happy with her newly decorated room and she seemed to have taken on a new lease of life. There was only one problem and it was the usual one – money!

'You've been kind to us, Kate,' she said one evening, 'but we can't keep taking your hard-earned cash. I'll have to go back to my job in the bagging factory soon and I'm dreading it. The thought of it sends shivers down my spine. There was so much dust and fluff in the air, you could hardly breathe. Sometimes I used to think I was going to choke. Your Aunt Sarah finds it the same.'

'I know how much you hate it, Mam, but if we're going to get Cissie and Danny home, we'll have to find a house to rent, and that takes money. They're under the Guardians till they're eighteen and they won't release them unless the place where they're going to stay has been passed by their inspectors.'

'I know that, Kate. We'll have to get a few bob together but I'm not even sure the bagging factory will want me back 'cos I had so much time off when I was pregnant. What I need is a job in the fresh air.'

'Somehow, Mam, I can't see you as a bricklayer,' I joked, 'or even as a labourer.'

'Don't talk daft, Kate. No, I'm thinking more of a job on a market stall, selling things.'

'What sort of things, Mam? What have we got to sell?'

'I dunno. Ornaments, hardware, second-hand clothes – stuff like that.'

Suddenly a thought struck me.

'Mam,' I exclaimed. 'I'm about to be brilliant.'

'Again?' She laughed. 'What's the brainwave this time?'

'When I worked in Macclesfield, the daughter of the house, Miss Emma, opened up a charity shop selling second-hand clothes and it made a small fortune. We could do something similar here.' I said nothing about the few items of clothing I'd nabbed.

'You've lost me, Kate. How would it work, this second-hand shop?'

I became keyed up as the idea began to take shape in my mind.

'You'll need capital. I can help you there. I could draw out some of my savings to get you started. We could bring in Aunt Sarah, if she's interested. That is, if she's forgiven me for insulting her by offering her money.'

'Of course she's forgiven you, Kate. She was a bit touchy that day as Barney had not been very well. Sarah will do anything to get out of that terrible bagging factory. I'm sure she'd take a chance.'

'As I see it,' I said, warming to my subject, 'you would need to go round the big houses in the posh districts and ask for their cast-offs. You wouldn't believe what rich people throw out. They're always changing their clothes to keep up with the latest fashions and they often give their cast-offs to their servants.'

'Wait a minute, Kate,' Mam said, her imagination now roused. 'I must bring Sarah into this.'

Sarah joined us and though she was a bit doubtful at first, she was soon caught up in the excitement.

'But the servants won't give their clothes away,' she objected. 'We'd have to offer them something in exchange.'

'We talk to the housekeeper or the house steward. They're always ready to do a deal, believe me. When Mam and I were shopping for crockery at Shufflebotham's on Rochdale Road, I noticed some beautiful china tea sets going at reasonable prices. I'm sure if you bought in quantity, you could get them at wholesale. You could also offer pot plants in exchange – aspidistras, cactuses, and so on. They're all the rage. We could offer these to the servants who would then approach their employers for their cast-offs. I know how the minds of these servants work. If we printed handbills and stuffed them in letter boxes, we're bound to get a response. It'll work, I'm sure of it.'

Once I'd stimulated the imagination of Mam and Aunt Sarah, there was no stopping them.

'What about selling the second-hand clothes?' Mam said. 'We'd need a stall on a market, say Tib Street.'

'I think we can do better than that,' I replied. 'What about renting a shop on Oldham Road? On the way to work, I've seen one to let not far from Westmacott's. If we opened one there, we'd attract the women from the factories and mills from around the district.'

'Let's do it!' Sarah said. 'I tell you, the idea of leaving that bagging factory fills me with joy. All my prayers answered. Why, we'd be our own bosses. We could choose our own hours. I'd be able to spend more time with Barney and look after him better.'

'Perfect,' Mam agreed. 'And if I were to leave the baby with you, Sarah, I could do the buying in the morning and you could do the selling at dinnertimes and in the evenings when the workers have finished their shifts.'

'We'd be glad to look after the baby and young Eddie as well,' Sarah said. 'Uncle Barney loves children and it'll give him an interest in life.'

For a brief moment I had visions of Barney coughing and spluttering over the two young ones but I dismissed it as unworthy.

'We're getting so carried away, Celia,' Sarah continued looking at Mam, 'we're forgetting to ask Kate what part she wants to play. Maybe she'd like to do the buying 'cos after all she'll be financing the operation. And there's the small matter of how we pay her back.'

'No need to worry about that. If this business is a

success and you make it work, that's enough reward for me. As for my own job, I'm happy washing bottles at Westmacott's as I've made lots of friends there. Besides, I think one of us should earn a regular wage in case anything should go wrong.'

'Don't talk like that, Kate,' they chorused. 'What could go wrong?'

That was the day Mam and Aunt Sarah changed their prospects. I drew out ten pounds from my savings and on Saturday afternoon the three of us, along with the baby and young Eddie, visited Shufflebotham's and chose a selection of beautiful tea sets in attractive packages.

'Sprats to catch mackerel,' Aunt Sarah remarked.

We were in business.

'It'll never work,' said Frank McGuinness when he heard about it.

He was wrong. The business did work. Pretty soon, Mam and Sarah were getting postcards from lots of people offering second-hand clothes and asking them to call. Mam showed a flair for buying good quality items from the toffs – dresses, silk underwear, men's suits and overcoats, and there was a steady demand for shoes for both sexes. Within six months, they were building up their own capital and the idea of finding a house to rent was definitely on the cards. Even Frank McGuinness was optimistic.

'We must keep our eyes peeled for suitable accommodation,' he said to me one day.

When I heard him say this, deep down I had a vague feeling of unease, even dismay, for I hadn't seen him as part of the overall plan. Besides, on one or two occasions, I'd found him, Mam and Aunt Sarah supping up at the Land o' Cakes when I'd visited after work.

'A business meeting,' they said. 'Planning our strategy for tomorrow.'

Huh!

The baby had been left with my consumptive Uncle Barney and they'd given our poor Eddie a packet of Smith's crisps to keep him quiet. He looked lost.

I pushed any niggling thoughts I had to the back of my mind. Everything, I told myself, would work out fine once we were back together again.

Around this time, we had a visit from Danny. He was now seventeen and was living in lodgings in Collyhurst. He was still under supervision by the Guardians but they'd allowed him to take a job as a carpenter. What a handsome young man he'd turned out to be. Tall, dark-haired and with those laughing blue eyes that reminded me of Dad.

'I'm hoping to join the Territorial Army when I'm eighteen,' he told us. 'I loved playing in the cadet band at Swinton, so it's the soldier's life for me. Meanwhile I'd love to have a room in the family house if we can swing it. My digs are OK but it's not the same as having your own home.'

'When you think about it,' I said, 'it makes sense for all of us to get back together. Here I am paying rent for a furnished room, so's Danny, and so's Mam, and Cissie is still in Swinton. Surely it'd be cheaper all round if we rented our own house. Provided we can find one, of course.'

We swung into action and began scouring the district for a suitable place. There were scores of houses of the two-up, two-down variety but we were looking for something bigger. If the Guardians were going to inspect it before releasing Cissie, it would have to have at least three bedrooms.

It was Angela's Jimmy who found it for us, or to be more precise, his uncle, a train driver with the LMS. The railway company had a few houses to rent and it was one of these that Jimmy's uncle earmarked for us. Number 5 Angel Meadow, overlooking St Michael's burial ground and opposite a goods yard. Angel Meadow. What a beautiful name! But many of the streets in the district had names equally beautiful: Blossom Street, Primrose Court, Hendham Vale, Red Bank. All slums. The people who named these streets either never visited them or had a sick sense of humour.

The house was exactly what we were looking for. It had three bedrooms, a parlour, a living room, a scullery, a nice big yard with our own lavatory. The LMS required references from an employer and for a while we thought we had a problem because Mam worked for herself and couldn't ask for one from the bagging factory where her reputation had not been so good. It was left to me to get the reference from Mr Dowd and I felt embarrassed approaching him as I had been working there only six months.

'A reference already, Kate?' he said, looking up from his desk in the office. 'Surely you're not leaving us so soon?'

'No, it's not that, Mr Dowd. We're hoping to rent a house so's the family can live under one roof.'

'No problem, Kate. I've been happy with your work and, more important, the way you get on with your fellow workers. I'll see the reference is typed and signed before you leave tonight.'

Happily, you might even say triumphantly, I carried the document home to Mam that night. She wasn't in when I got there. She was in the pub as usual with Sarah and the McGuinness man, planning their strategy. I was getting more and more worried about these so-called planning sessions. They were becoming a habit.

Chapter Twenty-Two

The work at Westmacott's was hard and the hours were long but I got used to the routine. Angela and Hilda became close friends and although we joined in the community singing and laughed with the others at the rude jokes and catty remarks, we didn't take an active part. We preferred quiet conversation amongst ourselves and we didn't go in for rowdy behaviour. Angela lived with her parents and two younger sisters in George Leigh Street opposite St Michael's Church. Hilda lived with her parents, grandparents, and her younger brother, Eric, in their pork butcher's shop on Dantzig Street. Her dad was also a bird fancier and bred racing pigeons in his backyard loft, she told us. Angela and I said we hoped he didn't use the birds as reserve for whenever meat was in short supply.

'It's strange what some of our menfolk do for a hobby,' I remarked. 'My Uncle Barney keeps rabbits and my Aunt Sarah threatens to use them for rabbit stew.'

'And I have an uncle who breeds whippets,' Angela said. 'They've never won anything but so far no one's talked about eating them. But you never know.'

Once or twice, we met Angela's boyfriend, Jimmy, when he collected her after work. He was certainly handsome but we found him to be a bluff and outspoken character. A true northerner who could always be relied on to tell you in a loud voice just what he thought, whether it embarrassed you or not. But Angela loved him, and since we liked Angela, we had to like him as well.

One evening Jimmy advised Hilda to wear built-up shoes, pile her hair up high, and try stretching exercises so she could look taller. He told me my eyebrows were too thick and I should have them plucked.

'Thanks very much,' I said and, not to be outdone, retorted, 'and *you* should find yourself a decent barber and not one who uses a basin to style your hair.'

'That's nothing,' Angela said when I reported the conversation to her. 'He once asked me if I'd got my coat off a rag-and-bone man's handcart. The cheeky bugger. But I love him 'cos he has no airs and graces, never beats about the bush, and always says what he thinks.'

Most nights when we finished the day's stint, we walked arm in arm down Oldham Road, laughing and talking, happy to be in each other's company. Though Angela reserved the weekends for Jimmy, that didn't mean us three couldn't go out occasionally during the week for a quiet drink and a visit to Queen's Park Hippodrome. We left the organisation to Angela as she seemed to know her way around. My only problem was my landlady who was a stickler for keeping early hours. Once or twice I'd persuaded her to extend my curfew to half past ten but I was only too glad when, in the spring of 1907, we moved into our new house.

First, we visited the railway office at Red Bank, handed over the reference and four weeks' rent in advance. In exchange we were given the key to the front door. We were in seventh heaven and we carried that key as if it would open the door to paradise.

I drew out the last few pounds from my savings and with Mam's profits from the business, we visited a second-hand furniture shop on Rochdale Road and bought some furniture for the bedrooms: three single beds, a couple of wardrobes, along with flock mattresses, pillows and bedding. One bedroom was to be for Danny and Eddie, another for Cissie and me, and the third for Mam. I wanted to put the cot and a single bed in Mam's room but she insisted on a double bed 'in case Frank stays over'. That was something I didn't want to hear but I was so happy at the prospect of moving in, I brushed the thought from my mind. We even acquired a little kitten, Flossie, from a neighbour across the street. Our home was complete.

That same day Mam flitted her stuff across and I collected my few bits and pieces from my lodgings.

'You've been a good tenant,' Mrs Hudson told me when I said goodbye. 'If ever you want to come back, you'll be most welcome.'

'Why, thank you, Mrs Hudson. And you've been a good landlady. If ever I want to come back, I'll remember your words.'

After the hustle and bustle of working in the Macclesfield household, I'd found life at Mrs Hudson's dull and restrictive. Not only because of the curfew she'd imposed but also because of the quietness, the solitude and the fact that there was, as we say in Lancashire, 'nowt to do'. I'd ended up counting the blobs on the wallpaper for a bit of excitement.

A little later, Danny arrived carrying his trunk on his shoulder. He'd taken up smoking a meerschaum pipe and it gave off a lovely smell when he took a puff.

'That's the St Bruno tobacco,' he told me. 'But I took up the pipe 'cos people treat you seriously. It makes a man look intelligent and wise.'

I could see my long-cherished dream coming true at last. As for Eddie, he was like a young pup, almost wetting himself with excitement as he dashed from room to room, asking over and over again, 'Is this ours? Really ours? Can I bring my pals to play in the yard?'

'Yes, yes – it's all ours! Course you can bring your pals,' we called, our bliss matching his. And when Eddie grasped that his big brother Danny was back and they were to share a room, his delight knew no bounds.

Next, we had a visit from the Guardians. They came and inspected every nook and cranny, every room, the back yard, the lavatory, the bedrooms, the kitchen. They checked the place for vermin – mice, rats, bugs, fleas. The house passed with flying colours. And so it ought 'cos Mam and me had spent a couple of days scrubbing the place out from top to bottom.

The following week, Cissie came home. We hugged and hugged and we cried a lot for we'd all been through so much since we were last together as a family. That night, watched by our little family kitten, I addressed my glass swan which had place of honour on the mantelpiece next to the boat-shaped teapot.

'Well, swan,' I said, 'we've been through some rough times together, you and I, but here we are in the place where we belong. Home!' I could swear I saw the swan smile. The kitten was looking at me curiously.

'I must be going mad, Flossie,' I said. 'What am I doing? Talking to a glass swan!'

This period was one of the happiest in my life. Everybody seemed content with the way things were going. Cissie helped Mam and Aunt Sarah with the clothing business, Danny went to his carpentry job in Newtown, Eddie was settled in at St Michael's School. As for me, I'd become an old hand at Westmacott's. I was good at my job, or so Declan assured me. Not that the job required much skill.

I had the respect of the other women, and the close friendship of Hilda and Angela. We continued to go out occasionally during the week but now I didn't need to worry about being told off by a landlady for coming back late. Our little weekday excursions were innocent enough – a shandy maybe in the Bonnie Gray or a visit to a fairground when there was one in town. One week, though, it was different.

'I've got a surprise for the two of you,' Angela announced one bright morning. 'I won't tell you what it is or it would spoil it. I'll just say that it will cost you threepence each. I'll call for you this evening at seven o'clock. So make sure you're wearing your best bib and tucker. We're going to town.'

Promptly at seven, Angela and Hilda called at Angel Meadow. I was ready – had been for half an hour – and wondering what she'd organised. Angela was always thinking up something new. I introduced my friends to the rest of the family and we were ready to go. Before we set off I couldn't help noticing the way Danny and Hilda looked at each other. Uh-oh, I thought. Cupid is around firing his arrows.

We took the electric tram into Piccadilly and walked to Oxford Street from there. Our destination? St James's Theatre. There was a massive placard advertising the night's programme: FOR ONE WEEK ONLY! STRAIGHT FROM THE BIOGRAPH, LONDON! MOVING PICTURES WITH SOUND EFFECTS!

'Oh, is that the surprise?' I said, disappointed. 'We've already seen moving pictures at the fairground. They were smudgy, jerky pictures of people walking up and down and a bunch of kids jumping about. Amazing but boring. Each picture was about one minute long. Cost tuppence. Daylight robbery, if you ask me.'

'No, happy Harriet,' laughed Angela. 'This is not the same as the freak show at the fairground. It's different, as you'll see.'

'It *looks* different,' said Hilda encouragingly. 'For a start, there are films with titles and the programme is forty minutes. And what do they mean by sound effects?'

Next to the silver screen the effects man sat at a table with two half-coconut shells for horses, a piece of sand-paper for water, and a box filled with pebbles for marching soldiers, and many other ingenious devices. His farmyard imitations supplied the animal noises whilst a heavily built lady provided atmospheric music on a battered piano.

There were five short films each telling a different story. The first one was called *Watering the Gardener* and showed how one man accidentally stood on the hosepipe whilst the gardener looked down the nozzle to see why there was no water. When the man stepped off the pipe, the gardener got it in the face. This short act brought gales of laughter from the audience and had them in stitches. There followed a series of films by a Cecil Hepworth. One entitled *Rescued by Rover* about how a dog rescued a baby had everyone hanging onto their seats, with the audience cheering, hissing and booing in all the right places. Last, there was a crime film entitled *The Life of Charles Peace*, about a murderer in Sheffield. I went through every emotion that night – laughter, joy, excitement, fear, and horror.

'What a wonderful evening and isn't it marvellous what they can do nowadays?' I remarked to my companions as we came out into a Manchester drizzle and to sober reality.

And what was waiting for me at home was reality all right but not the sober kind.

As I stepped off the tram at the top of Angel Meadow, I could already hear the human cats' chorus coming from Number 5. The voice of Frank McGuinness bawling out

'*Ta-ra-ra Boom de-Ay*' was louder than all the rest. I could hear baby John crying his heart out upstairs.

I turned the key in the front door and went into the living room. They were all there – Mam, Aunt Sarah, Frank McGuinness and half a dozen hangers-on from the Land o' Cakes. A large pitcher of beer and bottles of whisky and brandy stood on the table. Judging by the racket they were making, they'd been guzzling for a few hours. And there was that sickly sweet smell of alcohol that I forever associated with the McTavish family and the workhouse. The slightest whiff of whisky was enough to bring back the terrifying memory of the day Old Jock was poised to give Danny the flogging of his life.

'Hey up!' Frank bawled. 'Here she comes, our little Katie. Come and give us a kiss, sweetheart.'

'She's a love, is our Kate,' Mam said thickly. 'Come and have a drink with us, love.'

The scene filled me with dismay. Was this what I'd been making the effort for? Was this the dream I'd carried around in my head all those years? I ignored Frank's slobbering invitation and addressed Mam and Aunt Sarah.

'Can't you hear baby John crying upstairs?' I said.

'Ah, he'll be all right,' Mam said. 'Don't be so bloody miserable, Kate. Come and have a drink.'

'No, thanks, Mam. Not for me.'

'Get down from your high horse, Kate,' Mam drooled. 'There's nothing wrong with a little drink. We're only having a bit o' enjoyment. God knows we deserve that after all our work walking round Didsbury and Fallowfield.'

'I agree, Mam. Nothing wrong with a drink – I have one myself occasionally. But I hate heavy boozing and drunkenness, like this tonight. Besides, you're keeping half the district awake. And when people are in their cups, they don't know what they're doing.'

'We're not like that,' Sarah said, refilling her glass from the jug.

'Look, Aunt Sarah,' I said, 'this place smells like a brewery. Is this what you're going to spend your profits on – jugging it every night?'

Dropping the idea of greeting me with kisses, Frank McGuinness now changed tack. 'Listen you,' he spluttered, 'your mother can do as she bloody well likes in her own house. It's got bugger all to do with you. Who do you think you are, barging your way in and spoiling our party?'

'Look, Frank,' I exploded, 'your son's screaming upstairs while you're boozing down here. Why don't you push off and take your sozzled mates with you so Mam can attend to the baby.'

'I think we'd better be on our way, Celia,' one of the old hags in the party wheezed. 'We'll not stop where we're not wanted.'

The party began to break up and drift towards the front door.

'If things go on like this,' I continued, 'I'm tempted to return to my lodgings. At least there was peace and quiet there.'

'Ah, let the bugger go,' Frank McGuinness barked at Mam. 'She's brought nothing but misery since she came back from Macclesfield. She doesn't realise that you've got a new family now. Tell her the good news, Celia, about the baby.'

I felt the hair on my head stand up.

'I'm expecting again,' Mam mumbled. 'Frank and me are going to have another.'

The news hit me like a thump in the chest. Things were not going according to plan, at least not to *my* plan.

I went up to my room and found Cissie weeping.

'They've been at it since you went off with your friends,'

she said through her tears. 'Singing, shouting, swearing, dancing. I couldn't get to sleep and I'm so weary. My feet have been killing me. I must've walked miles with Mam today.'

We were joined by Eddie.

'I can't sleep,' he sobbed, 'because of the noise. It keeps wakening young John up in the next room and I have to go in and see to him.'

'How long has this been going on?' I asked.

'A long, long time,' Eddie replied. 'Not only tonight but all the time you were working in Macclesfield, Kate. I wish Frank McGuinness would go away.'

You're not the only one, I thought. I said nothing about the latest development which I hadn't fully absorbed myself. They'd find out in time.

Later, Danny came home and in hushed tones in the little bedroom the four of us discussed the situation.

'I gave up my lodgings and came home hoping for the best,' said Danny, 'but now I'm not so sure. I still have plans to join the Territorial Army. Probably the Manchester Regiment. There's always demand for men to join as bandsmen.'

'I feel the same,' Cissie said. 'I miss my friends and the teachers at Swinton. I think I'd like to get a job in service like you, Kate. Miss Morrell said I'd make a good under-parlour maid.'

Eddie felt he had to join in. 'I'd like to be a bandsman like Danny,' he said, 'if I could get a place in Swinton. Do you think they'd have me, Kate?'

'Of course, they would,' I said, 'but let's not rush things. I've spent half my life planning for this time and I don't want to throw it away so easily. Let's wait and see if there are any more of these binges and communal singing sessions in the living room. If there are, then we'll have to act.'

On that note, we said our goodnights. Before we settled down to sleep, Danny popped back for a moment.

'One last thing, Kate, before we turn in.' He grinned. 'What about that gorgeous girl you introduced me to? I'd love to get to know her better.'

'You mean Hilda,' I answered with a smile. 'I'll see what I can do.' My heart wasn't in the smile. I was still reeling from the shock of the news that had been dumped in my lap.

When things had gone quiet, I lay staring at the ceiling, my mind working overtime. The night's clash had been upsetting enough but Mam's announcement had knocked me for six. To me, it was becoming obvious that her first family had been relegated to second place. Had my dreams been in vain? Had I been kidding myself all this time with the crazy notion of re-creating the past? Living in a fool's paradise? That night, the wool had well and truly fallen from my eyes. Dad had died in 1897 and there was no way I could bring him or that idyllic family life back. The past was dead and gone; maybe that's where I should have left it.

Next morning, I could think of nothing but yesterday and as I crossed Oldham Road on my way to work, I was almost knocked down by a big dray horse and cart. I hardly noticed the young man who had greeted me each morning with a cheery 'Good morning. Sh-sh-should be a fine day, today.' I nodded to him absent-mindedly. He was not my type. The fortune-teller Susie and I had visited in a mad moment in Macclesfield had told me I would meet a tall, dark, handsome man. This man was only of medium build and when he raised his cap to greet me, I noticed his hair was light brown. Besides that, he wasn't handsome and there was that nervous stutter. Nice-looking maybe, but that was all. I had to admit, though, that he had a lovely, friendly smile.

At work, I joined my two friends and soon we were busy washing bottles. The talk was mainly about the cinema and the film *Rescued by Rover*.

'Did you notice the filthy attic where the young kid-napped kid was kept and the lovely home where he lived with his mam and dad?' Angela gushed.

'Yes,' said Hilda, equally enthusiastic. 'And the way the Gypsy was swigging from a bottle of gin. But I loved best the way the dog dashed through the streets. I don't know how they managed to get the camera to follow it so fast.'

'Marvellous,' Angela said. 'And I read in the *Evening News* that they produced the film for just over seven pounds.'

'Fantastic,' said Hilda. 'What did you think of it, Kate?'

'It was all right, I suppose,' I replied. My brain was occupied with other matters.

'Cheer up, Kate,' said Angela. 'It might never happen. Never trouble trouble till trouble troubles you.'

I gave my two friends a thin smile. 'Sorry, Angela,' I said. 'I've got things on my mind.'

'What sort of things?'

'Family things.'

'You're too serious about your family,' Angela told me. 'You worry too much. But we're friends here, Kate, and so you can confide in us.'

'It's the heavy drinking that's going on in our house,' I said. 'I know only too well from my workhouse days what terrible things booze can do. I've come to hate the smell of the stuff, especially whisky.'

'I'm sure your family will be all right,' Angela assured me.

Putting on a brave face, I said, 'Talking of family, Hilda. I think you've made a conquest. My brother Danny has taken a shine to you. He wants to know if he could meet you some time.'

Hilda's face lit up. 'I'd love to, Kate. Danny looks like a real gentleman.'

'Not only that,' laughed Angela. 'He's young, handsome and available. Look, I don't want to butt in here but why don't we organise a little party on Friday – pay day? We could book seats at the Grand. I hear there's a wonderful variety bill this week. The usual turns plus a big star – Harry Lauder. What about it, Kate?'

'Not for me, thank you, Angela,' I said. 'I'd be the odd one out. Five people going out together would seem a bit strange, to say the least. And anyway, I'm not in the mood, as I said before.'

Angela was insistent. 'You need cheering up, Kate, and a visit to the Grand is what the doctor ordered. I'll ask Jimmy if he knows anyone suitable, preferably a tall dark stranger.'

'Going out with an unknown man? You must think I'm desperate. Not for me, thank you, Angela.'

'We'll wait and see,' said Angela, smiling mysteriously.

The usual banter from the crowd left me just as cold.

'My old man's idea of helping with the housework,' Brigid announced to everyone, 'is to shift his feet when I want to sweep under his chair.'

'You're lucky,' yelled Tessie. 'Mine won't even move his feet except when he makes tracks for the boozer.'

I was not in the mood to join in. It was the same when the community chorusing started up. My thoughts were dark and depressing. I could see our little family breaking up – the family that I'd so painstakingly got together.

When I got home that night, Mam had gone to the pub for one of her business conferences and so I cooked the tea for the rest of the family. The evening passed quietly and there was no repeat of the drunken orgy. Mam came home with Frank McGuinness and later they went quietly to bed. Perhaps, I thought, they've taken my words to heart and decided to calm down.

On my way to work next day, the same man with the sandy-coloured hair passed me with the usual sunny smile. This time he managed to say a little more than he had on previous occasions.

'Good morning. A bit of sun-sh-shine at last, eh!'

'Good morning,' I replied. 'Yes, it looks promising, doesn't it?'

Friendly enough but not exactly a dazzling conversation. My personal weather man, I said to myself. If I ever want a weather forecast, I'll know who to ask.

When I went into the bottle-sluicing room, Angela and Hilda were already there.

'Great news, Kate,' Angela announced. 'I've booked a box for the second house at the Grand, Friday night.'

'A box! You must be mad or made of money,' I exclaimed.

'If there's going to be six of us, it's quite cheap. And if we go Dutch, it won't break the pockets of the men either.'

'I hope you're not including me in the six,' I said. 'I don't fancy the idea of going out with a bloke I've never met. He could be anyone, for all I know. Charlie Peace or even Jack the Ripper.'

'We're going out as a group,' Hilda said. 'I can't see any problem. Why not take a chance?'

'That's right, Kate,' Angela added. 'Take a chance! You might meet Charlie Peace but then again, he might be the man of your dreams. Nothing ventured, nothing gained.'

At home that night, I broached the matter with Danny. Unlike me, he didn't need to be asked twice.

'Thanks, Kate, for fixing it up for me. You're a great sister.'

'Don't thank me,' I said. 'Angela is the one to thank – she's a born organiser. At least you know who you're going with but she's trying to persuade me to go in the company of some mysterious friend of a friend. God knows who it is and what he's like.'

'I'm sure Angela wouldn't set you up with a rough, undesirable type,' he said. 'Why not come along and enjoy yourself? You take life too seriously.'

Next day, Angela and Hilda kept at me on the same subject for so long that for the sake of peace I reluctantly agreed. I hoped the peace was not of the Charlie kind.

'Just for this one night,' I insisted, 'and I hope the unknown gentleman, whoever he is, is aware of that.'

When Friday came, my two partners talked about nothing else – the show we were to see, the men we were going with, the dresses we were to wear. The prospect even brought the normally quiet Hilda out of her shell.

'I've got something wonderful to wear for this special occasion,' she gushed. 'My old grandma has given me a hat she once wore at an opera in Berlin. She preserved it in mothballs all these years. It's still like new. It does something for me – makes me look taller. Wait till I show you.'

At the dinner break, Hilda produced Grandma's gift from a battered leather hat box she'd humped to work that morning. The hat was one that featured an imitation bunch of cherries on the top and it was hard to tell the front from the back. It was a disaster. Proudly Hilda arranged the thing on her head. It made her look like something from a costermonger's barrow.

'Well, what do you think?' she asked, surveying our expressions anxiously.

'You're right, it does do something for you,' I exclaimed, turning to Angela for support.

'Yes, you'll certainly cause a stir in the theatre,' Angela said, smiling fixedly but taking great care to avoid my eye.

When Hilda took the hat box back to the staff cloakroom, we could no longer hold back the laughter. It burst forth like a dam breaking its banks and we couldn't resist a couple of choruses of 'Where did you get that hat?'

'What are we going to do?' I giggled. 'She can't go to the theatre wearing that monstrosity. But how are we going to tell her? She'll be so hurt – it's her grandma's pride and joy.'

'*We* mustn't be the ones to tell her,' Angela chortled. 'If she turns up in that hat tonight, Jimmy'll tell her and no mistake. She'll take it from him as she knows how blunt he can be.'

We thought the hooter would never go that night and when it finally did at six o'clock, we were halfway down Oldham Road before the sound had died away.

When I got home, I examined my wardrobe. What to wear? I remembered those wonderful garments I'd acquired at the Macclesfield charity shop. It was now that they would come into their own.

Watched by Cissie, I opened up the wardrobe and took out my purloined outfit – the long black velvet skirt and the cream silk blouse with the high neck, to which I fastened the cameo brooch given me by Gran'ma on my eighteenth birthday – thank God she hadn't given me one of her hats. Daringly, I applied a little face powder, a touch of rouge, a smidgen of lipstick, and finally I sprayed myself with the latest perfume, 4711. I wondered if the drop earrings might be overdoing it but I thought, in for a penny, and I put them on. I examined myself in the long mirror and saw a strange glamorous girl looking back at me – one wearing stolen clothes.

'Well, what do you think, Cissie? Will I do?'

'You'll do, Kate,' she said quietly.

Finally, I put on the fur-collared coat, my cream kid gloves with the pearl buttons and I was ready. The last touch was my evening bag containing a hanky, a powder compact, and a few coins for the tram.

I met Danny waiting on the landing outside the bedroom. He greeted me with a wolf whistle.

'Kate!' he exclaimed. 'You look like one of them debutantes you see in magazines.'

I should, I thought, as these garments once belonged to one.

'Why, thank you, Danny. You look pretty good yourself.'

Danny was wearing his best Sunday suit and a white shirt with a starched collar.

We called out goodnight to Mam in the kitchen and to Cissie and Eddie who were leaning over the upstairs banister.

'Shall we go, Lady Catherine?' Danny grinned and offered his arm.

The second house of the variety was due to begin at eight fifteen and we'd arranged to meet at quarter to eight outside the Grand, intending to have a quick drink before the show. Just after seven, Danny and I caught the tram to Piccadilly, walked down Mosley Street to Peter Street, and arrived at the theatre just on time. Angela and Jimmy were already waiting with warm, welcoming smiles. There were greetings all round with much shaking of hands but I could see no sign of my blind date, nor of Hilda. I looked around anxiously, expecting to see a one-eyed hunchback with a twisted mouth.

'What's that funny smell?' Jimmy grinned, looking straight at me. 'Has someone been using turps?'

'He's referring to your perfume, Kate,' said Angela. 'The

cheeky devil! It's his way of paying you a compliment.'

'Glad you like it, Jimmy,' I said.

Angela and I exchanged looks. The cracks about my perfume confirmed our opinion that we could rely on Jimmy to tell Hilda about the 'you know what'.

A few minutes later, Hilda arrived wearing *the hat*.

'Now for the fireworks,' Angela whispered to me.

'What a beautiful hat!' bellowed Jimmy when he saw her. 'It makes you look taller and definitely becomes you. And I love those cherry things on the top.'

Hilda flushed with pleasure, or so we thought. How wrong Angela and I had been about Jimmy's reaction! Hilda excused herself and went off to the ladies, no doubt to make last-minute adjustments to her hideous headgear. She was back in two minutes minus the hat.

'If Jimmy likes it,' she said to us in an aside, 'there must be something wrong with it.'

God works in mysterious ways.

'If you're looking for your young man, Kate,' Jimmy said, 'Tommy's gone to buy cigarettes and a programme. Don't worry, he'll be back – that is, if he hasn't developed a case of nerves at the last minute and done a bunk.'

Then I saw him. He was smoking a cigarette and he had a programme in his hand.

'But I already know him!' I exclaimed. 'I see him every morning. He's my weather man!'

'The real name of your weather man,' Jimmy laughed, 'is Tommy Hopkins and he's been a good friend of mine since we were at St Patrick's School together. Tommy, meet Kate.'

We shook hands. His grip was warm and reassuring.

'I hope you're not too disappointed to find I'm to be your partner for the evening,' he said with a smile.

'I should bloody well hope not,' said Jimmy, grinning at

me. 'Once Tommy knew that Angela was a friend of yours, he's not stopped pestering for an introduction. Anyway, let's not stand outside here in the cold, we're wasting good drinking time. Let's go in and have one at the bar.'

As we went inside, Tommy held the door for everyone. At least he has good manners, I thought.

This was my first visit to a theatre and there was something about it that I found strangely exciting. The sights, the sounds, and the smells combined to produce a special atmosphere. Perhaps it was the manager in his magnificent white tie and tails presiding over the well-dressed crowd thronging the foyer, or the smell of cigars merging with the heady perfumes of the ladies, or the bright lights and the colourful placards in the glass cases displaying past performances, or the thick plush carpets and the smart military uniform of the commissionaire. Maybe it was simply the sense of anticipation about the show we were going to see. But how I loved the gaslight glow in the foyer – back at home we still had oil lamps and candles – for it seemed to cast a soft light on the people's faces, giving them a gentle, friendly look.

The bar was on the first floor, and as we climbed the staircase my eyes took in the signs pointing the way to the different seats of the theatre – the gallery, the balcony, the stalls and one set of seats with a foreign-looking name – the fauteuils. And *we* had tickets for the poshest of them all – a private box. The saloon was crowded when we got there but we managed to find a table and the men went to the counter for the drinks – beer for them and port and lemon for us ladies.

'Well, what do you think of him, Kate?' Angela suddenly asked. 'Jimmy tells me that Tommy's been going out of his way each day to pass you on the road to say good morning. He must be pretty keen.'

'Too early to tell,' I said. 'He's good-looking, got nice eyes and he's well-mannered, I'll say that for him.'

'I think the three of 'em are good-looking,' Hilda said, 'and I'm so glad they don't have whiskers, moustaches or beards that hide their features. I think all that hair on a man's face makes him look ugly and a bit like an ape.'

'It's the latest fashion for young men to be clean-shaven,' Angela told us. 'Didn't you know that? Ever since they brought out that new safety razor thing to replace the old cut-throat.' Angela was well-informed about men. I suppose that was because she'd been going out with Jimmy a long time.

We turned our attention to the signed pictures of star artistes which decorated the walls, until the men came back with the drinks.

'Should be a good show tonight,' said Jimmy. 'Not only because of the top of the bill but for some of the other smaller acts as well.'

We finished our drinks and went into the auditorium. I think this was the first time any of us had had seats in a box because we were taken aback by how close we were to the stage.

'I don't know about coming to *see* a sh-show,' laughed Tommy. 'I think we're going to be *in* it!'

The safety curtain was down and we spent the first ten minutes reading the advertisements for the best places to eat, the best pubs to drink, and the best Turkish cigarettes to smoke – Abdullah of course. The murmur of the audience gradually quietened down when the musicians began filing through the door at the back of the orchestra stalls and started switching on their little lights and trying out their instruments. As the safety curtain rose – oh so slowly – the sense of excitement and expectation rose with it. The spotlights lit up, cutting through the tobacco smoke and tinting it with an assortment of beautiful colours. The conductor appeared, bowed and smiled to the audience, tapped his baton on his stand, and the orchestra let rip with a series of rousing, cheerful tunes. The theatre was like a huge palace but to me it seemed warm, cosy, and intimate.

The show began with a series of minor acts – acrobats, performing dogs, trick cyclists, jugglers, conjurers, a comedian telling bawdy jokes and making rude noises, and one or two singers who warbled about their lost mothers and unfaithful sweethearts. None of them to my taste.

After the interval came the star we'd been waiting for.

Harry Lauder dressed in his kilt, his tam-o'-shanter bonnet and carrying his familiar twisted walking stick.

Before he sang, he made a small speech to introduce himself. A speech which brought waves of laughter from the audience.

'I've just come down frae Scotland. It's a long way, I can tell you. But who'd waste twelve and six on the train fare when I've got a good pair o' walking boots. They say we Jocks are mean wi' our money but it's no' true – we're just careful with it. Mind you, tak ma Uncle Donald – please! Now he *is* mean. Why, the other day, he accidentally broke a bottle of iodine. So he cut his ain finger just to use it.'

He broke into 'I love a lassie, a bonnie Highland lassie (as pure as the lily in the dell)' in his own inimitable style.

He paused for a moment to make a request. 'I want everyone to join in when we come to the chorus bit for it'll save my voice, you understand. And if you can save a Scotsman anything at all, it'll be much appreciated.'

The audience didn't need asking twice. They lifted the roof off.

Harry sang only three songs, interspersing them with his patter about his relatives back in Glasgow.

'My brother Angus came round the other day and asked if I believed in free speech. When I told him I did, he asked if he could use my telephone.'

One of his songs caused a private chuckle in our party. When he announced that he'd be singing 'Stop your ticklin' Jock', we ladies exchanged knowing glances and burst out laughing, which left our escorts wondering what we'd found so funny. Needless to say, we sang the official version with the rest of the audience.

Harry's act was short. Too short as far as I was concerned for I could have listened to him for hours. He finished with a typical request.

'I hope you'll tell your friends and family about me and ask them to come and see ma show. I'm not wastin' ma money advertisin'. I believe in word of mouth.'

He left the stage singing 'Just a Wee Deoch-an-Doris'.

When he'd gone, we shook our heads in wonder for we knew we'd watched a great professional at work.

'Pure genius!' exclaimed Tommy. 'But I'll bet he's not popular with his fellow Scotsmen with those stories of their meanness.'

Too soon my first variety came to an end. Tommy helped me on with my coat and it was back to reality.

Outside the theatre, we shook hands and said goodnight.

'That was one of the most wonderful evenings of my life,' I said to Angela. 'Thank you for arranging it. And thank you, Tommy,' I added, 'for escorting me and looking after me. I'll expect your weather report on Monday morning when you pass me on Oldham Road.'

He nodded and smiled. 'I'll have to make sure it's correct then.'

'We must do it again,' said Angela.

'Leave it with Angela and me,' Jimmy said. 'We'll book for next Friday.'

'That'll be great,' Tommy said warmly, 'but maybe this time ordinary seats so that we're not part of the show.'

Everyone laughed and we made our different ways home.

It was gone eleven o'clock when Danny and I reached Angel Meadow. Outside Number 5 we found a small crowd of tut-tutting women, their shawls wrapped tightly round them. We were not left long in doubt as to what they were tutting about. From the front parlour of our house came the most awful caterwauling, along with wild music played on an out-of-tune fiddle. Judging from the screams and yells of delight, it sounded as if Mam had organised a *ceilidh* in the front room. The racket could be heard several streets away and the front door had been left wide open for anyone from the street to walk in.

Above the din could be heard the booming voice of Frank McGuinness belting out yet another Boer War song from his bottomless repertoire.

'What-ho!' she cried
On Mafekin' night! On Mafekin' night!
What happened outside?
On Mafekin' night! On Mafekin' night!

'That bloody row,' whined one of the women, 'has kept my kids awake for the last two hours.'

'We should set the law on 'em,' said another.

'It's bringing the tone of the bloody district down,' added her husband. 'It's enough to waken the dead. Riffraff like them should be locked up.'

Danny and I sighed in resignation and exchanged

glances which said 'What a scene to come home to!'

'Right,' Danny said. 'We've got to put a stop to this.'

First port of call was to check on the young 'uns upstairs. There we found Cissie and Eddie both tearful and trembling with anxiety. The baby in the front bedroom was bawling his head off.

'What are we going to do, Kate?' Cissie complained. 'We can't stay in this house with this row going on every night.'

My hackles rose. 'We've got to do something, Danny,' I said.

We stormed downstairs.

Danny flung open the door of the front parlour and we found a dozen men and women lolling about and swilling beer from two large pitchers. Once again, there was that awful workhouse smell of whisky. In the midst of it all stood Frank bellowing out his song about Mafeking. They were all well and truly sloshed.

'Well, lookee who's here!' McGuinness yelled, pointing to Danny and me. 'Saint Catherine of Ancoats! And her sidekick the Prince of Collyhurst! The two miseries!'

I wondered what he'd have said if he'd known that I was standing there in clothes I'd pinched. Still, we had to do something to break up this boozing session for the sake of the neighbours and the kids.

'It's our Kate and Danny,' Mam slurred. 'Won't you join us in a little drinkie?'

'Not for me, thanks,' Danny snapped. 'And I think you lot have had enough.'

Beer was spilt on the new table cover and the peg rug, the vase lay broken on the hearthstone, glasses and half-eaten sandwiches were everywhere. And tragedy of tragedies, my glass swan lay on the hearth – in pieces!

I blew my top. I was blazing.

'Out! Out!' I shouted, pointing to all the hangers-on. 'All of you! You drunken slobs! Out of the house! Now!'

Drunk though they were, the crowd got the message and began to slink towards the door. I felt like Christ ordering the money-changers out of the temple.

'Don't you talk to us like that, Miss High Horse,' Frank gibbered.

'You've made this house into a boozer,' I yelled, 'and brought your sozzled rowdy cronies home to go on with your drinking. You've disturbed the peace of the district and I'm surprised you've not had the police round. Not only that, you've terrified the life out of the kids upstairs. But that's it! I've had enough!'

'Now, Kate,' Mam wheedled. 'No need to be nasty! These are our friends, come for a little party!'

'Party? Party!' I yelled. 'I'll show you party!' With that, I picked up one of the pitchers from the table, carried it to the scullery and poured the ale down the sink.

'You've no bloody right to pour good ale away like that,' Frank McGuinness barked. 'I've half a mind to give you one,' he added, raising his hand.

'You try that,' Danny said dangerously, 'and you'll have to deal with me first.'

Big though he was, McGuinness saw through his glazed eyes that Danny was bigger and meant business. He lowered his hand.

'Either *he* goes or *I* do,' I snapped. 'But there'll be no more jugging it here tonight.' I picked up the second pitcher, intending to give it the same treatment as the first.

'You'll not bloody well waste another jug of beer,' McGuinness shouted, taking my arm.

'Hands off my sister!' Danny said, grabbing McGuinness's lapels.

Mam now joined in and cracked a plate over my head.

The jug of beer fell from my hand. Beer ran over the floor and a trickle of blood down my forehead.

The blow from Mam sent me reeling and left me in a state of shock, not so much from the physical damage or the pain in my head but more from the idea that my own mother could be so violent towards me. The hurt wasn't to my head but to my heart.

'That's the last straw!' Mam bawled. 'You can bloody well sling your hook. Pack your bags and bugger off. We don't want you here!'

Though still dizzy from the blow, I could see it was time to bring matters to a head.

'Right, Mam, That is *it*! I've reached the end of my tether,' I cried. 'I'll pack my bags tomorrow.'

'The same goes for me,' Danny declared. 'Tomorrow, I'm off back to my digs. I don't want any more of this yelling and scrapping. Right now, I'm going to bed.' He turned to face Mam and Frank McGuinness. 'And thanks for ruining one of the happiest days of my life.'

Danny and I returned to calm the kids who'd witnessed the scene from the landing.

'What about us, Kate?' Cissie whimpered. 'If you and Danny are leaving, I don't want to stay.'

'Neither do I,' Eddie sobbed. 'I want to go with you, Kate.'

I tried to reassure them both. 'Leave it to me,' I said. 'I'll not desert you. I'll fix up something for you.'

I didn't sleep a wink that night. My mind was racing with plans for the future, not only for myself but for Cissie and Eddie as well. Next morning, I packed my suitcase and went downstairs.

I met Mam in the kitchen. She was seated at the table with her head in her hands. She looked crestfallen and for a moment I felt sorry for her and the nasty hand fate had dealt her since the death of my father. But my mind was made up.

'Look, Mam,' I said, 'maybe I went too far pouring your beer down the sink but I do hate drunkenness. I came back from Macclesfield and tried to get the family together again. But I was wrong. Things have moved on and you now have a second family to think of. It's obvious that things are not going to work out between us and it's best I leave. Danny feels the same and is going back to his old lodgings.'

'I'm sorry about last night,' she said plaintively. 'We got carried away drinking and all that. When I hit you with that plate, I didn't know what I was doing. I hope it's not a bad cut on your head.'

'It could be worse.' I grinned ruefully. 'Only a scratch – I've got a hard head. A dab of iodine soon fixed it.'

'I know the way you feel about things here living with a stepfather,' she continued. 'So I'm not going to ask you to stay 'cos I think you may be right about me having a new family to care for. I have a young baby and another on the way, and it's as much as I can cope with at the moment. Frank isn't as bad as you make out, he does care about me and his kids.'

Yes, I said to myself, about his *own* kids but not us Lallys.

'Will you be able to manage?' I asked.

'We should be all right,' she said. 'The business is doing pretty well and Frank has his war pension.'

I thought this might be a good time to raise the matter of Cissie and Eddie but I wasn't sure how she would take my suggestion. She might think I was interfering. I had to tread carefully. I didn't want to stir up fresh trouble.

'I think Cissie and Eddie might also be better off,' I began tentatively, 'if they made a new start.'

Mam's reaction surprised me.

'They've been on my mind as well,' she said slowly. 'I don't think they're happy here with Frank and our new family. Do you have any ideas?'

Did I! I'd been up half the night thinking and worrying!

'Cissie is now fourteen and has completed a first-class education at Swinton. She could take up domestic service like I did. If you like, I could write to my old employer, Mrs Lamport-Smythe, and see if she knows of any vacancies. As for Eddie, he would like to go to Swinton and do a course in music and one of the manual skills, like carpentry or plumbing. He talks about following in Danny's footsteps.'

'Could you fix it up, Kate? I'd be so grateful,' she said earnestly. 'It would solve a lot of problems.'

When I left home that morning I wouldn't say I was on good terms with Mam but we'd come to an understanding. We'd settled our differences but things were no longer the same. Friendly but distant. The presence of Frank McGuinness in the house had driven a wedge between us.

It was a Saturday morning when I moved and it meant taking the day off work. I was sure my workmates would be making cracks on Monday morning about me going on the booze on Friday night and having a hangover the next morning. I'd laugh with the rest of them, and I couldn't see any great problem with Declan Dowd when I explained the circumstances.

I slunk back to Mrs Hudson's place in Sherratt Court to ask for my room back. She was glad to see me.

'You're welcome to come back, Kate, on the same conditions as before.'

'Thanks, Mrs Hudson, but I'm not so keen on those curfew hours you imposed. And this time I'd like a key to the front door.'

'Well, I suppose, since I know you, it'll be all right. But what would you be wanting a key for? You won't be stopping out till all hours, will you?'

'No, it's just that on Friday nights me and my friends like to visit the variety theatre and we may be back later than ten o'clock. Say around eleven or eleven fifteen.'

'Very well, I'll give you a key on condition you're back no later than eleven thirty. As for the variety theatre, isn't that where a lot of half-naked painted women prance about the stage?'

'No,' I replied. 'Variety's now respectable and has famous singers like Caruso and Dame Nellie Melba.' I hadn't seen either of them on variety programmes but Mrs Hudson wasn't to know that. It seemed to convince her that variety may have become respectable. What she'd have said if she'd known about Marie Lloyd's singing and kicking her legs, the Lord only knows.

In the following weeks I was busy arranging things for Cissie and Eddie. A visit one Sunday to see Mr Birkby at Swinton ensured a place in Mr Maguire's class for him and he also took up a musical instrument – the cornet. He was a quick learner and it wasn't long before he had a place in the army cadet band of the Manchester Regiment. I wrote to Mrs Lamport-Smythe about Cissie and as luck would have it, the under-parlour maid, Lottie, had recently left – a piece of news which did not surprise me, given all her blunders. Cissie had no problem in securing the position since she came highly recommended by Mr Birkby and Lucy Morrell. Danny finally joined the Territorials at the Ardwick depot and was soon promoted to corporal because of his early military training at Swinton.

As for me, I continued in my job at Westmacott's but in one important way I'd changed. I no longer harboured notions of re-creating the past. I could look back fondly on the happy times that used to be. Nothing wrong with that. But now I realised that the past was the past. Those days of childhood bliss had gone for ever and could never be brought back, no matter how much I dreamt and prayed. No, my thoughts looked to the future and all its possibilities.

Chapter Twenty-Three

Though I'd had the row with Mam and was living in lodgings again, there followed a happy period. The Friday night trip to the theatre became a regular feature for the six of us and one we looked forward to eagerly to round off the week. Manchester had its own theatreland concentrated along Peter Street and Oxford Street and many of the top artistes of the day came, sometimes to try out an act before putting it on in London's West End. If a show went down well in Manchester, it would have no problem elsewhere because it used to be said (mainly by Manchester people, I think) that 'what Manchester thinks today, the rest of the world thinks tomorrow'. So over the weeks we saw some of the greatest performers of the variety world, people like George Robey, George Formby (Senior), Harry Champion (*Boiled Beef and Carrots*), and Florrie Forde with her song 'Oh! Oh! Antonio!'.

One Friday, Angela booked seats at the newly opened cinema and we saw Mary Pickford in a film called *Her First Biscuits*. The placards outside described her as 'the world's sweetheart'. We loved her from the moment we set eyes on her.

'She's not a patch on you,' Tommy said to me as we came out.

'Flatterer,' I said. 'Mary Pickford is the most beautiful

girl in the world. It says so on the poster.'

'Nonsense,' he said. 'She's only a flickering shadow on a screen but you're the real thing, flesh and blood, and she can't hold a candle to you.'

After a while, Angela began organising outings for Sunday afternoons; she never seemed to run out of ideas. One Sunday, it was a cruise down the Manchester Ship Canal on the SS *Maud* which boasted its own resident banjo player to serenade us all the way to Warrington and back. Another week, we paid a visit to Belle Vue Zoo to gawp at the animals. In the elephant house, Jumbo held out his trunk across the little moat and touched Jimmy to beg for a bun. Jimmy shrugged his shoulders and held up his hands apologetically to show he had nothing. Slowly, the elephant withdrew its trunk, dipped it in the water and deliberately soaked Jimmy from head to foot. It wasn't funny and we had to go into a cafe to dry poor old Jimmy off. But if it wasn't funny, why were the rest of us giggling for the rest of the day?

'I don't know about that saying elephants never forget,' Tommy remarked. 'Somehow, I think Jimmy will never forget that elephant.'

As the months rolled by, we kept up our Friday night routine but we began to meet during the week as couples as well. Jimmy and Angela had a longstanding courtship, of course, but Danny now went out with Hilda, and I with Tommy.

One Friday night Tommy and I decided to go all posh and as a change from variety book seats to see a play by Stanley Houghton at Miss Annie Horniman's newly opened Gaiety Theatre in Peter Street. For me, it was a night of drama all right. At the interval, Tommy went into the crowded bar to buy cigarettes and a couple of drinks. I waited outside and then I saw him. Bernard Sheridan! He was talking with a group of friends. The sight of him set my heart fluttering wildly. I turned away, hoping he wouldn't see me, but too late! He broke away from his circle and with a broad smile on his face came over to me.

'Kate,' he said, kissing my hand. 'How wonderful to see you again. You look as charming as ever! What are you doing here at the Gaiety?'

'The same as you, Bernard. I've come to see the play. Is Miss Emma with you?' I asked, looking over his shoulder for her.

'That fell through, Kate,' he said, looking deeply into my eyes. 'Emma was so wrapped up in her social work and women's emancipation that she hardly had time for me. What about you? Are you still in service?'

'Not now, Bernard. I've changed my job. So many things have happened since the Macclesfield days.'

'Look, we must meet up some time and share our news. There's usually a change of play every week and if you're at the theatre maybe we'll see each other one of these nights. Perhaps we can have a quick drink in the interval or something.'

From the corner of my eye, I could see Tommy returning with the drinks.

'I don't think so, Bernard,' I mumbled. 'My life is different now and I . . .'

'I understand, Kate,' he said quickly. 'Not to worry. But it would be nice to have a chat about the old days in Macclesfield. I work in our bank's head office here in Manchester now so maybe we'll run into each other some time – the town can't be that big. Anyway, great seeing you again, Kate.' He shook my hand warmly and strode off to rejoin his friends.

'Who was that?' Tommy asked. 'He seemed to be on friendly terms with you.'

'No one important,' I replied. 'An old friend of the family I used to work for.'

Tommy seemed happy with my answer and changed the subject to a discussion of the play we'd come to see. I hoped my feelings were not apparent because inside I was in turmoil.

I hardly paid any attention to the play in the second half. All kinds of ideas buzzed round my head. I thought I'd forgotten Bernard Sheridan and that I'd got over him. I'd put it down to a stupid infatuation. If that was so, why did I feel so confused? I'd dismissed any feelings I'd had for him a long time ago and accepted that he and I lived in two different social worlds. When Miss Emma had announced her engagement on the morning I took in her tea, that had sealed it once and for all. Now he was back, as handsome as ever, and I was all mixed up. He seemed interested in seeing me again. Maybe there was a chance for me after all, now that Miss Emma had bowed out of the picture. Bernard was educated, well-off and in a job with wonderful prospects.

For the rest of that week, my head was in a whirl. What to do? Should I go to the theatre alone next week in the hope of meeting Bernard or should I stick to my early decision to forget him? Perhaps I was being stupid and letting my imagination run away with me.

Amongst my own little group, it was now accepted that Tommy and I were courting, or walking out. And when I use the word 'walking' I don't use it lightly because for Tommy, walking was walking!

'Going training tonight', he would say.

'What, on a Sunday night in winter!'

'Got to keep fit.' He would grin, hold out his arm, and say, 'Get your leg in bed.' That meant linking. Off we'd go and he walked my feet off. We weren't exactly the romantic types though we did manage the occasional kiss and cuddle, but that was as far as it went.

Tommy worked hard during the week but on Saturday afternoons he played football for a team on Newton Heath loco recreation ground. And for that he had to keep in training. All very well, but I didn't see why I had to keep in training as well. In the evenings we walked – maybe marched is a better word – for miles and miles. We'd set off from Ancoats and end up five or six miles away in places like Crumpsall, and on one occasion as far away as Moston. It was there that Tommy's stammer nearly got us in trouble. We went to quench our thirst in the Ben Brierley and I asked for a glass of shandy. Tommy went up to the bar to get the drinks.

'A pint of mild,' he said, 'and a glass of sh-sh-sh shandy.' He managed to get the word out at last.

'Here, you!' the bartender barked. 'No more for you! You've had enough already.'

'Don't you "you" me, you!' Tommy shouted angrily. 'Give me the bloody drinks before I land you one.' He grabbed the man by the lapels and was about to nut him. I could see there was trouble so I hurried over to the bar to calm things down.

'Sorry,' I said to the bartender. 'Tommy here has not had a single drink today, I can vouch for that. He has a slight problem getting the words out. Now please, could we have a pint of mild and a shandy?'

Tommy and the barman cooled down. We got the drinks and went to our places in the corner. Tommy took a Player's Weight from his packet and lit up.

'I don't really stammer, Kate,' he said. 'Well, not much anyway. Just with words beginning with "sh".'

'Then I won't ask you to say "Sister Susie's sewing shirts for soldiers," ' I said with a laugh.

Tommy returned the laugh. 'Nor tongue-twisters,' he said, 'like "She sells sea-shells on the sea shore".'

'But you said that perfectly. So what's the problem?'

'It's only when I have to speak to a stranger or I'm nervous that I get tense and start to stammer.'

'You're going to have to learn to relax, to take a deep breath before you speak. And when you do, speak slowly and calmly. Don't get excited. But apart from that, Tommy, how long have you had the stammer?'

'As long as I can remember. As a kid I got knocked around a bit and I'm not sure but maybe that has something to do with it.'

'Tell me about it.'

Tommy lit another cigarette. 'Are you sure you want to hear about it?' he asked anxiously.

'I'm sure.' And indeed I *was* sure as I'd never seen Tommy blow his top like he'd done at the bar. There had to be some explanation as he was usually gentle and as mild as milk.

'Very well, you asked for it. I don't remember much about my early childhood but my old Aunt Julia tells me my mother and father were a happy couple at first. He was a tailor in one of the rainproof factories in the Strangeways district and earned a good wage. They had their own little house in North Kent Street in Ancoats. Then tragedy struck. According to the death certificate, he died of spinal meningitis and my mother Mary was left to fend for herself.'

'That's terrible, Tommy. How old were you?'

'I was three years old and so I don't remember much about my father but he was only twenty-five when he died and my mother was twenty two.'

'Your mother must have been heartbroken. How did she get by with her husband gone?'

'She was a bracemaker at Blair's and though her wage wasn't good, she managed to make ends meet,' he said, pulling on his cigarette. He wasn't finding it easy to tell his story.

'I remember that firm on Oldham Road,' I said. 'They made braces and corsets with genuine leather – solid so that they lasted.'

'That's right. Anyroad, my mother had to give up the house 'cos she couldn't afford the rent and so we went into lodgings in North Kent Street. She used to leave me at the top of Gould Street with my butties whilst she went off to work. She would kiss me and say, "Now go straight to school, son. I'll see you tonight when I get home." All I had to do was run down Roger Street and she went to Blair's on Ancoats Lane.'

'Your mother was a brave woman.'

'She was that all right. When I was about seven – and I remember this part only too well – tragedy struck for the second time. You see, I slept in the same bed, it was the only bed, with my mother. During the night, she complained of a terrible thirst and asked me to get her a drink of water from the tap outside. I did so and she drank it right down in one go. She cuddled me in her arms and we settled down for the night.'

I hardly dared to breathe when I asked, 'What then?'

'Next morning when I awoke, she was still holding me tightly to her breast.'

'And?'

'She was dead. The doctors put her death down to angina pectoris – whatever that is. They had to force her arms open to pull me out.'

'Oh, my God, Tommy. And you only seven.'

'I was seven and my mother was twenty-six. I was an orphan and the big question was: what to do with me?

There was some talk of putting me in the workhouse.'

'I pray to God that they didn't,' I said. 'I've had some and I know what it's like.'

'No, I was spared the Bastille but sometimes I wonder whether it might have been better than where I landed up. My mother had a married sister by the name of Dorothy Langley and after a lot of humming and hahing, they agreed to take me in. Everyone knew me as Tommy Langley but I never forgot I was a Hopkins.'

'You said they were worse than the workhouse. I don't think anything could be worse, Tommy.'

Tommy's hands were shaking as he went on with his story.

'The Langleys lived in Almond Street off Rochdale Road and there was this old grandad who'd lost an eye in the American war. He used to belt the living daylights out of me with a horsewhip for the slightest thing. One day I was playing ball with some lads and we broke a street lamp. The others managed to get away but I was caught by a policeman and taken home by the scruff of the neck. That old grandad didn't half lay into me with his whip.'

'He reminds me of our workhouse master who tried to do the same thing with my young brother Danny. Such people should be locked up. But how did you come to end up in Smithfield Market?'

'Since I was an orphan, I was allowed to attend school part-time. So every afternoon they sent me to work in Smithfield Market driving a pony and cart delivering fruit and vegetables all round the district until late at night. I was so exhausted at the end of each day, many's the time I slept in the stable with the pony.'

'You must have got out of their clutches at the finish.'

'I did and all. Being market people, the Langleys were heavy drinkers. One Friday night when I was about sixteen

– I was a market porter by this time – I came home after a long day and found them all half canned. "Hey up!" I heard the grandad say. "Here's our Thomas home with his wages" (they always called me Thomas when they wanted something) – "we'll be all right now for a jug of ale." It was then that I wrapped up my shirt and got out.'

'That's when you got your present lodgings, I suppose.'

'Not by a long chalk. I had to go through a few before I found my present place.' Tommy chuckled at the memory of his first experiences at going it alone. It was good that he could see the funny side of a situation and a relief to know that hardship hadn't destroyed his sense of humour. Not only that, I loved his attractive, infectious laugh.

'A mate of mine in the market recommended a place called Cain's Lodging House on Shudehill. "You pay half-a-crown," this lad told me, "and you'll get a bed and a box to store your things." That meant my shirt! "You buy and cook your own food," this mate said. "Be independent!" I didn't much like the look of the place. There were a lot of old men and lots of boozers and that. Anyroad, I got myself a few groceries – bread, butter and tea – but the next morning when I went to get the stuff out, I found a great big beetle on the bread. That was enough. I lapped up my shirt for the second time and moved on.'

'It could have been worse.' I giggled. 'You could have *eaten* the beetle. Joking apart, your life story could have come straight out of Charlie Dickens. So what happened next?'

Tommy was now smiling broadly and enjoying himself. 'One of the lads called Billy Ingrams on Deakin's market stall told me that his mother – a widow – sometimes took in lodgers. I went along and she seemed a nice old lady and the house looked clean. Nothing can go wrong here, I thought. I'd been there about a week and I came home a bit late. They'd already had their tea – bacon and cheese – it sounded good. But when I saw their dog licking the frying pan that my tea was going to be cooked in, I thought it was time to call it a day.'

As I listened to Tommy, a part of my mind compared him to Bernard Sheridan. Tommy had neither prospects nor money. He certainly wasn't as handsome as Bernard, yet there was an indefinable something about Tommy that attracted me. Perhaps it was his quiet modesty and cheerful optimism that I found irresistible. Like me, he'd been through the mill and survived.

That night, he and I sat together in the corner of the Ben Brierley laughing and crying our hearts out, and when he'd finished telling his story, I knew that Tommy was the only man for me. We talked the same language and there was a bond of understanding between us. I forgot all about Bernard Sheridan and his glittering prospects. He could find one of his own kind to share his wealth. As for me, I'd spent half my life trying to recapture my early childhood bliss but from now on I decided I would devote my time trying to make up for everything that fate had done to this man sitting before me. I'd make it my aim to bring him happiness. We'd been through such rough times and had laughed at the same kinds of daft situations that I knew we were meant for each other.

Chapter Twenty-Four

At work, Angela continued to organise our social calendar. Every August Bank Holiday, she arranged a trip to the seaside for the six of us and we were happy to let her do so. On these day excursions, we covered about all of them – Blackpool, New Brighton, Morecambe, Llandudno.

Then early in 1910, Angela and Jimmy announced their forthcoming marriage. When I say 'announced', I mean they sent out fancy, engraved invitation cards to their selected guests, and Hilda and I were included as workmates. The wedding was to be celebrated in February at St Michael's Church, Ancoats, and Danny agreed to be one of the ushers, and Tommy to be best man. When I heard this last piece of news, I was concerned because that meant a speech and I wondered if Tommy was up to it. Whatever happened, I didn't want him to make a fool of himself.

'What about your stammer?' I asked.

'Not to worry,' he said. 'I don't get tense amongst friends, and anyway, I'm hoping you'll go over my speech to check it for me.' He took out a crumpled piece of paper from his pocket. I read it over quickly.

'Ladies and gentlemen, you'll be glad to know that my speech will be a short one. Jimmy chose me to be his best man and I don't know why unless it's because he's recognised at last that I *am* the best man. But Jimmy and Angela are a good match and I'm sure you will share with me in wishing the happy couple the best of luck in their future life together. Jimmy is a lucky man to have won Angela – she is a lovely girl and so are her sisters Rosa and Francesca. So now please stand and raise your glasses in a toast to the bridesmaids.'

'Well, what do you think?' he asked, anxiously scanning my face.

'Fine,' I answered. 'It's nice and short and that's what a good speech should be. But you might be nervous on the day and so I think we should take out words beginning with the sound of "sh", like short, sure, share, she.'

He readily agreed and rehearsed his speech aloud several times until he had it off pat.

An Italian wedding is not merely a ceremony – it's a spectacle. Three priests in full regalia and sung High Mass were needed to make sure the marriage knot was firmly tied. But the Mass was so long, I couldn't help thinking that not only was the knot *tied*, it was secured with a double padlock. Angela wore a white bridal gown and a tiara of flowers in her glossy black hair. She looked beautiful and radiant, and hardly recognisable as our fellow bottle-washer.

When they reached the exchanging of vows, always the most emotional part of the ceremony, there was a great deal of snuffling amongst the ladies and a few of the men. It was that talk of 'for richer or poorer, in sickness and in health, till death us do part' that triggered the weeping, as was to be expected. What was not expected was that the best man would keep turning round from his place in the front row to give me a shy smile and a nod of the head. Was he trying to say something?

The reception after church was held in the parish hall and the festivities were to go on all day. What with all the depressing news that was about – terrible earthquakes in Italy, suffragettes being force-fed in prison, Germany making threatening noises, and God knows what else – a wedding was what people needed to cheer them up. The celebrations were truly wonderful. There must have been a hundred guests, some dancing on the wooden floor, others sitting it out at tables piled high with rich food, demijohns of *vino*, and a dozen kinds of ice cream. Angela and Jimmy sat in splendour at a raised table and waved like royalty to the people below. At speech time, Tommy delivered his words with practised ease and I was proud of his achievement. There was a great deal of laughing and singing to the accompaniment of a mandolin. We were enjoying ourselves so much that we lost track of the time.

'It's a good job there's no work tomorrow,' Tommy remarked. 'I'd never get up for four o'clock.'

The word 'clock' brought me to my senses with a jolt.

'What time is it, Tommy?' I asked anxiously.

He consulted his waistcoat watch.

'By God, it's half past twelve already. How time flies when you're enjoying yourself.'

My heart skipped a beat. Mrs Hudson would have locked up the house. I'd told her that I'd be back around eleven o'clock.

Tommy and I got our coats, paid our respects to everyone, and left hurriedly. We walked swiftly across to Sherratt Court but I knew in advance what we'd find. The house was locked and in total darkness. We knocked carefully a few times but I knew it was no use. The door had been bolted and Mrs Hudson would not open it to anyone, not at one o'clock in the morning. What to do? Only one thing left. I had to go back to my mother's and beg a bed for the night. How I hated to do it! But what alternative was there? I'd had little contact with Mam since arranging things for Cissie and Eddie and I wasn't sure what kind of reception I would get. We set off walking again, and to make matters worse it started to tipple down. Tommy's getting plenty of training tonight, I thought.

It was one thirty when we reached Angel Meadow and we were both wet through. There were still lights on at the house, though the front door was shut. No doubt one of Mam's and Frank's drinking sessions had wound down and I had the awful job of asking them for a night's lodgings. How humiliated I felt! I was going to have to eat big pieces of humble pie and no mistake.

We stopped inside the doorway of a factory.

'Let's sh-shelter here out of the rain, Kate,' Tommy said. I noticed the slight stammer. He was jumpy about something.

'Kate, before you go in and ask for a bed,' he said, water dripping from his cap, 'let me ask you something.'

I looked at him closely. I knew what he was going to ask and I also knew he was not finding it easy. In his life, he'd been rejected so much, he must have been afraid that he was going to get hurt again.

'I love you, Kate. Have done ever since I saw you going to work on Oldham Road. I want to take care of you and look after you for the rest of your life. What do you say?' He gazed into my eyes anxiously; his life and his future happiness lay in my answer.

I didn't hesitate for a second. I'd known for some time what my answer would be. How I'd waited for this moment!

'Tommy,' I said, 'I knew what you were going to ask. And my answer is yes! A definite yes! Let's get married as soon as we can and set up a home of our own. You and I were made for each other.'

Tommy's look of relief said it all. He took my face in his hands and kissed me on the cheek. I wrapped both arms round him and held him close.

'Oh, Tommy, Tommy,' I said. 'I don't know why we've waited so long.'

'Thank you, thank you, Kate, for accepting me,' he said. 'I know I'm not much of a catch, and I'm sure you could have done much better than the likes of me, a market porter. But the one thing I can promise you is that you'll want for nothing. I earn enough in the market to keep us, if not in luxury, at least enough to keep a roof over our heads and we won't starve. I'll see to that. Now go in and face the music but remember, there's light at the end of the tunnel. I'll stand here with you to make sure you're all right.'

'Fine, Tommy,' I said, 'but leave the talking to me.'

My heart was bubbling with joy and now that Tommy had asked me to marry him, I could have faced anything or anybody – even the devil himself.

It was Frank McGuinness who answered the door. He didn't recognise me at first, probably because it was dark and it was raining. He also looked bleary-eyed as if he'd had a few. When the penny finally dropped, he rubbed my nose in it, good and proper.

'Well, lookee here! The Queen herself has come to visit us. And with her new boyfriend. What may we do for you, Your Majesty, on this dark and rainy night?'

He was soon joined by Mam who came down the lobby to see what was going on.

I explained the situation, how we'd been to a wedding and how my landlady had locked me out and I needed a bed for the night.

'Goodnight, Kate,' Tommy said cheerily when he was sure I was going to be all right. 'See you tomorrow.'

I gave Tommy a quick hug and whispered to him, 'No need to worry now, Tommy. Everything's fine. The way I'm feeling I could climb Mount Everest or swim the Atlantic but right now I'll settle for a bed and a roof over my head. Meet you tomorrow 'cos we've got lots to talk about.'

I turned back to Mam who was standing in the doorway.

'Kate,' she said, 'you look wet through. Come in at once.'

But Frank McGuinness wasn't going to let an opportunity like this go by and he couldn't resist gloating at my predicament.

'I think we should charge her for board and lodging,' he sneered.

'You can stop that talk, Frank,' Mam said. 'No matter what you think, Kate is still my flesh and blood and there's always a bed here for her if she wants it.'

I was moved when I heard Mam say this. She hadn't forgotten her first family after all.

'You can sleep in the back bedroom,' Mam said. 'You'll be with the kids. They're sound asleep and so I don't think you'll disturb them.'

There were now two children – John and the new baby, Henrietta, Hetty for short. Furthermore, they'd married in a hush-hush wedding at St Michael's. According to Angela, who lived in the same parish, the rector had leaned on them about having kids and 'living in sin'.

Frank looked put out by Mam's chastisement, not that anything Frank said or did could have taken away that wonderful warm glow of happiness I felt inside that night.

We chose Saturday, 7 May, as our wedding day. If Angela's wedding could be described as spectacular, ours was sombre by comparison. We planned for a ceremony to be held at St Chad's Church on Cheetham Hill Road, with a little reception afterwards for friends and relatives in the Knowsley Inn opposite. My own immediate family was there: Danny who was best man, Cissie the bridesmaid, and young Eddie – only now not so young at thirteen years of age. We had also invited Mam and Frank McGuinness but she had sprained her ankle – or so she said – and they were unable to come. I was disappointed that my own mother hadn't been able to make it for my big day and I suspected that Frank was somehow behind it.

Invited guests were few – Jimmy and Angela, already pregnant, Hilda, and one or two fellow workers from Westmacott's. We wanted a quiet wedding with no fuss. And that's what we got, only a little more than we bargained for. On Wednesday, 4 May, King Edward became ill with pneumonia and died on the Friday. Most inconvenient of him, we thought. At least he could have given us notice.

Canon McCabe asked us if we wanted to postpone since the whole country had gone into mourning. It was a repeat of Victoria's death only more so because Edward had been popular. People had affectionately called him Bertie or good old Teddie. Even the songs of the time had declared that there would never be war as long as Eddie was on the throne. Now there was gloom and misery everywhere. But with or without Edward on the throne, we were going on with our wedding. When we'd fixed the date, we'd had no idea that Edward was going to depart this life. The only thing we did cancel was the week's honeymoon in Blackpool since we felt that the place would indeed be *Black*pool. Furthermore, the money saved could be put to better use.

'I'm not joking,' I said to Tommy when we heard the

news of the King's death, 'the government thinks it can switch our feelings on and off like a tap. Now we're supposed to go around with long faces; there's to be no laughing or joking or dancing. In fact no enjoyment. But you watch,' I added, 'in a year's time, there'll be the coronation of his son, George, and the government will order us to start smiling and celebrating again.'

'You're right, Kate,' he said. 'I'm sorry the King's dead but it doesn't affect us, 'cos when all's said and done, we didn't know him personally. We've just got to get on with our lives.'

The ceremony went off without a hitch though Canon McCabe felt that a short, subdued affair was more suitable than the usual ritual. Half an hour after arriving at the church, we were man and wife.

It was the same over in the pub. Everything was draped in black and the landlord decreed that everyone had to talk in whispers and on no account was there to be any singing unless it was to be something like 'Down Among the Dead Men'. We had some lovely presents given us. A linen tablecloth from Susie in Durham, from Lizzie in America a ten dollar note for which the bank gave us fifty shillings, a crockery set from the girls at Westmacott's, a set of pans from Angela, sheets and pillowcases from Hilda and Danny, a biscuit barrel from Cissie. The biggest surprise of all came from Eddie. My glass swan! Almost as good as new! He'd picked up the pieces and glued them together again in the workshop at Swinton. This little act of Eddie's had me in tears for I felt that, although Mam wouldn't be at my wedding, Dad was present in that glass swan.

Jimmy had to have his joke though. He looked round at the depressing décor of the pub. 'Even if Edward hadn't died,' he chuckled quietly, 'I reckon the atmosphere is right for a man getting married. We can sing "At Trinity Church I met my doom".'

'You wait till I get you home,' Angela hissed, poking him playfully in the ribs.

Chapter Twenty-Five

We found a small two-up, two-down house in Back Murray Street off Oldham Road – what they called a working-man's home. We hadn't much money to spend because I'd used up all I had doing up Mam's house, and while Tommy had a decent enough job in the market, he had practically nothing in ready cash. It was a case of going back to Solly's to borrow money for furniture. At Cantor's on Oldham Street, we were able to furnish the whole house for under ten pounds. For the bedroom, we bought an iron double bed, with straw mattress, bolster and two pillows, a chair with a cane bottom, and to cover the bare floorboards, a bit of carpet. For the downstairs living room, we got a square table with four wooden chairs, two armchairs, a horsehair sofa, a fender and an ash pan. We covered the floor with a congoleum square and a peg rug. In the scullery, I had all that I could wish for to do the washing – a copper boiler, a mangle, a dolly, and a scrubbing board. A visit to Shufflebottom's for crockery and pans and our household was complete. Not palatial but for Tommy and me, heaven. A place we could call our own at last. No more lodgings, no more being blown from pillar to post. No more having to be in at ten o'clock or being locked out in the rain.

Tommy had traditional ideas on marriage and insisted

that I give up work and look after the home and become a housewife. I didn't need much persuading. Anyway, it would have been impossible to carry on at Westmacott's because Tommy started work in the market at four o'clock in the morning and I got up with him to make his breakfast and prepare his mid-morning snack.

We settled down to a comfortable routine and life ticked over happily. I loved housework. After all, it's what I'd been trained for and I was good at it. I shopped, cooked, cleaned, washed, black-leaded, polished the windows and sang my head off as I did so. At first I worried about disturbing the Kenyons next door with my rendering of the popular song of the year:

Ah! sweet mystery of life, at last I've found thee.
Ah! I know at last the secret of it all.

But my singing was nothing next to the row our neighbours made each weekend when they fought like cat and dog. At Mass on Sundays, Mrs Kenyon usually appeared with swollen face and a black eye.

'Bumped into the kitchen door,' she claimed, or, 'Slipped on the kitchen step.'

Tommy finished work around midday and when he'd promised me that I'd never starve, I found that was a serious understatement. Every day he brought home a shopping bag filled with a wide variety of produce – fruit, vegetables, fish, chicken, and even the occasional rabbit. Sometimes he carried home ribs or pork chops bought from Muller's, Hilda's parents' shop on Dantzig Street.

'What a lovely old couple,' he used to say, 'and they threw in half a pound of sausages free.'

But that wasn't all. Each day he left a sum of money on the table varying from three shillings on Monday to ten shillings on Friday. I'd never been so well off and it gladdened my heart to see Tommy so content when he went off to Smithfield Market whistling even on dark, rainy mornings.

And our joy knew no bounds when at the end of July I suspected I was pregnant. I had missed two periods in a row and, while I wasn't one hundred per cent sure about it, I was normally as regular as clockwork. So what else could it be? Besides, I'd been violently sick for a few mornings and I knew that was one of the signs.

It was a Monday afternoon when I thought I'd better tell him. I hoped he'd be happy but with men, well, you never knew how they were going to react to something like that. To put him in a good mood, I'd made him his favourite meal – cow heel stew – and he was tucking in and at the same time reading out bits of news from the *Daily Mail*. It was his way of keeping me up to date with current affairs, he said.

'I see they nabbed that Dr Crippen fella whilst he was at sea. They caught him using that thing called wire-less. I always knew it would work one day.'

I seemed to remember that he'd said the opposite at the time and that it would never amount to anything, not in a month of Sundays. Best not to argue, not at that moment anyway.

'Good news,' I said.

'Good news! I should think it was. Crippen had murdered his missus and buried her under the cellar floor.'

'No, I mean *we've* got good news.'

I told him about it. I needn't have worried about how he'd react. He was ecstatic. We both were. At the same time, we were also a little bewildered since our knowledge of sexual matters was rudimentary, to say the least. Nobody had told us anything. I had picked up a few snippets from my dubious experiences with Harold in Macclesfield and from the jokes being thrown around by the women in Westmacott's. But it was pretty sketchy. Of course Tommy and I knew how babies were made, we weren't that daft, but all the same, we found it difficult to take in how our kissing and cuddling could result in this miracle of creation. We'd had to find out about sex by instinct, as it were. By leaving it to Nature, as Gran'ma used to say. We'd had to learn our lessons the hard way. In the early stages, I'd found sex not only painful but unpleasant, while Tommy found it embarrassing to discuss it. After a while, I got used to it and it became less painful but I never lost the idea that it was something that women had to put up with to keep the husband happy.

As for the birth process itself, I was even more ignorant since everything to do with sex and having babies was shrouded in secrecy. Nice people didn't discuss such things. And being pregnant was embarrassing.

'We must keep this news to ourselves,' Tommy said. 'It's a private matter and has nothing to do with anyone else.'

'What about Mrs Kenyon next door?'

'Especially Mrs Kenyon.'

I hid my condition from others' eyes for as long as possible. Uncomfortable though it was, I tightened my corsets and wore a pinarette – the kind that ties at the sides – so that the growing bulge in my stomach was not apparent. When walking to the clinic on hot days, I wore my big winter coat to cover myself up and though the sweat was running down my arms, wild horses couldn't have made me take it off. I noticed that from this time on, Tommy never went out in public with me. At weekends we'd always gone out somewhere – the pictures, the Queen's Park Hipp, the local for a couple of quiet drinks. Now it all stopped. As if he didn't want to be seen with me now that I was starting to get big. Funny old world.

At five months, I could hide my condition no longer and the secret was out. Mrs Kenyon turned out to be helpful, for she had lots of suggestions. Little in the way of advice about actually having the baby – she was much too shy to talk about that – but she was well informed about predicting the sex of the baby.

'During pregnancy,' she told me, 'you'll get funny fanciful tastes. Ice cream with tomato sauce, sausages with jam, and God knows what else. Don't worry about it, eat what you like. A little bit of what you fancy does you good.'

'Strange you should say that,' I said. 'Lately I've had a craving for apple pie. It's odd because I don't usually like it that much.'

'That *is* good news,' she exclaimed. 'It's a sign. Apple pie means a boy. You're going to have a little boy! It's well-known in Lancashire that fancying cherry pie means a girl, and apple pie a boy. Your husband *will* be pleased.'

'Are you absolutely sure?'

'Absolutely! As God is my witness!'

'An old wives' tale,' Tommy said when I told him. Nevertheless he looked pleased at the prospect of a son.

'We'll call him Thomas,' I said. 'He'll be your son and heir.'

He gave a broad smile and looked as happy as a dog with an extra tail.

'What if it's a girl?' he asked.

'We'll call her Mary after your mother. But Mrs Kenyon is one hundred per cent positive it's a boy. So think boy.'

I began knitting. In the evening, no sound was to be heard in our living room but the clicking of needles. Everything was to be blue – bonnets, matinee coats, leggings, bootees, nighties – everything.

'I think this little bugger's going to be a Tory, judging by your knitting,' Tommy joked.

For the next few months, he thought and talked about nothing but his son.

'I'll teach him to play football. If he's going to make the team, he'll have to keep fit and that means long walks. Don't worry, I'll see to it that he keeps in training. There's the problem of his education. We must try to send him to a decent school and I won't stand for any kids bullying him. I'll show him how to look after himself. I've learned a trick or two in the market. Another thing, nobody will push him around the way I was pushed around or he'll have me to deal with. If I catch one of them teachers belting him, I'll be up at that school in two shakes and I'll give 'em what for. They're not going to treat my son like that, I can tell you.' He punched his hand and turned red with anger.

'Hold on, Tommy,' I said. 'The kid hasn't even been born yet and already you're getting into fights over him at the school.'

'We've got to think ahead. What kind of job will he have? I could show him how to be a market porter, it's not a bad job. Good money and lots of fruit and veg to take home – even fish. That's good brain food, you know. He'd never have an empty belly, that's for sure. But he'd have to be quick, strong and clever to do the job well.'

Every day, he brought home extra food as if we didn't have enough already. 'Rabbit – that's the meat to build you up,' he insisted. 'Best food there is to give you strength. Better than chicken. Better than steak.'

We ate rabbit till it was coming out of our ears, in every conceivable dish – rabbit pie, rabbit stew, rabbit casserole, and with dumplings for extra sustenance. I swear my two front teeth were beginning to take on the look of our furry friends.

From time to time, I wondered how and where the baby came out. I thought of visiting my mother for advice but Frank McGuinness was always present. I wanted to ask Mrs Kenyon but was too shy. And I'm sure it would have embarrassed her too. I remember my gran'ma saying, 'It comes out where it went in.' But that didn't seem to make any sense. Girls at Swinton School had always claimed it came out of the belly button which would open like a flower at the right time. It was hard to know what to believe and I didn't know what to expect. I stood over a mirror and had a look at myself 'down there'. What rubbish gran'ma had talked. There was no way a baby could get out from there! I had to go along with the belly button school of thought.

Towards the end of February in 1911 the pains began. I'd been doing the washing and had lifted the dolly tub filled with water and clothes when I felt something snap inside. When the contractions started a little later, I put them down to the rhubarb we had eaten the day before but then it dawned on me what they were. I'd arranged for Mrs Kenyon to come and help when my time was due. I had hoped to ask my good friend Angela to do this but she had lost her own baby in a miscarriage a few months earlier and I thought it might upset her. So I knocked on Mrs Kenyon's wall and shouted to her that she was needed. I sent Tommy to get our 'handy-woman' who lived two streets away. There were two handy-women in our district – Annie Swann and Bridget Coogan. I didn't want Annie even though she was an old friend because she was more used to laying out the dead and acting as pawnbroker's runner than delivering children. We'd plumped for Mrs Coogan as she'd had a little training in midwifery and what's more her fee was only a couple of bob.

I always kept the house spotless but Mrs Kenyon and I

had cleaned the bedroom from top to bottom just the same to make sure. I made the bed in readiness using the new sheets we'd got as wedding presents and I got dolled up in my best nightdress and cardigan. I sat there in all my glory waiting for Bridget Coogan.

Tommy was soon back with our woman who strode in, all businesslike. Her sharp manner gave us confidence. Here was a woman who knew what she was about.

'The first thing you can do is get out of that finery, put on your oldest things and get out your oldest sheets and lay out newspapers to protect your mattress.'

From what? I wondered.

'And you,' she said pointing to Tommy, 'can bugger off to the pub. You'll only be in my road here.'

Tommy didn't need telling twice. He looked relieved, nodded his agreement and had his cap on before she'd finished speaking.

When he'd gone, Mrs Kenyon heated up pans of water on the fire whilst Mrs Coogan tied a towel on the bedrail and told me to pull on that when I needed to. I hadn't the first notion of what was going to happen and I was beginning to get scared. She asked me the name of our doctor 'just in case' and when I told her it was Dr Cooklin, she seemed pleased.

'He's one of the best,' she said, 'not like some of these others who kill half the kids with their forceps and he charges only thirty bob. But you look young, fit and healthy, so I'm sure we won't need him. I hope you're going to have your baby without any fuss. None of that screaming or shouting or you'll frighten half the neighbourhood. The first one is always the most difficult but we'll see what we can do to speed things up.'

This reference to screaming and shouting did nothing to reassure me.

Bridget told me to walk about the room until the baby was ready to come. When the first white-hot spasm went through me, I was taken completely by surprise. I held onto the bed and I couldn't hold back the scream which came out of my throat. Bridget gave me a swift slap on the cheek.

'We'll have none of that!' she snapped. 'You must grin and bear it.'

I'll bear it, I thought, but I won't grin.

But Bridget was also kind and as I stood at the foot of the bed taking deep breaths, she stroked my back to try and deaden my agony. I lost count of the time and so I don't know how long we stood around like this. A couple of hours maybe. It got bad, and she told me to get on the bed and lie on my left side.

'Won't be long now, love,' she urged. 'Pull on the towel for all you're worth – that should ease things.'

I did as I was told but it didn't help much.

More searing pain. I thought this agony was going to go on for ever. Then at last it was over and I heard the most beautiful sound in the whole universe, the wonderful, wonderful cry of a newly born infant.

'It's a little girl,' Bridget announced. 'The bonniest baby you ever did see. An angel from heaven. And today is the coronation of King George and Queen Mary. So maybe you should call her Georgina or Mary.'

'It's already been decided and it's definitely not Georgina,' I said. 'Her name is Mary.'

She washed the baby and put her in my arms. She was right, she was indeed bonny, with light brown hair and hazel eyes like her father.

My first thought was that it should have been a boy, according to Mrs Kenyon and her apple pie theory, and I wondered how Tommy would take it after all that talk about a son and heir. But at that moment I was past caring and only glad that the ordeal was over and the baby was alive and well. Mrs Kenyon joined us and helped by taking away the blood-stained newspapers and the afterbirth to burn them on the fire which she had built up in the kitchen.

As for Tommy, there was no need to worry about his reaction. When he laid eyes on his daughter, a look of unutterable tenderness came over him and he took her in his arms delicately as if afraid she might come apart if treated any other way.

'It's OK to hold her firmly,' Bridget told him. 'It's a baby you're holding, not a meringue! It won't crumble in your grasp.'

But Tommy continued to treat Mary gently for ever after. It was as if having a daughter brought out all his tender instincts. Every night he cradled her in his arms and rocked her to sleep with soft words and gentle lullabies. He talked to her and told her how beautiful she was with her curly brown hair and the hazel Hopkins eyes. Mary gurgled and cooed with delight as if trying to answer him. During the night, the slightest cough or snuffle from the cradle and Tommy was up like a shot to attend to her. If he could have re-organised Mother Nature, he would have suckled her.

Shortly after Mary was born, Canon McCabe honoured us with a visit. It meant getting out the best cups and saucers. He congratulated us on our fine baby and arranged a date for the baptism. He questioned us closely about our chosen godparents. Were they God-fearing, practising Catholics who would take the awesome responsibilities of sponsorship seriously? We were able to reassure him on these points. We had chosen Jimmy and Angela for the simple reason that if they were destined not to have any children of their own, they could take over Mary's spiritual welfare if Tommy and me were knocked down by a tram or a runaway horse.

'After the christening,' the Canon said, 'we shall arrange for the churching and purification of the mother.'

'We don't want to put you to any trouble, Canon,' Tommy said. 'We'll just have the christening.' He was thinking that this churching thing might involve extra expense.

'Ah, but your wife must be purified after giving birth. It's an ancient Catholic custom to give thanks to God for a safe delivery and to make atonement for her sin.'

Sin? What sin?

'Sorry, Canon,' I said. 'I don't understand. Surely having a baby is not a sin.'

'Ah, indeed no,' the Canon answered. 'But the custom goes back to Old Testament times. The Jews considered a mother to be unclean for seven days – fourteen if God had sent her a girl, as in your case.'

It was the first I'd heard that I was unclean for having a baby and that I had to be purified. I couldn't remember old Shirty Gerty mentioning it at school.

Tommy frowned at this suggestion that I was somehow tainted for having given birth to his beloved Mary.

'And what happens, Father, if we decide not to have this ceremony of yours?' he asked testily.

'Well, I can tell you this,' the Canon snapped. 'In the old days in Ireland, we held that until she was churched, a mother would never get strong, and any food she cooked or served would do her family no good. And if she refused to be churched, neighbours were displeased, believing she would bring a plague of rats about the place. Kate here should not venture out of the house until she has been churched after the christening. Nor should she have any visitors, for it would only bring terrible misfortune on them. And bear in mind that it's a great privilege to be offered the ceremony because the church offers it only to respectable married mothers.'

A bit late to talk about not visiting or having visitors, I thought. There was the Royal London Club man who'd come round the first day to insure the baby for tuppence a week. There were Angela and Hilda who'd already been round to see the baby. According to the Canon, they were in for a run of disasters and bad luck.

Tommy now looked angry and was on the point of giving the Canon a piece of his mind. 'I've never heard such a load of—'

'We'll be glad to have the ceremony,' I said, interrupting him quickly before he could put his foot in it. Best not to get on the wrong side of the parish priest.

The following Sunday afternoon, we took Mary to be baptised. As well as Jimmy and Angela, we invited Hilda and Danny, and Mrs Kenyon. Eddie came over from Swinton and Cissie, who had managed to get the day off, came up from Macclesfield.

Mam and Frank McGuinness were also invited but were otherwise engaged. Aunt Sarah too was unable to come because of Barney's ill health. As we set off walking to the church, I couldn't help noticing how wistfully Angela looked at the baby as she carried it to the church. I sent up a silent prayer asking God to send Angela one of her own.

When we reached St Chad's, the main party made its way to the baptismal font but I was told to go to the side altar of the Blessed Virgin as I wasn't allowed to take part in the christening. I felt like one of the lepers I'd read about in history books. All I needed was a bell round my neck and I could enter the church calling out 'Unclean! Unclean!' so that everyone could keep away from me. I knelt there saying the rosary whilst Mary was baptised at the other end of the church. All I could hear was a lot of Latin words being mumbled over my daughter, with Jimmy and Angela promising to bring her up in the Catholic faith if it so happened that Tommy and me got hit by that tram people kept talking about.

When the christening was over, the Canon came down to me with an altar boy carrying a lighted candle and a bucket of holy water and went inside the rails of the side altar. I was told to hang onto the end of his stole and hold the lighted candle while he said more Latin words over me. He blessed me with holy water and made the sign of the cross with his thumb on my forehead. I was declared clean and told that I could join my family who were waiting for me at the end of the church. So both Mary and I had the devil taken out of us that Sunday afternoon. I don't know how Mary was feeling but I felt no different.

After the christening and the cleansing, it was back to Back Murray Street for tea and sandwiches. A proud and happy Tommy presided over it all. Danny and young Eddie gave us a lovely duet performance on clarinet and cornet, something from Mozart. Eddie was now fourteen years old and coming on well. Cissie told us how she was going out with a nice boy from Macclesfield. He was one of identical twins so like each other, she sometimes got them mixed up.

'Well, it's to be hoped that you marry the right one,' I said. 'You'll have to have him tattooed. Anyway, you're much too young to be going out with boys.'

'Kate,' she said, 'you're losing track of time. I'm now seventeen and old enough to think about getting married myself.'

It was true. Time was going by so quickly that I'd forgotten that my brother and sister were growing up fast.

Later, the three men went to 'wet the baby's head' in the Turk's Head, a popular pub for market workers on Shudehill.

Like most Smithfield market men, Tommy liked a drink but, thank God, he didn't overdo it like the loathsome McTavish in the workhouse, my own mother and Frank McGuinness, or our neighbour, Paddy Kenyon, who not only drank but beat up his wife every weekend. A few Saturdays ago, Madge Kenyon had come running to us with her two kids for shelter and Tommy and I had had to go round to confront Paddy. He'd been in a violent mood and had been using his wife as a punch bag after drinking Chester's beer in the Crown and Anchor. But he hadn't been so brave when faced by another man and I think I put the fear of God in him when I threatened to set the 'Cruelty Man' on him. I'd asked Madge why she stayed with Paddy when he was so vicious.

'It's only when he's had a drop too many, Kate. At other times, he's kind and considerate. Besides, where could we run to if we did decide to leave? I depend on Paddy for everything – food, rent, fuel, clothes. Without him, I've got nowt. We do at least get a bit of peace some weekends since he's joined the Territorials and has to go on manoeuvres. I think he's only enlisted as a cheap way of getting a training camp holiday.'

Tommy's drinking was confined to a couple of pints in the evening when he went to play his game of crib with his cronies and sort out world affairs, like what to do about the Chinese hordes, German re-armament, and the anarchists who were planting bombs in London. Tommy was always trying to involve me in the news by reading out bits from the paper. He always began with words like: 'Country's going to the dogs, Kate,' or 'I don't know what the world's coming to, I really don't.'

Sad to say, I was never interested unless it concerned me personally. After all, I didn't know any members of the Chinese hordes, or the German leaders who were building those Dreadnoughts. Whilst I was sorry to learn about the sinking of the *Titanic* and, like everybody else, made tut-tut and tsk-tsk noises when Tommy read it out, none of my friends had been on it and so it didn't affect me. And God forgive me, there was even the guilty thought that such a thing could never happen to me or my family 'cos we weren't in the habit of cruising on ships like that.

As the months went by, Tommy's attachment to Mary grew stronger. Soon she was making little happy babbling noises in reply to his serenading; they reminded me at times of two doves cooing to each other. He murmured to her how one day he would dress her in silk and satin and tie ribbons in her hair. She'd be the most beautiful little girl, all peaches and cream, in the whole of Manchester and win prizes at baby shows. I couldn't help thinking at times that he was overdoing it a bit but there was something about this little creature that brought joy to everyone's heart. For Tommy, she brought out his most protective feelings. Mary had only to whimper and he was there to pick her up and she immediately stopped and began her happy cooing sounds.

When she was one year old, we were wakened in the middle of the night by her making little wheezing and grunting noises followed by a bark-like cough. It was evident that she was having difficulty in breathing. We both became alarmed and didn't know what to do for the best. Mary turned her big eyes to Tommy, looking for help and relief, but he didn't have the answer.

He fell to his knees – a thing I'd never seen him do.

'Please, God,' he prayed, 'don't take my child away. Please help her to get better.'

'Don't take on so, Tommy,' I said. 'She's going to be all right. You'll see.'

First thing next morning we were round at the surgery waiting with the other patients for Dr Cooklin to arrive.

'Is it serious, doctor?' Tommy asked anxiously.

'It's a mild case of croup,' the doctor said after examining Mary. 'Steam inhalations will help her breathe more easily. Keep her warm and place a bowl filled with hot water and a few drops of Friar's Balsam near her cot. And most important of all, both of you stay calm! Fear soon communicates itself to little ones.'

It was useless telling Tommy to stay calm. His early childhood experiences had made him tense and expecting the worst. But there was nothing to be afraid of. Within a week, Mary's breathing returned to normal and she was her happy, gurgling self.

It was about this time that I found I was pregnant again.

Good, I told myself. Maybe this time it'll be a boy. I decided not to consult my fortune-telling neighbour with her apple-pie/cherry-pie theories. Best to leave it to Nature and accept whatever God sent us. Since Mary had been born Tommy had never said he would like a boy but nevertheless I thought that deep down he would welcome a son and heir to play football with and to follow in his footsteps in the market. As it turned out, I had another little girl whom we named Florence after my childhood heroine Florence Nightingale. She was as beautiful as Mary but definitely took second place in Tommy's affections. One good thing about another girl was that we were able to hand down Mary's clothes.

A year later, there was another baby on the way. By the law of averages, surely this one would present Tommy with a son. Our hopes were in vain. Another girl! We called number three Pauline, or Polly for short. Why Polly? It sounds daft, I know, but my favourite nursery rhyme at school had always been 'Polly put the kettle on' and I liked the sound of the full name Polly Hopkins. Somehow, it sounded so tasteful.

Of course Jimmy Dixon had a wonderful time with his snide remarks.

'Why all these girls, Tommy? Trying to produce a netball team or what?' or 'You want to get some more Boddington's bitter down you, Tommy. That should do the trick.'

Tommy took it in good part and simply laughed it off, even when Jimmy said one night, 'Here's Angela and me doing our best to have one kid and Tommy there has only to hang his trousers over the bed rail and there's another little Hopkins on the way.' It was meant to be a joke but the remark contained a certain amount of sadness because Angela still longed to have a child but there was nothing doing.

Whilst our home could not be described as crowded, it was gradually filling up. Everywhere there were baby things: clothes, rattles, prams, cradles, nappies drying on the line. What a job it was keeping the place clean and it was a constant battle to fight off the bugs, the fleas and the other pests. Cockroaches were my biggest worry; they usually came out at night and it was best to tackle them by putting talcum powder down. But one day, I had the shock of my life when I found Flo – who was now at the early crawling stage – had 'something' in her mouth.

'Come on, Flo, my little love,' I said softly. 'What's that you've got in your mouth?'

I managed to get the 'something' out. Imagine my horror when I found she'd picked up a cockroach! I redoubled my efforts. Tommy spent much of his time worrying about childhood illnesses – scarlet fever, bronchitis, whooping cough. All potential killers. He brought home jars of Virol and bottles of Scott's Emulsion, two products he swore by. And he was forever fretting that the kids might meet with some accident. One day, Mary slipped whilst playing hopscotch and bashed her head on the pavement. He carried her over five miles to the casualty department of Ancoats Hospital. It turned out to be nothing serious though it left a little lump on the back of her head for a day or two. But Tommy would take no chances.

How proud he was of the kids! Before our marriage, he hadn't gone to church much but now he became a regular sight, happily attending nine o'clock Mass every Sunday with me and his three girls dressed in their ribbons and silk finery. A pillar of St Chad's society is what he'd become.

He was anxious as ever to educate me in current affairs. One day, I was breast-feeding Polly and thinking about what I'd get Tommy for his tea – perhaps tripe and onions from the UCP, he always liked that – when he disturbed my train of thought by reading an item from the *Daily Dispatch*.

'The news looks bad, Kate.'

Here we go again, I thought.

'Irish at it again, Tommy?'

'No, not the Irish this time, Kate. It's abroad. Some mad bugger's killed the Austrian Archduke and his missus.'

What in God's name had that got to do with us? It was like all that stuff about famine in India and earthquakes in Turkey. As far as I knew, we didn't have any archdukes among our friends or neighbours. Best to humour him, though.

'Oh, aye,' I replied. 'Is that important?'

'It could be, Kate,' he said slowly. 'All the countries have signed agreements to protect each other if they're attacked. Gentlemen's agreements, they call them.'

'Sounds complicated, Tommy,' I said. 'A bit like when kids fight in the playground. Johnny hits young Alfie. Sid comes up and says to Johnny, "You hit Alfie again and I'll belt *you* one." Next Bert walks up to Sid. "And if you hit *Johnny*, I'll thump *you*." And so it goes on till everyone's making a fist at everyone else.'

Tommy laughed. 'It's what the politicians call the balance of power. Stalemate. That is, unless one of the crazy bastards does carry out his threat and then all hell will be let loose with everyone bashing each other over the head.'

'Do you think that's going to happen over this archduke fella? Is there going to be a war, Tommy?'

'Not a chance. Thanks to Queen Victoria and Prince Albert, all the European heads are related to each other – either uncles or cousins. Besides, nobody can afford it.'

Monday, 3 August, was a Bank Holiday.

'I think we'll go to Blackpool again,' Angela announced one weekend in July. 'I'll organise seats for us on the excursion from Victoria for Monday morning. Whatever we arrange, the men will agree as they always leave it to us.'

By 'us' she meant herself. We'd always left the choice of our day out to Angela, but this time Hilda and I thought we'd like a say – a sort of palace revolution.

'We've done Blackpool twice,' Hilda said. 'Let's try somewhere else for a change.'

'I suppose we could go to New Brighton again,' Angela said, not sounding too keen on the idea.

'Why not pick a different place?' I protested. 'Let's try Southport.'

'Southport!' Angela exploded. 'Who in God's name

wants to go to Southport? It's got the name of being the dead centre of Lancashire – a cemetery with lights. And the sea is so far out, you have to hire a cab to go for a swim.'

'We've never been there and I've heard it's a lovely place for the kids,' I argued, not to be talked out of it so easily. 'It's called the Seaside Garden City.'

'And I've heard it's quiet and refined,' Hilda added. She didn't mention that she and I had talked it over before raising the matter with Angela.

'So, who needs quiet and refined?' Angela scoffed.

'We do!' Hilda and I chorused.

'We'll vote on it,' I said. A bit unfair really, as we knew the result already.

Angela lost two to one. Southport it was.

'Don't blame me if you have a miserable time,' she said. Angela always had to have the last word.

From Ancoats to Victoria Station is only a short walk. Tommy carried Mary high on his shoulders and Jimmy carried little Flo, while I had charge of Polly in her pram. Danny and Hilda met us at the station and this time we were joined by Eddie who had got the day off from Swinton. We put the pram in the guard's van and caught the nine o'clock excursion, arriving in the resort an hour later. We stepped out of Chapel Street Station into glorious sunshine, and something strange came over the men. Perhaps it was the sea air or the freedom of a day off work. Whatever it was, they became little boys again – especially Tommy.

'First thing we do,' he shouted excitedly, 'is take a carriage ride through the town.'

Outside the station we chose a landau drawn by a pair of fine black horses and we were soon riding down Southport's magnificent boulevard that was Lord Street.

'I've always wondered what it felt like to be King for a

day,' Jimmy laughed as he gave a royal wave to passers-by on each side of the road.

'Let's hope some mad bugger doesn't shoot us,' Tommy called.

After the tour, we found our way to the so-called Pleasureland where our three men rushed about like kids in a sweets factory eager to try everything that met their eye.

They insisted we all have a go on the water chute. Us ladies politely turned the offer down as we didn't fancy it one bit and we hated paying out good money to be shaken about and frightened to death. Instead we took the children to the promenade paddling pool where Angela held Mary's hand tightly as she joyfully splashed about in the water. Hilda and I sat in the shade with the two younger ones. We could hear the men's ecstatic WHEEEE! as their wooden boats shot down the steel ramp at breakneck speed into the lake three hundred yards below. After that, it was the Maxim Flying Machine whirling them round the rim of the lake. With the children we preferred quieter activities like building sand castles or taking donkey rides. We couldn't leave Pleasureland without visiting the funfair and wasting a few pennies on the 'Try Your Luck' stalls. Good, harmless fun. At the 'Drop the Man Into the Water' stall Tommy succeeded in hitting the bull's-eye, so tipping the poor victim into the big barrel of water below.

There would have been more but I reckoned that it was time for a break, and anyroad it was one o'clock and we were ready for dinner. Near the railway station, we'd noticed a lovely restaurant called Hayes' which offered 'special terms for picnic parties'.

'I reckon seven adults make up a picnic party,' Danny remarked.

There was only one meal we could choose and that was

fish and chips cooked as only a Lancashire restaurant knew how.

Throughout the meal we could hear the newsboys calling out the headlines.

'LATEST NEWS! INVASION OF FRANCE! GERMANY ON THE MARCH!'

'I don't like the sound of that,' I said.

'Newspapers exaggerating as usual,' Tommy said. 'Nothing to worry about, it won't affect us.'

'And even if it does,' Danny answered, 'you can leave it to the army. We'll soon sort the Kaiser out if he wants war.'

'I hope there *is* a war,' Eddie exclaimed. 'I wouldn't mind getting into it.'

'Don't talk so daft, our Eddie,' I said. 'War's not a game. Besides, you're far too young.'

'I'm over seventeen now, Kate. Old enough to join up.'

'The army's not for baby boys,' retorted Danny. 'You're hardly out of nappies.'

'Huh!' Eddie replied. 'I've already done two years with the Swinton army cadets, so I'm an old hand. If there's going to be a war, I want to enlist fast before it's all over. I'll be in the Bugle Band.'

'That should terrify the Kaiser, all right,' Jimmy laughed. 'That means we'll have a short war.'

'For God's sake,' Angela said. 'Enough talk about war. We're supposed to be enjoying ourselves.'

After lunch, we decided on less hectic activity and strolled along the promenade licking our ice-cream cornets.

Our walk took us as far as the pier and we found we were in time for a performance of the Pier Pierrots at three thirty. We took our seats in a row of deck chairs arranged in front of the stage and we hadn't long to wait. The troupe came on singing 'I do like to be beside the seaside' to the accompaniment of several banjos; they were wearing the traditional costume of loose-fitting white silk shirts with four or five large black pompoms on them, dunces' caps and white face-paint. The entertainment was as advertised – a good family show, suitable for all ages. It began with a few songs sung around the piano, followed by a few simple sketches and monologues. Two comedians did a quick-fire double routine. The quips were topical and had an anti-German flavour. We wondered how Hilda would react having a German grandad but she seemed to take it in good part and laughed with the rest of us. Somehow the humour seemed to reflect the spirit of the times, unhurried, uncomplicated, unthreatening. The Germans wouldn't dare to start a fight with us – we were British. The show finished with a general sing-song of the popular tunes of 1914: 'Hello, Hello, Who's Your Lady Friend?' 'Keep the Home Fires Burning'. And finally Elgar's patriotic song which had become our second national anthem:

Land of Hope and Glory, Mother of the free,
How shall we uphold thee, who are born of thee?
Gird thee well for battle, bid thy hosts increase;
Stand for faith and honour, smite for truth and peace!

After the show, we ordered tea and cakes from a kiosk in the municipal gardens and found places near a beautiful fountain. Not far away was a bandstand and we settled down to listen to a military band playing a selection of airs from *The Merry Widow* until it was time to catch the excursion train back to Manchester.

We reached Victoria Station tired but happy. Angela was ready to concede that Southport wasn't so bad. But as we stepped out of the station, the terrible news hit us like a thunderbolt.

'EVENING NEWS SPECIAL! GERMANY INVADES BELGIUM! WAR IMMINENT!'

Tommy bought a paper and read the main items.

'A hundred thousand Germans march on Belgium and Luxembourg. Belgian King appeals to His Majesty King George the Fifth for help.'

'What does it mean, Tommy?' I asked. 'Is it war?'

'No two ways about it, Kate. It's war all right.'

'Oh, good,' Eddie exclaimed. 'Now I can join up. I'd better be quick though, before it's all over.'

Next day, Great Britain declared war on Germany. As if by magic, there appeared on hoardings and the sides of trams and buses and on pillar boxes government recruiting posters with the moustached face of Lord Kitchener and his pointing finger. 'In this crisis, your country calls on all able-bodied men to rally round the flag and enlist in the ranks of her army.'

Other posters appealed to the women of Britain to tell their men to go. Everywhere there were notices calling on army reservists and Territorials to report immediately for duty. Tradesmen had cards printed and exhibited in their shop windows: 'Business as usual during alterations to the map of Europe.'

Mrs Kenyon came round to tell us that her Paddy was a reservist and would be joining up the next day. 'He's been told by his bosses at the Salford Gas Department that each man's family will get fifteen shillings a week with a further half-crown for each child during his absence. That's in addition to his shilling a day. We've never been so well-off.'

When she'd gone, Tommy said, 'That bugger Paddy Kenyon can start taking out his anger by bashing the Boche instead of his wife. And she's going to get paid while he's doing it.'

On that first night of the war, Tommy and I got Mrs Kenyon to baby-sit while we went with Jimmy and Angela to join the crowds congregating in Albert Square. There we found a vast multitude of people celebrating, cheering and slapping each other on the back. They were waving Union Jacks and bellowing 'Rule Britannia'.

'Bloody fools!' Jimmy said. 'They don't understand what we've let ourselves in for.'

'Not to worry,' Tommy said. 'Asquith said it'll be over by Christmas.'

'Not according to Kitchener,' Jimmy replied. 'He reckons we're in for a long haul – a few years maybe.'

'He would say that,' I said. 'Being a soldier, he's hoping it'll last for a few years. More medals and glory for him. Maybe a statue in Trafalgar Square and a plaque in Westminster Abbey.'

A number of city councillors appeared on the town hall steps to address the throng through a public address system. The first orator whipped up hatred of the Germans by describing the atrocities their troops had committed: bayoneting babies, bricking-up mines containing Belgian miners, hanging Belgian priests head downwards as living clappers in their church bells, and raping nuns. Speaker after speaker spoke of 'foul crimes towards both sexes', the German hordes, the impending invasion, and the gallantry of our 'little British army'.

The final speaker turned to the real purpose of the meeting – the question of recruitment.

'Thousands, nay millions of men are to be rushed into the bloodiest of wars mainly, we are told, for a mere scrap of paper. But on that scrap of paper are written the words, "The honour of Britain".'

There were loud cheers and it was some time before he could go on.

'That is a fine idea, but we also have to remember that at the same time we shall be fighting for ourselves, for our wives, for our children, for everything that's dear to us. Fighting for our shores, the liberty of our country, for our hearths and homes. Can we sit comfortably at home while this is going on? I appeal to the men of Manchester to enlist today.'

As I listened, I wondered how much fighting he would be doing personally. Probably not much. His speech had the desired effect, however, for there was spontaneous applause and the crowd began singing the national anthem with great gusto.

The night ended when the Lord Mayor came onto the platform and shouted out, 'Are we downhearted?'

'No!'

'Shall we beat 'em?'

'YE-E-E-S!'

At home that night, Tommy said, 'I think that councillor was right. It's not fair that people like me should sit at home while others fight for our home and our children.'

'Don't talk so daft, Tommy,' I told him. 'You're thirty years of age and you have a family to think of. Leave the fighting to the young men.'

But he wouldn't hear of it. Next day, he took the day off to go down early to join the crush of hopeful recruits at Ardwick Artillery HQ. He was away all day and I was worried out of my mind. I prayed to God that something – I couldn't think what – would stop him from joining.

A sheepish-looking Tommy came back later that evening.

'Well,' I said anxiously, 'when do you go?'

'I don't,' he said. 'I didn't pass the medical.'

'Didn't pass the medical! But you're as fit as a fiddle! What's wrong with you?'

'My feet,' he said. 'They said I've got hammer toes and something called Hallux Valgus.'

Thank you, God, I said silently. Up to that point I'd never realised that the Almighty had a sense of humour.

'That Hallux thingamajig sounds serious,' I said. 'But surely those hammer toes would be useful in a war. You could kick hell out of the Germans.'

'It seems not, Kate. They reckon I wouldn't be able to do long route marches.'

That was a laugh. Tommy not able to do long marches! He'd marched me all round Manchester during our courtship and he'd have marched the British Army into the ground.

Chapter Twenty-Six

In the first week of the war, young Eddie got his wish and enlisted in return for the King's shilling.

When I asked him how he'd managed to get himself into the army at such a tender age, he gave me a big wink and said, 'Easy. I told the recruiting sergeant I was seventeen and one month. The sergeant said, "I didn't hear you properly. Did you say eighteen and one month?" "I did!" I replied. That was that and I was in!'

Like his schoolmates at Swinton Industrial School, Eddie was in the unusual position of having done his drilling and his square-bashing in advance, so he needed only a minimum of further training before joining the British Expeditionary Force which was being sent to France.

Manchester and Salford became garrison towns and Heaton Park in the north of Manchester had been turned into a vast military camp. In the early days, there weren't enough uniforms or weapons to go round and parades were taken in civvies, with sticks for rifles. As a sergeant in the Territorials, Danny had been sent to Heaton Park along with other experienced NCOs to begin the mammoth task of licking the thousands of raw recruits into shape and ready for battle. Danny was unhappy with this posting and was for ever bemoaning his fate.

'Why they have to send young whipper-snappers like Eddie to France whilst experienced men like me have to remain behind, I'll never know. This Kitchener's Army is a right bunch of riffraff. Fred Karno's Army isn't in it.'

'You count your blessings, Danny,' I told him. 'You're obviously needed more here training troops than going abroad yourself.'

Eddie, along with many of his Swinton companions, was amongst the first contingents to be posted to Heaton Park. The atmosphere there was more like a boys' holiday camp than an army training centre. On summer evenings, after their sons had finished gruelling military manoeuvres during the day, the families of the young soldiers would sometimes gather on the grassy knolls for a get-together. It was on one of these occasions that, thanks to Danny pulling a few strings here and there, we succeeded in getting a group of friends and relatives together for a farewell picnic before Eddie went to France. Hilda was there, and her brother Eric, and Angela and Jimmy. Cissie came with her intended, Keith Atherton, and his twin brother, Ernie, and it was true what she'd told us, they were like two peas in a pod, tall and thin, which prompted Jimmy of course to make his usual personal comment.

'You know, Cissie, if your man Keith there were to slip down a crack in the pavement, you'd have a back-up copy in his brother Ernie.'

'We're not exactly the same,' Keith grinned. 'For example, our tailor knows that we dress on different sides.'

For some reason I was never able to understand, the men roared with laughter when they heard this.

Eddie brought a few chums from Swinton but his special friend seemed to be Alf Higgins – they spent much of the time laughing and skylarking about. And finally, surprise of surprises, along came Mam with her two young ones,

John and Hetty, but no Frank McGuinness. We were so glad to see her because, although we had sent her an invitation, we hadn't expected her to turn up.

It was a happy meeting with lots of laughter and good-natured kidding. We had brought mountains of sandwiches, cheese and piccalilli, ham and chicken, to be washed down with a few bottles of Guinness and Mackeson's stout.

'Enough here to feed the whole battalion,' Eddie remarked as he tucked in.

Making use of one of the little stone fireplaces that were dotted conveniently about the park, the young soldiers demonstrated how they would light a fire when they got to the trenches and how they would make a brew-up in a billycan.

'First,' said Eddie, 'we build up the fire with thin chips of wood, next boil the water, then put the sugar and the tea into the can.'

'We always save a little tea,' added Alf Higgins, 'and dip the corner of a towel into it to wash our faces.'

Eddie grinned. 'Next we dip our shaving brushes into the bit remaining and work up a lather. Nothing's to be wasted in the trenches.'

It was left to Jimmy and Tommy to provide the light-hearted banter in a double act that wouldn't have been out of place at the Queen's Park Hipp.

'If you take that bugle of yours, Eddie,' Tommy quipped, 'and let off a few notes at the Jerries, you won't see their heels for dust. I'm only sorry I won't be there to witness it.'

'Shame about that, Tommy,' Jimmy countered. 'From what I've heard, your hammer toes are what's stopping you. I don't understand that. With hammer toes, you could have been useful at the front nailing barbed wire on the fences.'

'Funny man!' replied Tommy. 'I don't suppose you heard that I was also suffering from Hallux Valgus on each foot.'

'Yes, I did. I asked my doctor about it and he said you've got bunions.'

As everyone was laughing happily, I suddenly had a mental picture of these splendid young men facing the German machine guns on the Western Front, and an involuntary shudder passed through me. But the talk on this balmy summer evening was about the thrill and adventure of going abroad to fight a brutal enemy. It had little to do with King and country and flag-waving, and more to do with youth eager to prove its manhood. They talked as if they were about to have a fortnight's holiday in the Isle of Man. The young men seemed to regard the war as high jinks and an opportunity to sow their wild oats, a bit like the young Zulu warriors Gran'ma used to tell me about. Washing of the spears, she said they called it.

In his usual tactful way, Jimmy turned to Hilda's brother, Eric, to ask, 'How do you feel about going to fight your German relatives?'

Eric was equal to the question. 'About the same as King George fighting his cousin, Kaiser Wilhelm. He's a crazy Prussian and he's got to be stopped. Apart from that, Hilda and I are both as English as you are. Mancunians, in fact.'

'In many ways, I envy you young lads,' Jimmy continued. 'How I'd like to join Kitchener's Army and take a trip to France! A bit of excitement to pep up a dull existence would suit me down to the ground right now. Instead, I'm compelled by the government to stand operating a lathe for the duration.'

'If you want excitement,' Angela remarked, fluttering her eyelids, 'you've always got me. Anyroad, the army wants young fit men, not old fogies like you.'

Three weeks later, Private Eddie Lally and his mates sailed to France as bandsmen with the BEF. The other young lads at the picnic – the twins and Hilda's brother – joined the Salford Pals Battalion of the Lancashire Fusiliers. Six months later, they too were in France. Around this time, we celebrated two weddings. Cissie married her twin boyfriend, Keith, and Hilda and Danny finally tied the knot in a ceremony at St Chad's.

Tongue in cheek, Danny explained the reason for the wedding. 'Hilda may as well have the army marriage allowance,' he said.

'I see,' I replied. 'So love doesn't come into it. It's a business arrangement, is that it?'

'Exactly,' he replied, grinning from ear to ear.

Deep down, I was overjoyed to hear that Danny was to be married and to Hilda, such a kind, gentle girl. I loved the idea of my younger brother marrying, settling down and having children. I could see it in my mind's eye – his kids playing with mine in Queen's Park or going to the Saturday matinee together. It was all happening, my long-cherished dream of the extended family coming together.

As for Tommy, though he'd failed his medical, he was determined to do his bit for the war effort. Jimmy came to the rescue and found him a job doing night work at Henry Wallworks on Red Bank. The work would involve production of motor car parts for vehicles destined for the Western Front. Not that Tommy knew anything about engineering or had mechanical skills but he would be useful fetching and carrying for those who did. His hours were 6 p.m. to 6 a.m. but even that was not enough. Every morning he kept his hand in at Smithfield Market by doing a couple of hours on Deakins' stall. This meant that he stayed in touch with his old market friends and customers, and it also gave him the chance to pick up extra food for the family table.

Tommy was still a great believer in the value of the rabbit and he made sure we had a steady supply, with the occasional hare thrown in.

The autumn months of 1914 brought news of battles whose names were enough to cause a shudder – Mons, the Marne, the Aisne and, the bloodiest battlefield of all, Ypres, which our men called Wipers. Tommy bought a map of Europe with little packets of flags to mark the front line and he and Jimmy followed the war closely. As the line bulged into France towards Paris, they slowly came to accept that we would not be in Berlin by Christmas after all. Every day, we scanned the endless lists of casualties published in the newspapers, praying that none of our loved ones would be featured there. Sometimes, we recognised familiar names of soldiers killed in action – Lieutenant Harold Lamport-Smythe of the Cheshire Regiment, Danny's old friends from the workhouse and Swinton, the two Foley brothers of the Lancashire Regiment. And the war came close when we saw the name of our next-door neighbour, Paddy Kenyon, killed at Ypres. Madge, his wife, was inconsolable and she spent a great deal of time telling us what a wonderful husband he'd been. It was of some comfort when she found that the pensions awarded to her by the War Office and the Salford Gas Department were truly generous. In January 1915, we heard that Eddie had been hurt at the Marne. It wasn't serious, thank God – a broken arm and a fractured collarbone. Bomb blast had sent him flying through the air and he'd landed badly. Everyone said that Eddie had been lucky – he'd got minor wounds that would earn him a spot of leave.

In February of that year, Eddie came home with his arm and shoulder in a sling. It was a joy to see him, though somehow he looked different. Tired, older and more serious perhaps, though I think a better word might be solemn. When he told us that his best mate, Alf Higgins, had been killed whilst standing right next to him, I could understand why.

'A shell from a nine point two,' he said simply. 'It broke up into splinters about the size of my hand. It was one of those that sliced the top off Alf's head alongside of me. There was blood and brains all over the trench. Alf didn't even see it coming. It could have just as easily been me.'

After that, Eddie hardly said a word and we didn't press him. Whatever experiences he'd had were too awful to talk about. Maybe he thought that, as civilians, we wouldn't understand anyway. On his first night back, we organised a family gathering and adjourned to the Land o' Cakes to celebrate his homecoming. The usual crowd came round, including Mam and this time Frank McGuinness. Never one to miss a booze-up, I thought, but I dismissed it from my mind as uncharitable. Accompanied by our elderly resident performer on the old battered piano, we sang the songs of the day – 'Pack Up Your Troubles', 'Long Way to Tipperary', 'The Army of Today's All Right', and all the patriotic songs we could think of. Eddie sat there savouring every moment.

After the pub, we went back to the house for a bite to eat and a few extra drinks. It was then that Eddie opened up and told us all that had been happening to him.

'The Germans aren't the only enemy,' he said, rolling a fag and lighting it. 'Just as bad are the cold, the rain, the mud, and the vermin – lice, bugs, and rats which feed on the rotting corpses lying around us. In the trenches, you make the greatest friends you've ever had, true comrades because you depend on each other for survival. The old hands used to say that if you're going to get killed, it's best to get it at the beginning. That way, you don't suffer so much. There were so many deaths, we became hard and brutal. We had to be. On my first day in the trenches, our platoon sergeant kept coming to the dug-out to ask how I was. "Is Private Lally all right?" he'd ask. If he asked it once, he asked it a dozen times. "That sergeant's a really nice man," I said. "Looks after me like he was my father." Everyone roared with laughter. "You bloody fool!" someone said. "He's drawn your name in a lottery and stands to win the jackpot if you get hit." '

'The heartless bastard!' Tommy exclaimed.

'Not at all,' Eddie replied quietly. 'After a few months out there, I became as bad. But there was an incident I witnessed with my own eyes that'll remain with me for the rest of my life. It can only be described as a miracle because there's no explanation for it.'

The little company crammed into our front parlour sat spellbound, hanging onto Eddie's every word.

'It took place at Mons. The BEF had been almost wiped out. We'd started with about sixty thousand men and I don't think we had even half left. The Germans not only outnumbered us but they had better equipment and bigger guns. I was with a platoon of about thirty men and an officer called Lieutenant Willis. We were cut off in a trench and Willis said, "We can either stay here and be caught like rats in a trap or we can make a run for it. It's the only chance we've got.' We didn't have time to think about it. We dashed into the open and we heard the German cavalry tearing after us. We turned round to face them, expecting instant death, when we saw between us and the enemy a bright cloud and in it a whole troop of angels.'

'Come off it!' exclaimed Jimmy. 'You're having us on. This is *nineteen* fifteen not *fourteen* fifteen.'

'As God is my witness,' Eddie replied, 'I saw them, we all saw them, including the officer. The German horses were terrified and reared up then stampeded. The cavalrymen pulled at the bridles but the horses had gone mad and went off in every direction. This gave us time to reach a little fort and save ourselves.'

'Are you sure you hadn't just been given your ration of rum?' Tommy asked playfully. 'It sounds a bit far-fetched.'

'It doesn't matter whether you believe me or not,' Eddie said testily. 'I tell you I'm standing here talking to you tonight because of those angels. We took a few prisoners in that clash and they kept asking us who the horsemen in armour were who led the charge. They were seen by thousands of soldiers, English and German, religious and non-religious alike.'

'Well, I believe you, Eddie,' I said, 'because I read about it in *The Universe* last Sunday at church.'

'And so do I,' added Danny. 'Many of the walking wounded from Mons are back in Heaton Park. They swear they saw the angels and it was because of them that a massacre was prevented.'

There was a long pause while we took it all in.

'It's unbelievable,' Jimmy said at last, breaking the silence. He sounded sceptical.

'That's the whole point of a miracle,' said Angela. 'It's something that *is* unbelievable. Otherwise it wouldn't be a miracle, would it?'

Our lives were dominated by the war. Eddie was given a temporary post guarding German prisoners of war in Leigh where a big camp had been built. The situation on the Western Front became ever more desperate and every day we thanked God that the two men in our family had postings at home. Hilda's younger brother, Eric, was not so lucky. In the action at Ypres he lost both his legs at a place called Hill 60, a piece of derelict ground which the generals regarded as vital. At the cost of many lives, we had won it and then lost it again. To us at home, it seemed a terrible waste of young lives. Hilda and her family were distraught when their young man came back in a wheelchair to be rehabilitated at Whitworth Street Municipal School which had been converted into a hospital for the wounded.

My sister Cissie also suffered tragedy. In 1915 she had become pregnant and when her time was due, her husband Keith who was stationed at Heaton Park Camp had gone absent without leave to be by her side at the crucial time. The Red Caps were sent to bring him back and, as punishment, he'd been posted immediately to the front at Ypres. He was killed on his first day by a sniper's bullet. Cissie had a miscarriage, probably because of her grief. She eventually found happiness though, 'cos some time later she married his twin brother, Ernie. So Jimmy's quip about her having a back-up copy of Keith turned out to be true.

Our complacency about our own two young men was short-lived. So many soldiers had been lost in battle that the government gave up its policy of voluntary enlistment and announced plans for conscription. In April, Danny received orders to join a contingent of men going to France. It was a sad farewell when we took him to London Road Station. Poor Hilda, I thought, this war is hitting her badly. But that wasn't the end of it.

Late one night in May, Hilda came banging frantically on our front door.

'Oh, Kate! Tommy! For God's sake, please come and help us!'

'What in heaven's name has happened, Hilda?'

'Mobs have attacked our shop and set fire to it. My father and my old grandfather have been beaten up! The police said they can do nothing.'

Tommy and I got dressed quickly and hurried to the shop in Dantzig Street. There we found the place gutted and firemen dousing out the last of the flames. Mr and Mrs Muller and their aged parents were standing by in their dressing gowns and in great distress. It was not the time to be asking about the whys and wherefores.

'Come with us,' Tommy said immediately.

Shivering uncontrollably and without a word, Hilda's family followed us up Miller's Lane, across Oldham Road until we reached Back Murray Street. We soon had a cheerful fire going and we wrapped blankets round them in an attempt to stop their trembling. Only when we'd got a hot mug of tea in their hands did we ask what had happened and why.

'The angry mob was blaming us for the sinking of the *Lusitania* last Friday,' Hilda explained. 'About ten o'clock at night, a crowd gathered outside the shop and began chanting "German pigs! German pigs!" Then they began breaking the windows.'

The story was taken up by her father, Edwin.

'I have never seen anything like it,' he said. 'The shop has been completely wrecked and looted. The mob took everything. One thug took a flitch of bacon, another a whole side of pork, others our furniture. One hooligan pushed our piano out of the upstairs window onto the pavement below. They set fire to the premises while the police looked on. Last, they set about me and my father who is seventy-eight years old. It was to escape mob violence like this that he came with my mother to this country twenty years ago.'

Throughout this account, the ladies in his party wept quietly.

'It was not our fault that German submarines sank the ship,' the old grandad tried to explain. 'We're simple people and know nothing about politics.'

'And your pigeons, your lovely pigeons, Edwin!' Mrs Muller wailed. 'All dead.'

'The police said they could do nothing.' Edwin Muller held out both hands to indicate the hopelessness of it all. 'Now I don't know what's going to happen to us.'

'My place is small,' Hilda said, 'but you can stay with me until something's settled.'

The Mullers stayed with us for the rest of the next day and then moved across to Hilda's one-bedroom house. Later the whole family was interned in Lancaster 'as enemy aliens' for the duration of the war.

'They tried to intern me too,' Hilda said, 'until they found I'd been born in Manchester. But I'm so worried for my family in that camp.'

'It's probably best for your family's own safety,' we told her. 'At least they won't be attacked there.'

The camp at Lancaster was a disused wagon works close to the river, a filthy, draughty place, littered with rusty scrap metal and guarded by high barbed fences. Hilda told us there were more than three thousand prisoners there, with more crowding in every day – seamen, waiters from the Midland Hotel, and even a German band which had been in the wrong place at the wrong time.

The attack on the Mullers was only one of many throughout our region. Many shops were forced to display a notice which declared: 'This is not a German shop. God Save the King'. Anyone with a foreign-sounding name was suspected as a spy and when the crowd heard about Edwin Muller's racing pigeons, they were convinced he'd been using them to send messages to the enemy.

After the attack, we saw a good deal of Hilda and whenever she had a letter from Danny she came round to tell us.

'You can't imagine,' she said, 'how hard I find it waiting,

always waiting for news. Ordinary sounds become a torture – the mantelpiece clock ticking off each hour of dread, the knock at the door bringing perhaps the dreaded telegram, the postman delivering the awful news I can't even bring myself to think about. I've taken up work in a munitions factory in an attempt to stop worrying. And my own family interned like prisoners of war in the Lancaster camp.'

'It can't go on for ever, Hilda,' I said, trying to console her. 'One day this war will end and life will return to normal.'

I couldn't tell her that I was as worried as she was.

Just before Christmas, she came to see us with joy written all over her face.

'Kate! Oh, Kate! Good news at last! Danny has written to say he'll be home permanently on December the thirty-first. Now there's conscription, there aren't enough experienced men to train the new recruits. He's been posted back to Heaton Park! Nineteen sixteen! A new year and a fresh start for us!'

What bliss it was to see Hilda smiling again! She had suffered so much in the last year with her brother's crippling injuries and the internment of her family. On New Year's Eve, Tommy and I took the children over to Hilda's to await Danny's return. Young Mary and Flo were as excited as we were to see Uncle Danny again. At around six o'clock, there came the knock at the door.

'It's him! It's him!' Hilda called out happily and rushed down the lobby.

But it wasn't him. At the door stood a postman with a special delivery. My heart skipped a beat when I saw this.

'He's probably been delayed,' Hilda said as she tore the envelope open. The look of horror on her face said it all. Ashen, she handed me the letter, looking to me to tell her that somehow she'd read it wrongly and had misunderstood it.

> Dear Mrs Lally,
>
> It is with great regret that I have to inform you that your husband, Sergeant Daniel Lally, was killed in the first line trenches at Passchendaele on December 29th at about four o'clock in the afternoon. The Germans were shelling our trenches and he was struck in the head by shrapnel and killed instantaneously as he was entering his dugout. It may be of some consolation to you to know that he suffered no pain. Sergeant Lally was a brave man and he gave his life for his country. Writing as I am just before the New Year, I feel most deeply how terrible your grief must be at this time.

'Kate, Kate,' she sobbed. 'What am I to do? I don't want to go on living without Danny.'

It's said that when the body suffers a terrible injury, nature comes to the rescue and paralyses the senses so that you do not feel the pain. Something similar must happen when we have emotional shock, for as I read the letter, a mental shutter seemed to come down to protect me from the agony of taking in the full meaning of the disaster. I felt numb and could not believe the dreadful news. Danny, my young brother – dead! I felt so lost and so helpless.

I flung my arms round Hilda and we clung to each other for dear life as if that might somehow alleviate the pain. But of course it didn't.

Some people find consolation in the thought that the body is no more than a package or a shell that houses the soul. Though the package may die, they say, the real person lives on and is indestructible. For me the idea offered no solace. I only knew that I would never see Danny again, never see him smile or hear him crack a joke. Inside, my heart was breaking but for the sake of Hilda I had to be strong.

Hilda began to shiver with the shock. She let out a moan of anguish and broke into uncontrollable sobbing.

'Oh, Kate, Kate! Danny can't be dead. He was everything to me, the only man I have ever loved. Before Danny, there was nothing, no real purpose to anything. I met him and my life had meaning. Now he's gone and I am back where I started. My family's interned and my brother Eric is disabled. I can't see the point in carrying on.'

'Dear, dear Hilda,' I said. 'I am so sorry for all that's happened to you. I know it's not the same but we're your family now until you get your own back. There's hardly a family in the land that has not been hit by this dreadful war. But this slaughter cannot go on for ever.'

'Won't Uncle Danny be coming home today?' young Mary asked.

'No, Mary my love. Danny won't be coming home ever,' Tommy answered gently.

I stayed with Hilda the rest of that evening, trying to comfort her. It was getting late when I left and I thought it best to wait until the next day to tell Mam the distressing news. I would save her at least one night of grief.

The following day, Saturday, I left the children with Tommy and with heavy heart walked the short distance to Mam's place. I found her there with Frank and they must have sensed from the look on my face that all was not well for Mam said, 'Kate, you look as pale as a sheet. What on earth has happened?'

'I have some bad news, Mam. It's Danny.'

'What's happened to him? Has he been wounded? Is it bad?'

'I am afraid it's worse than that, Mam. Danny's dead.'

She frowned at me as if she hadn't understood what I'd said. 'Dead? But he can't be. He's due home on leave today. He can't be.'

'I only wish he weren't,' I said sadly. 'With all my heart, I wish he weren't.'

She continued to stare at me speechless, as if willing me to take the words back and say they weren't true.

Frank's expression was grave. 'Has it been definitely confirmed?' he asked hoarsely.

'Hilda had a letter from his officer telling her how he died of wounds last Wednesday, the twenty-ninth.'

On hearing this, Mam hugged herself closely and began rocking to and fro, sobbing quietly.

'Oh, my poor, poor Danny,' she sang over and over again. 'Oh, my son – my son.'

Frank made tea while I tried to comfort her by holding both her hands tightly but she didn't seem to notice. For many years and in so many ways, Mam and I had gradually drifted apart but now in this moment of shared anguish we came together once more. How my heart went out to her, for she had suffered so much in her life.

'He left some things with me in a suitcase before he went to the front,' she wept at last. 'Please take them across to Hilda. I think she should have them.'

At home later that day, in the privacy of my bedroom, I opened Danny's suitcase to pack it tidily before taking it across to Hilda. My eyes filmed over when I came across his cozzy with the badge for swimming ten lengths and the music of the duet he and Eddie had played at Mary's christening. Fighting back the tears, I straightened out the rest of his things but when I finally came across one of his meerschaum pipes and caught the smell of his St Bruno tobacco, I could hold back no longer and the tears overflowed.

My memories of Danny came flooding back. In so many ways, he'd been the unlucky one in the family. He'd been the one to get caught by the Railway Police as he helped little Cissie over the railway fence, the one to end up getting the loathsome job of oakum picking in the workhouse, the one to get punished unjustly by the illiterate teacher Harold Catchpole, the one to be whipped by Old Jock the cruel workhouse master, and now the one to get himself killed on the Western Front.

Chapter Twenty-Seven

Danny was buried in France with full military honours, and we arranged a Requiem Mass for him at St Michael's. Eddie got compassionate leave from the POW camp to be with us. He was grief-stricken at the death of his big hero brother and whilst we waited for Hilda to arrive, I told him about the letter that Hilda had received.

'His platoon commander,' I said, 'wrote Hilda a beautiful letter of condolence saying how brave Danny was, how he had given his life for his country; and how he had died instantly and suffered no pain.'

To my surprise, Eddie's grief turned to anger when he heard this.

'Kate,' he said, tears of rage springing to his eyes, 'don't give me that stuff about "dying for his country". I can tell you that in the trenches men are slaughtered like cattle and there's nothing heroic about it. It's a terrible waste of thousands and thousands of good ordinary men: plumbers, tram drivers, clerks, milkmen. They died like flies and for what? A few yards of filthy mud. Oh, yes, I saw our officer writing the letters to the loved ones, trotting out the same old words. "Died like a true soldier"; "His supreme sacrifice will not be in vain"; "He died instantaneously and felt no pain". I've heard them all. They're lies, Kate.'

'Surely they can't all be lies, Eddie!'

'They are for me, Kate. Most men die in agony and screaming for their mothers. Did you know it took hours to carry a wounded man by stretcher from the line to the first aid post? Many men didn't even die a soldier's death; they drowned in the mud and the slime. It seemed to me they died in vain.'

'Things can't be as bad as that, Eddie. You're depressed at Danny's death.'

'Sorry, Kate. I shouldn't have said all that, it's against the rules. Soldiers are supposed to gloss over it in case they demoralise the people at home.'

'Whatever you do, Eddie,' I said, 'don't talk like that to Hilda. Don't take away the only things that console her.'

When Hilda joined us, Eddie didn't let me down. Hilda repeated the platoon commander's assurance about the way Danny had died.

'It's a great blessing, Hilda,' Eddie said, 'that Danny died without suffering. We can be truly proud of him for he died to make a better world for those who remain. This is to be the war to end all wars and it's said that the greatest sacrifice a man can make is to lay down his life for his country. Danny died a hero's death and mark my words, one day his name will be inscribed on a memorial raised to honour the glorious dead.'

'Thanks, Eddie. It's good to know his death has some meaning.'

'And a special thank you from me, Eddie,' I whispered to him.

Canon McCabe preached a lovely sermon about how Danny had given his life so that future generations might be free. He ended up by saying, 'Death is nothing to be afraid of. It is only the beginning of eternal life. And remember: those who died in battle are helping us from up there in heaven. They are helping us to win the war.'

I couldn't help saying to myself, what about the German dead? Who are they helping?

So, that was how I began 1916. With a knife through my heart. I could remember Shirty Gerty at St Michael's telling us all those years ago about Queen Mary Tudor who was supposed to have said, 'When I am dead and opened, you shall find "Calais" lying in my heart.' For me, change 'Calais' to '1916'.

Shortly after the Requiem, there was a lot of talk about a massive new breakthrough to be launched in France. It was to be one big battle that would end the war once and for all. The newspapers were full of it and even published the name of the place where it would take place – the River Somme in Picardy. If us ordinary people knew about it, I thought, so did the Germans. All young able-bodied soldiers were transferred from non-essential duties to prepare for the big fight. This included Eddie who was taken off the job of guarding prisoners and sent back to Flanders. I prayed to God that He would keep him safe.

'Surely, Lord, one of my brothers is enough for you. Please send Eddie back to us in one piece.'

I think God must have been only half listening for Eddie was hit by flying shrapnel at Thiepval and he was returned to us minus fingers on both hands. Everyone said how lucky he'd been getting 'a Blighty one'. That may have been so but it meant his cornet-playing days were definitely over. At least he'd survived the Somme where thousands of men had been cut down in the first five minutes of the battle. The so-called Pals Regiments were amongst the worst to suffer. At the beginning of the war, the Earl of Derby had this bright idea of recruiting soldiers from the same town, the same workplace, the same street, even the same family. The appeal was for men to 'serve with their friends and not be put in a battalion with unknown men as their companions'.

'That's all very well,' Tommy remarked, 'not only can the men serve together, they can die together as well.'

And amidst all this tragedy, I found I was having another baby. Perhaps it was a glimmer of hope in that fateful year. Things were collapsing around us but at least our little family was safe and secure. It was the only thing that seemed to make any sense in this mad, crazy world. Maybe this time it would be a boy. I dearly wished it to be so for I still felt that a son and heir was needed to complete Tommy's life though he himself had never said as much. He was supremely happy with his three daughters whom he worshipped, especially his first-born, Mary, who had a special place in his heart. Tommy had never had a brother or sister and all his love was in that child. The princess, he called her, and if he could have put her on a pedestal, he would have done so, he loved her that much. She had a lovely nature and was a beautiful little creature with lovely curls. She always reminded me of the paintings of the cherubs I'd seen on the altar of St Chad's Church. Every day she ran to meet Tommy when he came back from work and, holding his hand, she would lead him into the kitchen and tell him what I'd made him for his breakfast. One day, Tommy had brought home a pound of delicious sausages which he'd bought at the local butcher's on his way home. Soon there was the sound of sizzling sausages and a wonderful smell coming from my kitchen. Tommy offered one to Mary.

'I don't like those sausages,' she said.

'Why not? They're delicious homemade sausages,' Tommy said. 'Made by Burgess, the butcher.'

'I don't like them 'cos they're red,' she answered simply.

'But you've never tasted them!'

'Doesn't matter. They're red.'

As Tommy worked on the night shift, he usually went for a sleep after his meal. At around five o'clock in the evening, I sent Mary into the bedroom to wake him up.

'Come on, Dad,' she would call, lifting one of his eyelids, 'it's time to get up for your dinner.'

He would pretend to be dead and as she was about to run to me, he would suddenly come alive, grab her and start tickling her. She would giggle in delight and hug him tightly.

'You'll spoil that girl,' I used to say.

'So what if I do?' he would answer. 'Where's the harm in that?'

Sometimes I thought Mary did become too wrapped up in her dad. One night Tommy was out at some meeting or other of market porters and was late getting back. Mary refused to go to bed until he returned to tuck her in and tell her a story.

'Look, Mary,' I said. 'It may be after eleven o'clock before he's home. You'll have to go to bed without him for one night.'

'Shan't,' she said, defiantly tightening her lips. 'He said he was going to bring a bar of chocolate. I'm going to wait up for him.'

It was one of the rare occasions when I had to tell her off. It ended up with me giving her a little smack and she went to bed weeping.

'I'm going to tell dad when he comes home,' she said.

Just before Easter, Mary had her fifth birthday. To my amazement, the School Board was round at the house the next day.

'Now she's turned five, she must start school,' he said.

'Give us a chance,' I answered. 'Surely it can wait until after the Easter holiday.'

'No, the law is the law. Children must attend school as soon as they reach the age of admission.'

Reluctantly, we got her ready the next day. A little girl called Alice who lived round the corner agreed to take her.

Mary was as bright as a button and took to school rightaway. Every day she came home with stories of what she'd done, the things she'd made in Plasticine, how she was learning to read, and what Miss Simpson, her teacher, had said.

It was after Easter, a Monday at the beginning of May, that she came home looking flushed and I could tell she wasn't well. I felt her forehead and there was no doubt about it. She was running a temperature.

'I've got a headache, Mam, and my throat's sore,' she said. I think it was the first time I ever heard her complain about anything. Probably croup again, I thought, but I wasn't taking any chances.

'Come on, Mary,' I said. 'You'd better go to bed and lie down. I'll bring you a drink of homemade lemonade.' Homemade lemonade was her favourite.

'I've got a sore throat as well,' little Flo whimpered.

Oh, aye, I thought. She wants a bit of sympathy as well.

'And so have I,' said two-year-old Polly.

Kids, I said to myself, they're so jealous of each other when it comes to seeking attention.

'Well, you'd all better get in bed,' I said, humouring the two young 'uns.

Tommy went up to see Mary when he came home. He came down looking concerned.

'Mary's throat looks very swollen. I think I'd better go and fetch Dr Cooklin.'

Tommy does get het up so easily, I thought, and as for calling the doctor, I hated bothering him 'cos not only was it expensive but I was always worried in case I called him out on a fool's errand.

Tommy came back a couple of hours later to report that our own doctor was away for a few days but that a locum, a Dr Hyams, would call in the morning.

During the night, Mary's condition grew worse and we could hear her gasping for breath. We didn't know what to do for the best. How we prayed for the morning to come so she could get some medical attention.

At eleven o'clock, the young Dr Hyams arrived and from the hurried way he came into the house, we could see that he had many cases to get round that morning. He gave Mary a rapid examination, took her temperature, listened to her heart, felt the glands behind her ears and pronounced his diagnosis.

'German measles!' he said. 'There's a lot of it about at the moment. No need to worry but she must stay off school and not mix with other children outside the family. Keep her comfortable and give her plenty of liquids.'

He noticed I was pregnant.

'When is your baby due?' he asked.

'In about two months,' I told him.

He heaved a sigh of relief. 'At least your new baby's out of danger. Thank your lucky stars that you're not in your first three months or you could have had serious problems.'

With that, he wished us good morning and was gone.

Mary died that night fighting for breath.

Dr Hyams wrote 'German Measles' on the death certificate but I didn't believe it. Not for a moment. Tommy reacted to it with disbelief. No tears. No weeping and wailing. Only an expression of utter bewilderment on his face. He kept shaking his head as if to show he'd lost all hope and faith in life itself and of ever finding happiness.

Mary was laid out under the window in the front room.

A beautiful little girl looking more like an angel than ever.

Outside in the street, life went on as usual and I found that hard to understand. The news vendors were shouting something about an Irish uprising in Dublin but what did that matter in comparison to the death of our little daughter, the light of our lives? How dare the world go on with its ordinary business when for us it had stopped.

From the moment of Mary's death I was in total shock. Angela and Hilda came over to help and without them I don't think I could have attended to all the things that needed doing but I was so run off my feet, registering the death, arranging the details of the funeral that I had no proper chance to grieve. I went about my business in a trance. I felt as if I had died inside.

'And to think,' I wept, 'a week before she died I gave her a smack for not going to bed when I told her. If only I could have the time over again.'

The Catholic undertaker, Mr Stiles, did his best to provide a decent funeral on the pittance the Royal London paid out on Mary's life insurance. He made her a lovely white coffin but there wasn't enough money for a grave of her own and we had to bury her in a public subscription grave with her name on it. I held onto Tommy's hand for dear life and I sobbed and sobbed until I thought my heart would break. All our dreams and all our hopes had been taken away in the space of twenty-four hours. It was goodbye to our smiling, happy little girl who was afraid of the dark, who hated spiders and red sausages, who loved going to school and looking at the moon and the stars, who, when scolded, could turn your frowns into laughter. There were many wreaths placed in the hearse; the neighbours collected for a special big one. The rest of the flowers were simple: pink and white carnations from friends, Jimmy, Angela and Hilda; a second of white carnations and blue cornflowers from our own family.

When the inspector from the town hall had visited us the day after Mary's death, I asked him for an inquest.

'It couldn't have been German measles,' I said. 'She was playing in the street on Saturday and on Wednesday she was dead. Such a lovely girl who should have walked in the procession at church on the first Sunday of May.'

'What's the use of an inquest?' the inspector said. 'It won't bring your little girl back.'

'I blame myself,' I told him. 'I knew all along it wasn't German measles. I should have asked for a second opinion.'

'How could you be expected to know what it was your little girl had?' he replied. 'You're not a doctor.'

But I couldn't shake off that feeling that I could have done *something* and not simply accepted the opinion of a stand-in doctor.

After the funeral, our own Dr Cooklin came with a nurse to check on our other two little girls who were still in bed with sore, swollen throats. After a thorough examination, he and the nurse stepped to one side and had a whispered conversation. Finally, he turned to me.

'Mrs Hopkins,' he said, 'I'm so sorry to see you like this. Your two little girls have the same illness that Mary had. Diphtheria. They must both go into Monsall Fever Hospital immediately. I shall arrange for an ambulance within the hour. You must prepare yourself.'

The big ambulance that came from the police station was brown, the kind that struck fear into the hearts of Ancoats people. The normal black ambulance always attracted a tongue-clucking, sympathetic gauntlet of neighbours. Not so the brown ones, for everyone knew they meant infectious and contagious diseases.

'Keep away,' mothers told their kids. 'We don't want you with diphtheria or scarlet fever. And don't play near grids in the street 'cos that's where you get these diseases.'

The ambulance men wrapped our two daughters in red blankets and carried them off in silence.

Tommy seemed hardly aware of what was happening. He sat looking blankly in front of him, his mouth shut tight. Desperately I tried to get him involved in the things going on around him.

'We can go over to see them later tonight,' I said to him when the ambulance had gone. 'Thank God we caught the disease in time for the other two little girls.'

'I suppose so,' he said dully. He went back to looking mutely into space.

I tried to snap him out of this sombre mood by talking about the baby that was due in a couple of months' time.

'Maybe this time it'll be a boy, Tommy. If it is, we'll call him Thomas. What do you think?'

'Just as you like,' he answered.

No matter how hard I tried, I couldn't bring him round to respond and take an interest in life or in the future. He stayed isolated and withdrawn in his own world as if he didn't want to know or be involved in anything to do with the family.

'Why don't you speak to me, Tommy?' I cried. 'Don't turn away and cut me off like this.'

'I'm so sorry, Kate,' he said. 'Nearly everyone I have come to love has been taken away from me. First, my own mother and father, and now Mary. It's almost as if I put the kiss of death on anyone I get too close to.'

I sympathised with him but how I wished he would snap out of it. There was nothing I could do except pray that one day soon he would. Meanwhile I had to get on with things without him.

At Monsall, Flo and Polly were put in steam tents and I was allowed to sit with them but they insisted that I put on a mask and a big white gown. I went back the next day and on this second visit, I had to look at them through a big glass window 'cos they'd both had tracheotomies to help them breathe. But at least they were still alive. At home, the town hall sent men to fumigate the house. We had to seal up doors and windows and the gas they used left a smell that stayed with us for ever afterwards. A few other kids in Ancoats got diphtheria and a couple of them died. The neighbours seemed to think that anyone who had had this sickness in the house was bound to pass it onto others. But not everyone thought like that, thank God. Kind-hearted Mrs Kenyon next door was always there ready to help whenever she was needed.

'I believe in fate,' she told me. 'If you or your kids are on God's list to get an illness, you'll get it no matter what you do.'

Whilst Flo and Polly were in Monsall, I had my baby, a month early. It was a boy and we called him Thomas. He had Tommy's eyes and nose. I thought how this tiny child might go some way to make up for our terrible loss. He was a good baby and gave no reason for concern as he slept peacefully through the night as if he somehow sensed the sad atmosphere in our home and had decided to lie low. I nursed him with all the love I could summon up. After feeding him, I didn't want to put him down in his cot in case something happened to him. I held him in my arms for an hour after he'd gone to sleep.

He lived for six weeks. They put it down to enteritis. It was all the trouble I'd had; I couldn't keep any food down. Crying, just crying the whole time over Mary's death.

There was a sum of two pounds due on the baby's insurance, so I went back to the undertaker to get a coffin for a little boy.

Old Mr Stiles said, 'I'm afraid they took the horses for

the war and I have no coaches available 'cos there's some big funerals on this week. All my hearses have been ordered. There's a lot of soldiers died of wounds and Moston Cemetery and the Chapel of Rest will be crowded. But I'll tell you what I'll do: I'll make you a little coffin with his name on it and how old he was. The only thing is, you'll have to carry it there yourself. You won't be allowed to take it on the tram as it's against regulations.'

It was no use asking Tommy to go with me. He'd made up his mind to run away from trouble and leave me to it. After we buried Mary, he used to go out and we'd never see him again until late at night. As soon as he came home from work, he was straight out again as if he couldn't face being in the house. He was so used to Mary meeting him when he turned into Back Murray Street. He'd stopped going to church and simply switched himself off.

Madge Kenyon proved to be a great help and comfort. The baby's clothes, his matinee coat, his knitted vests and dresses, his bootees and other things had been left lying on a chair at the time of his death and I didn't want to remove them. She called at the house and made me collect them together and take them round to her house.

'If you leave them there, Kate,' she said, 'you'll never get over the baby's death.'

Anyroad, we got this little coffin and Madge and I carried it to Moston. We had to walk. We lapped the coffin up like a parcel and took turns carrying it under our shawls. I cried quietly all the way there.

Why couldn't it have been me? Why a little baby that did no one any harm? I asked myself over and over again.

We reached the Chapel of Rest and we took our place on the right-hand-side. On the other side was a big crowd of mourners for a soldier who had died of his wounds. At the front of the church was the soldier's coffin and on the other side was my tiny thing on a little stool. The priest said prayers and everything for the soldier, how brave he'd been and how he'd given his life for his country, and all that. Next he turned to me and Mrs Kenyon and said, 'We'll not pray for this little innocent child for he is safely in the hands of God but we'll pray for the mother that's lost him. We'll pray for her that she'll have the strength to carry on.'

When I heard those words, something snapped inside me and I burst out crying from the depths of my being, from my innermost soul. As long as I live I will never cry like that again. The people on the other side of the church looked over at me sorrowfully and at the end of the service, they agreed to let the baby be buried with their soldier.

When the baby was buried, Madge and I walked back sadly along Moston Lane. As we passed St Dunstan's Church, we decided to call in for a short visit.

As I knelt there, a great sob swelled up in me and the tears flowed down my face almost without end. I was filled with despair. In six months I had lost so much, my brother, my first-born child and my first-born son. My husband had withdrawn into a world of his own. All my dreams of happiness had been shattered. I looked up at the big crucifix suspended over the altar and for the first time in my life I could understand the true meaning of those words of Christ on the cross: Why hast thou forsaken me?

'Why, oh why, God,' I asked, 'did you have to take first my brother, then my children? What's it all for? I feel there is nothing to live for. The world is a place of pain and suffering.'

Then a strange thing happened. I felt an inner calm and I remembered part of a prayer we said at Benediction, 'To you do we cry, poor banished children of Eve; to you do we send up our sighs, mourning and weeping in this vale of tears.' Deep inside me a small voice was whispering that things were going to be all right. Perhaps from our own suffering, I thought, we learn an important lesson: how to offer comfort to others. Apart from that, I had two other children still in hospital and it was time I started thinking of them.

I visited Flo and Polly every day and told them about Mary's funeral and the death of the baby, and how lucky they had been that Dr Cooklin had caught their illness in time. Six weeks later, they were released with a clean bill of health. What joy to have them back home! At least, I thought, God had left me two of my children.

Chapter Twenty-Eight

It took a long time for Tommy to recover from his depression, but that didn't mean he didn't look after us. Food was short and many people were hungry and on the point of starvation, especially in the poorest families. It wasn't only the war that caused the shortages. In Smithfield wholesale market, a second 'under-the-counter' market had sprung up. Profiteers bought up any food available at crazy high prices and sold it on to the filthy rich who were the only people who could afford it. Policemen who saw this going on were often given a sweetener to persuade them to look the other way.

I think we'd have starved if it hadn't been for Tommy and Jimmy. Tommy still had one or two contacts in Smithfield market and Jimmy covered for him at the Wallworks while Tommy slipped out to see what he could scrounge. If they'd been found out, it would have meant the immediate sack for the two of them but things were so desperate, there was little choice. On these sorties, Tommy managed to pick up a few vegetables and even the occasional fish. I never inquired how he'd come by them and he never volunteered to tell me.

One day, just before Christmas 1917, Tommy really did take a big chance. I was expecting again and finding extra fare was getting more and more difficult despite the fact that the government had brought in food rationing, and despite the Virol and the Scott's Emulsion Tommy was always plying me with every day. In honour of our good friends, we had decided to call this latest addition Angela, if a girl, and James, if a boy. That was, if it survived at all considering the inadequate nourishment it was receiving.

It was a cold December. Some Christmas we're going to have, I thought. Both the grate and the pantry were empty and me and the children were having to wrap ourselves in blankets to keep warm. To add to the general air of depression, the news from the front was not good and our soldiers seemed to be bogged down in Flanders mud.

About half past five on the morning of 24 December, Tommy appeared at the door. He was out of breath and kept looking over his shoulder. He was carrying a large shopping bag filled to overflowing with all kinds of food: eggs, butter, sausages, fish, a wide selection of vegetables, bread, and even a pot of jam.

'Quick, Kate, hide this stuff in the scullery!' he panted. He went to the window to check that he hadn't been followed.

'Where in God's name did you get this stuff?'

'Don't ask!' he exclaimed, then went on to tell me. 'The wide boys come into the market throwing their money around. There's nothing they can't buy if they wave a few fivers about. Well, this here crook swaggered round the stalls flaunting his wallet and buying up the best food in the market. At Deakins, he put his bag down for a minute and went to inspect some tangerines and dates. Dates! I ask you! Where in God's name had they come from? Anyroad, quick as a flash I picked up his bag and I was off and I haven't stopped running since.'

'Did anyone see you?'

'Not a soul. And remember, officially I'm still clocked

on at the Wallworks until the hooter goes at six.'

'Don't you think it's wrong, Tommy, stealing somebody else's grub?'

Tommy looked at me and his two daughters. 'No. This shyster had loads of money and can easily replace the food. We can't.'

Tommy went back to the Wallworks to clock off. Next day, Christmas Day, we had the most wonderful dinner I can ever remember. And did we feel guilty as we tucked in?

Not one bit.

And I'm sure the baby that was born the following month was also grateful for that meal. We called him Jim after our friend, as we'd promised.

'What a terrible time for a child to be born, in the middle of the worst war in history,' Mrs Kenyon said. Quoting from her endless list of old wives' tales, she continued, 'There used to be a saying in my family: a child born out of sorrow will be a happy child.'

'I hope you're right, Madge,' I said, thinking that somewhere there must be another saying to contradict it.

The food shortages continued well into 1918 and what little there was available was expensive, except for bread. That was sixpence for a two-pound loaf and the price never went up throughout the war. That's about the only good thing I can say for it because it was horrible stuff. Heavy, chewy and doughy, made from God knows what – spuds, I think. Still, we were glad to get it when we could. When word got round that the Maypole or the Co-op on Oldham Road had had a delivery, there was a frantic dash to get in the queue which formed at six o'clock in the morning. Often there were near riots, especially when after three hours standing in line the copper on duty announced, 'That's all there is, ladies. Time to go home.'

Priority in the queue was usually given to mothers with

babies and this was enforced by the policeman controlling the crowd. Not a popular rule this, as it was not unknown for a woman to borrow a baby in order to jump the queue. One bitterly cold February morning I'd been standing in line for a couple of hours. I had young Jim with me and to keep him warm I'd wrapped him up tight under my shawl. The policeman announced the bad news. 'Only ten more loaves left.'

He counted out the required number and told the others that they may as well go home and wait for the next delivery. I was number ten and so just scraped in among the lucky few. Three places ahead of me was another woman with a baby. The lady behind me, number eleven, suddenly went berserk.

'I know that woman ahead in the queue, the one with the baby! Her name's Edna Blenkinsop and she lives in our street. She doesn't have a baby! Why, she's not even married!'

I'm sure that, had it not been for the copper, the crowd, would have lynched the Blenkinsop woman, whether she was a Miss or a Mrs. The offending lady, along with the baby who was an accessory to the crime, was frog-marched roughly from the queue. I think in England queue-jumping was regarded as worse than stealing or baby-bashing. Anyroad, the attention of the frustrated woman was now turned on me.

'Ask that woman with the bundle under the shawl if that's her baby, if it is a baby she has there,' Mrs Nasty demanded.

'Well, is it?' the policeman asked.

There in the street, I had to unfurl my shawl to prove that indeed there was a baby and, furthermore, I was breast-feeding it! All for one loaf!

* * *

Later that year when it seemed that people could bear the misery of the war no longer, there came rumours of peace. Just as in August 1914 none of us believed that a war would happen, so now we couldn't believe that peace would come. Tommy had gone to work and I was giving the kids their breakfast when I heard the wild cheering on Oldham Road. Madge Kenyon came banging on the door.

'Kate, Kate! It's over! The war's over!'

In the next street, a barrel organ balanced on one long wooden leg played a medley of patriotic songs whilst the old women in their bonnets and capes danced a jig. The news finally penetrated my brain and for the rest of the day my eyes kept filling with tears as I remembered the dearly loved ones who would not be around to celebrate the peace. Four days after the Armistice was signed, there was a big celebration in Albert Square. There were hundreds of disabled young men, some on crutches, some in wheelchairs. They don't have much to celebrate, I thought.

After the cheering and the singing, Tommy and I returned home in sombre and reflective mood.

'Well,' said Tommy when we reached Back Murray Street that night, 'so it's over at last. And what was it all for? Millions of men on both sides killed and maimed so that we could keep our honour. It's been a high price to pay. We've suffered just about everything that fate could throw at us. War, death, famine.'

'If you're talking about the Four Horsemen of the Apocalypse, Tommy,' I said thinking back to my religious instruction lessons, 'you've missed one.'

'Which one is that?'

'Pestilence.'

'Don't tempt providence, Kate,' he said.

* * *

In our family Uncle Barney was the first to get it. Spanish flu, they said it was. I don't know why poor old Spain got the blame for it unless it was that their King was one of the early victims.

Barney's illness started one day when he was on his way home after looking for a job on a building site. His cough developed from the usual hacking noise to this terrifying dog-like bark. Soon he was gasping for breath and sweating like a bull. Dr Cooklin went round to see him and told him it was nothing to worry about, a case of three-day flu, that was all. The doctor said the usual thing, how there was a lot of it about and all that. Aunt Sarah put Barney to bed in the front parlour and dosed him with Veno's Cough Cure. She wanted to put a fire in there but there wasn't a piece of coal to be had anywhere. Tommy and I went round to see him. One look and we sensed it was the end for poor old Barney. His breathing was harsh and he complained of pains in his head, ears, and eyes. He himself seemed to know he'd reached the end of the road but he appeared more concerned about the fate of his rabbits than himself.

'Kate, promise me one thing when I'm gone,' he wheezed. 'Don't let Sarah turn my pets into rabbit pie. They've been my best friends for so long and I'd like them to have new owners who will take good care of them.'

When Sarah took Barney his tea on the morning following our visit, she found him dead. We were so very sorry to hear the news but weren't that surprised as Barney had been ailing for most of his life.

Tommy and I managed to sell his rabbitry to a pet shop in Tib Street. So Barney had his dying wish and his 'friends' hopefully found good homes. In many ways, he'd been lucky to have Sarah looking after him all those years. She had always been as strong as an ox and never had a day's illness in her life.

It was when *she* went down with it that we grasped that something serious was going on. Not only did she develop that peculiar cough that Barney'd had but there were flecks of bright blood coming from her mouth as well. After a couple of hours sitting in the doctor's waiting room, Mam and me managed to get Cooklin round to see her. Doctors were like gold, as there was such a shortage because of the war and that. Poor old Dr Cooklin! He wasn't looking too well himself; he looked jiggered as this wave of sickness had run him off his feet. What put the wind up us more than anything, though, was that he was wearing a flesh-coloured gauze mask which gave off a strong smell of cinnamon and cloves, making him look like a circus clown. What *was* all this about? He told us to bathe Sarah's forehead with cool compresses and to give her lots of fluids, especially hot soups. It was important to keep the room well-ventilated and no one must smoke. When I asked him what was wrong with her, he didn't seem sure and mumbled something about the grippe and pneumonia. Anyroad, Mam and me fixed up a roster to look after her. I arranged with Mrs Kenyon to baby-sit with the three kids whilst Tommy went to work and I took my turn to take care of my aunt.

We weren't needed long, though, 'cos she died two days later. Her last words were from the song she'd sung at my dad's funeral so long ago, 'Barney Take Me Home Again'. We hoped Barney was listening. Family and neighbours were deeply saddened by Sarah's death but Mam was heartbroken at the loss of her elder and only sister. As for me, I was beginning to accept death as a normal part of existence.

In early 1919, despite his gauze mask, Dr Cooklin himself died. A case of the same sickness, everyone said, but complicated by overwork and nervous exhaustion. With our doctor gone and no replacement available, there was nothing for it but to take care of ourselves.

There were so many deaths taking place that my little world seemed to be collapsing around my ears and I learned how fragile life was. Friends, relatives, neighbours who had always been there, a constant in the background, like the town hall clock or the wallpaper in the parlour, were going down like skittles. Uncle Barney should have been in his yard with his rabbit hutches, Aunt Sarah tending the second-hand clothing stall, Dr Cooklin in his surgery, but day by day the social landscape was altering beyond recognition. And it was happening so fast that everything seemed unreal and I felt hollow inside. Resigned to fate. Who knew what tomorrow would bring?

Tommy had told me about the spread of this influenza a few weeks back when he was reading bits of the news out to me. He said millions had died of it in China and India but I hadn't taken too much notice at the time. More of those hordes again, I'd thought, they're always dying of something in their millions out there in the Far East. A pandemic, Tommy said it was because it had spread right across the world and in some parts of Asia and Africa whole populations had been swept away like a tidal wave. The *Daily Express* reckoned that it killed twenty-seven million people across the world – twice as many as the war itself. The strange thing about this influenza, we were told, was that it was most deadly not for the elderly and young children, but for people in their prime, between the ages of twenty and forty, who either had a speedy recovery or a speedy death. Not always true, we thought, 'cos in our family our two deaths had been getting on a bit. Also not true for Lloyd George and President Woodrow Wilson who had also picked up the bug and they certainly weren't in their prime. That said, it was true for the thousands of brawny young soldiers who had managed to survive shot, shell and gas in the trenches but died swiftly when the 'Spanish Lady' came to visit. I know it was selfish of me but how relieved I was to know that my young children would probably escape the infection. Then it struck me like a bolt out of the blue. Tommy and me were in the danger age range! He was thirty-three and I was thirty-two.

'Please, God,' I prayed aloud, 'for the sake of our children, don't let Tommy or me get it.'

One night, Tommy came home from the pub where he, along with his cronies, had been thrashing out policies for dealing with the big problems of the day.

'I was talking with some of the lads in the Queen's Arms,' he began, 'and we reckon this flu bug is a secret weapon of the Germans like the mustard gas they used during the war. They've set it loose to get revenge for losing the war.'

'How do you account for the fact that Germany's had twice as many deaths as we've had?'

'I dunno. Maybe the wind blew the bugs back in their faces.'

'You and your cronies in the pub talk a load of rubbish,' I said.

Some newspapers said the bug had come from American pigs brought over by the soldiers and spread through the trenches. Others said it had come from France in those rat-infested trenches our Eddie had been going on about. I didn't know what to believe but whatever it was, now that the illness had touched our own family and folk in the next street were popping their clogs, I realised how deadly the disease had become. The *Manchester Evening News* told us that half the city was in bed with it, but in Ancoats it must have been more because whole families were going down like flies. Sometimes whole streets of families were dangerously ill with no one to look after them. The scourge became so widespread that it featured in kids' games. One day, I heard Flo outside in the street playing skip rope with her friends to the rhyme:

I had a little bird
Its name was Enza
I opened the window
An' in-flu-enza.

When the death toll in Britain reached two hundred thousand, Lloyd George began making regulations and issuing advice. Good ventilation and fresh air, he said, were the best measures for prevention, and any gathering which involved mixing of bodies or sharing of breath was banned. Schools, dance halls, and cinemas were closed and big public funerals were forbidden since they meant crowds. Trams and buses were thought to be a special menace because of their bad ventilation. Churches were allowed to stay open but were told to keep services short – which was about the only good news we had that year. At the Lent service at St Chad's where we were supposed to line up and kiss the feet on the crucifix, people didn't seem too keen on the idea, especially as the cloth the altar boy was using to dab the feet after each kiss didn't look too clean. I noticed that each sinner made sure he didn't make actual lip contact with the crucifix. And God help anyone who coughed or sneezed during Mass! In seconds they found themselves isolated on the bench. Even the shopkeepers weren't taking any chances. At the Maypole on Oldham Road, old Jed Waite, whom I'd known for years, didn't take his pipe out of his mouth as he sliced a pound of butter from the block.

'Smoking's good for you,' he spluttered to the housewives waiting their turn. 'It clears your pipes and keeps the Spanish Lady away.'

'I'm sure it does, Jed,' I said, 'especially if you smoke old socks like you do.'

Now many people wore flesh-coloured gauze masks and one or two of the women had pomanders round their necks. Lord knows what spices they had stuffed into them but judging from the pong, it was time many of them had a change.

The big question in everyone's mind was: who would it strike next?

The answer came for our family a couple of days later. Mam and Frank McGuinness. They both went down with it suddenly one night in the pub as they were knocking back their daily quota of stout. As well as the normal flu symptoms of headache and fever, they were struck down with dizziness, a harsh cough and endless sneezing. Once more, I left my good friend Mrs Kenyon in charge of my young family in order to care for my sick relatives and their two children. It was hard to know what to do as even the doctors were at a loss. All kinds of quack remedies were being bandied about. Snuff, one journalist claimed, was the answer; another advised a pack of towels soaked in hot vinegar; still others, strong doses of whisky and sugar in a glass of hot milk – very popular, that one. The *Evening Chron* advised people to stop borrowing books, stop shaving, and stop shaking hands. About as daft as the old folk remedies Mam was insisting on from her sickbed.

'In Ireland, Kate,' she said, 'we found that goose-grease poultices and salt up the nose always worked.'

'I'm sure they did, Mam,' I said. 'They either killed or cured.'

I ignored these crazy solutions and adopted my own common-sense methods by keeping them both warm and supplying them with lots of hot onion soup which I'd heard acted as an antiseptic. How effective it would be I wasn't sure but at least it was better than sitting around doing nothing.

I was kept busy ministering to the two victims as well as washing, dressing, and feeding young John and Hetty and doing the daily shopping. On the third morning, Mam opened her eyes with the fever and the cough completely gone. The flu had flown away as quickly as it had arrived. Not so with Frank. His condition was worse and he went into rapid decline.

He lay on the bed with bloodshot eyes, his face a bluish colour. He struggled for air and every cough brought up blood-stained saliva.

'You're going to be all right, Frank,' I lied.

Frank didn't say anything. He looked at me dully but didn't see me. In a strained voice he began a conversation with imaginary comrades.

'No need to worry, boys! General Buller will soon be here with reinforcements. And what a day that'll be! The relief of Ladysmith, eh lads! Medals for everyone!'

All that day he raved deliriously and was in and out of consciousness. The next day, he seemed to rally and our hopes rose. Perhaps he's going to pull through, we thought. But our hopes were dashed. Next day he was as bad as ever.

'I think it's all up with me, Kate,' he said between bouts of hacking. 'I'm sorry that you and I haven't always seen eye to eye but I want you to know that I've always held you in the highest respect.'

'Frank,' I answered, tears springing to my eyes, 'I'm so sorry too, though I think the fault has been mainly mine. I couldn't accept the idea of anyone taking the place of my dad. I was wrong and I had this mad notion of trying to go back to the old days. I was so stupid trying to live in the past. Can you ever forgive me?'

'Perhaps we were both at fault, Kate, in not seeing each other's point of view. I was an intruder and I made no allowance for your feelings. As for forgiving you, there's nothing to forgive.'

Frank died the next day.

Mam was beside herself with grief. In the space of three years, she had lost her son, her sister, and now her husband, not to mention two of her grandchildren. Her life had been turned upside down. Like me, she became resigned to death and the notion that suffering was a necessary part of life. I held her tight in a consoling embrace and in that moment we were closer than we had been for many years.

Arranging Frank's funeral was no easy matter. There was enough insurance money to cover it but there was a terrible shortage of undertakers and grave-diggers and the authorities had to make use of the cold meat storage depot as the bodies piled up. And it was a strange funeral service we held; regulations allowed us only fifteen minutes to get through it because there was another cortege waiting outside.

'This is like the Black Death and the bubonic plague we learned about at school,' I said to Tommy when we finally buried Frank at Moston Cemetery.

'It's worse, Kate,' Tommy said, 'because more people have died in this plague. If it goes on like this, I think it'll be the end of civilisation.'

But Tommy's fears did not materialise because mysteriously the Spanish Lady faltered and by the end of 1919 she was gone.

Chapter Twenty-Nine

The birth of our first son seemed to trigger an ability in me to produce males, for there followed a run of boys. Four years after Jim, I had another boy and after an interval of three years, yet another. I gave Tommy the job of finding names for each of them. He opted for the name of Sam for our third boy, for no other reason than he was born on 28 July, the feast day of St Samson.

'The name denotes strength,' Tommy remarked, 'and in this day and age that's something a boy could do with, especially if he follows in my footsteps and becomes a market porter.'

Sam was a handsome baby with thick black hair but I wasn't sure about the name Tommy had chosen. If it had been left to me, I'd have called this one Rip Van Winkle because he did nothing but sleep. To start with, he didn't want to get himself born as he was three weeks late and had to be induced. Perhaps he knew something we didn't. I think he was too comfortable in there and decided to have an extra lie-in. When it came to feeding time, he simply fell asleep in the middle of the meal. His personality was clear from the beginning, for when he came to the crawling stage, he wasn't too keen on going round on all fours in case he fell on his face. Instead he developed the skill of scooting around the kitchen floor on his backside at breakneck speed by using his arms as oars. Perhaps one day I could enter him for the Boat Race. And his obsession with pans and baking tins convinced me that one day he would become, not a market porter as Tommy hoped, but a chef in one of the top hotels.

Tommy named the next boy Les after the famous Manchester composer, Leslie Stuart. Boys now outnumbered the girls three to two. But with five kids, I sometimes forgot all the names and young Les was often called, 'Flo, Polly, Jim, Sam, I mean Les.' This new baby was as different from Sam as it was possible to imagine. For a start, his hair was as ginger as Sam's was dark, but more importantly he had a completely different personality. He arrived on the scene two weeks early as if he couldn't wait to get on with the business of living. And as for feeding, where Sam had been utterly relaxed and dozed off, Les was tense and could finish a whole bottle in one minute flat and look round for more.

'He certainly takes after you, Tommy,' I remarked. 'He can drink a bottle faster than you can get a pint of mild down your throat.'

Les ate everything in sight – books, newspapers, bed sheets – even the nose on Tommy's face if he got the chance.

'He keeps biting me,' Tommy complained.

'But he likes you,' I replied. 'Look how he smiles whenever he sees you.'

'That's because he thinks, ah, here comes dinner.'

When Les reached the 'suck it and see' toddler stage, the whole family had to be on permanent sentry duty. When Les was not asleep, he was sucking on something: his toe, a bunch of keys, buttons, coins. When we lost something like the slop-stone plug, we knew where to look: 'Check in the baby's mouth! Quick!' There was no point asking Les, 'What have you got there in your mouth, love?' for he never answered. On one or two occasions we'd had to hang him upside down and slap his back to recover our property, like a piece of coal, Tommy's tie pin, studs or cuff links.

It was good to see Tommy joining in family life again after his period of black depression. He even began giving Jim football lessons, at first in the back yard and later on a nearby croft. One day they came back from training and I was surprised to see Tommy had a bloody nose.

'What happened, Tommy?' I asked. 'Did you get the football in the face?'

'Nothing of the sort,' he laughed, holding a hankie to his nose. 'I dribbled rings round our Jim here and he started moaning about it. I felt sorry for him and I said, "Right, Jim. Just for that, you can punch me as hard as you like here." I meant my shoulder but the little bugger thumped me in the nose.'

Tommy had regained his enthusiasm for football and had become a keen supporter of Manchester City and was a regular visitor to the new Maine Road ground. His hero was Billy Meredith, the famous Welsh international. When City reached the Cup Final in 1926, Tommy booked his place on the coach to Wembley with the Queen's Arms crowd. He was away all day Saturday but back in the early hours of Sunday morning.

'How did they get on?' I asked.

'Don't ask,' he answered. 'Bolton Wanderers won by a fluke goal. The only thing I've got to say is that if we ever have another son, he won't be called David or Jack. That's for sure.'

'Why's that, Tommy?'

'Because that's the name of the bugger who scored for Bolton – David Jack.'

* * *

My life had become one long round of feeding faces, washing pots, cleaning the house, doing the laundry and the rest of it. I didn't begrudge a moment of it, I loved having a secure, happy family around me. During these years after the war, we saw big changes in our lives. After the flu epidemic came the 'roaring twenties', not that we heard much roaring in Ancoats – the miserable twenties more like it. Lloyd George had promised us a land fit for heroes but the Great War hung over everything. At every street corner there were men simply hanging about – the unemployed, the disabled, and the occasional shell-shocked victim babbling to himself about the trenches. Neurasthenia was the posh name they gave to the condition. Men were beginning to ask themselves what it was all for and they'd stopped whistling 'Pack up your troubles in your old kit-bag' and changed their tune to:

We won the war, what was it for?
You can ask Lloyd George, or Bonar Law.

There was one desperate man going around the streets in town with a placard round his back which said: I KNOW 3 TRADES, I SPEAK 3 LANGUAGES, FOUGHT FOR 3 YEARS, HAVE 3 CHILDREN, AND NO WORK FOR 3 MONTHS BUT I ONLY WANT ONE JOB.

Tommy was lucky because he had regular work in the market and so we didn't go short of food, not until the General Strike when the whole country nearly came to a halt. When the bakers joined in there were no loaves in the shops but we could get self-raising flour and so I made my own. When word got out that I knew how to bake bread, I had half a dozen neighbours in the house asking me to teach them. They brought their own stuff, flour, yeast and that, but they were using my oven non-stop and no one thought to bring coal or coke to help me out.

On the other side of the picture, the twenties were a time of great inventions, like the aeroplane and the motor car. We didn't mind the first one so much as there weren't many of them about but the second became a dangerous nuisance when some cars began driving at twenty miles an hour, and motorbikes roared round the streets.

There was the wireless. Tommy was always fiddling about with a crystal set, cat's whiskers he called it. One day he called out all excited as if he'd found a five pound note, 'Kate, Kate, come quick and listen to this. It's Dame Nellie Melba!'

I put on the earphones as instructed but I couldn't hear anything except a loud hissing noise. 'Wait, wait,' he said, 'while I tickle the cat's whisker.' He fiddled about but I still couldn't hear anything. It was much better when valve sets came in but I always preferred the HMV wind-up gramophone which he bought later, though we had only two records to begin with, Waldteufl's *Skaters' Waltz* and Susa's *Stars and Stripes Forever*.

Our local picture house was the Don on Beswick Street. Flo and Polly were always mythering me to take them to the first house. Not that it took much mythering to persuade me. We saw the latest films and idolised the stars of the day: Douglas Fairbanks, Mary Pickford, and the heart-throb Rudolph Valentino with his flashing eyes, but it was the comics that really took our fancy – Harold Lloyd, Buster Keaton, and best of all, our own Charlie Chaplin who could have you laughing and crying at the same time in films like *The Immigrant* and *The Gold Rush*.

The American troops came over to fight in the war, and after they'd gone they left their way of life behind, not only in their films but in songs, dances, and even their way of speaking. It was jazz, jazz, jazz, everywhere you turned. Jungle music, I called it. Flo was the first to be infected. She was fourteen and had taken her first job at Northcote's, the fur coat makers on Oldham Road. Some of the other girls at work must have put the idea in her head for after a couple of weeks she came home and said she wanted to be a flapper.

'A what?' I exclaimed. 'What is it? Some kind of bird with large wings?'

Flo explained that besides having her hair bobbed and shingled, it meant wearing a dress with tassels and beads and a raised hemline, rouging her cheeks, putting on lipstick, and taping her breasts flat – not that she had much breast to flatten.

'You'll do nothing of the sort,' I told her. 'You'll get locked up walking about like that. Besides, your father would throw a fit if he saw you in that get-up.'

'Aw, Mam,' she said, 'all the girls at work are doing it. And they're learning me to do the Charleston at dinner times as well.'

Every spare minute she got, she practised the dance using a kitchen chair as support to disentangle her legs. Music was provided by Polly and Jim on paper and comb.

'What's the world coming to?' I said to myself. 'I must be getting old! Women smoking, drinking, painting their faces and doing these wild dances.'

Eddie was a regular visitor to the house. His war wounds had not disabled him – he wore black leather gloves and people hardly noticed he'd lost his fingers – and he'd managed to get a job as a watchman at the Refuge Assurance on Whitworth Street. Since we were within walking distance he made a habit of calling on us after work. He spent his time with us drinking huge mugs of tea and teaching young Jim soldiers' songs of the trenches, sung to popular hymn tunes. Every day, Jim could be seen marching through the house and singing at the top of his voice the unauthorised version of hymns like 'Onward Christian Soldiers':

Forward Joe Soap's Army
Marching without fear
With our old commander
Safely in the rear.

This was fine as long as the songs were sung in the right place at the right time. The top of a public tram car was definitely not the right place as far as I was concerned. I was taking Jim into town to buy a new pair of shoes at Timpson's on Market Street. It was raining heavily and this prompted my young son to break out with:

Raining, raining, raining
Always bloody well raining
Raining all the morning
And raining all the day.

Sung to the hymn 'Holy, Holy, Holy', Jim's rendering was much appreciated by our fellow passengers who not only laughed loudly but rewarded him with a round of applause. I was glad to get off that tram at Piccadilly before Jim gave us the complete repertoire.

I bought Jim a nice pair of strong boots that would last him at least six months, given his habit of kicking a can or any other object that caught his attention on the way to school. As we came out of the shop, I bumped into an old friend. Miss Emma from Macclesfield! She looked older – as I suppose I did myself – but I'd have known her anywhere.

She didn't recognise me at first but when it dawned on her, her face lit up.

'Kate!' she exclaimed. 'How nice to see you after all this time! How long is it since we last met?'

'I daren't count the years,' I replied. 'But it's a long time.'

We found a nearby teashop and there we settled down and caught up on each other's news.

During the war, Emma had driven an ambulance but now she had taken a full-time appointment with the Women's Social and Political Union (WSPU) and was spending her time working for women's emancipation.

'There's still a lot to do, Kate,' she said. 'We've succeeded in getting the vote for women over thirty but we won't be happy until women have the same voting rights as men. Now tell me all that you've been doing since you left Macclesfield.'

I told her about my job at Westmacott's, my marriage to Tommy and the seven children and how I'd lost two of them in 1916. When Emma heard that I'd had so many children, she was aghast.

'All that child-bearing, Kate! How on earth did you manage? It must have left you utterly exhausted and drained!'

I didn't think my family was particularly big compared to some of the other families in the district. Ten children or even more were not unusual.

'We manage to get by somehow, Emma,' I replied. 'We have no choice – we have to.'

'Look,' she said, 'I think I might be able to help you. One of our most active members has written a couple of books for women like you. I have them here with me. They were intended for another lady but I'm sure I can find replacements for her.' She glanced round the room to check that she was not being watched. Reaching into her large portmanteau, she handed me a brown paper package tied neatly with string. 'Read these books when you get home but for God's sake be sure that nobody else sees them or we'll both end up in trouble.'

I took the package from her and thrust it quickly into my own handbag, feeling a bit like Mata Hari in a film about German spies. We parted company promising vaguely to keep in touch but both knowing in our hearts that we never would.

Next day, when Tommy had gone to work and the children to school, I put Les to sleep in his cradle and turned my attention to the package which I'd hidden under the bed. The two books were by a lady called Marie Stopes. I'd heard her name before because Tommy had read something out of the paper to me, something about her opening a 'family planning' clinic in London. Marie Stoppem, Tommy had called her.

The first one I opened was called *Married Love* and I could tell from the title that it was the sort of book that respectable people wouldn't look at. But surely Miss Emma wasn't the sort of person who would recommend a dirty book! I turned to the first page and began to read and even though I was alone, my face turned red with embarrassment. The book used expressions like 'sexual relations' and it seemed to be saying that a woman was supposed to enjoy it as much as a man. Marriage wasn't just for having kids but it was also there for having a bit of fun in bed with your husband. Not just when *he* felt like it and demanded his marital rights but when the wife was in the mood for it as well. Marriage was to be an equal partnership! This went against everything I'd ever heard or been taught. For a married couple love-making (or sexual intercourse!) in itself, she claimed, was a sacrament and a couple was entitled to take steps to prevent offspring being produced. In other words, a married pair could use – and I found it hard to bring myself to say the words even mentally – birth control! I'd seen the words before on the windows of a shop near Manchester Cathedral. The kind of shop that sold mysterious rubber devices and dirty books, and here was I reading about it in the privacy of my bedroom. If the first book was hot, the second entitled *Wise Parenthood* was torrid. It gave details of the methods that could be used to prevent babies: condoms, jellies, pessaries, potions, intra-uterine rings (whatever they were) and one that had me puzzled, a Dutch cap. I wondered how wearing a hat in bed would stop a woman from having kids.

I was so absorbed examining the books that I'd forgotten the time. Hurriedly I put them back in their package and tied them up. Whatever happened, I mustn't let Tommy see them. But what to do with them? I couldn't put them on the fire 'cos they'd set the chimney alight. For the time being, I put them on top of the wardrobe next to Tommy's pot hat. There wasn't much danger of him looking up there unless he had to go to a funeral or a wedding.

Of course I had to tell Canon McCabe in confession about the books. When I gave him the titles, I thought he was going to have a heart attack. He spluttered and was having difficulty in catching his breath.

'By looking at such books,' he hissed, 'you have committed a serious sin against the sixth commandment which forbids immodest songs, books and pictures because they are most dangerous to the soul. Do you understand?'

'I do, Father.'

'Do you still have these books in your possession?'

'I do, Father.'

'I shall give you absolution but it is conditional on your getting rid of them. And remember that the only family planning permitted by the Church is the rhythm method. Now for your penance say twenty-five Our Fathers and say the Rosary ten times.'

He said the words of absolution. '*Ego te absolvo . . .*'

A pretty heavy penance, I thought. Reading Marie Stopes's stuff must be on a par with burglary or trying to murder your husband. And what was that rhythm method he had talked about? It sounded like it meant doing it to music. I put such sinful thoughts out of my mind or I'd have to go back to confession before I'd got out of the church.

Confession wasn't the end of it though. The following Sunday at eleven o'clock Mass – the adult Mass – Canon McCabe based his sermon on the sixth commandment and in particular the reading of bad books. I'm sure he was looking at me the whole time he ranted on.

'My dear brethren,' he declaimed, 'it is my duty to warn you of a number of obscene books which have been featured in the press lately. I refer to the work of a Dr Marie Stopes and her works on family planning.'

You could have heard a pin drop in the church. This was a subject that never failed to win their complete attention.

'Dr Stopes's own marriage is hardly an example to us. She is on her second husband, having discarded the first for non-consummation. Now she is married to a rich man and the reports are that they follow a lifestyle of free love which is more suitable for animals in the jungle or cats in the alley than in civilised society. We live in sinful times, my dear brethren, when well-to-do families prefer a baby Austin Seven to a real-live baby. This Marie Stopes woman has now provided such materialist people with the means by opening a family planning clinic where her vile methods of contraception are practised. Such methods are little better than infanticide. Yet this woman would have you believe that God sent down this beastly, filthy message. I tell you, dear people, that it is more likely that she was visited by the devil himself, for make no mistake, Satan roams the world in strange guises.'

The congregation lapped this up. Tub-thumping preaching was music to their ears.

'Have fewer babies, she says,' Canon McCabe thundered. 'Apart from the sinfulness of her ideas, she is recommending a reduction in the population at the very time when we are suffering the terrible losses of the war and the influenza epidemic. At a time when we need more souls and every ounce of good solid flesh and bone, we are faced by a series of books on how not to provide sons and daughters to carry on our traditions. If any members of this congregation have copies of the books I am referring to, I order you now, in the name of God, to get rid of them.'

When he gave this last command, I was a hundred per cent sure he was looking at me.

The next morning, I got Les out of his cot, dressed him and went out to do some shopping, taking the books with me. At the first tram stop, I dumped them in the litter bin. As I hurried away, I glanced back in time to see an old tramp rummaging through the bin and discovering the brown paper package. I wondered what he and his mates in Barney's brickyard would make of it when they got down to reading its contents.

Chapter Thirty

So that's my story as far as it goes. What happened to the people I met in my life? They went their different ways.

In America, my cousin Lizzie remained as a nanny in the employ of the O'Hagan family on Long Island; she never married or had children of her own. Susie, the ex-parlour maid, stayed in Ferrygate and ran the post office with her husband, Bob. She had three boys and her husband survived the Great War though he lost his left arm. Danny's widow, Hilda, went back to live with her family when they were released from the internment camp. For many years they have run a highly successful and popular pork butcher's shop on the corner of Corporation Street and Miller's Lane. Madge Kenyon married again after the war. I suppose with her two pensions she was considered a good catch, though someone told me that a war widow lost her pension if she re-married. Eddie remained at his job as security guard with the Refuge Assurance but later married a nice girl called Mona and lives in Greengate, Salford. So far, they've had no children. Mam continued running her second-hand clothing business but she bought a small market stall on Frank's insurance money. She went to live with her two children in a little house in Salford.

Angela and Jimmy became our neighbours for, at their

suggestion, we flitted to a new home in the Artisan's Dwellings in Collyhurst. I was glad to move because every day I saw young Alice, the little girl who used to take Mary to school. She would be playing or skipping along the street and it always brought back painful memories. Our new tenement home was on the first landing whilst Angela and Jimmy lived on the ground floor. They never did have any children of their own but they were always kind to ours, especially at Christmas, like that of 1927. As usual I played the part of Santa Claus as Tommy always celebrated the birth of Christ in the Queen's Arms. Flo was out at a party but the rest of the kids hung up the biggest stockings they could find, not that it ever made any difference since they all got the same things every year. Like my own mam used to do, I kept the presents simple: a Woolworth's torch, a tangerine, an apple, a few grapes, and half a bar of Cadbury's fruit and nut. On Christmas Eve, I crept into their bedroom, though I knew they would all be pretending to be asleep. Polly and Jim knew I was Father Christmas, and I knew that they knew but we kept up the pretence for the young 'uns. As soon as I'd gone, they'd be up eating their chocolate and shining their torches – making monster faces and playing at shadows on the wall. By the time morning came, the torch batteries would be used up. They wouldn't be able to get any more 'cos they wouldn't have the money and anyway, the shops would be closed. This particular Christmas was different because after Mass, Angela and Jimmy came round with expensive presents for everyone: a record of selections from *The Desert Song* for the family, dresses for the girls, a fort and toy soldiers for Jim, a drum for Sam, and a squeaky rubber doll for Les. We were truly grateful to them, except maybe for the drum.

Cissie, who was married to Ernie, the twin brother of

Keith who was killed at the Somme, had four children – all girls. She gave up trying for a boy when she had the fourth. Cissie lived in Salford but was a regular visitor to us in Collyhurst Buildings.

On 1 January 1928 Cissie brought her family round to celebrate the New Year.

'Well, Kate,' she sighed. 'Another year, eh?'

'Another year,' I said. 'The years simply whiz by.'

'We've seen some rum times, you and me, haven't we, Kate? Glad times and sad times. What were they all about?'

'Who knows? But you're right about us seeing both joy and sorrow. Maybe that's what life is – tears and laughter, joy and sorrow.'

'Aye, but it's usually the poor who have the sorrow, Kate, while the rich have the joy.'

'Not always, Cissie. Wealth has nothing to do with happiness. It's more the way you feel inside and the way you look at things. I always try to look on the bright side if I can, and I think caring for other people and listening to their problems are the things that really matter.'

'That's true. Weren't we always taught at school, Kate, that it's better to give than to receive?'

'That's right, Cissie, as long as it's not Spanish flu.'

She laughed. 'Or a Gypsy curse. But I often wish we could go back to those happy days before the workhouse when Dad was still alive.'

'I used to long for that as well, Cissie, but not any more. There's no harm in reminiscing and thinking back about the good old days but the one thing I *have* learned is that you can never turn the clock back.'

'I agree, Kate. We must turn our minds to the future, mustn't we?'

'I'm not even sure about that, Cissie. As I see it, there's more to life than dwelling on the past or worrying about tomorrow. The important thing is to get on with things *now*.'

'It sounds a bit of a miserable way of looking at things, Kate.'

'Not at all. I live for each day and I've come to appreciate the wonderful things around me, like the family sitting round the table or the smile on a neighbour's face when you've shown her how to bake bread. That sort of thing. That's what makes me happy.'

'And so you ought to be. You've got Tommy and five wonderful kids. Your family's complete and you can start to take life easy.'

'All true, Cissie. Except for one small thing.'

'What's that, Kate?'

'I'm pregnant again.'

Headline hopes you have enjoyed reading *Kate's Story* and invites you to sample the beginning of Billy Hopkins' *Our Kid*, which takes up the story of the Hopkins family where *Kate's Story* leaves off. *Our Kid* is also available in Headline paperback.

Prologue

Another Bloody Mouth to Feed

'Come on now, Kate. Y're no' really tryin',' said the midwife. 'Pull on the towel and push! Push!'

'I am bloody well pushing,' Kate shouted back. 'I can't push any harder. Pull and push. It's like rowing a boat on Heaton Park lake. You'd think God would have thought of an easier way of having kids.'

'It won't be long now, luv,' said Lily Goodhart, her next-door neighbour, wiping Kate's glistening forehead.

'That dose o' castor oil should speed things up,' said Nurse McDonagh. 'Anyway, it's no' as if it's your first wean.'

'Aye, but it never gets any easier, no matter what they say,' said Kate.

A sudden contraction convulsed her.

'Glory be t'God, that was like a red-hot poker going through me!' she gasped.

'Bite on your hanky when it gets too bad, Kate,' said the nurse. 'We don't want the neighbours to hear. And your kids are in the other bedroom. Is your husband no' around?'

'No, I told him to take himself off to the pub outa the road. He'd only be in the way. Besides, he doesn't like trouble, y'know.'

'Lucky for him! Just the same, I think he should be here, just in case we have to fetch Dr McDowell. Lily, you'd best go across to the pub and bring Tommy over.'

'Eeh, I don't think he'll like that,' said Lily.

'Never you mind whether he likes it or no'. Tell him he's needed over here. Dinna come back without him.'

'Very well, if you say so,' said Lily doubtfully as she left the little cramped bedroom.

'I do hope we don't have to bring no doctor. I'd be so embarrassed, like . . .' said Kate after Lily had departed.

'But he's a *doctor*.'

'It doesn't matter. He's a man, isn't he? I don't want no man – not even me husband, for that matter – to see me like this. And anyroad, I think . . .'

But the nurse did not discover what it was she thought, for Kate was racked by another agonising spasm and was busy stifling a scream.

'Come on now, Kate,' urged the midwife. 'Nearly there! Now, pull and push! Pull and push!'

It was eight o'clock on that Sunday night in 1928. Tommy was already on his third pint and a feeling of bonhomie and goodwill had begun to flow over him. He felt completely at home and in his true element.

'This is the place for me,' he said to Jimmy Dixon, his bosom pal. 'This is where I really belong. The vault of Tubby Ainsworth's. Best bloody pub in Collyhurst.' Its real name was the Dalton Arms, but hardly anyone called it that.

The thick tobacco smoke and the excited babble of twenty male voices talking at once combined to produce in

Tommy a deep sense of contentment and comradeship. In here, he felt safe and away from all those goings-on at home.

He took out a packet of Player's Weights, extracted the last remaining cigarette, tapped it slowly on his yellow, nicotined thumbnail, and struck a match. Puffing contentedly on his fag, he looked up from his cards and gazed round the vault, taking in the picture of the pasty-faced men in their flat caps and woollen mufflers which they wore like a uniform.

'Eeh, what a bloody fine bunch o' working men they all are,' Tommy said.

'Whadda you mean? Working men! Most of 'em are on the dole!' said Jimmy.

'Doesn't matter, they're the salt o' the earth. Except for that bastard Len Sharkey over there,' he added quickly as his eye lighted on his hated enemy, guffawing as usual with his mates over some joke or other.

They took a long pull at their pints.

In the main, then, Tommy was happy. A pint, a pal and a bit of peace – that was all he wanted. That wasn't asking too much, was it? But that Sunday night, he had more. It was his lucky night. He was on a winning streak, having just pegged twelve on the cribboard with a double pair royal. No doubt about it. He was well on the way to taking not only the game but the shilling bet that was riding on it. Mind you, Jimmy Dixon was a real Muggins and wasn't quick enough to add up even his own score, never mind Tommy's. But what the hell! Friend or no friend, a shilling was a shilling in this rotten old world. He downed the rest of his pint and stood up.

'My twist, Jimmy. Same again?'

Jimmy drained his own glass. 'Aye, ta. Don't mind if I do, Tommy. And see if you can't buy me a bit o' bleeding luck while you're at it.'

Tommy pushed his way through the men standing at the bar.

'When you're ready, Tubby. Pint o' usual for me and a pint o' bitter for Jimmy there. Oh aye . . . and ten Weights as well. Must have a smoke for the mornin'.'

'Right, Tommy. Pinta best mild, pint o' bitter, an' ten Weights. That'll be one and eleven altogether,' Tubby Ainsworth said, drawing the pints.

Tommy paid up, collected the beers and his cigarettes and returned to his seat at the card table.

'All the best!' said Jimmy.

'Bottoms up!' rejoined Tommy.

It was at that precise moment that his peace of mind was shattered. As he tilted his head back to drink, he saw through the bottom of his glass the shawled figure of Lily Goodhart hurrying towards him.

'Bugger it! Don't turn round now, Jimmy, but have you seen who's coming?'

'No. How the bloody hell could I?'

'It's Lily Goodhart, me next-door neighbour. And I know why she's here.'

As Lily threaded her way through the unyielding male bodies, she was greeted by various cat-calls.

'Women not allowed in the vault!'

'Men only in 'ere.'

'Go and fill your bloody jug at the snug.'

'S'all right,' she said. 'I just want a word with Tommy there.'

She went up to the card table. Tommy put his pint down.

'Yes, what is it, Lily?' he asked irritably – put out by her appearance in the vault and the fact that all eyes were on him. Especially those of Sharkey, who seemed to be enjoying yet another horse-laugh with his cronies.

'It's time, Tommy,' she said in an urgent whisper. 'It's Kate. I think you'd better come now. Her waters broke and the pains are coming faster. I don't think it'll be long now.'

'Bloody hell. No peace for the wicked – not even in the bloody pub. But what do they want me for? Kate told me to bugger off out of the way.'

'I think it's in case there's complications like, and they have to call the doctor.'

'A doctor! I can't afford no two quid for a bloody doctor. Besides, I've heard they kill more than they cure with their bloody instruments.'

'I'm only telling you what they told me.'

'All right, Lily. I'll finish this game first. Mind you, I can't see what bloody use I'll be. She'd be better off if I just stop where I am. How long's the midwife been there?'

'Over half an hour. I think she's doing her best to hurry things along like. Anyroad, Tommy, I'd better get out of the vault afore these men here chuck me out. But I promised to come and fetch you. Shall I wait for you?'

'Look, Lily, there's no bloody need for that. I've said I'll come when I've finished the game, and I will.'

'All right. If you say so.'

As if for protection, she pulled her shawl tightly around her shoulders and hurried out.

[*Tommy finishes the game, but his heart is no longer in it. After some lively exchanges with his drinking cronies, he calls it a night.*]

Leaving the smoky atmosphere behind, Tommy emerged from the pub into the Collyhurst evening air. It was half past nine and not quite dark, but already the lamplighter was going his rounds down Collyhurst Road.

Tommy crossed over the road. With his strange,

shambling gait, he hurried along by the side of the River Irk – known simply in the district as the Cut.

As he approached the iron bridge which led to the Dwellings, he spotted Polly playing 'Queenie-o-Co-Co, who's got the ball?' with a lot of other kids. 'See I haven't got it!' 'See I haven't got it!' they chorused as they offered alternate hands for inspection.

'Come on, our Polly,' he ordered. 'Time you was in. And bring Jim with you. It's past his bedtime.'

'Aw, Dad. Can't we stay out a bit? S'only early.'

'No you can't. Up you go.'

'Yes, but Dad . . .'

'Will y'do as you're told, y'cheeky little sod. And less of your ole buck. Now get up them bloody stairs afore I land you one. It's time you packed up them bloody daft games. You're thirteen and you'll be starting work next year. You should be giving help at home, not playin' out here. Your mother's not well, y'know.'

'Yeah, I know. She's got that stomach ache again. It's through eating all them kippers on Friday. But we're out 'ere 'cos they chucked us out when the nurse came. Sam and Les are already in bed, though.'

'I should bloody well think so. But now it's time the two o' you was in. So up the Molly Dancers!'

Reluctantly, Polly collected her ball and her younger brother. Squeezing past a courting couple who were at it on the steps, she followed her dad up the stairwell until they reached the landing and the lobby which led to their tenement – number 6, Collyhurst Buildings.

The door was ajar. Inside, they found Lily stoking up a big fire at the black-leaded kitchen range. Flo, the eldest daughter, was filling a large iron kettle from the tap in the corner of the room.

'It's a boy, Dad,' announced Flo. 'Seven pounds. And he's lovely.'

'Oh aye,' sighed Tommy, resignedly. 'I thought it might be a boy the way your mother's been eating all that apple pie lately.'

'How d'you mean?' asked Lily.

'Well, fancying apple pie means a boy, and cherry pie, a girl. S'well known, that, in Lancashire. But by God, another boy, eh! Another bloody mouth to feed! That's six kids we've got.'

Nurse McDonagh, all bustling and businesslike, appeared from the bedroom carrying a brown paper parcel, which she thrust into the fire.

'What's that? It's not the baby, is it?' asked Jim, his little face aghast.

'Never you mind what it is, young man,' Nurse McDonagh said. 'And no, it's no' the baby. The very idea, indeed!'

She turned to Tommy.

'So the prodigal son has come back to the fold, eh? And you look as if you've been in the wars, as well.'

She fished in her medical bag, pulled out a small bottle of iodine, and applied a little to Tommy's wound. Tommy winced.

'It's only a scratch. Not worth botherin' about.'

'Dinna fash yoursel'. I'm no botherin' that much. If you daft men want to punch each other's heads at night, it's no skin off my nose. More like skin off your heid, I'm thinkin'!'

'You're a hard woman, Nurse.'

'Ye've got to be in my job. But you took your time gettin' here. Timed it just right, didn't you? Like the last time – arrivin' home when it's all over. Typical man! You think when you've put your wife in the puddin' club, that's you out. Your contribution to the birth process!'

'Now, you know very well I'd have been no use to you. I know nowt about bringing kids into the world, except that you need a lotta hot water.'

'Aye, and I suppose you think that's for mixing with your whisky to make yoursel' a hot toddy! All things considered, though, I think maybe you were better taking yoursel' off to the pub and keepin' outa ma way.'

'But how's Kate? How's me wife doing? Is she all right?'

'You've no need to worry on that score. I thought at one point we might need the doctor, but everything's turned out fine, and mother and son are both doing well. You've got a strong, healthy wife there. She had her baby without any fuss – hardly made a sound. The only noise was from your son, and judging by the strength of his lungs, there's not much wrong with him either.'

'I know I picked a good 'un when I picked Kate,' he said proudly.

'Well, anyway, I've cleaned things up as best I can. And now I suppose you'll be wanting to go in and see the bairn. I don't see any way I can stop you.'

'I should bloody well hope not,' he said indignantly.

'I don't suppose there's any harm as long as you don't go breathing your beer fumes and germs all over the baby. Not too much noise, either,' she said, looking pointedly at the younger end of the family. 'Now, I'm awa'. I've got another case over the road – a lot more urgent than yours. I'll call in again tomorrow morning to see how things are. See that Kate gets a good sleep tonight.'

She began packing up her mysterious black bag, and Polly asked:

'Is that what you brought the baby in?'

The nurse gave her an old-fashioned look, hesitated, looked as if she were going to say something, then changed her mind.

'In a way it is, I suppose.'

'We had a listen at your bag before, and we didn't hear no baby in there,' said Polly.

'Don't be daft,' said Jim. 'Everyone knows that babies are brought by an angel. Don't you know nowt, Polly?'

'How d'you make that out?' asked Polly.

'Well, when one person dies, another one gets born.'

'Straight away?'

'No, stupid. When a person dies, he has to go up to this room in the sky where he has to wait for, I dunno, maybe a hundred years until it's his turn to get born again.'

'I dinna ken what they're teachin' 'em at school these days,' said Nurse McDonagh, shaking her head.

Tommy gave the nurse a sealed envelope.

'Ta very much for all you've done, Nurse. Though I think we should be getting a discount for quantity.'

'That'll be the day – when a Scotswoman gives a discount!' And with those words, Nurse Flora McDonagh departed from the scene.

Our Kid

Billy Hopkins

It was on a Sunday night in 1928 that Billy Hopkins made his first appearance. Billy's tenement home on the outskirts of Manchester would be considered a slum today, but he lived there happily with his large Catholic family, hatching money-making schemes with his many friends.

When war came, and the Luftwaffe dominated the night sky, Billy was evacuated to Blackpool. There he lived on a starvation diet while his own rations went to feed his landlady's children – 'I might as well be in Strangeways!' But even the cruel blows that were to be dealt to the family on his return to Manchester would not destroy Billy's fighting spirit – or his sense of humour.

Nostalgic, sad and funny, OUR KID recalls an upbringing and an environment now vanished.

OUR KID, originally published under the author name Tim Lally, was warmly acclaimed:

'How wonderful to have a book like this. A book . . . that pulls readers back to that different world . . . A glimpse of a lost reality' *Manchester Evening News*

0 7472 6153 9

headline

High Hopes

Billy Hopkins

'Off to some la-di-dah college,' said Dad. 'You'll pick up bad ways from them toffs down there. I've read all about their goings-on in the Manchester Evening News.'

It's September 1945 and Billy Hopkins is off to London to train as a teacher. Despite his dad's warning, Billy survives two years in the Big City, and returns to take up his first teaching job in Manchester – on £300 a year! The catch is his first class, Senior Four, who bitterly resent the raising of the school leaving age, and are all set to take it out on their teacher – luckily the kid from Collyhurst has some tricks up his sleeve. And Billy's about to fall in love with the beautiful Laura. But is she, as his dad says, 'too good for the likes of us'?

Nostalgic, funny and romantic, HIGH HOPES vividly evokes northern life after the Second World War, and will keep you laughing till the very last page.

'A cracking yarn' *Warrington Guardian*

'How wonderful to have a book like this. A book that . . . pulls the reader back to that different world' *Manchester Evening News*

0 7472 6604 2

headline